TREASURES OF CASTLE ROWLEY

A Rowley Family Romance Novel

Matilda Lockwood

Nimble Pig Press

ISBN 979-8-9892935-4-4

Published by Nimble Pig Press

PO Box 489

Indianola, WA 98342

Printed in the United States of America

First Edition

This book is dedicated to artists.

Especially my daughter Bailey, who has already created more books

that I ever could.

CONTENTS

CHAPTER ONE

A HIDDEN SQUIRREL

The evening sun's fading light filtered through the grimy panes of the neglected orangery, casting jagged shadows over the runaway tangle of vines. Cecelia pressed her back against the stone wall and listened. The air was silent, but heavy with the musty scent of rotting wood, damp earth, and wild herbs left to wither untended. Abandoned for six years now, the greenhouse had become a shell of its former self, glass streaked with grime, wooden frames sagging and splintering.

But this was why it suited her. No one came here, and no one would think to look for her in this forgotten corner. As minutes passed in solitude, Cecelia's shoulders eased. Carefully, she drew out the stub of a pencil and her nearly completed leather-bound sketch pad, sweeping her eyes around to ensure she was truly alone.

The walls were now overrun by persistent creepers. Honeysuckle and clematis had invaded the space, their tendrils winding through broken panes like desperate hands grasping for sunlight. Cecelia grimaced as the familiar nausea surged, one hand resting protectively over her slight belly as she reflected on how months along, the queasiness had become a daily companion. She reached into a hidden pocket tied under her skirts and retrieved a salted nut, chewing slowly. The salt stung her lips, but it cut through the nausea, if only for a moment.

"Oh, the grand old Duke of York…" she sang softly, her voice a low rasp, filling the hollow space. "He had ten thousand men."

This overgrown ruin was a reflection of her own tangled chaos, which was as comforting a thought as it wasn't. Clumps of lavender sprouted wildly, while yarrow and brambles emerged between shattered stones. Here, she could breathe—free from judging eyes, whispering tongues, and her mother's endless demands.

"He marched them up to the top of the hill," she murmured to the growing child within her, her voice barely audible. "And he marched them down again."

Above her, the castle went on without her—its secrets swirling like autumn leaves, uncaring of her absence. In this moment of time the abandoned greenhouse was hers alone.

"And when they were up, they were up…" Her charcoal-stained fingers traced the familiar lines of Annabel's face—her best friend's likeness emerging slowly on the rough paper. "And when they were down, they were down." The soft curve of Annabel's smile, the way her eyes lit up when she spoke of her fiancé—as these details came to life, they momentarily distracted Cecelia from her own worries.

Here, among the shattered glass and wild vines, she was not the pregnant, unmarried maid with a stained reputation. Here, she was simply a woman with her art. No watchful eyes, no probing whispers. No one to ask about the father of her child. God help her if anyone found out the truth.

"And when they were only halfway up, they were neither up nor down," she muttered, her voice bitter as she glanced at the nearly finished sketch. Satisfaction was always intertwined with the weight of responsibility that never lifted.

Cecelia's foot shifted, and she felt her scuffed patten caught on something hard beneath the dirt. Frowning, she set her sketch pad aside and crouched down. Her fingers scraped through the loose earth, unearthing a small, tarnished object. She held her breath as she wiped it clean on the hem of her skirts—a ring, long buried and forgotten.

The last rays of sunlight glinted off the metal, revealing a delicate engraving: a falcon on one side, a horse's head on the other. The ring's craftsmanship was fine, but its edges were worn, weathered by time and neglect. Who had left it here? Cecelia turned the ring over in her hand. It must have belonged to someone from the castle, perhaps slipped from a careless hand years ago. But how long had it lain hidden beneath the tangled vines, waiting to be found? Her heart quickened and without thinking she slipped the ring into her pocket. As the last light faded, a strange sense of resolve settled within her, even as uncertainty lingered.

A rustling sound interrupted her thoughts. Cecelia's gaze shifted to the source of the noise, her daydream slipping away as a squirrel darted from behind a toppled stone urn, its wide eyes fixed on her.

A smaller squirrel was clinging to its mother's fur. Cecelia grinned in delight. Carefully, she reached into her pocket and pulled out three more nuts, placing them gently on the ground a few feet away. "Go on," she whispered, her voice gentle.

The squirrel darted forward, snatched a nut, and fled into the undergrowth. Cecelia watched it vanish, her smile fading. How simple it was, she thought, to run. To take your child and disappear. No judgment, no barriers, just freedom. It was a kind of escape she could only dream of.

Her fingers returned to the sketch pad, flipping the page, moving with a renewed sense of purpose. The squirrel's quick movements took shape on the paper—the curve of its tail, its small body poised to leap. Animals were easier to capture than people, Cecelia reflected. They didn't judge, didn't whisper. They simply existed, free of human complications.

"Cecelia!"

Her heart leapt at the sudden voice, her pencil freezing mid-stroke. She looked up to see Annabel standing in the shattered doorway, cheeks flushed and a lantern in hand. "Yes?"

"Your mum's looking for you," Annabel called, stepping lightly over broken tiles, her breath visible in the cool air as the acrid scent of burning tallow filled the space and her lantern cast sharp shadows on the overgrown vines. "Says she needs help with the flax."

Cecelia quickly closed her sketchbook, tying its leather string with swift, practiced movements. She slid it into the larger of the hidden pockets beneath her skirts, feeling the fabric's worn edges against her fingertips. "Who ratted out my drawing nook, then?"

"No one but the rats," Annabel teased, looking around warily. "Well, Cassidy thought you'd be here."

"Little sneak," Cecelia muttered, rolling her eyes. "Does she need to know everything? I'll have to find a new hideout."

"I wouldn't worry about it," Annabel replied with a shrug. "Everyone else still thinks this place is haunted. Lise swears that's the true reason it's never been repaired."

"Good," Cecelia quipped, brushing bits of moss from her skirts. "The better to keep my mother off my scent. If there's anything she hates more than me shirking my duties, it's my drawing. Of course, she thinks the latter leads to the former." With a scoff, she added, "And they're squirrels, not rats."

Annabel wrinkled her nose, glancing at the vines holding the building together above them. "Squirrels are just rats with better lineage, aren't they?"

Cecelia laughed. Linking arms with Annabel, the two women stepped out into the crisp autumn air. The chill bit at their cheeks, the scent of fallen leaves filling their noses—a bracing reminder of the changing season.

"Lineage matters," Cecelia said dryly. "Look at Frederick Rowley. A month ago, he was practically crushed under his father's thumb. Now, with Henry out of the picture, he's about to be the new castle Baron."

"Does he feel lucky?" Annabel asked quietly, her smile fading. "He seems more wary than anything else. I wouldn't want the weight of the Rowley secrets."

"Fair enough." Cecelia hesitated, her expression darkening. "I've seen that weight before. My father wore it as we fled France after the Edict of Nantes was revoked, and I don't think he's ever fully recovered."

"I don't think I would either." Annabel's eyes softened. "Your family had to leave everything behind."

"Yes," Cecelia said, a trace of bitterness creeping into her voice. "Protestants like us became targets overnight. My family went from being respected to being hunted. My father had built a life, earned noble status—gone in the blink of an edict."

"How awful." Annabel tightened her grip on Cecelia's arm. "That must have been terrifying."

"It was," Cecelia admitted. "We lost our estate, our wealth, and our standing. We had no choice but to flee, and England offered safety, but not much else. My parents were desperate when they found work at the castle. And old Baron Henry Rowley was willing to employ desperate people."

"Even if it meant keeping them low," Annabel said softly. "Henry is a cruel opportunist."

"Yes," Cecelia replied, shuddering. "But Frederick's not like Henry. We've got a fighting chance of happiness now, with him in charge, everyone who lives here does...he behaves more like his true father Lucas, who was as common as the rest of us."

"Oh, you're hardly common, dear friend!" Annabel's voice took on a playful edge, trying to lift the moment. "You've got a few drops of noble blood running through your veins, even if it's been chased out of one country and disguised in another."

"How lucky I am to have a friend like you." Cecelia smiled. "Here's to commoners with complicated pasts, then."

Annabel laughed, nudging Cecelia as they approached the fork in the road. The castle loomed to one side, the farmhouse path to the other.

"Annabel!" A voice called from the castle gates. "Cecelia!" It was the butler, waving urgently. "You must come at once. Master Frederick is asking for you."

They exchanged quick, worried glances before hurrying toward the castle. The massive oak door creaked when Cecelia pushed it open, revealing the dimly lit great hall, and they made their way to Frederick's room, Cecelia wiped her smudged hands on her skirts. When they stepped inside, the sight stopped them cold.

Frederick lay pale and still in the grand oak bed, his skin almost translucent. The smell of fresh vomit lingered in the air. Baroness Philippa knelt at her son's bedside, clutching his hands. In the corner, the castle physician, Doctor Archibald Fenton, hovered over a cart of medical tools, his expression grim.

Annabel inhaled sharply, while Cecelia moved closer, her sorrowful gaze shifting from Frederick to Charlie, who stood at the opposite side of the bed.

Cecelia's heart pounded, the air in the room feeling suddenly suffocating. "What's wrong?" she whispered, breaking the oppressive silence. "Begging your pardon."

The physician cleared his throat. "Frederick has consumption," he announced, the words dropping like stones. "He has months left. Perhaps only weeks."

The words seemed to hang in the air, heavy and irreversible. Cecelia's vision blurred as the weight of the news sank in. Frederick—perhaps their only friend in the Rowley family at the castle grounds they called home, the one who was supposed to take over from his cruel, oppressive father—was dying.

The shock echoed in her mind as Annabel let out a choked sob, and Cecelia's heart crumbled under the unexpected blow.

Frederick was dying.

Chapter Two

A Dying Man's Wishes

The tension in the room was suffocating, the air thick with grief. Frederick, the young man set to be Baron of the castle, lay crumpled like a marionette in his bed. His skin was ashen, slick with sweat, and his fine doublet was spattered with blood. His breath rattled, a hollow, labored sound. At the foot of the bed stood Annabel's husband Charlie, wide-eyed and pale, his hands clenched in worry. The scent of burning herbs from the nearby hearth mixed with the damp chill that clung to the castle's ancient bones.

Frederick's body jerked suddenly, a fit of coughing wracking him. New blood speckled the sheets, his trembling fingers barely managing to wipe his lips. "I can't... even hardly speak without..." he rasped.

"You must not," Dr. Fenton cut in sharply, his tone slicing through the air. The dim candlelight cast harsh shadows across his gaunt face, accentuating the hollows of his cheeks. "Each word has the capacity to strain your lungs further."

Lady Philippa Rowley looked shattered. Her usual regal bearing faltered as she dabbed at her eyes with a lace handkerchief, her hand trembling when it rested on Frederick's arm. She was no longer the indomitable Baroness, but simply a mother on the verge of losing her child. "Doctor... it can't be true," she murmured, stepping closer to the bed. Her voice broke, a plea for hope in a room where hope seemed to have fled. "Is there truly no chance?"

Dr. Fenton's expression was grim, his voice steady but void of comfort. "I'm afraid the symptoms are unmistakable, my lady. Blood in the cough, fever, exhaustion—there's no mistaking consumption." He turned to Frederick, his eyes briefly softening with pity. "I've seen it enough to know."

Frederick's bloodshot eyes shifted to his mother. His voice was barely a whisper. "How long...?" The words lingered, heavy and desperate.

The physician paused, folding his hands before him. "Months, perhaps. A year, if you're fortunate." He seemed resigned, as if already grieving for the baron's inevitable fate. "We will make you as comfortable as we can."

Philippa's breath hitched. "My boy..." she choked out, her hand hovering above Frederick as if afraid to touch him, as if his fragility might shatter further under her fingers.

Frederick's chest rose and fell slowly. He seemed to withdraw into himself, as though seeking a place where the pain couldn't reach him. Watching him, Cecelia felt her throat tighten, guilt clawing at her insides. Frederick was not the father of her child—a lie she'd told too often the past month, both to protect him from his father's wrath and buy her time. Now, as she stood here watching him slip away, she wondered how much longer she could carry the weight of her deception.

Charlie, who had remained silent until now, cleared his throat, his voice hesitant but filled with concern. "Begging your pardon, Baroness, but... are we certain it's consumption? This came on so sudden. We were just at the market a fortnight ago, and..."

Dr. Fenton's eyes narrowed, the irritation clear in his tone. "You're a merchant, not a physician. Your assumptions are misguided."

"Keep your tongue civil, doctor." Frederick's eyes opened, a flash of defiance cutting through his pain. "Or ...even with my ill health, I'll see you dismissed."

Philippa's breath caught at her son's sharp rebuke, her gaze shifting between him and Dr. Fenton. "Leave us," she ordered, her voice suddenly. "All of you. Except my son, of course."

Charlie bowed his head, retreating swiftly. Dr. Fenton hesitated, his face tightening with disdain, but he turned and left, his cloak sweeping behind him, and Annabel followed with Charlie. Cecelia made to do the same, but Frederick's hand—weak but insistent—closed around her wrist.

"Stay," he whispered, the plea in his voice stronger than his grip.

Cecelia stopped. She glanced at Philippa, whose eyes were sharp with suspicion, her lips pressed into a thin line. "Of course, my lord," Cecelia murmured, bobbing a curtsy, her voice low but steady.

Frederick's eyes locked onto hers, with a mix of desperation and resolve. "I promised to help you, as you helped me," he said, his voice barely more than a whisper.

Philippa's face hardened, her voice carrying a warning. "Frederick, this girl lied. She claimed the child she carries is yours, yet you insist it is not so. The slander is rife throughout the castle and I will not have her stay under this roof."

Cecelia's heart pounded, but she kept her gaze lowered, her silence heavy. "I'm so sorry, my lady."

Frederick's breath was labored, but his words were clear. "Mother, she lied to protect me. To keep Father from disowning me." He paused, the effort evident in his drawn features. "Without her, I'd have lost everything."

"That cannot possible be true," Philippa dismissed.

"It is true," he retorted hotly. "You don't know what it was like here, alone with him. Besides, Cecelia's made it clear to all that she was telling tales to appease father. No one truly believes she carries my progeny, trust me."

"I see." Philippa's lips thinned. "And now you expect me to reward her?"

"She helped get you out of that dungeon," Frederick shot back, his breath ragged. "You owe her as much as I do."

Philippa's eyes narrowed, and she turned her gaze to Cecelia. "Very well. But she cannot stay here. The scandal is too great. She must go to Rowley Manor."

Cecelia's chest tightened. "Please, Baroness," she pleaded. "This is my home."

"Oh?" Philippa's eyes were cold. "Tell me—who is the father of your child, who you plan to raise in my home?"

Cecelia swallowed her nerves. "A fisherman," she lied. "We were meant to wed, but he was killed in a skirmish with a sailor."

Philippa's expression shifted. "What was his name?"

Before Cecelia could falter, Frederick interjected, his voice firm despite his condition. "She needn't answer that. If she wishes to stay, she will."

Philippa's jaw tightened. "You are in no position to dictate terms, Frederick. But I will consider her situation... if she agrees to leave within a month."

"No." Frederick's voice was faint but resolute. "She deserves a dowry first. And a husband who will care for her and the child."

Philippa gave a shark little laugh, disbelief on her face. "You expect me to arrange a match for her, after everything she's done?"

"Yes," Frederick answered. "She's done more for this family than you realize."

For a moment, Philippa stood frozen, her face flushed with anger and confusion. She turned abruptly, muttering, "This is madness. I'll not be—"

Frederick's eyes opened, his gaze sharp despite his weakness. "Mother... did you take Father to the constable? Henry's not still down in the dungeon, is he?"

Philippa hesitated, a shadow passing over her face. She glanced toward Cecelia, who stood with her eyes cast down. The air in the room seemed to thicken with the shared, unspoken truths and too many secrets. Philippa's hand trembled as it rested on Frederick's clammy forehead. "I haven't yet," his mother admitted, her voice low and reluctant. "Geoffrey needs to settle the family's affairs before we act. I'll speak to him tomorrow."

Frederick's expression hardened. "He must be turned in, Mother. We cannot take the law into our own hands."

Philippa's fingers brushed over her son's damp hair. "Yes... of course," she murmured absently.

"He will be brought to justice," Frederick insisted, his voice faltering. Suddenly, he was seized by a violent coughing fit. His body convulsed, his fingers clawing at the bed linens. Blood sprayed across the delicate fabric of his shirt, staining it crimson.

Panic flared in Philippa's eyes as she rushed to the door, her voice urgent and raw. "Doctor! Doctor Fenton, come quickly!"

Frederick's gasps filled the room, his body shuddering under the strain. Cecelia pressed a trembling hand to her mouth, tears blurring her vision as she silently prayed for mercy that seemed distant and unreachable.

When Philippa's frantic footsteps had faded down the corridor, Cecelia knelt beside Frederick, her hand brushing his cold, clammy fingers. "You shouldn't have done that," she whispered, her voice thick with unshed tears.

Frederick managed a weak smile, the effort visible in his strained features. "It was... the least I could do," he murmured, each word a struggle.

Cecelia's chest tightened, her emotions tangled in a web of gratitude and guilt. She longed to tell him the truth about the child, to confess the lies they had spun to protect each other. But now, as he lay so fragile before her, she couldn't bring herself to burden him further.

"Thank you," she whispered, the words heavy on her lips.

Cecelia left shortly after, Philippa's eyes burning hours in her back. It was time to go home for the night.

Ten years ago, home was a beautiful building in France, but now it was a small stone cottage she shared with her family on the crumbling English castle grounds.

For a moment she stopped on the path and tilted her head at the poky little house, where she still shared a room with her parents. At least she had her own bed—which had been a gift from Charlie and Annabel after her old one from childhood had collapsed.

With a grim sigh, she pushed open the weathered wooden door, stepping into the dim interior filled with worn furniture. The hearth crackled feebly, and the familiar scent of peat smoke added a faint warmth to the chill that seemed to permeate everything. She stepped in to see her parents sitting at the rough-hewn table, as she knew they would be, but Cecelia was startled to see their faces etched with worry.

James leaned forward, hair falling into his eyes as his arms rested on the table, his right hand picking anxiously at his sleeve. When he saw her approach, he smiled weakly.

Her father may have been anxious, but her mother was clearly angry. Bridgette sat rigid, arms crossed tightly, her lips pressed into a thin line of disapproval.

They both looked as though the weight of the world had settled on their shoulders.

"What's happened now?" Cecelia asked, her voice breaking the heavy silence.

For a moment, neither of them spoke. The tension in the room felt thick, almost suffocating. Finally, James lifted his gaze, his voice rough and weary. "Your mother's been searching for you, Cecelia. You worry us when we can't find you, dearest."

"I was on castle grounds." Cecelia's chin lifted defiantly. "And I'm not a child," she added, her tone firm as her hand instinctively moved to rest over the growing swell of her belly.

James looked away, his discomfort evident, while Bridgette's frown deepened, the flickering light accentuating the lines of worry on her face. "Don't start with us, Cecelia," her mother snapped, the strain in her voice making her sound older and harsher. "Things are about to change, and you'd best be ready for the tide to turn."

Cecelia gasped. "What does that mean?"

"Never mind." Her mother stood, standing and walking to the bedroom, pausing as she gave James a long-suffering look before flicking her eyes back to her daughter. "You and I are going to market in the morning, so don't run off at dawn."

"The market?" Cecelia's brows arched in surprise. "You haven't taken me there in ages."

"That's because you can't stay focused," Bridgette muttered, her voice low and clipped. "When I took you as a child you were always trying to spend the meager coins you have on trinkets, always distracting the merchants with rude sketches. But you're older now, and I'll have to trust that, as there's someone I need you to meet. Tomorrow, there's no room for idleness."

Cecelia opened her mouth to argue, but the stern look in her mother's eyes silenced her. With a resigned sigh, she followed Bridgette into the bedroom, falling asleep soon after her head hit the pillow.

In the morning, at her mother's prodding, she swung her feet out of bed and headed for the room's small washbasin, splashing cold water on her face. The chill bit into her skin, waking her senses. She quickly smoothed her hair back and changed into a clean frock—simple and rough, but serviceable.

As she moved toward the door to follow Bridgette's retreating back to the Rowley carriage, her father's voice stopped her. "Wait, mon petit cœur."

Cecelia paused, the familiar endearment softening her furrowed brow. She turned to see James pulling something from his vest pocket. A small smile tugged at the corners of her lips as he handed her a new sketchbook.

"Merci, Papa," Cecelia whispered, her eyes brightening. "Mine is almost full." She ran her fingers over the smooth pages, taking in the comforting scent of leather and paper. This one was smaller, easier to conceal from her mother's watchful eyes.

James's expression softened, the hint of a smile briefly lifting his tired features. "Don't mention it," he said gruffly, though his tone was warm. "And don't let your mother catch you neglecting your work for it."

"I won't," Cecelia promised, her voice filled with affection. "I love you." She carefully tucked the small book under her mattress, ensuring its safety before hurrying outside to join her mother. The carriage stood waiting, its wooden frame creaking as Bridgette climbed aboard, her expression still set in that familiar mix of disapproval and impatience. Cecelia followed, her heart heavy with the weight of her family's unspoken burdens, but somewhere deep inside, she clung to the fleeting joy that her father's quiet gift had brought her.

Chapter Three

THE MARKETPLACE

The driver, a weathered old man with a hunched back and hollow eyes, barely acknowledged Bridgette and Cecelia as they climbed into the creaking carriage. When Bridgette shut the door firmly behind them, the wooden frame shuddered against the cobblestones, and when it began to move each jolt sent vibrations through the seats, rattling the bones of its occupants.

"It's time you knew—we're leaving Castle Rowley," Bridgette declared suddenly, her voice cutting through the rumble of the wheels. The words came with an unsettling finality, a tone that left no room for argument. "Within weeks."

"What? Why now?" Cecelia's tone was frustrated. "Mumma, Frederick has convinced the baroness to arrange a match for me. She's promised a dowry, after everything—after nearly throwing me out. I begged her to let me stay..." Cecelia's voice cracked, her gaze turning desperate as it fixed on her mother. "I beg you now, Mumma. Please, not again. Not after France."

Bridgette's expression remained unreadable, her features flickering in the shifting light as the carriage rolled onward. "The shadows of Henry Rowley's sins run deeper than you can imagine. We've been caught in his schemes, and when his crimes come to light, there will be no mercy. We must leave before that day comes."

"That's madness!" Cecelia's voice rose, her frustration palpable. "Frederick will protect us. You did what anyone would do to survive under his father's rule." But even as she said the words, she wondered how Frederick could help them once he was gone.

Bridgette's lips tightened into a hard line and her hateful words echoed Cecelia's own guilty thoughts. "Frederick is not long for this world, Cecelia. He cannot save us from the consequences that will follow his father's exposure. We cannot afford to place our trust in a dying man." Her voice softened slightly, as if trying to offer a small glimmer of hope. "We're setting our sights on America."

"No!" Cecelia's breath caught. "America? But why? What could possibly await us there?"

"Indigo," Bridgette said quietly, her eyes gleaming with a rare hint of ambition. "The dye, Cecelia. We'll oversee a plantation, manage the crops. Fifty acres for your father, fifty for me, and fifty for you. We'll make a bloody fortune."

"Indigo?" Cecelia repeated, the word foreign and strange on her tongue. "You mean... running a plantation?"

"It can't be much harder than running this household and all these farms." Bridgette nodded. "Your father's old connections have secured the opportunity, ones who remember our time in France. We're offered us this chance in the colonies, far from the prying eyes of England or France."

Cecelia's mind reeled at the idea. "But what about everything here? My friends? The baby?" Her voice trembled. "Within weeks... how long would the voyage take? Will you have me give birth on a ship, in the middle of the ocean?" Cecelia began to feel sick, but when she dipped her hand into her pocket she found herself out of nuts.

Bridgette's laugh was sharp, almost mocking. "I birthed you in a carriage, but I survived. You will too. Besides, we should be there before you give birth, God willing." Her tone shifted, now filled with forced optimism. "My dearest, just think. In America, you'll have space, freedom—a room of your own, even. You'll find a husband there, someone who will look past your... circumstances."

Cecelia felt a bitter taste rise in her throat as Bridgette's eyes lingered pointedly on her growing belly. "Perhaps someone else could go in my place?" she offered weakly. "Bring a friend of Father's with you to America to help with the plantation. My friends—Annabel, Charlie, Lise, Agatha, Frederick as much as he's able—they would help me with the baby. I know they would. After all I did to help them..."

"Friends." Bridgette scoffed. "Annabel has her own troubles. Frederick is barely clinging to life. Lise and Agatha are planning their own escape, and you think they'll stay behind for you? No, Cecelia. No one here will save you."

Cecelia lowered her gaze silently, the harsh truth sinking in.

"And what of the child?" Bridgette pressed, her voice sharp. "Raising it alone, under judgment, without a name or support... Is that truly the life you want?"

"No," Cecelia admitted, her voice barely a whisper.

"Then you understand why we must leave," Bridgette continued, her tone brooking no argument. "There are no second chances here, not for us. We'll go quietly, make no fuss. Frederick's favor can no longer shield you. The baroness is furious about your lies—pretending Frederick was the father. I overheard her. She's watching you, waiting for you to do something wrong. And when you do, she'll cast you out without hesitation."

"I understand," Cecelia said softly, her shoulders slumping under the weight of the realization.

"And your sketches," Bridgette added, her tone cutting. "Don't think I haven't seen you skulking around spending hours on that nonsense. No more of them. You're a maid, not an artist. You can't afford to draw attention, now, either. I need time to prepare for our departure, and it would be most inconvenient if she pushed you out before that day comes."

"My art is all I have," Cecelia protested, though her voice lacked its usual fire. "I work quickly. It doesn't interfere—"

"Not when you lose focus," Bridgette interrupted sharply. "You must leave your fantasies behind. We have one goal now: survival, not scribbling." Her gaze bore into Cecelia's, demanding obedience. "Promise me, Cecelia. You'll stay focused."

Cecelia met her mother's eyes reluctantly. "I promise."

The carriage jolted to a stop as they reached the marketplace. Bridgette was quick to fling open the door, stepping down into the vibrant chaos of the market square. "Stay close," she ordered. "This is no time for wandering."

The market was alive with energy, the hum of voices a dull rumble compared with the sharp cries of merchants hawking their goods. Cecelia's senses were immediately overwhelmed in a way she felt strangely drawn to.

"Stay focused, Cecelia," Bridgette snapped, her voice slicing through Cecelia's thoughts. "This is no time for distractions."

Cecelia trailed behind her mother, navigating through the crowd. The air was filled with the pungent scent of spices. Cinnamon, cloves, and cumin wafted into her nostrils, followed by an earthy aroma of freshly dug potatoes and the tang of overripe apples. The sounds and smells were overwhelming yet exhilarating, a stark contrast to the dim and controlled halls of Castle Rowley. Stalls brimmed with goods—bolts of silk in jewel tones, wooden crates overflowing with rosemary and borage, barrels of salted fish, and wicker baskets piled with eggs.

As Bridgette haggled fiercely over a bundle of linens, Cecelia's arms obediently held a bundle of candles, a roll of twine, and a string of onions slung over her shoulder. She could barely keep pace with her mother, who moved swiftly from one stall to the next, her bargaining tone sharp and precise.

Finally, they reached a small leather stall tucked near the market's edge. Its owner, a grizzled man with rough hands and a worn apron, looked up as they approached. His eyes crinkled in recognition. "Bridgette Rousseau," he greeted, his voice as weathered as his goods. "And Cecelia—no longer a girl, but a young woman now."

Bridgette allowed a tight smile. "Yes, Harold. Cecelia's grown." She turned to Cecelia, her voice softer but firm. "Stay here a while, and don't stray from Harold." To Harold, she said quickly, "I've business here I can't bring this one to. Is that all right?"

Harold gave a small nod, already focusing back on the leather straps he was mending. Without another word, Bridgette disappeared into the crowd, her steps brisk and purposeful.

Cecelia lingered near the stall, her gaze wandering over the chaotic sprawl of the marketplace, a surreal blend of familiar scents and unfamiliar faces. For a moment, she felt as if she were standing between two worlds—one she was leaving behind and another she was yet to understand. She was pulled from her thoughts by Harold's voice.

"Apple?" he asked, holding out the small fruit.

Cecelia smiled gratefully and reached for it, but the apple slipped through her fingers, tumbling across the cobblestones. "Sorry!" She cursed under her breath and darted after it, her heart sinking as it rolled toward a nearby stall. Before she could reach it, a tall figure scooped it up, his hand wrapping around the apple with ease.

"Is this yours?" he asked, his voice gentle.

"It is." Cecelia's cheeks flushed as she dipped into a quick curtsy. "My apologies, sir."

"No need for that." The man chuckled. "It's just an apple."

She stole a glance upward, taking in the warmth of his smile and the kindness in his dark brown eyes. Mumbled thanks escaped her lips as she hurried back to Harold's stall, her heart pounding unexpectedly.

Moments passed, and Harold seemed to nod off in the midday heat, his head bobbing forward. Cecelia's gaze drifted again, this time toward a nearby stall selling small wooden carvings. The merchant—a middle-aged man in a well-worn coat—was carefully arranging figurines on the table. The vendor who'd rescued her apple stood across from him, deep in conversation.

The vendor's presence commanded attention. He spoke rapidly, switching from a language she could not discern to English with ease as he negotiated the price of a set of carved bangles. His tone was calm yet firm, his words imbued with a natural authority, and his gestures were fluid, the embroidered cuffs of his tunic catching the light as he moved. Around his neck hung a small silver pendant, something so beautiful it had to be an a heirloom, which gleamed against his dark skin.

The merchant nodded in agreement, and the vendor's face broke into a wide smile. As he counted out coins, he made a jest that sent the merchant into a fit of laughter. Despite the crowd and chaos, the confident vendor seemed at home, effortlessly weaving through the mass of bodies, stopping occasionally to greet familiar faces.

Cecelia found herself captivated by his ease. In the midst of the market's noise, he seemed to bring a sense of calm—an energy that stood in contrast to the often frantic English traders around him. She caught snippets of his conversations with various vendors, a mix of languages flowing smoothly from his tongue: the unfamiliar one when speaking to spice sellers, French with cloth merchants, and English with customers debating over prices. Soon, a conversation drew Cecelia's attention.

A gentleman, clearly of some means, was examining a small wooden box. "I need something like this, but the lid with a design that represents my mother's spirit," he said earnestly. "Something strong, but not ostentatious. A bird, ideally."

The confident vendor, his smile as inviting as his tone, encouraged, "Tell me about her; perhaps then we'll find the perfect match."

Describing his mother, the man painted a picture of a woman of strength and tenderness. "Nighttime finds her sewing or lulling the little ones back to sleep. She's been a sanctuary for any soul in need."

"She indeed sounds like a rare gem." Admiration warmed the merchant's voice, and as he opened a small book. Cecelia caught a flash of painted wings and her interest flared further. "What about a peacock? A creature of beauty and stature. Bold and majestic!"

But the man dismissed the suggestion. "No, that's not her. Too ostentatious."

The merchant, undeterred, offered, "A robin, then, or a sparrow? Both are emblems of care and industriousness."

"They don't capture her adventurous spirit, her independence." His brows knit together.

"An eagle, perhaps?" A hint of desperation began to catch in the vendor's voice. "The epitome of strength and freedom, wouldn't you say?"

"Too showy." The gentleman shook his head. "She's quiet, but enduring."

"A sparrow?" the vendor suggested. "Simple and persistent."

The man frowned. "Not quite right. She's more... watchful, protective."

"Perhaps if you take a look at a few of the samples here..." The vendor leafed through his book, but as he did so, the other man shook his head.

"There's still something missing." He stroked his beard thought-fully "Perhaps this is folly? I wonder if I'm chasing a fantasy, seeking a piece that fully encompasses what she means to us." He chuckled to himself and took a step away from the booth as the merchant's kind face crumpled.

Unable to resist, Cecelia leaned forward and spoke. "What about an owl?"

Both men turned to her, surprised by the interruption. "What was that?" The vendor's voice was kind. "I could not hear."

Emboldened, she said louder, "Owls are wise and silent, protectors of the night. They observe, even when unseen."

The gentleman's eyes lit up. "An owl... Yes, that's perfect. Thank you, my dear." He turned back to the vendor. "Can you carve one into the box?"

The vendor nodded eagerly. "Certainly, sir. I'll make it the finest owl you've seen."

Cecelia's cheeks flushed as the transaction continued and she real-ized she had spoken out of turn. She ducked her head, intending to re-treat, but after bidding his customer farewell, the vendor approached her.

His eyes crinkled with a friendly curiosity. The sunlight shining through the market's awnings caught the edges of his features, highlighting his warm brown skin and casting him in a soft glow. "You have quite an eye for symbolism," he said smoothly. "Sometimes that's all it takes to capture someone, isn't it?" His voice was low and inviting, with a melodic rhythm that carried hints of his upbringing.

"Yes," Cecelia said as she gazed at him. "Right. Er...my name is Cecelia. May I buy a pencil?" she added, feeling a bit foolish, but searching for a reason not to walk away.

"Of course! I'm Kunal Sutar," he said, extending a hand. His name rolled off his tongue with an unfamiliar cadence that danced into her ears. Her own name felt plain by comparison. Hands trembling slightly, she clasped them together to hide it. "Are you also an artist?"

Cecelia scoffed before she could help herself. "I'm no more an artist than I am a squirrel." She surprised both of them with an impish grin. "That is to say, I deeply wish I was one, I practice often, but I fear it is not to be."

Kunal threw back his head and laugh, a sound that tickled her insides in the most delicious way, and reached for a pencil. "I promise you, we all wish we were squirrels at times. Me, more than most."

"I... I've actually heard of you," she realized, digging in her pocket for a shilling, blushing and wondering what her mother would say to see her speaking to a man in the middle of the marketplace. "My friend

Annabel Barlow has mentioned your name. She spoke well of you and your family."

Kunal's smile widened, his eyes crinkling further, the warmth of his expression genuine. "Annabel and Charlie are indeed dear friends. It's always a pleasure to meet someone connected to them." His gaze lingered on Cecelia for a moment, not intrusive but intense, as if he were truly seeing her.

"Have you not been there in a while?" Cecelia asked, curious despite her usual caution with strangers, her hand extending the shilling she'd retrieved. "I don't remember seeing you."

"No charge." He shook his head and held out the pencil. "I'm afraid the Baron Henry Rowley isn't one for entertaining merchants on his grounds."

"The Baroness has returned to power." Cecelia took the writing tool too quickly to brush his fingers with hers, feeling a pang of regret. "The old Baron is... indisposed."

Kunal's eyebrows rose, his curiosity piqued. "Indisposed?"

"Locked away," Cecelia whispered, glancing around to ensure no one was listening. "It's complicated. I'm sure Charlie would tell you the story."

"Then I shall have to call on him soon." Kunal's eyes gleamed. "This may indeed be a boon to our family, who were good customers to the

Baroness once upon a time. "What an intriguing tale. Lady Rowley was always much more appreciative of the arts than her husband."

"I hope you're right." Cecelia smiled nervously.

"Cecelia!" Her mother's voice called out, and Cecelia flinched to see Bridgette approaching, her face stern and lined with impatience, followed by surprise.

CHAPTER FOUR

A SUDDEN STORM

"I thought I told you to stay put," Bridgette's voice snapped through the thickening air as she approached, her skirts brushing up a faint cloud of dust from the uneven cobblestones. Her eyes were sharp as they landed on Cecelia, then shifted to the man beside her. "The person I'd hoped you could meet was called away. What are you doing away from Harold's stall, bothering this merchant?"

"No bother at all, good woman," Kunal replied, his voice low and steady, with an undercurrent of confidence that softened Bridgette's sharp tone. His respectful nod and calm presence contrasted starkly with her mother's cutting edge. "Your young charge..."

"My daughter," Bridgette corrected, her fingers tightening around the frayed edge of her shawl. "I hope she wasn't getting into trouble."

"Far from it." Kunal's gaze held steady as it returned to Cecelia. "In fact, she helped me close a sale I might have lost without her eye for detail."

Bridgette's brows raised skeptically, and her narrowed gaze darted between Cecelia and Kunal. "Is that so?" she asked, her voice laden with doubt. Cecelia met her mother's piercing look with steady resolve, refusing to avert her eyes despite the rising tension.

Kunal remained composed, dipping his hand into his coat pocket. "Indeed. She's earned a commission." He offered a pound coin to Cecelia, his warm smile disarming the sudden chill of the conversation. "For her effort."

Cecelia's fingers closed around the coin, its weight and coolness unfamiliar. A small, hesitant smile tugged at her lips, but her gesture was fleeting as she dutifully handed it to her mother. "Thank you, sir," she said, her gaze briefly flicking back to Kunal.

Bridgette's expression softened—barely—as she accepted the pound, though suspicion lingered in her eyes. "Fair enough. We appreciate your kindness." She turned abruptly toward Cecelia. "Come along, dearest. We've much to do before the day is done."

"Yes, Mumma," Cecelia replied, her voice subdued, but her feet felt leaden as she prepared to leave. Her eyes lingered on Kunal, drawn by his easy manner and the confident way he occupied space without arrogance.

As her gaze shifted to the finely crafted items on his stall beyond pencils—delicate instruments, polished frames and figurines, intricately carved puzzles—an unexpected pull tugged at her heart. Her steps faltered, and just as she turned to leave, Kunal reached forward, his fingers brushing hers as he slipped something else into her hand. The contact was brief, but electric, and Cecelia's heart leapt.

"Thank you again," he murmured, his dark eyes locked onto hers, filled with warmth and mystery. For a moment, the bustling market faded around them, replaced by the quiet intensity of their shared gaze.

Cecelia nodded, her voice momentarily lost. She dipped her head quickly and hurried to catch up with her mother, her pulse loud in her ears. Her fingers tightened around the second pound coin and a small wooden object, its shape indistinguishable beneath her skirts. Curiosity itched at her, but she resisted the urge to investigate further, slipping both into a hidden pocket.

As they climbed into the carriage, Cecelia noticed the sky darkening in the distance—thick, roiling clouds gathering ominously, like a warning. The ride back to the cottage was filled with a charged silence. Cecelia's mind swirled with questions, each one as tumultuous as the clouds beginning to blanket the horizon.

When they reached the cottage, the smell of damp earth mixed with smoke from the hearth, creating an odd comfort. Bridgette wasted no time, ladling thick stew from the cauldron over the fire. "Eat quickly," she instructed. "Then head to the rose beds. Deadhead the spent blooms and check for pests before the rain comes."

"Yes, Mumma," Cecelia muttered. She hastily ate the stew—an earthy mix of potatoes, onions, and scraps of salted meat—barely tasting it as her thoughts returned to the hidden objects in her pocket. As soon as she finished, she bolted the door and drew the small wooden object from her pocket, turning it over in her hand.

Her breath caught.

The piece of wood, carved with intricate vines and leaves, seemed to hold a life of its own. She pressed gently on a seam, and it extended to reveal a thin stick of graphite—a pencil, cleverly disguised. Cecelia's heart swelled with unexpected emotion. The craftsmanship was too fine to be ordinary, and its secret function seemed made just for her. How had Kunal known she needed a way to hide a pencil even more than the tool itself?

She traced the delicate carvings with her fingertips, recalling the moment he'd slipped it into her hand. His touch had been so brief, yet it had left a mark that felt as real as the tool in her palm. Cecelia whispered a soft, "Thank you," the words barely audible.

But reality closed in quickly, and Bridgette's stern warning echoed in her mind: No more distractions, no more drawing. Cecelia bit her lip, torn between the promise she'd made to her mother and the undeniable urge to create. The pencil felt warm, as if it were urging her to defy the constraints placed upon her, to keep alive the one thing that brought her solace.

Her decision came swiftly. She snatched her hidden sketchbook from beneath the mattress, tucked it into her largest tied-on pocket, and grabbed her gloves and gardening tools.

The sun hung low in the sky as Cecelia reached the garden. The scent of roses mingled with the dampness of freshly turned soil. Her hands moved swiftly, snipping away spent blooms with practiced efficiency. Each cut sent petals fluttering to the ground, the rhythmic snip of the shears echoing like a countdown—one step closer to a departure she dreaded.

But her thoughts were not entirely on the roses. The small pencil, hidden safely in her pocket, seemed to pulse with a life of its own. Her mind wandered to the sketches she would soon create in secret, and a surge of rebellion rose within her, defying the constraints that had been imposed upon her. As she bent over a particularly dense rosebush, Cecelia's fingers tied twine around a stem infested with aphids, securing it with a taut knot. Yet her thoughts continued to drift to Kunal—his steady gaze, the quiet confidence in his voice, and the unexpected connection that had sparked between them. It was a dangerous distraction, and she knew it.

The sky darkened further, the heavy clouds rolling in like silent predators. Cecelia glanced up, feeling the weight of the air shift, charged with the promise of rain. She hurried through the final rows of roses, her hands quick but unsteady.

As the last of the rosebushes was tended to, Cecelia straightened up, wiping sweat from her brow. The garden was eerily quiet now, the usual chirps and rustles of nature stilled by the looming storm. Cecelia looked around, ensuring she was alone, before pulling the pencil from her pocket. She retreated to the shaded alcove at the far end of the garden, hidden among the thick foliage where no one would think to look. There, she opened her sketchbook and let the pencil glide across the page, her movements quick and deliberate. Each stroke felt liberating, as if she were releasing a part of herself she had kept locked away. Her sketches captured the market scene—Kunal's face, the carved owl, and the bustle of vendors. She drew feverishly, the urgency in her work matching the tension in the sky above.

But as she finished a sketch of Kunal's eyes, a rumble of thunder startled her. Cecelia snapped the book shut, tucking it back beneath her skirts. Her heart raced—not just from the storm's sudden ferocity, but from the realization that her brief moment of defiance was over.

She stepped back onto the main path, her smile fleeting as reality weighed down once more. Her father's sudden appearance caught her off guard, his grim expression mirroring the storm's approach. James looked older than she remembered, the lines on his face deepened by worry and fatigue. His hair, damp with sweat and humidity, clung to his forehead.

"Father?" Cecelia asked, her voice cautious. "What brings you here?"

James appeared startled by her presence but recovered quickly, his sigh heavy with weariness. "Just needed a moment," he said, though his words sounded hollow. "Your mother's told you about our plans?"

Cecelia's jaw tightened. "She has," she replied, her tone sharp with resentment. "And I'm to have no say in it, as usual."

Her father stepped closer, his gaze softening. "I understand how you feel. Leaving France was just as hard for me—harder, perhaps. But home isn't a place; it's the people we hold dear."

The storm finally broke with a deafening clap of thunder, sending a cascade of rain crashing down. Cecelia yelped, instinctively crouching to shield herself from the sudden deluge. Panic surged as she remembered the sketchbook hidden beneath her dress. If it got soaked... if she ran home her mother would certainly discover it, along with the forbidden drawings.

Heart pounding, Cecelia made a split-second decision. Instead of rushing back toward the cottage, she bolted in the opposite direction—toward the artist cabins, their dilapidated shapes barely visible through the curtain of rain. Mud splashed up around her ankles as she ran, each step uncertain on the slick ground.

The cabins, long abandoned, stood as relics of the castle's past—a place where artists once found refuge. Now, they offered Cecelia a different kind of shelter. She reached the closest one and threw her shoulder against the door, desperate to find cover.

Her father's voice rang out from behind over the storm's roar. "Cecelia! What are you doing?"

Cecelia hesitated, glancing back. Rain blurred her vision, but she could still see her father's confusion. "Why did you follow me?" she shouted over the roar of the storm, her voice edged with frustration and panic.

James, now soaked, pressed on beside her. "I thought you saw something I needed to see," he admitted, bewilderment clear in his tone.

With one last shove, the door to the cabin finally creaked open, and they stumbled inside, dripping wet. The musty scent of rotting wood filled the air, a sharp contrast to the fresh, rain-drenched world outside. Though the cabin was damp and dark, it was a welcome refuge from the unrelenting downpour. James removed his sodden jacket, shaking off the excess water before hanging it on a peg near the door. A pool of water quickly formed at his feet.

Cecelia shivered as the cold air hit her damp skin, her hair plastered to her face. She stomped her boots to shake off the mud. "The Baroness had these outbuildings put up yes? I don't think anybody's been here in ages, but it's still fine shelter during a storm."

"It's been years, and it wouldn't have been my first choice for shelter." James grimaced, rubbing his hands together to ward off the chill. "But yes, this cabin and the others was commissioned by the Baroness to be studios for painters and sculptors," he mused. "Back when the Rowleys still valued art."

His words hit Cecelia with unexpected force. The cabin, with its crumbling walls and faded remnants of creativity, felt like a physical manifestation of her own predicament—an abandoned artist, forced to hide her passion. She stood, dripping and silent, the sketchbook still clutched protectively beneath her damp skirts.

"What's really troubling you, then?" James asked gently, stepping closer. "It's not just about leaving, is it?"

The question pierced through her defenses, the storm outside mirroring the emotional turmoil inside her. "I don't want to be forced away again," she admitted, her voice cracking with suppressed emotion. "I want to decide for myself, to have a say in my own life."

James's expression softened. "I know, child," he said, his voice heavy with regret. "But survival comes first. We have to make sacrifices, sometimes more than we can bear."

"I'm not a bloody child." Cecelia's anger flared anew. "It's always about sacrifices," she muttered bitterly. "But what about the things that keep us whole? What about the things that make us who we are?"

James didn't respond immediately. Instead, he looked around the small cabin, his eyes taking in the cobweb-covered easel in the corner, the faded murals on the walls—evidence of the creativity that once thrived here. "Perhaps," he began slowly, "there's a way for you to hold onto who you are, even while we prepare to leave."

He reached into his coat pocket and pulled an old key off a crowded iron ring, its metal tarnished with age. "This is the key to this cabin," he said, extending it to Cecelia. "I could assign you here—officially, as part of my steward duties. You could clean and prepare the space for any artists who might return... but in the meantime, you'd have a place to draw, without anyone knowing."

Cecelia's heart leapt at the suggestion, hope rekindled amidst the storm's fury. "Oh, Papa!" she exclaimed, throwing her arms around him in sudden, unguarded affection. "Thank you."

"There, there," James murmured, patting her back with a small, weary smile. "Would that lift your spirits? Enough to get by until we have to leave?"

"Yes," Cecelia said, stepping back, her eyes bright with gratitude. "It would mean everything."

James nodded, his expression a mixture of relief and sadness. "I've always known you had a gift," he admitted quietly. "I'm sorry we couldn't afford proper instruction here like we did in France. But maybe... things will be different in America."

Cecelia's smile faltered at the mention of their impending departure, but she nodded. "Maybe," she said softly, clutching the key tightly.

James cleared his throat, a hint of emotion slipping into his voice. "Now, let's find our way back through the tunnels," he suggested. "If no one sees you coming and going, there'll be no questions."

Together, they lifted a loose floorboard and descended into the dark passage beneath the cabin. The tunnels were narrow and damp, their stone walls glistening with moisture, and Cecelia held her breath as they navigated the twisting path, each step echoing in the silence.

They finally emerged in the castle cellar, where the familiar scent of stored grain and drying herbs greeted them. The sound of hurried footsteps reached their ears, and Cecelia spotted Lise, one of the maids, frantically gathering towels into a basket. She looked pale, her movements rushed and anxious.

"Lise?" Cecelia called out, her voice breaking the eerie stillness.

Lise spun around, clutching the basket to her chest. Her wide eyes were filled with a mix of fear and surprise. "Cecelia!" she gasped, glancing nervously toward the stairwell. "What are you doing down here?"

"My father helped me get through the rain. We came through the tunnel," Cecelia explained quickly, sensing the urgency in Lise's demeanor. "You look like you've seen a ghost."

"What's happened?" James asked, his voice low and urgent. "It is Frederick? Is he..."

"No." Lise shook her head, her lips pressed tightly together, and when she spoke, her voice trembled. "It's Charlie."

"Charlie!" Cecelia felt her stomach clench, dread washing over her. "What do you mean?" she demanded, her voice sharp.

Lise swallowed hard, her eyes downcast as though she couldn't bear to meet Cecelia's gaze. "The baroness—Philippa—she pushed him," she said, her voice barely audible. "She pushed him right down the stairs."

A stunned silence fell over them, broken only by the distant rumble of thunder outside. Cecelia's heart pounded, her mind struggling to process the horror of what she'd just heard.

Chapter Five

INSULT TO INJURY

"Philippa pushed Charlie down the stairs," James repeated, his voice catching in disbelief. "Are you... quite sure?"

Lise, her arms full of linen, cast him a scathing look. "Sure as I'm standing here," she snapped. "Now if you'll excuse me, I've got to get these to the physician."

She shoved past them, moving swiftly toward the infirmary, with James and Cecelia following her through the stone corridors. The sound of their footsteps echoed and the tension seemed to press down on Cecelia, a weight as palpable as the ancient stone walls.

"Is he badly hurt?" Cecelia asked, her voice barely above a whisper. Her ankle throbbed slightly from the hurried pace—she must have twisted it in her haste, but she gritted her teeth against the pain.

Lise didn't slow down. "Not as badly as he could have been, no thanks to that woman." Her voice was edged with anger. "If it weren't for Annabel being there, I might have stayed and said something I'd regret." She shuddered. "We're leaving this place. We'd be fools not to."

"You're leaving?" Cecelia stopped short, disbelief coursing through her. The sudden halt sent a jolt of pain up her leg, and she winced. "Surely there's some misunderstanding. Why would she—"

Lise turned sharply, her eyes narrowing. "Misunderstanding? The Baroness knows the truth of Frederick's father—same as I do, same as she does. Her cruel husband demanded children and she marched out and got pregnant from the first merchant she admired on the property. And that truth's a threat to her and her line. Mark my words, Cecelia, she'll cut down anyone who gets in her way."

James sucked in his breath, his face pale. Lise didn't wait for either of them to respond but strode ahead, pushing open the door to the infirmary, leaving Cecelia and James to exchange anxious glances before following her inside.

The air inside was thick with the scent of herbal salves—comfrey for bruises, yarrow for cuts—blended with the acrid tang of dried blood. A small table near the bed held an assortment of earthen jars, a wooden bowl of poultices, and a cup filled with what looked to be willow bark tea.

Cecelia's breath hitched as she stepped inside, feeling a wave of fatigue wash over her. Her ankle's dull ache worsened. The flickering candlelight illuminated Charlie's bruised face, where he lay still, but his breathing sounded healthy. Annabel sat beside him, eyes red from crying, while Frederick stood near the physician, his expression tight with concern.

"Charlie!" Cecelia's voice broke as she rushed forward. Pain shot through her ankle, but she forced herself to keep going. "Are you all right?"

Lise set the towels down with a harsh thud, her lips pressed into a thin line. "Look at him," she muttered, shaking her head. "He's been lucky, but still..."

"Watch your tongue, laundress," Philippa's voice cut through the air, cold and unyielding, from where she stood in the corner. Her figure was stiff, her face cast into stark relief by the dim light—a mask of indifference.

Frederick turned toward his mother, his brow furrowed. "Mother... what happened?"

Philippa lifted her chin, her voice smooth, almost too composed. "Nothing happened. Mr. Wright here simply had the misfortune of falling while attempting to retrieve one of my precious artifacts. A terrible accident." She placed a hand to her chest. "I'll never forgive myself if the young man is hurt."

The physician, having finished his examination, straightened and began packing his tools—Cecelia's curious eyes spotted a small saw for splinting, clean bandages, and a jar of honey for wounds. "No lasting harm," he said brusquely. "Cuts and bruises, yes, but no broken bones. No internal damage that I can detect. He'll heal soon enough."

Philippa stepped forward, her eyes searching the physician's face. "Are you certain?"

Doctor Fenton glanced at her, his voice flat. "I am."

"Thank the Lord," Philippa murmured, but there was something hollow in the way she said it. Frederick's gaze lingered on her, a storm brewing in his eyes.

"Oh, thank heavens," Annabel whispered, clutching Charlie's hand tightly. Her relief was palpable, though her voice still shook. "You're so lucky, Charlie. To think of what could have happened..."

"I'm fine," Charlie croaked, wincing as he shifted slightly. "When can I leave? If nothing's broken..."

The physician sighed, waving a hand dismissively. "Another quarter hour at least. We need to ensure there's no delayed head injury."

Frederick's expression darkened. "Mother, may I speak with you in private?" His voice was strained but steady.

Philippa arched an eyebrow but allowed him to escort her from the room. The door closed softly behind them, leaving a thick silence in their wake.

Annabel exhaled deeply, rubbing at her temples. "Lise is right," she whispered. "We need to get out of here before something worse happens."

Charlie shifted uncomfortably on the bed. "It could've been an accident," he said, though even he didn't sound convinced. "Even if it wasn't, I don't want to go on the run with a body full of cuts and bruises."

Annabel's eyes flashed. "It wasn't an accident, Charlie. I saw her. She thought I wasn't looking, but I was. She pushed you." She turned to Cecelia, her voice trembling with urgency. "Tell him. The Baroness is mad, isn't she?"

Cecelia hesitated, her fingers curling into the fabric of her skirt. The pain in her ankle was becoming harder to ignore, but it also mirrored the deeper ache of her own fears. "I don't know," she admitted softly. "But she's been trying to send me away to Rowley Manor. And she still hasn't called the constable on Henry."

Annabel crossed her arms, her voice hardening with resolve. "I'm not staying in a place where the woman in charge tried to kill my future husband. I mean it, Charlie."

There was a soft knock at the door, and Frederick entered, closing it quietly behind him. His expression was weary, as if the weight of the world sat squarely on his shoulders. "Friends... I fear my mother meant to harm Charlie."

Annabel gasped, her breath catching in her throat. She sank onto the stool beside Charlie's bed, her fingers trembling as she reached for his hand. "Forgive me, but I didn't think you'd admit it, my lord. We fear the same."

"She knows I know he is my half-brother, and the thought worries her." Frederick's shoulders slumped as he stepped further into the room, his eyes dark with a heaviness that went beyond fatigue. "I've spent my life disappointing my parents," he said quietly. "My mother... she's been locked away for six years, thanks to my father, who is locked up now. But I know the look of disappointment. I've seen it on their faces too many times." His voice cracked. "And today, when the physician told her Charlie wasn't badly hurt, that same disappointment was there. It was unmistakable."

Charlie shifted in bed, grimacing with the effort, but remained silent. Annabel's grip on his hand tightened, her knuckles white. "She pushed him," she whispered, voice low and urgent. "I saw it. She thought I wasn't looking, but I was."

Frederick nodded slowly, running a hand through his disheveled hair. "She's been in the dark for so long, locked away in that dungeon... I don't think she knows how to act around anyone she perceives as a threat."

Annabel's voice tightened with worry. "We can stay with friends of mine, fishmongers in the village. We don't need to stay here. Not after this."

Frederick shook his head. "I had a different idea."

Annabel's breath hitched, her eyes searching Frederick's face. "What is it?"

Frederick hesitated, his gaze dropping for a moment before he spoke. "My mother knows she's unwell. She's agreed to stay with Geoffrey for a while, and she'll take the twins with her. Geoffrey's staff will look after her until she's feeling more stable." He smiled weakly. "She just needs time."

Annabel frowned. "And what happens when she returns?"

Frederick's expression grew serious. He reached into his coat and pulled out a folded sheaf of parchment, holding it out to Charlie. "You won't need to worry about that. You'll be as far from the castle as you can be without leaving the grounds, before she returns. This is the deed to the Wright house—I've had this ready for you since yesterday. You deserve it for all you've done to help me get my mother back."

Charlie's brow furrowed as he unfurled the parchment, his eyes widening. "The farmhouse by the river... the one my family used to rent." His voice was thick with disbelief. "Frederick... we never owned it."

"Well, you do now," Frederick said, his voice rough with emotion. "As my brother, you deserve far more, Charlie, and I'm sorry it has to be a secret. Giving you the house where your family lived is the least I can do... I wish it could be more."

"I can't believe it." Charlie struggled to maintain his composure. "A house... that's... Thank you, Frederick." He glanced over at Annabel, who sat in stunned silence, her fingers still laced with his. "Darling? What do you think?"

Annabel's lips parted, but her voice was barely audible. "I think... I think leaving is still our best option, at least by the time Philippa returns." She slipped her hand from Charlie's, wrapping her arms around herself as though trying to hold onto some semblance of control.

"Do what you will." Frederick let out a long, tired sigh, his eyes drifting to Cecelia. "You're surprised my mother agreed to leaving me behind, aren't you?" he asked quietly. "I know I am."

Cecelia nodded, her own body aching with fatigue, her ankle throbbing beneath her weight. "It seemed... strange. She's been so protective of you, especially with your illness."

Frederick's smile was small, sad. "Part of her doesn't want to leave. But she knows I need time. Time to prepare for what comes next." His voice trailed off, the weight of the future pressing down on him like a heavy cloak, matching the burden Cecelia felt in her own chest.

A sudden knock interrupted the moment, followed by the door creaking open to reveal two young children. Their faces were a mix of frustration and sorrow. The boy, Talon, glared up at Frederick, his hands clenched into fists. "So the day's finally come," he spat. "You're kicking us out, is that it?"

Frederick's face softened, the usual calm in his voice now tinged with sadness. "Of course not, Talon," he said gently. "You're going to stay with Uncle Geoffrey and Mother for a while. When you come back, things will be better."

"I don't believe you," Talon hissed, his voice sharp with anger. "Where's Father? Why is Mother back all of a sudden? No one's told us anything! I should bloody push YOU down the stairs."

Annabel sucked in her breath sharply and the girl beside him, Cassidy, gave her brother a reproachful look. "No one's going to tell us anything," she sighed, her voice weary beyond her years. "Not with you yelling like that. We'll be lucky if they EVER tell us what's really going on. You ruin everything."

"You say that to the wrong brother," hissed Talon, glaring at Frederick.

"Talon, Cassidy," Philippa's voice rang out from the hall as she approached, her presence casting a long shadow into the room. "The carriage is ready. Say goodbye to your older brother and tell him you'll see him in a fortnight."

Talon muttered a sullen goodbye, while Cassidy unexpectedly rushed forward, throwing her arms around Frederick in a tight hug. Frederick, caught off guard, returned the embrace awkwardly, his eyes distant as he watched his mother and the twins leave the room.

As the door clicked shut behind them, a heavy silence fell over the room. Annabel turned to Cecelia, her voice soft but serious. "How are you feeling, really?"

Cecelia let out a long sigh, exhaustion weighing on her limbs. "I'm fine," she said, though the tremor in her voice betrayed her vulnerability. "Healthy enough, and my family is helping." Her chest tightened as she imagined losing that support. "I don't know what I'd do without them."

Annabel's smile was small but kind. "I'd like to say you have us, too, but... I think we'll need you more than you need us, at least for a while."

Cecelia smiled, squeezing Annabel's hand. "I'll be here for you, as long as I can."

"Thank you," Annabel whispered.

"Show her your pages," Charlie mumbled, eyes still closed as if drained by the conversation.

"Pages?" Cecelia tilted her head, curiosity piqued. "For the book?"

"Charlie!" Annabel frowned, casting a sharp look at him. "They're not ready. You know I wasn't going to show her yet."

Charlie waved a lazy hand, his voice thick with the lingering haze of herbal medication. "Doesn't matter if they're finished. She can't read anyway—won't know if it's rubbish or not."

Annabel flushed a deep pink, her fingers twitching nervously. "Oh, Cecelia... I'm sorry. The medicine is making him bold."

Cecelia laughed lightly, waving off Annabel's concern. "He's right—let's have a look. I'll need to fetch my sketch pad later, though. Mumma threatened to take it if she catches me 'wasting time' with art again."

Annabel chuckled, though there was sympathy in her eyes. "Your mother and I haven't always seeing eye to eye, that's for certain."

Cecelia nodded. "Do you need anything while you sit with Charlie?"

"That would be perfect, thank you. In fact, if you wouldn't mind waiting here with him, I'll fetch a few things." Annabel stood, placing a gentle kiss on Charlie's forehead before slipping out the door. As she exited, nearly colliding with Rhys, a castle guard, a flurry of awkward apologies passed outside before the door closed once again, leaving Cecelia and Charlie alone.

Charlie groaned softly, shifting in bed. "I can't believe any of this."

"Quiet now," Cecelia soothed, tucking the blanket back over his shoulder. "You're in the best position possible for someone who's been pushed down the stairs. Did you hear Frederick? He said he'd give you a house. He'll spare no expense for your recovery."

Charlie grimaced. "I don't want money spent on me if I'm not earning it. What am I to do? Lie here all day, thinking about how I might be crippled for life at some point because of that madwoman, while Annabel wastes her days tending to me?"

"Well, that's why I'm here," Cecelia said, straightening her back with determination despite her own aches. "I'll help both of you."

He smirked, wincing as pain creased his brow. "You're a pregnant girl about to be dragged off to America within weeks."

Cecelia's eyes widened, panic momentarily breaking her composure. "How did you know? No one's supposed to know."

Charlie chuckled softly, a raspy sound that seemed to cost him effort. "Your father's been running his mouth, as usual. He's trying to get supplies for the journey. He told me the real reason over a few ales and a game of cards."

Cecelia's shoulders slumped, frustration bubbling to the surface. "That was quick. I'd rather stay here, you know. I don't want to go to America. But what choice do I have? You're right ...I'm unmarried, pregnant, and at the mercy of my parents."

Charlie's expression softened, though his words were pointed. "You've plenty of excuses, but excuses aren't the same as choices. Make your own choices. Make your own luck."

Cecelia scoffed, crossing her arms. "That's rich, coming from someone who's never had to empty a chamber pot every day."

Charlie's brow arched, undeterred. "I was mucking out stables until recently. Henry Rowley saw to it that I was given the dirtiest, most odious tasks."

"That was because of the old baron's grudge against your father. You were a merchant once, and you'll be one again, now that Henry's out of the way. It's not the same."

He shrugged, his face softening further. "It's not. But you weren't born to be a maid either. I remember when they tried to educate you with the other children. You ran away from the tutor. That's when your mother put you to work, wasn't it?"

Cecelia's lips pressed into a thin line, her silence speaking volumes.

Charlie sighed, voice gentler now. "Look, all I'm saying is I didn't have to go after Annabel. But I saw the world she was creating for herself, and I realized I wanted to be part of it. So, I jumped in. It was the best thing I ever did. If I'd listened to that voice in my head—the one that told me I was useless, that I had to follow the path others saw for me—I wouldn't be here today."

Cecelia's eyes softened. "Both of your parents died just a few years after I arrived, yes? You had to make your own way."

"And yet, here you are with living, loving parents," Charlie said, a hint of a grin tugging at his lips. "So, in that sense, you're already two steps ahead."

Cecelia allowed herself a small smile at that, her heart lifting just a little. "Perhaps."

Chapter Six

LEARNING TO READ

The next day, Cecelia made her way to the old Wright house, where Annabel and Charlie were already settling in. The cottage, nestled at the edge of a wood, had a thatched roof curling with age yet still sturdy. Thick stone walls bore the marks of time, and the overgrown garden hinted at years of neglect. Yet, despite its wear, the house had a charm, as if it had sprung naturally from the surrounding land, its crooked lines speaking of history and endurance. Cecelia carried beeswax and rags, intent on helping with the cleaning.

As she stepped inside, the scent of fresh lavender welcomed her. Sunlight streamed through the doorway, glinting off the newly polished wood floors and furniture. "Goodness, Annabel. What have you done?"

Annabel, her sleeves rolled up and hair slightly tousled, stood in the center of the room, smiling with a mix of pride and exhaustion.

"I know, I've practically scrubbed down the entire house with just a bit of help from Lise and Agatha. Charlie's been helping carry thing in—he just left to fetch supplies from the far side of the castle." She gestured around the room, her smile fading slightly. "The place is lovely, isn't it? The craftsmanship is remarkable; every beam and joint fits so cleverly. It's almost as if it were built with us in mind." Her voice grew quieter, ripe with unease. "But I can't shake the feeling that we've been manipulated into staying. My mother's thrilled about the engagement—she's coming out to chaperone me until the wedding this weekend."

"I can't wait to properly meet her." Cecelia set her rags on the table, taking in the freshly aired linens draped over the chairs and the hearth swept clean. "If you really wanted to leave, Frederick wouldn't stand in your way."

Annabel sighed, running her hand over a newly polished chair. "I know. But how can I? Refusing a free house—especially one tied to Charlie's past—feels foolish." Her voice faltered, revealing a hint of vulnerability. "Yet, after what the Baroness did, I don't think I'll ever truly feel safe here. Whether it's two weeks or two months, the fear won't just disappear."

Cecelia nodded, a sympathetic frown forming. "I've never felt safe, not really. Life's always been like walking on a knife's edge, never knowing if there'd be enough food or shelter. Anxiety's been a constant companion."

Annabel's eyes softened with understanding. "Yes... it's been that way for many of us, hasn't it? But sometimes, I find relief in reading or writing. It's as if the world pauses for a moment, and I can breathe." A blush crept over her cheeks, and she ducked her head, embarrassed. "I hoped this house might offer a small slice of happiness. A little less dread, a little more joy."

"But the Baroness tried to kill your sweetheart," Cecelia said bluntly, breaking the brief moment of optimism. "And that's difficult to move past."

"Yes." Annabel's expression darkened. "Though Charlie seems more worried about me than himself. If it had been my life at risk, he'd be beside himself." She shivered, her resolve hardening. "I'll stay vigilant. Maybe Frederick's right—perhaps a change of scenery will help the Baroness, and Geoffrey's supposed to turn in Henry once everything is set. It can't happen fast enough."

Cecelia suppressed a shudder of her own, nodding in agreement. "No, it can't."

Annabel looked at her with a gentler expression. "Is there anything that makes you feel safe? Something that quiets the anxiety?"

Cecelia hesitated, then allowed a slow smile to spread across her face. "Drawing. When I'm sketching, the world becomes manageable. The chaos fades away."

Annabel's smile turned wistful. "I understand. Writing does the same for me." She paused, then added resolutely, "You can come here to draw anytime. I won't tell your mother."

Cecelia's smile widened as she ducked her head. "You're a good friend, Annabel."

"And you to me." Annabel moved to a small wooden desk by the window, where she carefully unpacked a sheaf of papers from a worn leather satchel. She spread the sheets out methodically, securing each corner with small sandbags—an improvised but effective solution. The soft rustle of old parchment filled the quiet room, blending with the faint crackle of the hearth.

Cecelia leaned closer, squinting at the neat, looping handwriting. The letters looked like a series of intricate patterns to her—beautiful, but utterly indecipherable. "Will you read it to me? I don't remember where we left off. It's our story about the horses, right?"

"Yes." Annabel's expression softened, a fond smile creeping onto her face as she picked up the first page. She pointed to a word near the top. "That's 'horse' right there, see? And..." Her gaze lifted to meet Cecelia's. "I've decided whatever happens with our book, to put down a false name. A pen name, like with my plays, but a different one... I want readers, not trouble. But what about you—do you want your true name on it?"

Cecelia recoiled slightly, her brows furrowing. "Absolutely not. I want the joy of it and, hopefully, some money—not the attention. Let someone else handle that part."

Annabel's laugh was gentle but understanding. "What name should we use, then? Something elegant? Strong?"

Cecelia shrugged, a familiar tightness knotting in her stomach. "Does it matter? I can't read it, anyway. Just make something up."

Annabel's expression grew thoughtful, her voice softening. "Cecelia... do you truly want to learn to read? Deep down?"

Cecelia's shoulders stiffened, frustration bubbling to the surface. "Of course I do," she hissed, her voice raw with emotion. "But I was too stupid as a child, and I'm no better now. The words... they swim before my eyes. Always have."

"You're not stupid," Annabel said firmly, her tone unwavering yet kind. "My little brother and sister—Jacky and Lenora—had the same trouble. They said the words moved, like ripples on water. It was harder for them than for the other children, but I found ways to teach them differently."

Cecelia's suspicion flickered. "Who taught you?" she asked, wary but curious.

Annabel's eyes lit up with a warm memory. "An older, childless woman from the church—a saint in her patience and kindness. She had a gift for helping those whom others overlooked. My parents were farmers and mostly illiterate themselves, so every time I did something to help her, she took the time to teach me." Annabel picked up a small, well-worn hornbook—a wooden tablet with a sheet of parchment covered by a thin layer of horn to protect it. She placed it gently on the desk, then reached for a sandbag. "Here, let's try something different." She paused, extending her hand toward Cecelia. "May I use your fingers? Which hand do you favor?"

"My right," Cecelia replied hesitantly, then extended her hand. "All right... what are you doing?"

Annabel took Cecelia's right index finger, guiding it to trace a semicircle into the soft sandbag. "There. That's a 'C,' the first letter of Cecelia."

Cecelia closed her eyes, focusing intently on the sensation of her finger's path in the sand. The curve was a shape, solid and real. "C," she whispered.

"Exactly," Annabel encouraged, her tone filled with pride. "And now for the next letter—'E.'" She guided Cecelia's finger again, this time creating a shape that resembled a three-rung ladder with one side missing.

Together, they continued tracing each letter of Cecelia's name, Annabel's hand steady and patient as she guided Cecelia through the exercise. The room was bathed in soft, flickering candlelight, the scent of beeswax mingling with the faint, earthy aroma of the wood walls. Cecelia kept her eyes shut, relying entirely on the feel of each shape beneath her fingertip. When she finally opened her eyes, Annabel's face was glowing with pride and encouragement, her eyes bright in the dimly lit room.

"I could see them in my mind," Cecelia whispered, wonder filling her voice. "The letters... they weren't just strange marks anymore. They were shapes I could understand."

Annabel's smile widened, her excitement almost palpable. "That's exactly it! Each letter has its own form and path. Once you start feeling them, you'll begin to recognize them, like familiar faces."

But Cecelia's face soon clouded with doubt, her shoulders slumping. "It'll take ages to do this for every word in a book."

Annabel nodded, her expression turning serious but hopeful. "Yes, it will take time. But this is just the foundation. We'll start with short stories—I'll read them to you, and we'll pick out the words together. As you get better at tracing the letters, you'll need to do it less and less. You'll see."

Cecelia studied her, disbelief mingling with a growing sense of hope. "And you don't mind?" The words came out in a rush, her voice tinged with vulnerability. "You don't have to teach me..."

Annabel's response was immediate and filled with warmth. "It's my pleasure, truly. I'd be honored to help you, Cecelia. Besides, I need something to keep me busy while I adjust to this new life—becoming a merchant's wife and, with any luck, a published writer. We'll both be learning together."

Cecelia's laughter bubbled up, shaking her head. "You're a whirlwind."

Annabel's eyes twinkled, but she said nothing, just nodded in agreement. She then stood, moving with a sense of purpose. "Now, you've worked hard today, and I promised a reward, didn't I?"

Cecelia watched as Annabel went to a small side table, retrieving a wooden tray that held a small plate of jam tarts, their golden crusts still warm from the hearth and the vibrant red filling glistening under the candlelight. Annabel placed the tray on the table between them.

"Jam tarts," Annabel said, her smile widening. "A little treat to celebrate your first lesson."

Cecelia's eyes lit up at the sight of the tarts, and she eagerly picked one up. The sweet, sticky jam burst on her tongue, and she closed her eyes, savoring the moment. "These are lovely," she murmured between bites, her voice full of genuine appreciation.

Annabel picked up her own tart, raising it playfully in a mock toast. "To learning—no matter how long it takes."

Cecelia laughed, raising her tart in return. "To learning."

After finishing the tarts, Cecelia stretched and moved toward the door, the wooden floor creaking gently beneath her feet. "We should make sure a guard is stationed at your door tonight," she suggested with a yawn, fatigue catching up with her. "Just in case..."

Annabel's brow furrowed, a note of unease in her voice. "In case what?"

Cecelia turned back, her expression serious. "You suspect it too, don't you? That Philippa might still be plotting something."

Annabel sighed, her shoulders drooping as the truth settled heavily between them. "We freed her from the dungeon, for goodness' sake. Why would she want to harm us after that?"

Cecelia gave a small, knowing shrug, a wry smile tugging at her lips. "Rich folks aren't very good at gratitude, are they?"

Chapter Seven

A REAL ARTIST

Her mother's watchful eyes followed Cecelia everywhere the next day, leaving her no chance to sneak away and retrieve her hidden drawing pad. It wasn't until Maggie, the castle chef, discreetly pressed a box of gingerbread into Cecelia's hands—along with a shilling for her trouble—that she found an excuse to leave the house. The errand: delivering the gingerbread to Annabel and Charlie in celebration of their recent engagement! It was a task Cecelia would have gladly done for free, but the extra coin was a welcome surprise.

As she approached the tiny riverside cottage where her best friend and Charlie had settled, Cecelia breathed in the scent of slow-moving water and damp earth. The afternoon sun reflected off the river's surface, casting a shimmering glow that played through the windows of the modest home. Upon entering, she noticed how the warm and inviting atmosphere was such a stark contrast to the chill of the castle. The cottage was small but welcoming, with polished wooden beams above and a freshly swept stone hearth below. The faint scent of wood smoke hung in the air, blending with the sweet aroma of something citrusy.

Cecelia settled into a wooden chair, letting the cozy ambiance wrap around her like a comforting embrace. She watched as Annabel ladled lemon posset into a pewter cup, its tart aroma mingling with the soft sounds of the river just beyond the open window. The cottage exuded a sense of peace, one Cecelia rarely felt within the castle's drafty stone walls.

Annabel handed Cecelia the cup, smiling. "I can't tell you how wonderful it is to have a place of our own. I'm so glad you came to call. Did you manage to bring your sketchbook this time?"

Cecelia sighed, shaking her head. "No, I couldn't retrieve it. My mother's eyes have been on me constantly." She gestured toward a stack of freshly laundered linens on a nearby chair. "But what's all this? I didn't see them yesterday."

Annabel groaned, rolling her eyes. "My mother brought them over to embroider my new married name on every piece. Better her fingers than mine." She laughed. "She's gone to the castle now, fetching supper from Maggie while we prepare for the wedding."

Cecelia joined in the laughter. "That's lovely of her. I'd be honored to help, too, if there's anything you need."

Annabel's laughter softened, and she leaned in to whisper, "Please don't offer too much help, or my mother will start embroidering baby clothes next!" Her expression grew serious, and she added, "But of course, you're always welcome here, Cecelia. I hope you'll stay at the castle after your baby's born, won't you?"

Cecelia stiffened at the mention of the baby, her mother's warnings echoing in her mind. Had Charlie not told her of their move to America? "I—" she began, fumbling for an answer. Fortunately, the door creaked open, sparing her from a conversation she wasn't prepared to have.

Charlie entered, his strong arms wrapped around a large bundle of wood that filled the room with the scent of fresh-cut timber. Cecelia exhaled, grateful for the interruption, and watched as he set down the load with a grin.

"Welcome home, love," Annabel greeted him, her face lighting up as he moved closer.

Charlie grinned widely. "Good morrow, my love, and to you as well, Cecelia. And do you see what I've brought?"

"It looks like... bundles of wood?" Annabel laughed, tugging at the burlap covering to uncover a pile of planks and sticks. "Is that what's got you so excited?"

Charlie's grin widened as he began to unpack. "Yes, but not just any wood! Manik has gifted me some of his finest, to mark my return to the trade." He held up a piece of dark walnut. "Look at this!"

Annabel reached out, brushing her hand against Charlie's arm as she admired the wood's rich grain. "It's beautiful," she murmured.

Cecelia nodded. "What will you make with it?"

He pulled out a polished piece of yew. "This yew is perfect for something intricate, like a carved box or a decorative panel. And this oak," he said, tapping another bundle, "will become part of a grand chair for our hearth, with carved armrests and a high back—something to last for generations."

As Cecelia observed him, a mix of admiration and envy rose within her. Here was Charlie, full of purpose and plans, while Annabel, too, had written two completed plays and a book. Both were shaping their futures, driven by clear goals. Cecelia, in contrast, felt like a drifting leaf, her own path as undefined as the rough wood scattered across the table.

Her hand drifted to her belly, thoughts turning to the unborn child within her. Would she be able to create a future for her child that was free of the uncertainty that had plagued her own life? The rough, untouched planks in front of her seemed symbolic of her own raw potential, waiting to be carved into something meaningful.

Annabel nodded encouragingly. "It sounds like you have a lot of work ahead to set up your booth, love. I'm glad the fall hasn't slowed you down." Her fingers traced the rim of her cup thoughtfully. "I was thinking we should invite the Sutar family over for dinner to thank them... but—"

Cecelia's eyes widened.

"Sooner than you think," Charlie interrupted with a wide grin. "I just spoke with Frederick, and he may be ill, but he's still eager to commission a series of younger up-and-coming artists. Guess who's first on his list?"

Annabel's brow furrowed in surprise. "Not Kunal?"

Charlie's grin widened. "Exactly."

"Kunal Sutar..." Cecelia's voice trailed off, her pulse quickening. "Frederick hired him?"

Charlie nodded, his expression bright with enthusiasm. "Yes, the very same. Manik is his father. It's wonderful, really, to have such talent nearby. I didn't expect anyone to occupy the artist outbuildings so soon. They've been abandoned for years—what a waste of space." He shook his head. "But no better time to bring them back to life, eh?"

Cecelia's blood ran cold at the mention of the outbuildings. Her thoughts whirled. The artist outbuildings... "How right you are. When does he move in?" she asked, trying to keep her voice light.

"He's already there," he said with enthusiasm. "Kunal came back from the market with me and is picking out a studio now. He'll sign the contract with Frederick later today."

"Already... there?" Cecelia managed to say, her mind spinning.

"Yes," Charlie confirmed, noting her sudden distress with confusion. "James said he had offered one of the outbuildings to *you* earlier? ...but when I mentioned Annabel had a spot for you to draw here, he unlocked them and said he'd just give Kunal his pick. You didn't leave anything in there, did you? James said they were all empty."

Cecelia's face drained of color. "My sketches!" Without hesitation, she shot to her feet. "I'm so sorry, but I have to go!"

Charlie and Annabel exchanged startled glances as Cecelia bolted from the cottage, her breaths coming in short gasps. She started with urgency, but soon slowed, instinctively cradling her growing belly. The baby's well-being had to come first. Yet anxiety gnawed at her relentlessly, and her stomach churned violently at the thought of Kunal stumbling upon and scrutinizing her raw attempts at art.

The path from the riverside cottage to the dilapidated artist outbuildings wound through a cluster of ancient oak trees, their gnarled branches casting eerie shadows across her path. The scent of moss and decaying leaves filled the air. Cecelia's heart pounded as she neared the ivy-choked cabin she had secretly claimed, her legs trembling beneath her. She paused at the door, a mixture of dread and hope tightening her chest. Please, let my work be untouched...

The sound of footsteps from a neighboring cabin made her freeze, her breath hitching. But there was no movement from inside hers. Swallowing her panic, she gripped the handle and turned it slowly to find it was indeed now unlocked. To her immense relief, the door creaked open to reveal no inhabitants, the hinges groaning in protest. The interior was dark and still, undisturbed. A flicker of a smile crossed her face as she closed the door firmly behind her and locked it with the key her father had given her. Safe... for now.

A thin beam of sunlight filtered through a crack in the shutters, casting a pale stripe across the floorboards. Cecelia's eyes adjusted quickly, and she moved toward the small loft where her precious sketchbook was hidden, a surge of urgency propelling her forward.

As Cecelia approached the ladder, something snagged her foot. Startled, she looked down and saw not a random stick, but an intricately carved pencil... and her heart fluttered with a familiar cadence she remembered from her recent trip to the marketplace. The craftsmanship was exquisite, and was that a tiny *squirrel* perched on the end, its tail seemingly bristling with life? She ran her fingers over the delicate carving, marveling at the precision, and her pulse raced when she wondered how it had come to be there.

Quickly she pocketed the pencil, rummaging her hands in the small tied-on pocket that seemed now to be empty, and her heart sank. Where had the greenhouse ring gone? Raising her eyebrows in alarm, Cecelia grimaced as her fingers found a hole in the linen, and she shook her head and slipped the pencil into the larger tied-on pocket that usually housed her sketchbook. No time to worry on it now.

A sudden snap of a twig outside shattered her thoughts, sending a jolt of panic through her. Cecelia hurried toward the ladder, hands shaking, and she climbed, the weight of fear, along with the growing life inside her, seemed to press down with each step. The old ladder creaked and groaned, but she pressed on, determined to retrieve her sketchbook.

Just as she reached the top rung, there was a loud crack. Cecelia's breath hitched as the rung gave way beneath her weight. She scrambled for the next one, only to feel it splinter under her grip. Her heart pounded as she clawed desperately for a stable hold, finally managing to hoist herself into the loft with a burst of adrenaline. Below, the ladder crashed to the floor.

Cecelia lay in the loft, panting, her body trembling from the close call. The dusty linens beneath her offered no comfort. *That was too close.* She quickly checked herself for injuries, relieved to find nothing worse than scrapes and bruises, but her relief was short-lived when she realized of her sketches had slipped from the sketchbook and drifted to the floor below.

Terror gripped her. *What if someone finds it? What if Kunal sees it?* The thought of him discovering her work, scrutinizing her unpolished lines—she couldn't bear it. No one must see my drawings. She shoved the sketchbook into her largest tied-on pocket.

With a new surge of urgency, Cecelia leaned over the edge of the loft, eyes locked on the stray drawing lying like a fallen leaf on the floor below. She couldn't leave it there. *I have to get it back.* Her heart hammered as she considered her options. With the ladder broken, if she really wanted to descend, she'd have to descend the rickety shelves nailed to the wall.

Setting her jaw in determination, Cecelia reached for the nearest shelf.

Before she could make another move, a sharp knock at the door jolted her. "Hello? Is someone in there? Do you need help?"

The voice was unmistakable—Kunal's. His presence had lingered too long in her thoughts since their first encounter.

"No!" Cecelia's reply came out more panicked than she intended, her cheeks burning with embarrassment at the thought of him discovering her sketches. She lay flat on her right side in the loft, her arm stretched futilely toward the collapsed ladder below. *If only I were taller...*

"Are you sure?" Kunal's voice grew more insistent. "I heard a crash and thought I heard a cry. Are you hurt? May I come in?"

Her heart pounded louder and faster in her chest. "The door is locked," she called back, frustrated almost to the point of tears. "I'm in the loft, and the ladder... broke. I couldn't let you in even if I wanted to."

There was a pause, followed by Kunal's calming tone. "All right, just stay where you are. I'll see what I can do."

Cecelia huffed in frustration, retreating deeper into the shadows of the loft. She heard his footsteps circling the cabin, then the faint sound of gentle tapping—testing the doorframe. The rhythmic chiseling that followed was delicate but determined. Moments later, she heard the click of metal on metal, and the door creaked open, a rush of cool air sweeping into the room.

Kunal stepped inside, silhouetted by the sunlight streaming in behind him. His dark eyes, sharp and curious, scanned the room before finding her in the loft. "Cecelia Rousseau." His voice was light, teasing even. "I thought I heard a familiar voice."

Chapter Eight

PROPERLY MEETING

Cecelia's breath caught as Kunal stepped closer, his presence filling the small cabin with an unexpected warmth. He looked as handsome as she remembered—tall, broad-shouldered, with a quiet confidence radiating from his relaxed posture. His finely embroidered tunic, though marked by the dust of his day's labor, only accentuated the strength of his long, muscular arms.

When Kunal's gaze fell on the sketch fluttering on the floor, Cecelia's heart sank. She tried to steady her breathing as he bent down with a graceful ease, retrieving the drawing with a touch so gentle it felt almost reverent. He glanced up at her, a smile forming at the corner of his mouth. "I had a suspicion you might be an artist when you asked for that pencil," he said. "As I recall, you denied this."

"I'm not," Cecelia mumbled, her cheeks burning with embarrassment. She wished she could melt into the shadows of the cabin. "Truly, I'm not. I just—" She faltered, unsure of how to explain herself.

Kunal's dark eyes softened as he studied the drawing, his fingers lightly tracing the rough lines. He absorbed the details with surprising attentiveness, as if seeing more in the incomplete work than even Cecelia herself had dared to acknowledge. His presence felt both soothing and disconcerting, like a hearth fire in a cold room.

"This *is* yours, isn't it?" he asked, lifting the paper towards her, his tone sincere.

Cecelia forced herself to meet his gaze, feeling exposed in a way she hadn't anticipated. "Yes," she admitted quietly. "It's... just a sketch. No one was ever meant to see it."

"I consider myself lucky, then." Kunal chuckled softly, a warm sound that filled the chilly room. "I think you're more of an artist than you realize, Cecelia."

His words, paired with the teasing warmth in his voice, made her feel unsteady. Despite herself, a small smile crept onto her own face. "And as an artist yourself, you must know it's improper to judge an unfinished piece," she quipped, attempting to mask her vulnerability with humor.

"True enough," Kunal agreed, returning the drawing with a smile. As he handed it up to her, giving her a glimpse of sculpted forearms, his fingers brushed hers briefly—a touch that sent a surprising spark of warmth through her. "But from what I've seen, there's already something remarkable here."

Cecelia's pulse quickened, her fingers trembling slightly as she took back the sketch. She quickly tucked it away, her heart pounding. "Thank you," she managed, her voice barely above a whisper.

Kunal turned his attention to the fallen ladder, his expression becoming practical. "Let me fix that for you." He moved with purpose, setting the ladder upright and testing its stability before holding it securely. "If you'd like to descend, I shall not let you fall."

Cecelia gathered her skirts and carefully descended, her steps tentative as she navigated the broken rungs. Her breath came out in a shaky sigh of relief as her feet touched the ground. "I'm sorry for the trouble," she murmured. "You shouldn't have had to come to my rescue."

He stepped back, giving her space, but his eyes twinkled. "It was no trouble at all," he said. "I rather enjoy rescuing fellow artists in distress." His tone was playful, and his words made Cecelia's heart flutter.

She shook her head. "You're too kind, really. But... I'm just a maid here, Kunal. I assure you, you're wasting your time and charm."

His eyebrows lifted, surprise and confusion crossing his face. "A maid?" he repeated, as if trying to reconcile her words with the talent he had glimpsed. "Forgive me, but I thought you were one of Frederick's friends. He speaks of you as though you're part of his world."

Cecelia hesitated, unsure how much to reveal. "Frederick didn't have many friends while his father was around," she said quietly. "I suppose servants were the closest thing he had."

Kunal's expression shifted into understanding. "I see," he murmured. "So, you've known him a long time, then?"

"Yes," Cecelia replied, memories of her years at the castle flooding back. "I've been here ten years." She glanced down, suddenly feeling vulnerable beneath his gaze.

Recognition brightened Kunal's eyes. "Wait... you're the ginger-haired maid Charlie mentioned from his youth," he said with a chuckle. "The one always found sketching in hidden corners?"

A blush crept up Cecelia's cheeks, but she laughed despite her nerves. "Yes, that was me. And now, I'm an unwed and pregnant ginger-haired maid," she added, her voice dry but edged with defensiveness. She half-expected Kunal to withdraw or look down on her.

But he did neither. Instead, Kunal's eyes filled with unexpected compassion. "Everyone's journey is different," he said gently. "Yours is no less worthy than anyone else's."

The sincerity in Kunal's voice took Cecelia by surprise. She hesitated, then reached into her pocket and pulled out the intricately carved pencil, feeling the weight of its craftsmanship in her palm. "This belongs to you, doesn't it?" she asked.

Kunal's eyes lit up as he recognized the small object. "Ah, yes! I told you I like squirrels," he said, a broad smile breaking across his face. He gently took the pencil from her, their fingers brushing once more, the brief contact sending a familiar warmth spiraling through Cecelia's veins. He turned the pencil in his hand, holding it up to the dim light filtering through the dusty cabin. "I spent an entire evening getting it just right, then thought I'd lost it. Thank you."

Cecelia's heart was still racing, her pulse pounding in her ears. There was something genuine behind his smile and smooth words, a layer of earnestness she hadn't expected in this confident merchant. The realization unsettled her more than she cared to admit.

Kunal's gaze lingered on Cecelia's face. "Thank you for finding it," he repeated, his tone warm. "I came into this outbuilding first, but I wanted to explore the others before making a final decision." He paused. "And you—were you hoping to claim this space for your own?" His eyes danced curiously, but the question held no judgment, only interest.

"No, no," Cecelia stammered, her cheeks flushing. Her heart continued to thud rapidly in her chest, as if trying to break free of its confines. But Kunal's gentle patience seemed to coax the truth from her. "Well... yes," she finally confessed, her voice faltering. "But Annabel has offered to let me keep my drawing pad at her place."

"Why all the secrecy?" he teased, a hint of playfulness in his tone. "Are you a spy, Cecelia Rousseau?"

She let out a nervous laugh, trying to mask her discomfort. "No. My mother simply wishes me to focus on my duties, rather than indulge in what she calls 'nonsensical creative pursuits.'" The words tumbled out like an overdue confession, laden with years of silent rebellion.

Kunal's expression softened, understanding and sympathy crossing his face. "In Amber, where I'm from, many don't have the luxury of pursuing art," he said, his voice quieter. "But those who are encouraged to find beauty in the world and share it."

A strained laugh escaped Cecelia's lips. "My mother insists on diligence above all else. But I've always found ways to steal moments for my art." She glanced toward the door, half-expecting her mother's stern figure to appear at any moment. "Please... don't tell her. If I were a wise woman, I'd abandon my sketches altogether," she said, her voice filled with bitter resignation. "It seems my future lies solely in servitude and motherhood."

Kunal's brow furrowed. "That would be a true waste," he said earnestly. "You have a talent, Cecelia. It deserves to be seen."

She scoffed lightly, brushing off his words. "You've only seen a squirrel," she mumbled, her voice betraying her self-doubt.

Kunal's gaze held steady as he extended his hand. "May I see the sketch once more, please?" he asked, his voice gentle.

Cecelia hesitated, then reluctantly handed the page back to him. She watched, her breath hitching, as Kunal examined the drawing with a kind of appreciation that made her heart flutter. His dark eyes roamed over the details of her work, each line seeming to draw him deeper into her world. He held the paper with care, as if it were more than just a maid's idle doodle.

"This," he said slowly, his voice rich with admiration, "is a beautiful work." He traced the outline of the squirrel's fur with his finger, not quite touching the page, as if respecting the sanctity of the lines. "Your attention to detail is extraordinary—the texture of the fur, the liveliness in its stance. You've captured a moment in motion, a creature poised within its own world. And your use of light," he added, his tone thoughtful, "gives the drawing a softness and depth."

Cecelia's cheeks burned with an unfamiliar mix of pride and embarrassment. No one had ever spoken of her work this way. She looked down, unsure of what to say.

Cecelia blinked back the sudden rush of tears pricking at her eyes. His words, so generous, stirred something deep within her—something she hadn't allowed herself to feel for a long time: hope. "Thank you," she whispered, her voice barely audible. "You certainly have a way with words."

Kunal glanced down for a moment, a faint blush coloring his cheeks. When he looked up, his gaze was steady, his dark eyes holding a kind intensity. "You should not abandon your art," he said, his voice firm yet gentle. "Nor should you be ashamed to call yourself an artist. It is not a title of shame but one of honor. Your work speaks volumes, Cecelia, even if you do not yet hear it."

The words settled over Cecelia like a soft, unexpected warmth, making her feel both vulnerable and seen. She let herself look at him, her breath hitching as she took in the sharp angles of his face, the defined nose, the graceful curve of his lips, and the dark waves of hair escaping his cap. The room's rustic, drafty chill seemed to recede, replaced by the sudden intimacy of his presence. Her heart fluttered, a reckless thought crossing her mind: What would it feel like to close the space between them, to let their lips meet? It was an absurd notion—wild and wholly inappropriate—but the very thought sent a shiver down her spine.

Realizing the absurdity of the moment, she forced herself back to reality. "Very well," she replied lightly, trying to maintain a semblance of composure.

Kunal's brows lifted in surprise. "Sorry?"

"I shall not squirrel away my talents," she quipped, a shy smile tugging at her lips, attempting to play off the moment's intensity with a touch of humor.

To her surprise and delight, Kunal laughed—a rich, hearty sound that filled the small cabin, warming the air. "A clever turn of phrase, Cecelia."

Just then, a voice called from outside, breaking the spell between them. "Kunal? Are you in there?"

The voice was female, firm and purposeful, and Cecelia instinctively took a step back. "Is that... your wife?" she blurted, a sudden pang of disappointment gripping her.

Kunal's eyes widened in surprise, then amusement. "I'm coming, Rupa!" he called back, before turning to Cecelia with an apologetic smile. "My sister," he explained gently. "She's helping me settle in while our parents manage the market." His tone softened, as if wanting to reassure Cecelia.

They stepped out of the cabin together, and Cecelia's breath caught as she caught sight of Rupa. She was striking—tall like her brother, her posture commanding, with dark braided hair woven with a maroon scarf that matched her finely embroidered gown. Her piercing eyes swept over Cecelia with quick assessment, her smile warm yet edged with practicality.

Kunal gestured toward her with pride. "Cecelia, this is my sister, Rupa Sutar. She's considering staying here at Rowley Castle with our mother while Father oversees the business. Rupa, this is Cecelia Rousseau, an artist of considerable talent."

"A pleasure," Rupa said formally, eyes gleaming with curiosity. "It's always refreshing to meet a fellow artist."

Cecelia managed an awkward curtsy. "The pleasure is mine," she mumbled, feeling acutely aware of the rough edges of her patched dress and the dust still clinging to her skirts from the loft.

"We're attending a gathering tomorrow evening at the Le Fouquet house, along with Frederick," Rupa continued, her tone brisk and businesslike. "They're considering commissioning work from us—perhaps other artists as well. You should join us."

A surge of excitement flared within Cecelia, but she quickly quelled it. "That's terribly kind of you," she said cautiously, "but I'm only a maid. I wouldn't wish to impose on such company."

"A maid!" Rupa's brow furrowed as she glanced at Kunal. "You two seemed rather familiar when I arrived..." Her words were pointed, though not hostile. "How did such intimacy come to be?"

Kunal quickly stepped in, his tone light but firm. "Rupa, don't embarrass her. Cecelia and I first met in the marketplace. She's clever and resourceful—she helped me with a client and brought me the important news about Lady Philippa Rowley which led to this commission."

"I see." Rupa's lips twitched, her expression both intrigued and skeptical. "So, you're the castle gossip?"

"Rupa!" Kunal's voice was sharp. "Cecelia, I'm sorry..."

"No, I'm sorry." Cecelia's face burned, unable to bear the scrutiny any longer. "Excuse me," she whispered. Without a second thought, she turned and fled from the cabin, running until the rough cobblestones beneath her feet gave way to softer earth. She didn't stop until she was safely inside her parents' farmhouse, where she collapsed against the door, her breath coming in shaky gasps.

Chapter Nine

FIRESIDE TALK

The rest of Cecelia's day unfolded in monotonous drudgery. The weight of Castle Rowley's cold stone walls seemed to press down on her as she polished the silverware until her fingers were red and raw, each piece gleaming but providing no comfort. Emptying chamber pots—an endless, humiliating task—made her stomach turn, while the constant tending of the fire left her flushed with heat but never truly warm. The chill from the stone floors beneath her feet seemed to seep into her very bones, a constant reminder that this castle, for all its grandeur, was not her home but her cage.

By afternoon, she found herself on her knees, scrubbing the cold, unyielding floor behind a towering walnut cabinet in the solar. The cabinet loomed over her like a behemoth, its dark, intricately carved edges catching what little light filtered through the narrow, leaded windows. The weak, watery light cast spindly shadows across the room, as if the castle itself conspired to keep every inch shrouded in darkness. The musty scent of old wood mixed with the faint odor of extinguished candles.

The repetitive motion of scrubbing sent dull aches through her back, but she dared not stop. The rhythmic sound of the brush scraping the stone created a dismal sort of music, accompanied by the occasional crackle from the nearby hearth. Though the fire blazed, its warmth never seemed to reach her. She paused only briefly, resting back on her heels, her breath coming in shallow bursts. One hand slipped unconsciously to her belly. Barely noticeable under her coarse work clothes, it would soon be impossible to prevent questions from all she met. *What will I do then?* She bit her lip, pushing the thought aside with a familiar, weary resolve.

The cabinet's imposing shadow engulfed her, cloaking her from the world outside—a small mercy. The muffled thud of footsteps on the polished floor startled her, breaking through the stillness. Voices followed—low, hushed—and Cecelia froze, her hands gripping the scrubbing brush tightly.

Who's that? she thought, lowering herself carefully to the cold stone floor. She craned her neck to peer under the cabinet, eyes wide with surprise when she saw them—the Sutar family.

Annabel had told her all their names, and she recognized them quickly from her friend's description. Manik Sutar, tall and commanding, led the way with the quiet authority of a man who knew his place yet wore it with humility. His dark eyes swept the room, sharp and calculating, like those of a master craftsman assessing raw material. Behind him followed Sarala, her back straight and her chin lifted high. A shawl of deep blue wool was draped across her slender shoulders, fastened with a delicate gold pin. Her movements were fluid, graceful, like a woman who had learned the art of silence and strength. Next came Kunal, and her heart gave a little flutter. Cecelia noticed his brow was creased with thought, as if the weight of expectation had settled there, while Rupa walked with her mother's quiet elegance at the rear.

"Beta," Manik's voice was deep, smooth as aged oak. "Pass me your pencil."

"Of course, Pitaji." Kunal reached into his jacket, producing a slender pencil, hand-carved and dark with age. He passed it to his father, his eyes lowered in deference—a gesture of respect rather than submission.

Manik took the pencil, turning it over in his hands with a critical eye. "Kunal," he said, his voice soft but firm, "you must stop carving these animals onto your pencils. The wood weakens; the integrity is compromised." He ran a thumb over the small carved squirrel at the end of the pencil, shaking his head slightly. "Imagine how easily this will snap. Carve your creatures on something more substantial—a walking stick, perhaps."

Hidden in the shadows, Cecelia's heart gave a little lurch. She remembered the squirrel she had admired—small, intricate, the kind of work that spoke of an artist's care. She watched as Kunal bowed his head slightly, accepting the advice without protest. Despite the correction, Cecelia could see a flash of regret in Kunal's eyes, a quiet, familiar rebellion that she found oddly comforting.

"You're right, Pitaji," Kunal murmured, though the faint sadness in his tone was unmistakable. "I won't do it again."

Manik gave a brief nod, returning to his precise measurements. "Stick to the straight lines. The balance between simplicity and complexity—that's what sets our work apart, here and back home."

Sarala, standing beside him, adjusted her shawl, her bangles jingling softly with the movement. The sound was like a whisper of the faraway lands they had left behind. Her gaze swept over the room, proud yet reserved, holding a quiet dignity. Though outsiders in this foreign land, the Sutar family carried themselves with a sense of purpose that commanded respect.

Before any more words could be exchanged, the unmistakable rustle of silk skirts announced the arrival of Philippa Rowley.

The Baroness swept into the room with a regal air, her pale blue gown trailing like the tail of a serpent. Her sharp, appraising eyes scanned the Sutar family with the calculated precision Cecelia had come to recognize. Her lips curved into a smile—polite, but without warmth, a mask of civility often worn by those of her rank.

"Manik Sutar," Lady Philippa purred, extending a hand in a gesture of courtesy. "It's a pleasure to see you again. And your family, too." Her gaze lingered on Kunal. "I hear you will lead the efforts for our new commission? My son has spoken highly of you, Kunal Sutar. You must be very talented."

Manik shook her hand with calm confidence. "Baroness Rowley, this is Kunal. Yes, he will oversee the work. We are honored by your trust in our craftsmanship. Shall we discuss the details?"

Philippa's eyes gleamed as she outlined her vision. "For the library, I want four cabinets. Two for the botanical texts, two for the natural specimens. Ten feet high, five feet wide, with shelves and glass fronts, of course."

She moved toward the wall with an elegant sweep of her hand. "And here, I'd like two friezes. One for this wall, one for the gallery. Fifteen feet long, depicting mythological and natural motifs. I expect the craftsmanship to be flawless."

Sarala, her voice low but clear, responded with a respectful nod. "We will ensure that each piece reflects the grandeur of your home, Baroness."

Philippa nodded once, her eyes sharp and assessing. "Good. And what price do you ask?"

Manik paused, exchanging a brief glance with Kunal before replying, "Three hundred pounds for the entire commission. That will cover all materials and labor."

Philippa's expression tightened, her fingers tapping lightly against the fabric of her gown—a gesture of deliberation. "A considerable investment. But I shall pay it." She let the words hang in the air before adding, "I expect at least one cabinet, the friezes, and several carvings to be ready before Frederick's birthday celebration in two months."

Kunal, with a deep bow, responded confidently, "It will be done, Baroness." His voice was steady, though Cecelia noticed a slight tightening in his jaw.

As the Sutar family began to make their way out, Cecelia remained perfectly still, her body tense and heart pounding. She felt the weight of the exchange, a delicate dance of power and negotiation that left her both awed and envious. The Sutars' composed navigation of the castle's social dynamics was impressive—graceful, yet firm.

What grand things they will create, she thought, a quiet longing stirring within her. The idea of their finished works—elegant cabinets, intricate friezes—adding warmth to the cold, calculated halls of Castle Rowley filled her with both admiration and yearning.

Letting out a slow, shaky breath as their footsteps faded, Cecelia sank deeper into the shadows, resuming her scrubbing. The rhythmic strokes of the brush were the only comfort in the frigid stillness, the only sense of control she had in her constricted world.

But her thoughts soon drifted from the stone floor to Kunal. She pictured his skilled hands bringing wood to life in this place that had always felt lifeless. The castle had never been a place of creation—only one of maintenance and survival. Yet now, the promise of something beautiful seemed to linger in the air like a whispered secret. For the first time in years, Cecelia felt a small spark of hope.

That night, her hopeful thoughts were replaced by restless nightmares. They dragged her into terrifying visions: a ship bound for America, her belly swollen with child, only to lose everything to the raging sea; harsh labor under an unforgiving sun, her hands cracked and bleeding, her body prematurely aged. Each ghoulish scene left her breathless, her heart racing with fears she couldn't escape.

Waking with a jolt, cold sweat slick on her skin, Cecelia swung her legs over the side of her narrow bed, shivering as her bare feet touched the icy floor. She reached for her coat, then quietly pulled on her boots and crept out of her room, moving through the dark house with the caution of a thief. Outside, the biting night air hit her face, sharp but oddly comforting—a contrast to the suffocating heat of her dreams—and as her eyes adjusted to the darkness, she noticed a flicker of light beyond the old stone wall, a curl of smoke rising against the black sky. Smiling, one of her favorite memories resurfaced: Annabel and Charlie and Lise inviting Cecelia to join their fireside dinner. Drawn to the glow, she stepped cautiously across the frosty ground, her boots crunching loudly in the silence.

She hesitated. *What if it's not Annabel and Charlie?* Then laughter—light and familiar—drifted on the breeze, urging her forward.

Thankfully, huddled around a crackling fire were Annabel and Charlie, each holding a small pastry. The firelight danced across their faces, casting a warm, golden glow. Cecelia's smile widened, but then she noticed Kunal beside Charlie. The sight of him made her heart leap, but memories of the pity she'd seen in his eyes resurfaced, twisting her stomach.

Annabel's face lit up when she spotted Cecelia. "Cecelia! I'm so glad you've come. We weren't too loud, were we?"

"No, no," Cecelia said quickly, stepping closer. "I saw the fire and thought I might join you, if that's all right."

"Of course, it is!" Annabel patted the empty log beside her. "Come, sit. Warm yourself. It's freezing out tonight."

Despite her nerves, the pull of the fire and friendship was too strong to resist. Cecelia crossed the last few steps and sank onto the log, allowing the fire's warmth to envelop her chilled body. The comforting heat contrasted sharply with the castle's pervasive coldness, but it did little to settle her fluttering heart as Kunal acknowledged her with a quiet nod.

"Would you like a samosa?" Kunal asked, his voice gentle as he held out the small, golden pastry. "My parents made them. They're best enjoyed warm, especially on nights like this."

Cecelia managed a faint smile as she accepted the offering. "Thank you," she murmured, the rich spices and warm pastry easing the tension in her chest. The act of sharing food by the fire created a sense of intimacy, as if this moment were a stolen reprieve from the harsh realities waiting beyond the fire's circle of light.

"Cecelia," Annabel began gently, her tone careful. "You know you could always move in with us if you're worried about staying at the castle. There's a detached room that would be all yours."

The unexpected offer caught Cecelia off guard, stirring a cautious hope within her. She shook her head, however, trying to keep her voice steady. "You're about to start a family. You don't need the likes of me getting in the way."

"We've already talked about it." Annabel leaned closer, her voice warm and firm. "You're no burden, Cecelia. You're family."

The word family hung in the air, its weight both comforting and overwhelming. Tears pricked Cecelia's eyes, but she quickly brushed them away, laughing softly to mask her emotion. "Family," she echoed, the word feeling both sweet and bittersweet on her tongue. "Are you sure you wouldn't mind? After the baby is born, I mean…"

Annabel's hand gently patted Cecelia's arm. "We'd help each other. You with your baby, me with mine when the time comes. That's how it should be."

Cecelia swallowed, her throat tightening with unexpected emotion. "You don't know what that means to me," she whispered, clutching the small handkerchief in her lap. "But I don't think the Baroness would allow it. An unmarried, pregnant maid living with a newlywed couple? It wouldn't look right."

Annabel shrugged, unconcerned. "Who cares what it looks like? We can make it work. All you have to do is ask her."

Kunal's deep voice cut through the conversation with thoughtful intensity. "If you're looking for a way to earn money without being on your feet all day, why not sell your drawings? I've seen lesser work fetch a fair price."

Annabel's eyebrows shot up in surprise. "Kunal's seen your sketches?" She laughed softly. "I've known you for ages, Cecelia, and you guard those drawings as if they were made of gold."

Kunal's lips curled into a playful grin, his gaze lingering on Cecelia. "Just one sketch," he admitted. "But it was enough to see you've got talent."

Cecelia crossed her arms defensively. "I'm right here, you know," she muttered, glancing between them. "And no one's ever paid real money for my work."

Charlie chuckled from across the fire. "That's not entirely true. You had half the village bartering with you until you angered the bailiff's wife and your mother put a stop to it."

Cecelia shook her head, her voice filled with self-doubt. "Apples and bread aren't the same as a shilling."

The firelight flickered in Kunal's eyes as he leaned forward, his voice soft yet resolute. "What if your sketches came framed with intricate carvings? Would you think them worthy then?"

Suspicion crept into her tone. "Why would you do that? Out of pity?"

Kunal's expression softened. "No," he said, his voice sincere. "Because I feel a kinship with you, Cecelia. Maid or not, it doesn't change what I see in you. If you ever want guidance in your art, I'd be honored to help."

Cecelia's chest tightened, but it was with a mix of relief and new-found respect. He wasn't pitying her; he was offering partnership.

"Would you carve acorns into the frame for the squirrel?" she asked, her voice softening.

Annabel, intrigued, raised an eyebrow. "Squirrel?"

Cecelia shook her head, smiling, while Kunal nodded with understanding. "Exactly," he agreed. "We could sell it at the market and split the earnings."

Despite the excitement that fluttered in her heart, Cecelia's voice remained cautious. "But won't your father mind? He seemed... particular about the commission earlier."

Charlie looked curious. "Is he still overseeing it? I thought this was your first solo project."

Kunal rubbed his neck, frustration evident. "He was supposed to leave it to me, but he can't help stepping in." Turning to Cecelia, he asked, "When did you overhear him?"

Cecelia's face reddened. "I was scrubbing in the solar," she admitted. "Your family came in while I was on my knees. I should have spoken up, but..." She trailed off, feeling awkward.

Kunal waved away her concern. "You were doing your work."

Still, Cecelia couldn't shake the feeling that he might suspect her of eavesdropping. She nibbled on the samosa, its once-comforting flavor now heavy with unease. When Kunal offered her another, she accepted with a nod of gratitude.

Annabel's face turned serious as she hesitated before speaking. "Cecelia, if you do stay with us, we need to know... Is there any chance that the baby's father could return?"

Chapter Ten

CONFESSION

The weight of the question hung heavy in the cold night air.

Cecelia almost wished she hadn't come. The warmth of the fire and the taste of the samosa felt distant now, her stomach twisting as the reality of her secret pressed relentlessly against her chest. She lowered her gaze, voice trembling. "I haven't told anyone who the father is. Not even him. And he must never know."

Annabel's brow furrowed, her features softening in the flickering firelight. "I see..." she murmured, her voice low with concern. Then, gently but insistently, she asked, "And his family? Could they find out? Could they come for you?"

Cecelia swallowed the lump in her throat as Annabel's words hit home. What if the family *did* find out? What if they *did* come for her and the child?

After ignoring these questions for months, it suddenly felt as though her future dangled by a thread, one wrong move threatening to send everything spiraling into ruin. She opened her mouth to speak, but the words stuck in her throat, tangled with shame and fear.

Annabel, sensing Cecelia's hesitation, offered a reassuring look, then turned to Charlie. "Dearest," she said softly, her voice laced with gentle urgency. "Would you and Kunal gather more wood for the fire? Perhaps one of you could hold the lantern while the other gathers the wood." Her smile was coaxing.

Charlie nodded. "Of course," he replied, rising with ease.

Kunal's gaze lingered on Cecelia, concern in his expression. "Are you sure you'll be all right?" he asked, his voice low, betraying a quiet protectiveness.

Charlie let out a soft chuckle, trying to lighten the mood. "Last time a man crossed Annabel and Cecelia, he ended up in the dungeon. And before that, it was pepper in the eyes. They'll be fine."

Cecelia's lips twitched into a faint, reluctant smile. "That was all Annabel," she muttered, her voice barely audible.

Kunal's worry eased slightly, though a shadow of concern still flickered in his eyes. With a nod, he followed Charlie down the path, the lantern's glow soon swallowed by the darkness.

Once the men were gone, Annabel turned back to Cecelia, her voice low and filled with tenderness. "Is it easier to tell me now, with them gone?"

Cecelia's shoulders slumped, and she lowered her head, her voice barely holding steady. "If I tell you," she whispered, "you must swear not to pity me. And you cannot tell a soul, Annabel. Not a soul. It wouldn't be safe for me."

"You have my promise." Annabel's hand settled gently on Cecelia's arm, her eyes sincere. "On my honor, I will not breathe a word."

Cecelia's pulse thrummed loudly in her ears as she leaned closer, her words barely more than a breath. "When you first came to this castle, I warned you against it."

"I remember." Annabel's brows furrowed, confusion flashing across her face. "You told me the place was full of ghosts." She scowled. "Though, it turned out the only thing to fear at the castle was Baron Henry Rowley."

The name hovered between them like a curse, drawing a shudder from both women. Silence settled heavily over them, broken only by the crackle of the fire, as Cecelia struggled to gather the courage to speak the truth that had been festering inside her.

"Henry Rowley," Annabel repeated, her voice filled with loathing. "That monstrous man. The same who threw his wife into the dungeon for not giving him an heir quickly enough."

Cecelia nodded, her lips trembling as she tried to force out the words she had long kept buried.

"The same odious pig who took Charlie's eye," Annabel continued, her voice growing colder with each word. "Likely the one who had his parents killed too. That man robbed our future children of their grandparents."

Cecelia's hands clenched in her lap, her whole body shaking as she prepared to reveal the darkest part of her past.

"The man who forced me to read vile filth to a room of drunkards," Annabel growled, her hands balling into fists. "And then he burned my bookbinding kit. He even burned Cassidy's book her mother gave her, what was it called..."

"*Aesop's Fables*." The truth clawed its way up Cecelia's throat, but only a choked whisper emerged. "And he disinherited Frederick for... for loving men. Until I lied and said I was carrying Frederick's child to save him."

Annabel let out a weary sigh, her voice thick with disgust. "We could list that evil tyrant's sins until dawn." Her tone softened as she reached for Cecelia's hand. "But Cecelia... who *is* the father?"

The weight of Cecelia's confession hung between them like a suffocating fog, as thick and tangible as the damp chill clinging to the night air. She stared down at her feet, her voice barely more than a whisper, as though saying it aloud might make it even more unbearable. "Some time before you arrived," she began, her words faltering as her voice shook, "Baron Henry Rowley started... putting his hands on me. Slipping them up my skirt when I was cleaning."

Annabel's breath hitched sharply, her eyes wide with horror. "You never told me."

"We all hated him," Cecelia continued, her voice breaking under the strain. "But he was the master of the castle." She glanced around, as if even the shadows might betray her secrets. "I tried to fend him off, to brush away his advances without angering him. But when I did, he docked my pay, claimed I was neglecting my duties. My mother was furious. I was too ashamed to tell her the truth, so I hid. I tried to be where he couldn't find me."

Tears pooled in Annabel's eyes as she gripped Cecelia's hand, her voice a low murmur filled with guilt. "Why didn't you tell me? We could have done something, anything to help."

"You had your own troubles," Cecelia whispered, her voice barely audible, raw with pain. "Everyone did."

Annabel's eyes, wide and sorrowful, glistened with the flickering light of the fire. "I'm so sorry, Cecelia. I should have known. I should have—"

"You did help," Cecelia interrupted, a bitter laugh escaping her lips. It was dark, jagged—filled with a mixture of regret and relief. "He became quite distracted with you. The idea of a farmer's daughter who could read, married to a respectable man no less... It was as if he saw you as an omen, a curiosity. And because you were married, he never dared touch you. Or... did he?"

Annabel's expression darkened, her mouth tightening into a thin line as she slowly shook her head. "No. He didn't try until the very end... when he threatened to right before Philippa pushed him into that cell. Thankfully nothing came of it, but..."

Cecelia's breath caught in her throat. "I remember now," she said. "He said he would try to get you with child—to create children who would be strong and literate."

Annabel shook her head slowly, disbelief and anger flashing in her eyes. "For all his titles, Henry Rowley was a simpleton when it came to understanding the world," she muttered, her voice dripping with contempt.

The tears Cecelia had tried to hold back pricked at the corners of her eyes, a heavy cloak of shame settling over her shoulders. Her voice wavered as she confessed, "I carry his child."

For a moment, the only sound between them was the crackle of the fire. Annabel's face crumpled with emotion, and she wrapped her arms around Cecelia, her touch warm and unwavering. "Oh, Cecelia... I'm so sorry." Her voice was thick, her words barely a whisper. "You've been carrying this burden alone, all this time."

The dam broke. Cecelia's shoulders shook as the tears poured freely, the pain and shame she had bottled up for so long spilling out in sobs.

"I'm so ashamed," she choked out, her voice ragged. "No one else knows."

Annabel's voice dropped to a fierce whisper, full of urgency and fear. "And no one else must know," she said, her eyes darting around them, as if the darkness itself might be listening. "You're right to keep this secret, Cecelia." Her gaze sharpened, and her voice was filled with dread. "Are you certain Henry doesn't know? When... when did this happen, if you don't mind telling me?"

"It was after Hattie was sent away," Cecelia replied, her voice trembling as the painful memory surfaced. "When you and Lise went to that play. Henry... he struck Hattie when she refused him, pushed her into the fireplace, then threw her out of the castle. When I was alone, he found me in the kitchen. He made me bring him a cold supper in bed. When I arrived..." Her voice faltered, as if the memory itself burned. "He shut the door behind me."

Annabel's face contorted with sympathy and rage. "You were afraid he'd do the same to you—throw you out, just like Hattie."

Cecelia wiped at her tears, her voice thick with bitterness. "It wasn't being thrown out that scared me. I could find work somewhere else. But Henry threatened to throw out my parents too, and made it clear that no one around here would hire them, on his orders." The bitterness in her voice deepened as she continued. "We struggled so hard to rebuild our lives in England after everything went wrong in France."

Annabel's eyes brimmed with compassion. "And now they're leaving again... and they have no idea of the price you've paid."

Cecelia lowered her voice, casting furtive glances as if the very walls might betray her secret. "They mustn't know," she whispered. "When I woke, he'd rolled off me just enough for me to slip away. I dressed and left as quietly as I could."

Annabel's face turned ashen, the horror of the revelation sinking in. "He was drunk, wasn't he?" she asked, her voice barely audible. "Do you think he remembers?"

Cecelia nodded slowly, her voice flat. "He's known for it. The next day, he asked if I'd brought him the cold supper. I told him I had, that I'd left it on his dresser while he was asleep. He seemed to believe me." Her gaze shifted to Annabel. "I heard about what you did at the play—throwing pepper in that man's eyes. After that, I started chewing cloves of garlic and rubbing pepper *and* onion behind my ears. It kept Henry at bay." She gave a stilted little laugh. "I stopped when he went in the cell."

Annabel stared at Cecelia, her expression grim. "If Philippa finds out you're carrying Henry's child, she might have you killed," she whispered urgently. "And if Henry discovers the truth... God, Cecelia, he might do even worse. He's always wanted a legitimate heir."

"When I realized I wasn't merely nauseous, but pregnant..." Cecelia sighed heavily, feeling the truth settle over her like a weight she could no longer bear. "I thought Henry couldn't have children."

"So did I," Annabel murmured, her tone taut with fear and sympathy. "But if you've been with no one else..."

"I haven't," Cecelia confirmed, her voice breaking as tears streamed down her cheeks.

Suddenly, a sharp snap echoed from the darkness beyond the firelight, causing both women to flinch. Their hearts pounded as they strained to listen, their breaths shallow.

Charlie and Kunal emerged from the darkness, their arms full of firewood, but the pale look on their faces stopped Cecelia cold. A sinking feeling twisted her stomach, and she exchanged a worried glance with Annabel.

"Charlie, did you hear us?" Annabel asked quietly.

Charlie's eyes flicked away from Cecelia, his voice low and raspy. "Just the last part," he admitted. "I'm sorry. We didn't mean to overhear..."

Kunal crouched by the fire, his gaze fierce as it locked onto Cecelia. "I'll kill Henry Rowley myself," he said, his voice deadly calm, brimming with conviction. "I swear it."

Annabel and Charlie exchanged startled looks, but Cecelia's heart gave a foolish flutter at Kunal's words. They reminded her of when Charlie had made a similar vow after Henry had humiliated Annabel by forcing her to read lewd words to a crowd. Trying to regain her composure, she managed a trembling smile, her voice shaky. "That's very noble of you, Kunal. But maybe, instead, you could promise me something else: don't speak a word of what you heard tonight."

Kunal's intensity shifted into earnestness. He nodded solemnly. "You have my word. Not a soul will know." Then, after a pause, he added thoughtfully, "But you could do better than telling people the father is a fisherman, Cecelia. It could ruin any chance you have for a decent marriage."

Cecelia frowned, her voice tinged with frustration. "What else can I say? Who else could it be?"

"Why not claim he was an out-of-town merchant? You could say you married him, and he was killed before you knew you were with child. Merchants are always coming and going. It would make more sense than a fisherman."

Charlie, standing by the fire with his hands on his hips, shook his head doubtfully. "Inventing a nameless fisherman is one thing. But creating a whole story about a merchant tied to trade? That's a lot to juggle—especially if someone like the Baroness starts asking questions."

Cecelia chewed her lip, anxiety tightening her chest. "The Baroness already suspects me. Lying about a fisherman was hard enough, and I'm sure she's just waiting for a reason to have me thrown out of Castle Rowley."

Annabel tilted her head thoughtfully. "What if we said the baby was Charlie's? We could claim it happened before we were engaged."

Charlie's eyes widened at first, but then he seemed to consider it, his brow furrowing. "It... might actually work. It'd explain why Cecelia's staying with us."

Cecelia gawked at them, her voice incredulous. "You can't be serious. You want me to pretend I'm carrying Charlie's child?"

"Why not?" Annabel shrugged nonchalantly. "We're friends. It's nobody's business but ours. As long as it seems plausible, the villagers won't care. We know the truth."

A surge of gratitude swelled in Cecelia's chest, but she shook her head again, her voice firm. "Thank you, truly. But no. I can't ask that of you." She managed a small, grateful smile. "But would you still let me stay, even without the lie?"

Annabel didn't hesitate. "Of course," she said, pulling Cecelia into a warm embrace.

Cecelia's voice wavered. "Frederick promised to give me money after we shamed Henry into restoring his inheritance, but now the Baroness watches his purse like a hawk. She thinks I manipulated him, rather than telling a simple lie to save him." Her gaze fell to the ground, her words heavy. "But that's nothing compared to how I judge myself."

Annabel shook her head vehemently. "I know you better than she does, and I don't see it that way at all."

Charlie's voice was soft but resolute. "Neither do I."

Kunal's voice was a gentle murmur, filled with admiration. "And neither do I. You've shown more courage than most."

Cecelia let out a small, broken laugh, her eyes shimmering with unshed tears. "I wish I could believe all of you," she said, her voice thick with emotion. "I didn't come here seeking pity, yet here I am, demanding it."

"You're not demanding anything," Kunal said quietly, regret lacing his tone. "I misjudged you. I thought your hesitation with art was due to modesty, not the sacrifices you've made."

"She is talented," Annabel chimed in, her voice strong and unwavering. "You should see her sketches. They're remarkable."

Charlie nodded in agreement. "Don't let that talent go to waste."

A surge of frustration bubbled up in Cecelia. "I have neither time nor means. Kunal's family are renowned woodcarvers; Charlie's family were craftsmen. You've had the luxury to follow your passions. I can barely keep my hands clean enough to touch paper, let alone create something worth selling. I'm just a maid. Bathing isn't even something I get to do often."

"I understand, believe me." Annabel's expression softened with sympathy. "So why America? Why are your parents so eager to leave, if they don't know the truth about the father?"

"Oh, the trouble is still Henry." Cecelia's shoulders slumped. "They're terrified that when he is handed over to the authorities, Henry will drag them down with him. They're fleeing to avoid being implicated in the many crimes they assisted him with."

"I see." Annabel leaned in closer, her voice conspiratorial. "I wouldn't want to go to America either. It's still developing—hardly any doctors, and so dangerous."

"I don't mind the idea of travel," Cecelia admitted, her voice filled with quiet resignation. "But I don't want to give birth on a ship. I don't want to be on the run with parents who feel like fugitives." She let out a small, mirthless laugh. "I don't want to leave all of you."

Kunal, still looking puzzled, raised his hand like a student with a question. "Wait—did I hear correctly? You conspired to throw the Baron into the dungeon?"

Annabel's eyes sparkled with mischief as a grin spread across her face. "Oh yes. And it's quite the tale. Let us tell you how it all unfolded...the secrets of Castle Rowley."

Chapter Eleven

MASQUERADE

The next morning, the house was cloaked in an oppressive silence when Cecelia awoke, a faint chill in the damp air. The worn hearthstones offered no warmth, their fire long extinguished. She shivered, pulling a thin shawl tight around her shoulders and reached for a shriveled piece of dried apple and a handful of nuts. As she chewed, the stale flavors seemed to mirror the bleakness inside her, and her eyes drifted to the enormous basket of feathers that needed sorting—a task that, like her life, felt endless and suffocating. She sighed, poking at the stubborn lump of barley that still hadn't softened in the cooling kettle.

The creak of the door cut through the silence. Cecelia glanced up to see Bridgette entering, her steps brisk and determined, her face lined with a familiar tightness. "Morning," Bridgette said tersely, her sharp eyes catching Cecelia's meager meal. "Good, you're eating. I couldn't keep anything down when I was carrying you." Her tone was clipped, more dutiful than warm. She gestured to the basket. "These feathers won't sort themselves, and it's a manageable task, given your condition. I'll even help. The masquerade tonight is going to have everyone in the castle on their feet—let's take advantage of the calm before the storm and set."

"Yes, Mumma," Cecelia murmured in what she hoped was a respectful tone. Yet the tension that hung in the air was too thick to ignore, pressing down on Cecelia like the dampness of the walls. She cleared her throat, mustering the courage to break the silence. "Mumma, could we... talk for a moment?"

Bridgette paused, her fingers already plucking at a cluster of feathers, her expression guarded. "What now?"

Cecelia inhaled deeply, feeling the words tremble on her lips. "Annabel and Charlie offered me a place to stay with them. In their spare room. I want to accept it, Mumma. You and Papa can still go to America, but I— I want to stay here."

Bridgette's hands stilled, and her eyes hardened as if she had expected this but dreaded hearing it aloud. "Not this nonsense again," she muttered, voice tight with barely concealed frustration. "Enough, Cecelia."

But Cecelia's resolve only grew stronger, fueled by an anger she had kept buried for too long. She set down her spoon and looked directly at her mother. "I don't want to go to America. I've thought about it, and I've made up my mind. If you and Father have to flee, then go. But I'm staying here."

The silence that followed was suffocating, broken only by the soft rustling of feathers. Bridgette's face seemed to pale, her eyes darting briefly toward the basket as if it held answers she could not find. "No," she said finally, the word heavy with finality.

"I've thought it through," Cecelia pressed, her voice unsteady but determined. "I had no part in Father's debts or the Baron's schemes. You're running from problems that aren't mine. I can stay, have the baby here, and send word when it's safe for you to visit."

Bridgette's mouth tightened, and her hands resumed their sorting, each movement sharp and methodical, as if the task could distract her from the truth. "You have no idea what you're talking about," she said coldly.

"Then explain it to me," Cecelia demanded, her frustration breaking through. "What's really happening? Why must we leave everything behind?"

Bridgette's hands trembled, her voice lowering to a bitter whisper. "It's not just the Baron's crimes. Your father owes a fortune to the Rowley estate, more than we could ever repay. He gambled on a wool merchant, secured the loan with the castle as collateral. The flock was diseased, and the buyers refused it all. Then there was the coal mine—he sank everything into it, and it flooded. We've nothing left to show for it. I could go on, but I hope that's enough."

Cecelia's stomach churned. "I didn't know," she managed.

Bridgette laughed bitterly, the sound hollow and edged with despair. "Even worse, Philippa won't turn a blind eye like Henry did. She'll call in every debt, and we'll be ruined. Your father will be jailed, and they'll come for me next. When I can't pay, it'll be debtor's prison for me too."

The weight of the truth settled over Cecelia, heavy and suffocating. "And if you both run... you leave me to face it all alone."

Bridgette's eyes turned cold. "Yes. You'll be left with debts you can't pay."

Rage surged through Cecelia, her fists clenching. "That's not fair," she spat. "Father should stay and face what he's done. It's his fault."

Bridgette's gaze flashed with anger. "Do you want him to rot in prison, then?"

"Maybe he deserves to," Cecelia snapped, the words escaping before she could stop them. The moment hung between them, raw and unforgiving. She braced for a slap, but none came. Instead, Bridgette's eyes filled with tears, her lips trembling as she struggled to keep her composure.

"I hope the child you carry is just like you," Bridgette whispered, her voice cracking, her back turned as she walked toward the door. "Always a disappointment."

Cecelia's own anger flared anew. "I hope it is," she shot back, her voice rising as tears blurred her vision. "At least it'll try to be better than its own parents."

Bridgette paused at the threshold, her voice a low, venomous hiss. "Don't you dare speak a word of this to anyone," she warned before slamming the door behind her, the sound echoing through the small room.

Cecelia tarried in the small, damp room, her shoulders hunched as the bitter chill pressed in, heart still raw from her mother's harsh words and the reality of her family's circumstances. She clenched her fists, trying to shake off the burden, but the ache lingered, relentless.

Thankfully, by nightfall, Castle Rowley had transformed into a haven of opulence. The masquerade ball was in full swing, its lively energy permeating the grand halls. For the first time in years, the castle felt truly alive. Echoes of violins filled the air, mingling with spirited laughter. The warm, heady scent of rosewater mingled with musk, and the flickering glow of beeswax candles—which smelled far better than the cheap tallow-fat ones in the farmhouse—cast intricate shadows on the polished floors.

With Philippa away, Frederick seemed almost reborn, his pale complexion flushed with excitement, a new confidence visible in his stride. Word among the servants was that he hadn't been this spirited in years, having spent the day indulging in elaborate preparations: a perfumed bath, a meticulous shave, and several glasses of Madeira wine to bolster his nerves.

Meanwhile, Cecelia, seized by a mix of determination and rebellion, made her own preparations. She had stolen a bucket of lavender-scented water reserved for linens, scrubbing away the grime of the day. She sliced a lemon and rubbed its juice over her skin, masking the faint scent of the kitchen with its sharp citrus tang. Her best gown, faded but still serviceable, was hastily mended at the hem, and her hair, plaited into an intricate half-crown braid by Annabel's skillful hands, gave her what she fervently hoped was an air of understated elegance.

Despite her growing belly, still mostly hidden beneath her skirts, Cecelia's resolve remained strong. As she made her way toward the grand hall, she felt a surge of excitement—an intoxicating blend of fear and anticipation.

The ballroom was a spectacle to behold. Candlelit chandeliers bathed the room in a soft, golden glow, illuminating the elaborate tapestries draped along the walls. Silk gowns in every hue—emerald, sapphire, crimson—moved like waves, each adorned with shimmering brocade, lace ruffles, and embroidery depicting mythological scenes or floral motifs. Gentlemen in velvet frock coats, elaborate wigs, and Venetian masks completed the lavish tableau.

In the center of it all stood a grand buffet, laden with delicacies. Towering marzipan sculptures, sugar-paste swans, and gilded peacock pies formed a decadent display, while servants moved gracefully with trays of spiced wine and rosewater cordials. The hum of violins shifted to a lively Sarabande, and the clacking of heels marked the intricate dance steps on the marble floor.

Cecelia hovered by the entrance, a mix of awe and uncertainty in her expression as she watched the swirling colors and masked faces until a sudden nudge jolted her from her thoughts.

She spun around, startled, to find Gwyneth beside her, a mischievous grin on her face. "Evening, love. Here to catch a glimpse of the finery, are we?" Gwyneth's familiar rough accent coupled with her cheeky tone clashed humorously with the elegance of her surroundings.

Cecelia forced a nervous laugh. "Just for a moment. I daren't linger."

"Nonsense!" Gwyneth, holding a half-empty goblet, chuckled. "There's a cloakroom set up nearby, and no one's minding it. Could use an extra pair of hands. Come along, then."

Cecelia hesitated, knowing the risks. "I'm stationed in the kitchen. If my mother finds out, she'll have my head."

Gwyneth waved a dismissive hand. "Let's say Frederick's given the order. He's far too busy and soused for anything to check truths with him. You're safe for tonight. Besides," she added, her tone conspiratorial, "the cloakroom's a perfect place to catch whispers—secrets worth keeping, if you know what I mean."

"You do know my weakness, don't you?" With a deep breath, Cecelia nodded. "All right. Just for a bit."

The cloakroom, dimly lit and slightly musty, was a small reprieve from the lively ballroom. Gwyneth guided Cecelia to an overstuffed chair near the door. "Make sure the tags match the symbols inside their cloaks, and if anyone causes trouble, call for Lavin," she instructed before slipping away with a wink.

Alone at last, Cecelia exhaled deeply. The quiet offered a brief escape, a chance to gather herself. She retrieved a small scrap of paper and a pencil from her apron and began to sketch. Her hand moved quickly, her strokes fluid as she captured the elegant curves of a masked reveler she had seen in the ballroom. The act of drawing calmed her, the familiar motions bringing a sense of control amid the chaos.

Suddenly, the door creaked open, and Cecelia hastily tucked her sketch away, replacing her nervousness with a bright smile. A flustered woman, her blonde curls disheveled, entered the room. "Oh, bless you for being here!" she exclaimed. "I'm Susan, Gwyneth's assistant. She told me you were filling in."

"You're welcome to take over," Cecelia offered, feeling a twinge of relief.

"I've had quite the ordeal." Susan shook her head. "Our horse spooked at a snake, nearly tipped the carriage. Took ages to get here." She sighed, brushing a stray curl from her face. "I must look a mess."

"Not at all." Cecelia managed a sympathetic smile. "That sounds dreadful. But the peace here is welcome."

Susan eyed her curiously. "You're not local, are you? A friend of Frederick's? You don't look like any of the bawds we hired for tonight."

"I know; my dress isn't nearly fine enough." Cecelia's laugh was soft, nervous. "It's... complicated."

Susan grinned, her eyes twinkling. "Isn't it always? But you're too pretty to be hiding away here. Come, let me paint your face for the ball. You'll fit right in."

Before Cecelia could refuse, Susan had already whisked her to a low stool, deftly applying rouge to her cheeks and kohl around her eyes. Cecelia closed her eyes, surrendering to the unexpected luxury.

"You've lovely features," Susan murmured. "This will enhance them beautifully."

When Cecelia finally opened her eyes and caught sight of her reflection, she was momentarily stunned. Her cheeks were flushed, her eyes more defined, and the subtle tint on her lips transformed her usual smile into something almost regal.

Susan wasn't finished. She pulled a violet gown from a nearby closet, its lace trim delicate and intricate. "Try this. It's mine, but it'll fit you well enough. I'm a bit bigger around." Cecelia hesitated, but Susan insisted, pressing the gown into her hands. "Trust me."

The violet silk slid over Cecelia's skin, its luxurious weight both foreign and tantalizingly familiar. She caught her breath as she faced the mirror, surprised by the figure that stared back—poised, elegant, and cloaked in mystery. The delicate lace ruffles at her neckline and cuffs framed her with an air of regality. For the first time in years, she felt... beautiful. The woman staring back wasn't just a maid; she was someone who belonged.

"You look like a princess," Susan proclaimed, her face radiant. "Now, all you need is a mask."

She fanned out five options, and Cecelia put on a peacock's eyes, covering most of her face and leaving only her lips and eyes free. But before Cecelia could respond, the door swung open, revealing Gwyneth with a mischievous smile. "Well, well, Cecelia," she teased, surveying her from head to toe. "You've transformed, haven't you? If I didn't know better, I'd mistake you for a lady."

"Hardly," Cecelia replied, her tone tinged with uncertainty. She shifted in the gown, feeling its unfamiliar stiffness. "I've no idea how to walk in this properly, let alone hold my own in a ballroom full of nobles."

Gwyneth waved her hand dismissively. "You're doing fine, love. Besides, all the best secrets are learned on the job." She paused, then let out an exaggerated sigh. "I'd gladly swap places with you tonight. But as luck would have it, I'm in dire need of a girl who speaks French."

Cecelia's brow furrowed. "French? What for?"

Gwyneth's eyes sparkled with amusement as she sipped from a half-empty goblet of wine. "Special request, darling. One of our esteemed guests has a penchant for such a thing. Too bad none of my girls can manage it."

Cecelia's heart quickened. "And who, pray tell, made such a request?"

Gwyneth's grin widened. "Kunal Sutar, Frederick's new artist-in-residence. Poor man's been dragged here by Frederick himself and offered the evening's entertainment—on the house." She took another sip, then continued with a wry smile. "Kunal tried to refuse at first. Can you imagine? But Frederick insisted. So Kunal, in his infinite politeness, finally requested someone who could speak French. Odd fellow, that one. Standards, I suppose."

A strange mix of curiosity and apprehension knotted Cecelia's stomach. "How... thoughtful," she managed, her voice slightly strained.

"Right?" Gwyneth chuckled. "But alas, it seems the man will be disappointed tonight. No French-speaking courtesans in sight." She shook her head as if in mock pity. "His loss."

Before Cecelia could respond, another knock interrupted them. Gwyneth opened the door to find a short, dark-haired woman, who whispered urgently in her ear. Gwyneth nodded, then turned to Susan.

"It seems you're needed," Gwyneth said apologetically. "Cecelia, can you manage here a while longer?"

"Of course," Cecelia agreed, eager for a moment alone.

Gwyneth gave Cecelia a playful air kiss, then swept out with Susan. As the door clicked shut, the sudden silence enveloped Cecelia. She sank back into her chair, her heart still racing from the unexpected revelations.

The room was warm, the fire crackling softly in the hearth. Cecelia pulled out her pencil and a scrap of paper, retreating into her sketching. Each stroke steadied her, grounding her in the familiar rhythm of lines and shapes. The moments passed quietly, with only the soft scratching of graphite to keep her company.

Then came a sudden noise—a swift, decisive rustling at the door. It opened with deliberate urgency, and a figure stepped inside, closing it quickly behind him. Cecelia's heart leapt, her fingers freezing over her drawing.

She hurriedly tucked the sketch down the front of her gown, her breath catching as she rose slightly to peek over the desk's edge.

It was Kunal.

He stood with his back to her, his movements stiff and hurried. His shoulders were taut, and his breath came in uneven bursts. He scanned the room briefly before collapsing onto the edge of the bed, burying his face in his hands. He muttered under his breath, the words too faint for Cecelia to hear, and her eyes softened as she watched him. She recognized the anxiety in his posture, the way he kept glancing at the door. It was a familiar kind of fear—the kind born from hiding and uncertainty. For a moment, Kunal seemed less like the mysterious artist and more like a kindred spirit, trapped by circumstances and seeking refuge.

Her initial pity for him when he entered the room deepened into something more intimate—a shared understanding. In that moment,

Cecelia felt a surge of boldness, a desire to close the distance between them. She saw not just a man cornered by society's expectations, but someone whose vulnerability mirrored her own.

Then, a daring idea formed. Gwyneth's words echoed in her mind, and Cecelia's late grandmother's voice seemed to rise within her—a voice that had insisted Cecelia master French as a child, no matter how much she resisted. Tonight, that voice would serve a different purpose. Standing tall, Cecelia reached for the voice she had nearly forgotten. Her late grandmother, a woman of French descent, had been insistent that Cecelia learn her language, no matter how resistant she had been as a child. Now, she summoned that voice, the firm, no-nonsense tone her grandmother had used when she was displeased, and let it roll off her tongue with precision.

"Bonsoir, monsieur," she said, her voice low and rich, distinctly different from her usual tone.

Chapter Twelve

ESCAPE

Kunal jolted, his whole body tensing as Cecelia emerged from the shadows like an apparition cloaked in mystery. His wide-eyed confusion quickly morphed into something calmer when he caught her demure smile. The transformation she felt in her silk gown, masked face, and painted lips emboldened her—she was someone new, someone bolder, and she relished it.

"I... I beg your pardon, miss," he stammered, his words faltering as he struggled to recover from the surprise. "I didn't realize someone was here. I'm—"

"Tu te cachais?" *You were hiding?* Cecelia teased, her voice low and silky, head tilting playfully as she invoked her grandmother's French. The familiar cadence felt strangely liberating, as if she were shedding her usual skin.

Kunal's surprise melted into a warm laugh, its richness sending a welcome shiver down Cecelia's spine. "Vous m'avez démasqué, douce dame," *You've caught me out, gentle lady.* he replied, his French accented but endearing. The tension in his shoulders eased, and the spark in his eyes glinted under the lantern's soft glow.

Her lips curled into a mischievous smile, her confidence growing. In the dim light, she felt the role she was playing take hold, each word she spoke thickening the air with tension. "J'avais cru comprendre que vous cherchiez une prostituée qui parle français," *I thought you were looking for a prostitute who speaks French?* she purred, leaning closer, the words a dangerous blend of seduction and jest.

Kunal's face paled, and he visibly floundered, the innuendo hitting him like a slap. He dropped his gaze, awkwardly rubbing the back of his neck. "Je... je ne pensais pas que Gwyneth avait des Françaises dans son personnel," *I... I didn't think Gwyneth actually had any French girls.* he stuttered, his embarrassment both endearing and amusing.

Cecelia laughed, her voice a mix of genuine amusement and wicked delight. "Veinard," *Lucky you.* she murmured, her eyes gleaming.

Kunal's awkwardness shifted to a hesitant smile, but then his expression grew thoughtful as he studied her closely. "*Cecelia?*" he asked, incredulity mixing with a hint of relief.

She grinned, dropping the charade. "Yes," she confessed, her voice filled with laughter. "I couldn't resist. I was lurking about the party, and Gwyneth roped me into helping with cloaks. So here I am—playing dress-up."

His shoulders relaxed completely, and he shook his head with a soft chuckle. "Well, you certainly had me fooled. I thought..." He trailed off, gesturing at her gown and powdered face. "You looked like one of Gwyneth's finest."

Cecelia raised an eyebrow, still amused. "I'm afraid not. Susan made me up for fun, and now I'm masquerading as someone else for the night."

His eyes rested on her face, and a flicker of naked admiration passed over his features before he stumbled over his words. "It's... beautifully done. Not that you needed it, of course—you're lovely as you are. I mean... without all this." He gestured to the elaborate makeup, his cheeks flushing with awkward sincerity. "I only meant... it's well done."

A strange warmth bloomed in Cecelia's chest, and she quickly steered the conversation in a different direction to avoid lingering on his compliment. "What exactly were you hiding from?" she asked, her curiosity genuine. "I thought an artist like you would be soaking in the sights, maybe even finding inspiration—or a potential commission."

Kunal's expression shifted, his earlier mirth replaced by something more solemn. "I've never chosen my own commissions," he admitted, a hint of bitterness in his voice. "My father's always controlled that. I want to change things, but... it's not as simple as I hoped. I became quite overwhelmed. Besides, this kind of revelry feels out of place for me... I only came because Frederick insisted." He scratched the back of his neck nervously. "I don't suppose you know a way out of here, do you?"

Cecelia leaned forward, her eyes dancing with playful mischief. "So, because I often hide in dark corners, you assumed I know all the secret passageways?"

Kunal's alarm was immediate, and he shook his head hastily. "No, no, that's not what I meant—"

"I'm teasing." She cut him off with a grin. "And you're right. I do in fact know a way out of here, but it's not exactly straightforward. It involves the old tunnels beneath the castle. Are you up for a bit of adventure?"

His eyes lit up in excitement. "Absolutely."

Without hesitation, Cecelia rummaged through an old desk drawer, retrieving a thin metal ruler. She led Kunal to the back of the room, her movements confident and precise as she knelt to pry open a panel hidden beneath the floorboards. A small, dark passageway lay beneath, and she handed him a torch with a dramatic flourish. "You first, monsieur."

Kunal accepted the torch, a hint of wariness in his expression. He descended carefully, and Cecelia followed close behind, just as a sharp knock echoed from the door above. She pressed a finger to her lips, quickly replacing the panel and covering it with a rug before rising to her feet.

Susan burst into the room, slightly breathless but cheerful. "All done!"

"That was fast," Cecelia said lightly, her voice steady despite the adrenaline pulsing through her veins.

Susan grinned, tossing her bag onto a chair. "So was he," she quipped. "I should be fine here now if you want to head back. But—oh! Could you keep the dress on for the rest of the night? You can return it tomorrow."

Cecelia nodded, her gratitude genuine. "Of course. Thank you."

Susan flashed a smile and slipped out, leaving Cecelia alone once more. She took a steadying breath, her earlier boldness beginning to falter. Despite the excitement of the masquerade above, the room felt colder now, like a pause before a plunge.

She turned back to the hidden panel, lifted it quietly, and grabbed a lantern from the hearth. The passage below beckoned, shrouded in darkness. The underground corridor stretched ahead, damp and dimly lit by a single torch Kunal had already placed in a holder along the wall. Its flickering light cast elongated shadows that seemed to shift and twist with each breath of air. Kunal stood just ahead, his form almost blending into the stone, but he straightened sharply when he heard her approach. "Do you need help?" he asked, his voice low.

Cecelia shook her head. "I've been down here more times than I can count." As she stepped closer in the tight space, her hand brushed unexpectedly against his chest, the warmth and firmness of him surprising her. She pulled back quickly, cheeks burning. "Sorry," she mumbled, and then, more confidently, added, "This way."

They moved deeper into the narrow corridor, the lantern swinging between them and casting eerie patterns across the walls. The air grew colder, thick with the musty scent of damp stone and aged earth. Above them, the muffled sounds of violins and laughter filtered through, a faint reminder of the opulent world they had left behind.

"Stay close," Cecelia urged. The tunnel felt as if it were closing in, the walls narrowing with every step. She took the torch from its holder and jammed it into a crevice. "We should leave this here. Too much light will give us away. I know the way."

"Understood," Kunal whispered, his voice sounding different—softer, less guarded. The darkness pressed against them, making it hard to breathe.

"Why did Frederick make you attend tonight?" Cecelia asked quietly, breaking the silence.

Kunal let out a dry chuckle. "He claimed I needed 'artistic inspiration.' Apparently, debauchery counts as muse material. I suppose he thought the courtesans might awaken some dormant genius." The humor in his voice was bitter.

"Does it work?" she teased, trying to lighten the mood. "Do women in scandalous gowns ignite your creativity?"

"No," Kunal said flatly. "Only more nerves."

Cecelia's heart skipped at the finality in his tone, but she quickly masked it. "You should embrace your own style," she said. "Carve squirrels if you like."

Kunal hesitated, his voice raw with vulnerability. "It's not just the squirrel. It's my father's every expectation. Each time I try to carve freely, I hear his criticisms—'Too ornate,' 'Won't last.' It's paralyzing." He paused, then added quietly, "Sometimes I fear I'm not an artist at all—just a mimic."

The weight of his confession hung between them. Cecelia reached out instinctively, her fingers brushing his arm. "You are an artist, and a magnificent one," she insisted, her voice fierce.

Before Kunal could respond, a noise echoed from behind them. Cecelia's body tensed, her heart pounding. "Oh no," she whispered. "There shouldn't be anyone patrolling this stretch of the tunnels."

"What do we do?" Kunal's voice was tight, his earlier vulnerability replaced by fear.

"Hide," Cecelia commanded, her eyes darting around. Her fingers found the edge of an old tapestry hanging loosely on the wall. She tugged it aside to reveal a narrow alcove behind it. "In here. Hurry!"

Without hesitation, Kunal squeezed into the cramped space, Cecelia following close behind. The alcove was small, forcing them to press close together. Cecelia felt the heat of Kunal's body, his breath warm against her hair.

Footsteps approached, slow and deliberate. Cecelia's heart hammered in her chest as she strained to listen.

"You've reached her parents?" The voice was muffled but unmistakable—her father's. Cecelia's blood ran cold.

"They refuse involvement until they're sure she's cured," replied another voice, nasal and unpleasant. Cole, Henry's former right-hand man.

"That's absurd," James muttered angrily. "She's their daughter."

Cole's tone turned conspiratorial. "Perhaps we should keep her hidden down here, away from Philippa's eyes. Henry won't be imprisoned forever, and once he's free, he'll want to know why we released Marguerite."

"Tell the Baroness that yourself," James shot back, irritation clear in his voice.

There was a pause, then the sound of boots shuffling. "I'll move the Comtesse Marguerite to a guest room," James muttered, his voice growing distant. "It's better for her recovery."

"No need," Cole protested desperately.

"I've had enough of your nonsense," James snapped, footsteps echoing as he brushed past Cole.

Cecelia held her breath until the sound faded entirely. Slowly, she exhaled, her chest aching from the effort of staying silent. She glanced up at Kunal, his face inches from hers, his eyes wide with fear and confusion.

"What was that about?" Kunal's voice was barely more than a whisper, rough and urgent.

"Complications," Cecelia replied, her voice strained, raw with emotion. "And secrets I didn't want to hear."

The air between them crackled, the distance more charged than physical—a silent invitation hanging in the darkness, unanswered yet palpable.

Cecelia remained still, her breath heavy in the silence save the slow drip of water echoing through the stone corridor. Just as she began to regain her composure, Kunal's arm brushed lightly against hers. The touch sent a jolt through her, her breath hitching as his lips came close to her ear, the warmth of his words almost tangible. "Are you alright? You're trembling. I'm afraid too, but..."

"I'm *not* afraid," she hissed, the fury in her voice sharp and brittle. "I'm *angry*. How could my father not tell me? We've pulled three women from those dungeons in the past month, all locked away by men trying to break their spirits." Her fists clenched, her nails digging into her palms. "And now, another one. How is this the only answer they have?"

Kunal's brow furrowed, concern mingling with confusion. "And your father was involved?" he asked softly, the disbelief clear. "He was one of those men? I thought his voice sounded familiar."

Cecelia nodded, her eyes flashing. "He was the one who ordered her release. I need to find out who this woman is, and if there are more like her. The old Baron locked his own wife in these cells. God knows who else might be suffering in there."

"Why not let the authorities handle it?" Kunal's voice held both caution and bewilderment.

"Not until the Baroness is ready, is what I keep hearing," Cecelia retorted, her tone exasperated. "She's waiting to confront Henry's brother before making it public. But I can't wait for her to decide when to do the right thing. There could be more women trapped, and I can't let that sit on my conscience." She pushed back the heavy tapestry, her frustration manifesting in sudden, decisive movements. "Come on, let's get you out of here first."

Kunal reached for the lantern hanging on the wall at the same moment she did, their fingers colliding, and it ended up in his hand. His touch was warm and his gaze suddenly held hers, searching, intense. "You'd risk everything for people you don't even know?" His voice was incredulous, but something deeper lurked beneath it, a vulnerability that mirrored her own.

"Of course," Cecelia shot back. Her freckles stood out starkly in the flickering light, her eyes burning with defiance. "How could I stand by and do nothing?"

Kunal's expression sharpened, a new intensity in his dark eyes. "How do you live like this?" he demanded quietly, as if searching for an answer he could not comprehend. "How can you do the right thing, even at your station, without a second thought?"

"For God's sake," Cecelia huffed, her frustration flaring. "How could one *not*?" She made to grab the lantern again, determined to lead them both out of the darkness.

But before she could grasp it, Kunal moved closer. The sudden shift in proximity was electric, and before she could react, he leaned in and kissed her.

The kiss stole her breath, catching her off guard. His lips were cool at first, then quickly warmed against hers, the sensation startling in its intensity. Cecelia, accustomed to the feverish heat of her own skin, felt a shock of clarity in Kunal's touch—a solidity, a refuge she hadn't realized she'd been longing for. Her initial hesitation dissolved, and she kissed him back, her response fierce and raw, fueled by anger, fear, and a longing she could no longer deny.

The kiss deepened, a hunger they both recognized but had never dared acknowledge. Cecelia's fingers tightened on Kunal's arm, seeking stability as the dizziness of the moment overwhelmed her. The scent of damp stone mixed with the musk of Kunal's skin, the cool air of the tunnel sharp against the warmth of their breath. Every nerve in her body seemed to sing, the darkness around them becoming less a place of confinement and more a world where they could momentarily escape the burdens that had brought them here.

The distant echo of footsteps in the corridor jolted them, and they broke apart abruptly. Cecelia's breath came in ragged gasps, her pulse still racing—not only from the fear of discovery but from the sheer intensity of the kiss they had just shared. Instinctively, her hand found Kunal's, and the warmth of his long fingers against hers sent a shiver through her. His thumb traced a slow, reassuring circle over the sensitive skin between her thumb and forefinger, a tender gesture that lingered.

The flickering lantern in Cecelia's other hand cast fleeting shadows across the cold stone walls, their shapes twisting like secrets trying to escape. She gestured toward the way out, her voice barely a whisper. "This way."

Kunal nodded, his hand still firmly clasping hers as they hurried down the passage. His stride, longer than hers, matched her urgency with ease. The intimacy of the moment—their intertwined hands, their shared silence—felt both dangerous and exhilarating.

At last, they reached the ladder. Cecelia climbed first, pushing aside the heavy stone cover that concealed their exit. The cold night air hit her flushed face, the sudden chill startling after the closeness of the tunnel, and the stars above seemed brighter than usual, scattered across the sky like diamonds on black velvet. The artist outbuildings were just visible, their shapes softened by moonlight.

Kunal followed her up, taking a deep breath as he emerged. His cap sat askew, and his hair, mussed from their escape, added an air of disheveled charm. For a moment, in the soft glow of the moon, he looked like a hero from one of Annabel's favorite romances—brave, brooding, and unexpectedly vulnerable. "Quite convenient that the tunnel leads here," he remarked with a wry smile, his voice low, as if still afraid to disturb the quiet night.

Cecelia hovered near the edge of the disguised exit, unsure whether to flee back to the familiarity of the castle or linger a moment longer. "It pays to know one's way out," she replied, trying to keep her tone light, though her heart was still heavy with the unspoken emotions of the night.

Kunal turned to face her fully, his dark eyes glimmering with something akin to hope. "Cecelia..." he began, his voice thick with unspent words.

For a moment, Cecelia feared he would take back the kiss, declare it a mistake now that they stood under the stark reality of the stars. Bracing herself for disappointment, she straightened. "You needn't say anything," she said quickly, her voice more formal than she intended. "We should both return before we're missed."

But Kunal's hand reached for hers again, stopping her. "Would you..." he hesitated, then blurted, "Would you like to come in? For something to eat, I mean. As a thank you."

Caught off guard, Cecelia blurted, "I may be pregnant, but I'm not one of Gwyneth's bawds." As soon as she said it, she winced. Perhaps he did not mean to bring her inside to finish the kiss.

A deep blush crept up Kunal's cheeks, visible even in the moonlight. "I didn't mean..." he stammered, then regained his composure. "I mean, my family is here—my mother and father are asleep in what will be my room, and my sister Rupa is in the main room. She's waiting up for me, fretting as usual."

"Oh?" Cecelia tilted her head, intrigued by his unexpected honesty. "And how can you be so certain she's still awake?"

Kunal's smile turned rueful. "I promised I'd be back within the hour. And Rupa, she's... persistent."

The sincerity in his voice paired with the gentle amusement in his eyes warmed Cecelia more than the night air ever could. The invitation felt genuine, a quiet plea for more time together rather than any calculated seduction. "I suppose I am hungry," she admitted, her voice softening.

Kunal's gaze grew more intense, his eyes locking with hers as he took a small step closer. "I swear, I have no ill intentions," he said, the rawness of his confession breaking through the formalities of the evening. "I've never done this before. I've never even kissed a woman before tonight."

The honesty in his words, so different from the polished flirtations Cecelia had often encountered, disarmed her completely. She found herself drawn to him, not just physically but in a way that felt deeper, more urgent. "Neither have I," she whispered, surprising herself with the admission. Her cheeks burned, but she met his gaze with unflinching courage. "But I'd like to share that meal... and perhaps more words, if you have them."

CHAPTER THIRTEEN

SHATRANJ

The room, bathed in the warm glow of beeswax candles, was unmistakably Kunal's domain. The scent of freshly carved cedar intermingled with the rich tang of wood oil spoke to hours of careful craftsmanship. On the floor lay curls of wood shavings, each one bearing witness to the delicate work that had transpired here. Tools—chisels, mallets, gouges—were arranged with meticulous care on a broad workbench, their handles worn smooth from frequent use.

Rupa sat at a long wooden table, her fingers deftly polishing a newly carved flute. The oil-soaked rag in her hands left a gleaming sheen on the wood, releasing a subtle, musky fragrance. As the door creaked open, she glanced up, her sharp eyes narrowing slightly at the sight of Cecelia. "Good evening, brother," she said with a hint of wry amusement. "I see you've brought someone to tidy up after you."

Kunal, closing the door behind him, smiled easily. "Rupa, you remember Cecelia," he said. "She helped me escape the party." His tone was light, but his eyes betrayed a deeper relief at the unexpected retreat.

Rupa's brow arched, a mix of fondness and reproach in her gaze. "You should be forging alliances, not running back like a boy avoiding chores. Baron Rowley might be curious to know why his artist-in-residence prefers the company of shavings over silks."

Kunal gave a soft, unbothered laugh. "The event is less a party and more a poorly disguised orgy," he said dryly. "Even Frederick called it such. No one will miss me as long as I feign enthusiasm in the morning."

"Ah, matters of pleasure," Rupa remarked, her voice taking on a playful edge as her gaze shifted to Cecelia. "Have the two of you—"

"No," Cecelia interjected, her cheeks flushing as she looked away. "Of course not. We merely crossed paths at the ball."

Rupa's lips twitched with faint amusement, but her eyes remained sharp. "And yet here you are, in my brother's quarters. It seems a curious turn for a maid, even a helpful one. What precisely is your role tonight?"

Kunal stepped forward, his expression calm but resolute. "Cecelia is a creative soul in her own right," he said, pulling out a sturdy wooden chair for her. "You and Mother always say that artistry thrives in many forms, don't you?"

Rupa's expression softened for a moment, as if conceding his point. But her tone remained pointed. "Does our family not also teach respect for propriety? Is it proper, Kunal, to bring a maid here while our family rests beneath this roof?" She paused, her eyes searching Cecelia's face. "Tell me, Cecelia, what do you hope to gain from this... hospitality?"

Cecelia, feeling her face flush anew, lowered her gaze as she remembered Gwyneth's boast that Frederick was too drunk to remember assignments he'd made tonight. "Forgive me, Miss Rupa. Baron Rowley asked that I check in and see if you needed assistance. Truly, I am here on his behalf," she lied, her voice humble and apologetic. "Helping your brother was simply part of my duties as a maid, ensuring the comfort of our guests."

Rupa's shoulders relaxed slightly, but her gaze remained wary. "I don't need help cleaning," she said finally, her voice weary. "Leave the shavings. We'll manage."

Cecelia bowed her head in understanding, a pang of disappointment swelling in her chest as she turned to leave.

"Wait," Rupa called, her tone less sharp. "What kind of maid—"

"You don't need to answer that," Kunal interjected sharply, his tone unexpectedly protective. Cecelia flinched at the intensity in his voice, both surprised and heartened by his defense. Kunal stepped forward, his dark eyes locked on Rupa, the flickering candlelight reflecting a challenging glint. "Cecelia is my guest, and as the commissioned artist here at Castle Rowley, *I* decide who stays."

The words hung in the air, charged with quiet authority. Cecelia's breath caught; she felt the room's tension wrap around her like a second skin. Was it an offer of protection or something more? Her pulse raced as she waited, unsure whether to retreat or hold her ground.

Rupa's lips curved into a faint, reluctant smile, her gaze shifting between Kunal and Cecelia. "Of course. Cecelia, please, make yourself comfortable."

Relieved, Cecelia exhaled and took a seat, her heart slowly settling back to its regular rhythm. Kunal struck a match and lit a beeswax candle, its sweet, warm scent mingling with the faint aroma of cedarwood. The space, simple yet inviting, felt like a glimpse into their shared world—a blend of artistic ambition and familial warmth. Cecelia ran her fingers over the sturdy oak table, marveling at the small touches that made the room feel like home. "You've made this place truly lived-in," she murmured.

"That's Rupa's doing," Kunal said, nodding toward his sister. "She has an eye for making things both functional and beautiful. I may have moved the furniture, but she's the one who made it feel like ours."

Rupa let out a dry chuckle. "If only our parents believed that. They still credit Kunal with every little improvement." Her voice carried a hint of affectionate sarcasm. "Mother even suggested I take inspiration from him when organizing my own belongings."

"I'll set them straight," Kunal promised, his brow furrowing slightly. "But why let them believe otherwise? You might have spoken up in your own defense."

Rupa waved a dismissive hand, her focus already back on the delicate wood flute she was crafting. "Let me finish this piece," she muttered. "I'll be too tired to argue soon enough."

The fire cast long shadows across the room, the soft glow enveloping them in a cocoon of warmth. Cecelia rose from her seat, drawn to a game set on the opposite side of the table. Her footsteps were muted by the rushes scattered across the stone floor, which absorbed the noise and added a rustic charm to the chamber. As she approached, the faint scent of rosewater mixed with cedarwood hung in the air, making the moment feel both foreign and familiar.

The game board was exquisite—each piece carved from polished wood, bearing intricate details that hinted at a long history of craftsmanship. She carefully picked up a small elephant figure, its features so finely detailed it seemed to breathe under her touch. "Is this a different kind of chess?" Cecelia asked, her voice tinged with curiosity. She turned the piece in her hand, captivated by its lifelike form.

Kunal moved closer, leaning over the board beside her. "It's shatranj, an ancient version of chess," he explained. "This set was carved by my grandfather back in India. It's one of the few things we brought with us when we left."

Cecelia's gaze lingered on the board, the weight of its history settling heavily between them. The elephant felt cool in her hand, as if imbued with the distant warmth of its origins. She gently placed it back on the board, a silent acknowledgment of the journey it represented. Before she could find the right words, Kunal lifted the lid of an earthenware dish nearby, releasing a wave of aromatic steam. "Would you like to try some? It's Gajar Ka Halwa, carrot pudding with nuts. My mother made it."

The sweet, earthy scent carried memories of kitchens past—of simple English pies and rustic stews. But this dish was different, richer, more complex. Cecelia nodded, settling onto a cushioned bench as Kunal ladled a portion into a small bowl and handed it to her. She took a tentative spoonful, savoring the fragrant blend of cardamom, warm milk, and crunchy nuts. "It's delicious," she whispered, the unexpected sweetness a comforting surprise.

As she ate, Cecelia watched Kunal's hands move with a quiet certainty. There was a subtle grace to his movements, a careful attention to detail that matched his intricate carvings. Each gesture seemed deliberate, as if carrying the weight of his family's legacy. Her eyes traced the strong lines of his face, softened by the candlelight.

"How do you play?" Cecelia asked lightly, breaking the comfortable silence. Her voice carried a hint of challenge, a playful nudge that sought to ease the lingering tension. "And are you any good?"

Kunal's eyes brightened, a spark of warmth and mischief illuminating his gaze. "I'd like to think so," he replied, a crooked smile tugging at his lips. There was a faint tease in his tone. "Care to find out?"

"Oh, I do," she admitted with a grin. "But I fear you'll trounce me."

His chuckle was low, deepening the warmth in his gaze. "My father is the true master," he said with a nod, acknowledging his own limitations. "But I'm learning. It's all about strategy, foresight." He gestured toward the board. "These aren't mere kings and queens. It's the shah and his army." Picking up a piece resembling a small castle, he added, "This is the Rukh, the tower—it strides boldly across the battlefield."

Cecelia's fingers hovered above the board, her curiosity piqued. "And what about the queen?" she asked, her voice filled with playful intrigue.

"Not quite a queen," Kunal corrected gently. "This is the Firzan. She moves only one square at a time but wields tremendous influence, commanding from the heart."

"I like that," Cecelia said, her smile softening as her gaze lingered on the piece.

He continued, motioning to the row of smaller pieces at the front. "These are the pawns—Baidaq. They're the soul of the army, advancing step by step, protecting the shah."

Her hand moved toward a piece with a familiar shape. "And this one?" she asked, tapping it gently.

"The Asp," Kunal explained. "It moves in an L-shape, just like the knight in your chess. Agile, unpredictable, leaping over obstacles."

"And what about this one?" Cecelia pointed to a diagonal piece with a distinctive notch.

"That's the Pil, the elephant," he said, his voice taking on a note of pride. "It strides diagonally, like your bishop. Strong and capable, but deliberate in its movements."

As he described each piece, Cecelia listened intently, absorbing every detail. She had never played chess, yet the board captivated her. "And this one, with the carved top?" she asked, her curiosity deepening.

"The Farzin," Kunal replied. "It moves one square diagonally—cautious, yet essential. The advisor, always close to the shah, always guarding."

"And this last one?" Her fingers hovered over the most ornate piece, its intricate carvings commanding attention.

His voice softened, carrying a weight beyond the game. "That's the Shah. The king. If he falls, everything crumbles." His dark eyes locked onto hers. "In life, it's much the same. All decisions lead back to the safety of the king."

The unspoken meaning lingered between them, heavy and loaded. Then, Kunal broke the silence, his tone lighter. "Shall we play?"

"I shouldn't," Cecelia murmured, her voice reluctant yet tempted. "You've already thanked me for helping you escape the party. I don't want to intrude further."

"Please," Kunal urged with a soft laugh as he began resetting the pieces. "You've been speaking of shoulds and shouldn'ts since we met.

Must everything be about duty?" He tilted his head, his expression inviting yet challenging. "You sound like the women in my life—always weighed down by expectations."

Cecelia arched an eyebrow. "And you sound like a man haunted by his father's demands," she countered, a playful yet pointed retort.

Kunal paused, then nodded, conceding the truth in her words. "Touché," he admitted, a hint of admiration in his voice. "You're perceptive, Cecelia."

The room's flickering shadows danced on the walls, casting shifting patterns over the carved wooden pieces. The scent of cedar mingled with the faint musk of earth and sawdust, remnants of Kunal's craft beneath the workbench. Small and unassuming, the space was filled with the warmth of hands that had shaped each item carefully—tools with worn edges, intricate carvings catching the soft glow of the fire.

Cecelia's gaze settled on the board. "It's beautiful," she said, almost reverently. "I'm afraid to touch it, really. It feels like it belongs in a museum, not in the hands of someone like me."

Kunal's smile was warm, almost inviting. "My grandfather always said that wood craves the warmth of human touch," he mused, his fingers lightly tracing one of the carved pieces. "Each game leaves an imprint—a story embedded in the grain. If we never touch them, those stories fade." He set the piece back on the board, his hand lingering momentarily as he caught Cecelia's gaze. "These pieces are born from the earth, carved by hand. They're meant to be held, to feel the intentions of the player."

The words seemed to stir something within Cecelia. She glanced from Kunal to the board, then back again. The idea that even simple objects could carry stories—shaped by hands, molded by touch—made her curious. Tentatively, she reached out, wrapping her fingers around a Firzan. It felt warm against her skin, solid yet fragile, as if it held the spirit of past games. "I like that," she murmured. "A good story is something I can never resist."

A spark of interest lit Kunal's eyes. "Do you? Then my mother would like you. She's a keeper of our family's stories."

"Tell me one," Cecelia urged, leaning forward with genuine intrigue.

He paused, as if deciding where to begin, then shifted a piece on the board. "Here's a favorite," he started, voice dropping to a more intimate tone. "Long ago, beneath the vast skies of Amber, there lived a bird—known as the Sun's First Child. Each morning, it spread its golden wings to catch the dawn's first light. This bird possessed a gift—it could see beyond appearances, sensing the essence beneath."

Cecelia's lips curved into a faint smile. "A wise bird, then."

"Very," Kunal agreed. "One day, the hidden spring that sustained a village suddenly vanished. The desperate villagers sought the bird's help. At dawn, it soared high, seeing what others could not—beneath the barren earth, the spring had merely shifted underground. Guided by the bird's path, the villagers uncovered the water, saving their home."

She listened intently, absorbing every word. "It's a beautiful story," she said quietly, her expression thoughtful. "Seeing beyond the surface... sometimes, it's the only way to survive."

"Indeed," Kunal agreed. "The lesson is simple: true wisdom lies in what others overlook. We must be like the Sun's First Child—seeing what remains hidden."

He sighed then, as if revealing a secret. "But there's a riddle within this story, one I haven't solved."

"A riddle?" Cecelia's eyes sparkled with excitement. "I love riddles. Charlie and Annabel solved quite a few last year."

Kunal's gaze was playful. "I heard you had a hand in that."

"A small hand," Cecelia replied, a hint of pride slipping through.

Kunal stood, moving toward a wooden shelf in the corner. He returned holding a bundle wrapped in dark fabric. Unwrapping it carefully, he revealed an intricately carved sandalwood chest adorned with floral designs and brass inlays. "This is a family heirloom," he explained. "My great-great-grandmother crafted it. Before my grandmother died, she told me to always keep it away from sunlight—under this embroidered bird." He pointed to the woven design on the cloth. "We've tried for years to uncover its secrets."

Cecelia's breath caught at the sight. "It's exquisite," she whispered, running a tentative finger over the delicate carvings. "Whoever made this was an artist."

"She was," Kunal said softly. "And before she died, my grandmother charged me with solving its mystery. I've never brought it out in daylight, as she insisted. I was a rebellious child, often defying her wishes. After she was gone, I became more careful—more determined to honor her memory."

Cecelia's eyes twinkled mischievously. "I imagine she knew you better than anyone. Perhaps she expected you to break the rules. What if the riddle can only be solved in sunlight? Maybe that's the very challenge she intended."

Kunal laughed at the bold suggestion. Before he could respond, Rupa—who had been sitting quietly nearby—let out a sleepy yawn. "Don't you dare," she warned. "You'd upset a ghost."

Kunal shook his head, amused. "Perhaps," he conceded. "But I like the way you think."

The night grew deeper, and Kunal began to teach Cecelia shatranj. As they played, each move felt purposeful, a dance of strategy and foresight. Rupa polished her flute nearby, occasionally joining the conversation but mostly leaving Kunal and Cecelia to their quiet focus on the board.

To Cecelia, the game was both a distraction and a revelation. Each piece, each move, mirrored the complexities of her own life—a world full of strategies, alliances, and unexpected shifts. Yet within the game, there was a simplicity that contrasted the chaos of her reality. It was about choices—measured, deliberate, and entirely her own.

As they played, there were moments when Kunal's fingers brushed hers. The firelight cast soft shadows, illuminating the space between them. For brief seconds, the world outside felt distant and unimportant.

Finally, as the game reached its climax, Cecelia moved her piece with precision. "Échec et mat," *Checkmate.* she declared, her voice triumphant.

Kunal's smile was one of genuine admiration. "You learn quickly," he said, his voice low as their eyes met across the board.

CHAPTER FOURTEEN

SWEET POETRY

"How did you manage that?" Kunal's gaze was fixed on the board, his brow knit in disbelief. "I could've sworn I had you cornered."

Cecelia leapt from her seat, the thrill of victory rushing through her veins. "I won!" she exclaimed, twirling in place, her laughter echoing off the stone walls. But just as suddenly, a wave of dizziness washed over her. Her legs buckled, forcing her hands to grasp for the table's edge.

Kunal reached her in an instant, his arm wrapping around her waist with unexpected gentleness. His hand trembled slightly. "Are you alright?" Concern lined his voice.

"I'm not sure," she admitted, her voice thin and breathless. "One moment I was fine, and then—" She winced, the sudden onset of pain stealing her words.

Rupa, barely glancing up from her work across the room, offered a dry observation. "She's pregnant. Get her off her feet, Kunal, before her ankles turn to tree trunks."

Kunal managed a nervous chuckle as he looked down, then back at Cecelia. "There's a hammock in the corner. Or I can call for your father—"

"No," Cecelia interrupted softly, leaning into his support. "I haven't lain in a hammock since I was a child. It sounds wonderful."

He guided her gently toward the cushioned swing, his grip steady yet cautious. As she sank into the soft fabric, Cecelia felt a rush of unexpected relief. Her legs finally free of pressure, she exhaled deeply, blinking away sudden tears. Embarrassment flushed her cheeks. "I don't know what's wrong with me. You've been so kind, and here I am... falling apart."

"It's been an unusual night for all of us," Kunal replied, his voice a mix of reassurance and a touch of vulnerability. He cleared his throat, as if uncertain of how close to stand. "You're not a burden, Cecelia. You're good company." His smile was small, hesitant.

Her cheeks warmed at the words. "You're kind," she managed, her voice soft. "I haven't had this much pleasant company in ages. My days are filled with chores, and I've been trying to learn to read a book—"

She paused, frustration threading through her words. "It's so much harder than I expected. Annabel makes it look effortless, but for me…"

Kunal's eyes softened. "Reading books isn't for everyone. I prefer plays or poems, myself. They're shorter, easier to grasp, and often have music to break the silence."

Rupa finally stood, casting a knowing look at the pair. "I'll be rinsing my face," she announced, her tone casual but deliberate. "Try not to wake Maa." Her steps faded, leaving Cecelia and Kunal alone.

He leaned closer, a hint of mischief in his expression. "I might have something in my collection you'd enjoy."

Cecelia arched a brow. "I'll take that challenge."

With a grin, Kunal crossed to a small bookshelf, his fingers brushing over the worn spines. "Let's see…" He paused, his brow furrowing in concentration. A moment later, he returned to the hammock, a slim volume in hand.

"My sympathies, Cecelia," he said softly, his voice filled with empathy. "You've been through much. It's clear you've endured, but it must feel heavy at times."

Cecelia's throat tightened, caught off guard by his unexpected tenderness. "Perhaps," she whispered, "but others have suffered more."

"And modest, too," he teased gently, though his eyes held a spark of admiration. "You don't find that in many artists." As she opened her mouth to protest, he shook his head, smiling. "We've settled that already." The confidence in his tone silenced her objections, bringing an unexpected warmth as she smiled and shook her head back at him.

Relaxing into the hammock, Cecelia watched as Kunal opened the delicate pages. "This is Hafez," he explained, his voice reverent. "A Persian poet from centuries past. He often uses nature as metaphors for the heart's deepest emotions."

Cecelia's mind drifted to her own sketches—the squirrel, the trees, the winding path that seemed to promise freedom. Could her drawings hold meaning she hadn't yet realized?

Kunal's voice dropped, more intimate now. "Here is the Persian: Delam be havaye kouye to khosh ast vali; Be jan to ke janam az ghamat azardeh ast."

The words spilled like music, soft and melodic. Cecelia closed her eyes, letting the foreign cadence envelop her, warm and inviting. "It's beautiful," she murmured, the language curling around her like a tender embrace.

Kunal's voice grew thoughtful as he translated. "The meaning would be, more or less, or at least my interpretation this night..." he began, choosing each word carefully. "My heart is content with the thought of your street, yet by your life, my soul is pained by your sorrow."

The translation landed with a quiet weight between them, and Cecelia's breath hitched. Their eyes locked, and the room seemed to shrink, their unspoken longing filling the silence. In that suspended moment, the world beyond the walls vanished, leaving only the raw intensity between them.

"You're right," she managed to say, her voice hushed. "I like it."

Suddenly, Rupa reappeared, breaking the fragile spell. She seemed blissfully unaware of the charged atmosphere. "Oh, it's gotten so late!" she exclaimed. "Cecelia, you should head home."

"Yes, you're right," Cecelia replied, her voice steadier now, though she felt a pang as the moment slipped away. She rose, feeling the ache in her legs from the day's work, while Kunal reached for the lantern. He hesitated at the door, as if reluctant to part.

"It's not far," Cecelia assured him, gesturing toward the dim outline of her parents' cottage in the distance. "I can manage on my own."

But Kunal shook his head, unwavering. "I know you can. But I won't let you walk alone in the dark, not even with a lantern. I'd never forgive myself."

Side by side, they stepped into the crisp night air, the lantern's flickering glow casting long shadows over the rugged path. The castle loomed behind them, a silent sentinel in the moonlight, while the earthy scent of the Yorkshire fields mingled with the distant call of owls and rustling leaves.

"Thank you," Cecelia said quietly, her voice soft against the night's stillness. She was acutely aware of the space between them—too little, too much. "It's comforting to have company. Tomorrow will be another long day of chores. I expect I'll be asleep the moment my head touches the pillow."

"I hope they don't have you on your feet too much," Kunal replied, his voice low. "Given your... condition."

"I'm pregnant, not an invalid," Cecelia retorted, her tone light despite the fatigue lacing her words. "But my mother's been kinder lately, making sure I get lighter tasks. Still, I'd trade scrubbing floors for a day spent sketching." The confession tumbled out before she could stop it. She paused, feeling exposed, and added quickly, "I don't mean to make you feel guilty."

Kunal chuckled softly. "No guilt, I promise. Yes, I've had the luxury of painting for a living, but I understand hard work." He paused, then asked gently, "How did you learn to draw so well? Were you self-taught?"

"I wish I could say I was born with a pencil in hand," Cecelia laughed, the sound quiet but genuine. "I took lessons as a child, back in France. My teachers thought I had promise, but when we lost everything, my art became a luxury we couldn't afford." She looked up at the stars, her voice softening with the memory. "We lost our home, our money... everything changed. And sacrifices had to be made."

Kunal's eyes softened. "I'm sorry," he said simply. "That must have been hard."

They reached the cottage, its dark silhouette resting peacefully under the starlit sky. Cecelia turned to him, her voice barely a whisper. "Thank you for walking me home." She hesitated, the words slipping out before she could stop them. "And please... don't tell my mother."

A slow, understanding smile spread across Kunal's face. "Your secret is safe with me."

The next morning, Cecelia awoke before dawn, the memories of the previous night still fresh. She moved quietly through the sleeping castle, her thoughts tangled and restless. In a haze of duty, she dipped candles and polished silver with brisk efficiency. When the tasks were done, she slipped into the kitchen, snagging a piece of gingerbread Maggie had baked the day before. Tucking it into her apron, she headed toward Kunal's cottage.

As she approached, she halted abruptly. Voices—sharp and low—emanated from within.

"...put it in the light after all this time?" Rupa's voice was laced with frustration. "Why now, Kunal? You've kept to tradition for years, and now you risk everything. For what?"

Kunal's reply was quieter but steady. "It's my choice. And I don't think I've ruined anything. After speaking with Cecelia—"

"Cecelia? She's a lovely girl, but really, Kunal," Rupa's tone sharpened, each word a pointed jab. "You've been practically courting her. She's a scullery maid! Do you want to upset everything for someone who has no place in our world?"

Heat flooded Cecelia's cheeks—anger, shame, and a strange pang of hurt. Her hand trembled as she fumbled the gingerbread parcel, setting it on the windowsill before stumbling back. The porch creaked beneath her feet, and in her haste, she knocked over a stool, the clatter breaking the still morning air.

Her heart pounded, but she forced herself to keep moving, her head high despite the tears stinging her eyes. The door creaked open behind her.

"Cecelia, wait!" Kunal's voice was urgent.

Ignoring him, she quickened her pace until she reached the castle gates, her emotions a whirlwind of humiliation, anger, and confusion.

Inside the kitchen, Bridgette was mid-conversation with Maggie when she noticed Cecelia's flushed face and tear-bright eyes. Her gaze narrowed.

"What's wrong?" Bridgette's voice was sharp.

"Pregnant and alone," Cecelia shot back, her tone clipped. "What's my next task?"

Bridgette's eyes widened, unprepared for her daughter's rawness. "You can rest if you want. I saw the work you did this morning; it was commendable."

"No need," Cecelia retorted, her voice tight with frustration. "I need a distraction. Might as well be useful, isn't that what you always say?"

Bridgette hesitated, her tone softening. "Yes, that's true. Actually, Barnaby offered me a crate of apples if someone could muck out his stables today." She cast a wary glance at Maggie before lowering her voice. "I was going to ask Hattie, but we'll need her for making fruit leather..."

"Fine," Cecelia cut her off. She turned on her heel before Bridgette or Maggie could respond and headed toward her father's study.

James looked up as she barged in, startled by her abrupt entrance. "Ma coeur, what's the matter?"

"Where is Marguerite?" Cecelia demanded, her arms crossed. She shifted uncomfortably as the pressure on her belly reminded her of her condition.

James's face paled. "Where did you hear that name?"

"Doesn't matter," Cecelia snapped, stepping closer. "Have you brought her up from the dungeon yet?"

"Keep your voice down," James hissed, his eyes darting to the door. "Yes, she's in the third guest bedroom. Frederick hired a new physician for her, one specializing in... women's issues of the brain."

"Women's issues of the brain?" The revelation struck Cecelia like a physical blow, the room spinning around her. "What on earth do you mean?"

"She was kept in a gilded cage, like Philippa," James explained carefully. "Marguerite's from a noble family, but it seems she tried to give away her family's wealth to the wrong people. Her family sent her here to be 'cured.'"

"Cured," Cecelia repeated, fury barely contained.

"Yes. Any more questions?" Her father sighed.

Before Cecelia could respond, the front door creaked, and Bridgette's stern voice cut through the tension. "Cecelia! You wanted work; now go muck the stables."

Without a word, Cecelia shot her mother a tight smile and stormed out, her anger simmering beneath the surface.

The stables were dim, the faint morning light filtering through the cracks in the wooden walls. Cecelia pushed open the doors with more force than necessary, startling the horses. The sharp scent of hay and manure filled the air as she grabbed a pitchfork and attacked the soiled straw with aggressive vigor. Each thrust was a release, each movement fueled by the anger roiling inside her. "Bloody fool," she muttered under her breath, directing her venom at herself.

With each jab, the straw piled higher in the wheelbarrow, the rhythmic clatter punctuating the silence. One of the horses neighed uneasily, and Cecelia paused, her breathing ragged. She reached out, stroking the horse's nose gently. "It's alright, Leo. None of this is your fault." The horse nickered, as if offering its silent agreement.

"You're probably the only one who listens," she murmured, smoothing his mane with a tenderness that contrasted her earlier fury. "I work as hard as any of them, yet I'm invisible. A servant, like this straw. But I know my worth. Maybe not today, but one day."

Time blurred as she worked tirelessly, mucking out the stalls. Sweat dampened her brow, and exhaustion pulled at her limbs, but she pressed on, determined to prove something—to herself, to the world, to anyone who had ever doubted her.

Finally, she leaned against Leo's stall, her hand resting on the horse's flank. "Maybe I should just stay here," she mused aloud, her voice soft. "It's simpler, isn't it?"

Leo snorted in response, and Cecelia found herself laughing, the sound surprising her. But her brief moment of peace was cut short by the creak of the stable door.

"Hello?" she called, stepping cautiously out of the stall. To her surprise, it was Kunal.

She inhaled deeply, steeling herself against the sudden rush of emotions. Emerging from behind the stall, she became acutely aware of her disheveled appearance—dirt-stained dress, sweaty hair, and the unmistakable scent of hay clinging to her skin. Despite everything, she met Kunal's gaze head-on, her expression a mix of defiance and vulnerability. "Yes?"

CHAPTER FIFTEEN

CHICKEN CHASE

"Did you come to the studio this morning?" Kunal asked, his voice low but urgent. His eyes never left Cecelia's face, piercing through the shadows that clung to the dim stable.

"You shouldn't be here," Cecelia muttered, her gaze shifting to the floor. The stable felt oppressively small, sunlight slicing through cracks in the wooden walls and catching on drifting dust motes. The musty scent of straw mixed with the pungent smell of manure, heavy and unrelenting. She gripped the pitchfork tighter, her knuckles stark white, as if it could somehow anchor her. "This place is filthy. You'll ruin your fine clothes."

He took a step closer, straw crunching beneath his boots. "I don't care about the dirt," he insisted, his voice steady, "I care about you."

The words struck like a physical blow, and her heart lurched unexpectedly. Still, she kept her tone sharp, unwilling to show any cracks in her armor. "If you need a horse, I'll fetch you one. There's no need to linger."

He ignored her offer. "So, you did come to the studio?" he pressed, a note of regret shadowing his voice. "Cecelia, I'm so sorry. Rupa's words... she didn't mean them. I don't know how much you overheard, but—"

"I heard enough," she snapped, crossing her arms, though the defensive posture couldn't hide the slight tremor in her voice. "Please, just go. I don't know what I was thinking, letting myself..." She trailed off, biting her lip hard enough to draw blood, unwilling to finish the admission. She wouldn't let him see how deeply it hurt.

"Rupa spoke out of turn," Kunal pleaded. "If she'd known you were there, she never would have said those things."

"It doesn't matter," she whispered, her voice barely audible. The familiar mix of hay and dust scraped against her throat, as did the bitterness lodged deep in her chest. "I am beneath you both, Kunal. You shouldn't even be speaking to me."

"Don't say that," he murmured, stepping closer, the space between them shrinking until she could feel his warmth. His voice, raw with emotion, was insistent. "You have no idea how much I admire you."

Her eyes burned, and she fought back the tears that threatened to spill. "Don't patronize me," she choked out. "And don't pity me, either." She turned away abruptly, pressing her palm to her forehead, her composure fraying like old linen under strain.

"There is no pity," he assured her, a note of desperation creeping into his tone. "Only respect. And... something more."

She stilled, her breath catching. Something more? Against her better judgment, she glanced at him, her heart thudding painfully as she registered the intensity in his gaze.

"I want to court you, Cecelia," Kunal said, his voice dropping to a hoarse whisper. The confession hung between them, unexpected and vulnerable. "If you'd have me."

Her fingers, still resting on the stable door, faltered. Every rational part of her screamed to turn away, to protect herself from this dangerous possibility. But the warmth in his voice, the urgency in his eyes—it was unraveling her defenses. The air around them thickened, as if the stable itself were holding its breath.

He closed the distance between them, and before she could process what was happening, his hands cupped her face gently. His touch was warm and unexpectedly tender, his thumbs brushing the curve of her jaw. His lips captured hers in a rush of longing, stealing her breath in the process. Her body, fueled by weeks of unspoken desire and simmering frustration, responded instinctively. She kissed him back with a fervor that surprised even her.

The stable seemed to hold its breath, the world outside fading into oblivion. Kunal kissed her hungrily, but with a tenderness that made her knees weaken. His hands slid down to her waist, pulling her closer, as if he never wanted to let go. Cecelia's hands found his vest, her fingers curling into the fabric as she pressed against him, matching his intensity with her own.

The rough scent of hay mingled with the intoxicating feeling of being wanted—truly wanted. Cecelia almost laughed at the absurdity of it all: here, in the filth of a stable, she felt more alive than she had in years.

His lips trailed down her neck, sending a shiver through her body. Cecelia opened her eyes just enough to see him—his face flushed, his dark eyes half-closed with desire. Her breath hitched, a thrill running through her. For the first time, she saw a man utterly consumed by her, and it made her heart soar.

"I've been captivated by you since the moment we met," he murmured against her lips, his voice rough with feeling. "Your strength, your fire... you've bewitched me."

Her chest tightened with a mixture of disbelief and longing. "And yet, you make no effort to escape?" she asked, her voice shaky, barely more than a whisper.

"I have no desire to escape," he said, resting his forehead against hers. "I'm bound to you, Cecelia, in ways I can't explain." His hands moved from her waist to her shoulders, pulling her closer still, and he kissed her again—this time slower, more deliberate.

Emboldened by his words, Cecelia's hands slipped beneath his vest, her fingers grazing the warmth of his chest through the thin fabric of his shirt. The contact sent a spark of pleasure down her spine, and she deepened the kiss, losing herself in the moment.

The soft rustling of their clothes, the faint snorts of the horses, the smell of straw and sweat—it all seemed distant, drowned out by the thunderous rhythm of her heart. She had never felt more wanted.

For the first time, she wasn't just a maid, a servant, or a burden. In Kunal's arms, she was a woman.

Every movement between them felt charged, the air thick with the tension of unspoken desire—desire that had lingered between them for weeks, now surging forward, finding release in the soft press of lips and the lingering touch of hands. Cecelia had never been this close to anyone, not truly. Yet here she was, her body betraying her with its yearning, allowing herself to be drawn into the moment's heat, knowing it was a dangerous place she might never escape.

"May I court you officially?" Kunal whispered, his voice rough and filled with emotion.

"Kunal..." Cecelia's heart raced, torn between hope and dread. "I am not only beneath your station, but I carry another man's child. You should run from me as far as those long, beautiful legs can carry you."

"Perhaps I should," he agreed, a playful grin breaking across his face, his eyes intense. "But I find I have no wish to." He tilted his head with a teasing lilt. "And you've been observing my legs, have you?"

Cecelia stifled a laugh, her breath hitching. "The way your legs remind me of a fine stallion is neither here nor there." She took a step back, trying to steady her breathing, suspicion mingling with vulnerability. "Are you just trying to cheer me after Rupa's harsh words?"

"When I first saw you, your eyes lit up at my drawing tools," Kunal said, taking a slow, measured step toward her. "It was the same fire I feel when I work—something I've never forgotten. It drew me to you, Cecelia."

Her throat tightened, words caught somewhere between fear and desire. She shook her head, still unsure if this was some sort of cruel jest.

"I'll be honest," Kunal continued, his voice steady, raw. "It's not often I consider courting a woman with child. But your circumstances are not your fault. The way you've reacted to them is admirable. And this feeling I have for you, Cecelia—it's not a passing whim." He paused, his gaze open and earnest, a question in his eyes.

Cecelia inhaled deeply, the weight of her thoughts pressing against her chest. After a long, silent moment, she managed a tight laugh. "I want to kiss you again, if I'm being truthful. But this isn't right for you, Kunal. I would ruin you."

Kunal's lips found hers again, firm but tender, cutting off her words. "You will do no such thing," he murmured against her skin, his thumb brushing a stray curl from her cheek. His hand cupped her face gently, and Cecelia shivered at the tender warmth of his touch.

The dim light of the stable, mingling with the earthy scent of hay and horses, faded from Cecelia's awareness as they stood close. The judgments of society, the whispers of propriety, the unyielding rules of class—all seemed to melt away. She leaned into Kunal, her heart pounding, their chests pressed together as he kissed her again. His lips trailed down her neck, lingering on her collarbone. Cecelia's body trembled, and for a fleeting moment, she wanted to be swept into the hay, her need so fierce she nearly begged for more. But sense clawed its way back, the reminder of the risks pulling her from the precipice.

"We have to stop," Kunal muttered, breaking the kiss with clear reluctance, his breath ragged. "I've never... been with a woman, and if we go further, I'm not sure I'll be able to walk away."

Cecelia's heart pounded, her voice barely above a whisper. "I won't pretend I didn't enjoy it."

His grin returned, his thumb gently tracing her flushed cheek. "I enjoyed it more than I should have." His eyes softened, lingering on her face. "I've enjoyed everything about you—your boldness, your wit, your fire." His fingers gently tangled in her curls. "And your hair... it reminds me of a wood nymph's."

Cecelia snorted softly, pushing her rebellious red curls under her bonnet. "These wretched things? They catch every bit of straw and leaf."

"Then you truly are a forest pixie," he teased, coaxing a smile from her.

"Did you come here to steal kisses?" Cecelia asked, raising an eyebrow. "Or was it to charm me with those legs?"

Kunal chuckled, his gaze warm. "I came to bring you to my sister. She wishes to apologize."

Cecelia's brow furrowed. "She sent you, did she?"

"She had no idea where you were," Kunal explained. "Barnaby mentioned seeing you in the stables, so I came to find you."

Cecelia's expression hardened, her arms crossing protectively over her chest. "And I suppose what just happened between us will be kept... secret?"

Kunal hesitated, shifting slightly. "I'm not ashamed of how I feel," he said quietly, his voice firm. "But if you won't let me court you—"

"Aren't you ashamed, though?" Cecelia interrupted, her gaze sharp. "Isn't that part of the thrill? That you shouldn't want me? I'm no fool, Kunal."

His face flushed, but he met her gaze steadily. "If only I were a master of love and seduction," he said wryly. "But I'm not. You underestimate my sincerity."

Her tone softened, but she kept her guard up. "I know sincerity, but I also know reality. You're a Sutar—part of one of the most respected trade families in England. What would people say if you courted a disgraced maid?"

Kunal stepped closer, his voice low and impassioned. "I may not know much about love, but what I feel for you, Cecelia, is real. If we were to marry..."

Her heart ached at his words. She had never felt so torn between reality and the fierce longing to hope for more. But she couldn't let him sacrifice everything for her. She wouldn't allow it.

"Regardless," Cecelia said, voice laden with both tenderness and resolve, "I cannot let you throw your life away. You must not speak of this to anyone. And..." Her voice broke, her throat tight. "And you must not pursue me. I won't have England laugh at you, nor at your family."

Kunal's eyes searched hers, a storm of emotions swirling within them—defiance, longing, and something like hope. "If that is truly what you wish," he murmured, though his gaze told a different story, one of stubborn yearning. "But I care not who laughs," he declared, his voice filled with quiet conviction. "I swear it."

Cecelia's throat tightened, and she shook her head firmly. "Then you do not understand." She gestured to herself, hands trembling. "Look at me. I'm only a scullery maid, Kunal." Her voice was raw, echoing the words he'd once used against her, and Kunal flinched. "I've been mucking out stables. A single straw on your tunic could ruin it."

With a glance down at his fine tunic, Kunal managed a wry smile. "This tunic is tougher than it looks, but the barn air is getting rather close." He stepped toward the door and gave it a push, letting in a gust of fresh air. Suddenly, Cecelia heard the familiar shout of the neighboring farmer calling his chickens. The dry rattle of corn in the wind warned her of what was coming.

Before she could say a word, a noisy flood of feathers erupted from the barn. Kunal's eyes widened in alarm as the birds charged into the yard. "Oh no!" he exclaimed, hands flailing in panic. "Cecelia, I didn't mean to—where are they going? Should I... should I go after them?"

Cecelia watched him, momentarily speechless. What was he thinking? The chickens knew where the food was; they'd be back by dusk. But before she could explain, Kunal bolted into action, sprinting after the runaway fowl.

She could only stare as he chased the squawking flock, his tunic flapping behind him like a banner of sheer determination. Dust rose around him in chaotic clouds, his boots thudding against the ground as he managed to capture two old hens, one tucked under each arm. He stumbled back toward her, triumphant yet breathless. Tossing the birds into the barn, he tried to shut the door—only for a cunning hen to dart right between his legs and escape once more.

"What in the—" Kunal spluttered, looking utterly bewildered. "Do chickens never give up?" He spun around, searching the yard as if more surprises might spring upon him. "And is that... a cow? Do cows eat chickens? Should we call for the guard?"

"Call a guard?" came Annabel's amused voice from behind, making Cecelia jump. "What in heaven's name is happening here?" She squinted through the barn door, then burst into laughter at the sight of Kunal's desperate pursuit. "Is he... trying to catch chickens?"

Cecelia pressed a hand to her forehead, groaning. "Yes, Annabel. He's trying to catch chickens."

Annabel's grin widened, clearly enjoying the spectacle. "And you're just letting him make a fool of himself?"

"I have no idea why," Cecelia sighed, her eyes lingering on Kunal's floundering attempt. "But he... he wants to court me."

Annabel's eyes sparkled with mischief. "I thought I sensed something between you two." She paused, watching Kunal's relentless chase, then added, "But..."

"But I'm not good enough for him," Cecelia blurted out, waving a hand toward Kunal's flailing efforts. "Look at him, Annabel. Just look."

Annabel's expression softened, but her voice was firm. "Oh, I am looking. I'm looking at a man who's willing to chase chickens for you." She leaned closer, lowering her voice. "Are you really going to deny him just because you think you're not worthy? Or are you afraid to let yourself be loved?"

Cecelia felt a pang of something akin to hope, but she squashed it down. "It's not that simple."

"Isn't it?" Annabel's tone was gentle, but insistent. "Maybe you're cutting off your nose to spite your face, Cecelia."

The words lingered, like a challenge. Cecelia's heart pounded in her chest as she watched Kunal pause, wiping sweat from his brow. She drew in a deep breath, then called out, "Kunal!"

He stopped dead, turning toward her with a mix of guilt, hope, and a dash of bewilderment. "If this causes you trouble..."

"It won't," Cecelia assured, her voice stronger now. "But you can't catch chickens that way. They always come back on their own."

"They do?" His voice carried a hint of disbelief, his gaze darting between her and the fleeing birds. "I thought..."

"You didn't let me finish explaining," Cecelia chided gently, crossing her arms, a reluctant smile tugging at her lips.

Kunal scratched his head, clearly sheepish. "Ah. I suppose I didn't."

Annabel, still watching with amusement, stepped back. "I'll leave you two to sort this out. But Cecelia," she added with a wink, "don't be too hard on him. He did try."

Kunal let out a heavy sigh, shoulders sagging. "I've made a complete fool of myself," he said quietly. "Clearly, I am not suited to your world."

Cecelia's expression softened. "And yet," she replied, her voice barely above a whisper, "you stopped when I called your name."

Kunal's gaze was intense, filled with vulnerability. "I'll stop now as well, if that's what you wish," he said, his tone raw. "No more kisses, no more courtship. If you truly do not want me, I'll walk away."

"Kunal," Cecelia cut in, her voice steady but soft. "You may court me."

His eyes widened with disbelief. "Are you jesting?"

Cecelia's cheeks flushed, but she kept her gaze steady. "Partly, yes. Watching you chase those chickens... seeing you ruin your clothes for me, and then stop at my call—it made me reconsider." Her voice warmed with a hint of laughter. "And maybe Annabel's words hit home as well."

Kunal's face broke into a radiant smile as he reached for her hand. "Then I am grateful—to Annabel, to you, and even to these miscreant chickens."

Chapter Sixteen

GIBBERISH

After another lingering kiss, Cecelia pulled back, gently brushing dirt from Kunal's tunic with quick, practiced movements. "I can help with this," she said, her voice softer. "The laundress who worked here taught me some tricks for getting dirt out of finer fabrics."

"Dirt out of silk?" Kunal teased, his smile broadening, eyes crinkling at the corners. "I'd be grateful, but maybe you'd prefer seeing what Rupa found in the chest instead."

Cecelia hesitated briefly, then nodded. "I'll come," she agreed. "But... maybe we should keep this courtship to ourselves for now? Just until we're more certain."

His gaze softened, understanding flickering in his eyes. "Of course. We'll take it as slow as you need. For now, I'll return you as a dear friend."

A short while later, after rinsing her face and hands in the cold well water, Cecelia followed Kunal back toward the cabin. The evening sun cast long, slanted shadows across the grass, the air growing cooler with each step. Inside, warmth greeted them—a mix of cedar, wood shavings, and the low, comforting crackle of the hearth.

"Cecelia," Rupa called from the table, her tone less guarded than before. She set aside a small carving, a frown creasing her brow. "I've spoken with Annabel and Charlie. I didn't realize you were involved with Annabel's book when I—" She paused, as if weighing her words. "When I called you a scullery maid."

Cecelia's cheeks warmed. "She's writing it," she clarified quickly. "I'm just doing some of the drawings." She hesitated, then added, "And I am a scullery maid, but not just that. It wasn't always like this."

Rupa's expression softened, as if she understood more than she let on. "I see. Please, have a seat."

Cecelia eased into the worn wooden chair, the tension between them easing slightly. Her eyes flickered to the parcel of gingerbread she'd left behind earlier, now resting neatly at the center of the table.

"Mara's gingerbread?" Kunal asked, his eyes lighting up with recognition. "Charlie's mother's recipe, right? I can smell the rosewater."

"Yes," Cecelia replied, her voice taking on a warmer tone at the mention of Mara. "She was a good friend to my mother—clever, resourceful, always making people feel cared for. Maggie bakes this often now. I thought, since you liked the spices I used last night, you might like this too."

Kunal broke off a piece and tasted it, a satisfied smile forming. "You were right. Your sense for spices is sharp."

Cecelia blushed at the compliment, but quickly shifted the conversation. "What's the next clue?" she asked, popping a piece of gingerbread into her mouth before setting the pouch aside.

Rupa leaned forward, her voice growing serious. "We set the chest in the sunlight, and a hidden compartment was revealed. Inside was a plaque with an inscription in our language." She opened a small notebook, where she had carefully copied the inscription.

Curious, Cecelia leaned closer. The letters flowed in elegant, looping lines, more like art than words.

"It's in our mother tongue," Rupa explained, tracing the symbols with her finger. "'Path to the infinite,' it says."

"Path to the infinite," Cecelia echoed, feeling a shiver down her spine. "What does it mean?"

"In our language, 'Anant' means infinite, and 'Marg' means path," Rupa explained.

"Anant ko marg," Kunal added softly, as if the words carried weight. "Our grandmother used to speak of it when she spoke of life's deeper mysteries."

The phrase seemed to hang in the air like an unanswered question, both poetic and profound. "It sounds like there's something more to it," Cecelia murmured, the words resonating deeply.

"There always is," Rupa said with a wistful smile. "Our grandmother loved riddles. She passed this chest to us, expecting we'd unlock its secrets someday."

"But there's something else," Kunal interjected, his voice tinged with frustration. "It's written in English below, and I can't make sense of it."

Cecelia frowned, leaning over to peer inside the chest. "What does it say?"

Rupa lifted the trunk's lid, revealing an inscription hidden beneath the velvet lining. Cecelia squinted, then laughed lightly. "I can't read, but even I know—that's just gibberish."

Kunal let out a long sigh, running a hand through his tousled hair. "Exactly."

Cecelia bent closer, inhaling the mingled scents of aged wood and earth. "Odd, though—English letters, but nonsense?"

Rupa shrugged. "Not that odd. Our great-great-grandmother Sunni married an Englishman. She often wrote in a mix of both languages."

Cecelia tilted her head thoughtfully. "It reminds me of the coded letters we used to deliver as children. My parents sometimes had illiterate servants run messages for others in the castle who didn't want to use the usual messenger—they'd sometimes check them first. Some looked a bit like this. In code." She paused. "I talked to Charlie about one of them once, and he said it was the kind of code his father used to write to his fellow Freemasons—something to keep prying eyes away."

Rupa laughed warmly, her tone unguarded. "Of course, Charlie would know about codes, then—I forgot Lucas was a Freemason."

"But he never joined," Kunal added, his voice tightening. "Charlie was too young when his father died. And now? I doubt he'd be interested. It's still a sore spot, and he's got the market stall to worry about."

"Certainly, but..." Rupa clucked her tongue teasingly, her eyes glinting. "He'd be upset if we left him out. It's a family riddle, after all. He wouldn't miss the chance."

A reluctant nod from Kunal. "Perhaps. But he's busy at the market today."

With a decisive brush of her hands, Rupa stood. "Then we'll speak to him tomorrow. For now, I'd like a proper tour of the castle grounds." She shot Cecelia an appraising look. "I also need to move my things to the next studio. Living out of a suitcase in my brother's room is hardly ideal."

She disappeared into Kunal's room without further word, the wooden door creaking softly behind her.

A charged silence lingered while Cecelia and Kunal exchanged a look, a slow smile tugging at Cecelia's lips. "It seems I've regained your sister's favor," she whispered, her eyes bright.

Kunal leaned closer, his voice a playful murmur. "I'm glad to hear it. Now... when may I kiss you again?"

But the moment was fleeting. Rupa reappeared, now clad in a heavier woolen shift and sturdy boots fit for a trek across the castle grounds. She sat, lacing her boots with quick efficiency, then turned to Cecelia with a determined expression. "I have a proposition for you. A way to start making amends."

Cecelia's brow arched. "What sort of proposition?"

Rupa's eyes gleamed with pride. "Frederick has commissioned my brother *and* me to craft something special. As part of that, I've been granted the services of a personal maid for three months. That maid, Cecelia, is you."

Cecelia's breath caught. "Me?"

"You'll come here daily," Rupa continued, rising and smoothing her skirts. "Perhaps sweep a bit, help with some tasks. But otherwise, you're free to do as you please—draw, rest, whatever suits you."

The world seemed to tilt. Cecelia struggled to comprehend. "I..."

Kunal's voice cut in, low and concerned. "You didn't mention this plan to me. If she's caught—"

Rupa waved his objection aside. "Her life is her own to decide, not yours. If she chooses, she can come."

Kunal's jaw tightened. "Of course, but—"

"Yes, I'll do it," Cecelia said suddenly, her voice unsteady but firm. "I'll come."

"Excellent," Rupa declared, her grin triumphant. "Frederick wants a harpsichord for the great hall—a grand one. And smaller instruments for the new theater. I'll be working here for the next few months. If I have a maid, I can rent one of the outbuildings as my workshop."

Kunal protested again, softer this time. "But Cecelia's family... they won't approve."

Rupa's patience was wearing thin. "That's not your concern. Let Cecelia decide her own fate."

He sighed, defeated, his gaze searching Cecelia's. "It's your choice, then."

Cecelia managed a reassuring smile. "My mother won't mind. She worries too much, but there's no real danger."

"Mothers, and indeed life itself, have the ability to destroy dreams we don't hold onto. Ours has been known to favor stability over passion." Rupa's laugh was knowing. "My advice? Tell her something far worse first. The truth won't seem so bad afterward."

Kunal frowned. "When has our mother ever stopped you from following your dreams? It's me she pressures to marry."

The mention of marriage sent a jolt through Cecelia. Her chest tightened, the weight of unspoken hopes pressing on her.

Rupa laughed, a bell-like sound. "That's because I'm nearly affianced to Tazir back in Amber. Once you're engaged, she'll shift to pestering you for grandchildren."

Cecelia tried not to meet Kunal's eyes, heat rising to her cheeks.

Eager to steer the conversation away, Kunal pointed ahead. "Is that the cabin? Looks like we've arrived."

The door creaked open, revealing Annabel's warm, welcoming smile. "Oh, do come in! You've arrived just in time for pie."

Charlie, already nestled by the hearth, waved them over with a grin. Once pleasantries were exchanged and everyone settled at the rough-hewn table, Kunal pulled out his notebook, its worn leather cover hinting at years of use. Cecelia smiled to see how close it resembled her own.

"Charlie," Kunal began, his tone shifting to seriousness, "we've made a discovery—a clue in the chest Cecelia found. It's a code, and I remember you mentioning your father taught you some things about codes. We could really use your help."

Charlie's expression darkened, as if Kunal had struck a nerve. "Codes?" he echoed, a bitter edge to his voice. "I haven't touched those since Da had me working on Freemason puzzles."

Annabel's eyes widened in surprise. "I never knew you were involved with the Freemasons."

"I wasn't," Charlie replied, voice rough with the weight of old wounds. "I just helped Da prepare. But after my parents disappeared, after I lost my eye... and everything that followed—I let the skill rust. I won't be one of them, not now."

Cecelia leaned forward, her voice soft yet steady. "Don't say that, Charlie. You're capable, and you know it."

His jaw tightened. "It's not that simple. Freemasons value physical wholeness, and I'm not... complete. And hiding my craft for so long has made it feel lost to me."

Kunal's eyes met Charlie's, unflinching. "You're wrong. Your worth isn't tied to being whole. You still carry your father's legacy, and that's not diminished by your injury. You're more than capable of reclaiming what's yours."

"Freemasons can cling to tradition, but even they are changing." Rupa lifted her glass. "A missing eye doesn't define you—your skill and spirit do."

Charlie's gaze flickered and he hung his head, a hint of vulnerability breaking through. "I don't know... I've been in the shadows for so long. It's hard to believe I'll even be at the market next week."

"You've been in the dark long enough," Kunal said with quiet conviction. "It's time to step into the light."

Rupa gave him a playful nudge. "And you can start by solving this code."

A soft chuckle escaped Charlie's lips, his tension easing. "Alright, let's have a look."

He leaned over the notebook, studying the string of letters:

XCGDKZYKOFLNHDZKWHVVJNAESJUGCY

Murmuring to himself, he took out a large book and a length of parchment, and began testing different ciphers, fingers shifting letters, his brow furrowed in concentration. Each attempt only resulted in more jumbled nonsense. Cecelia and the others watched in fascination.

"Not a Caesar cipher," he muttered, rubbing his chin. "Could be polyalphabetic, something more intricate..."

As they ate and drank, Charlie continued working in focused silence, the candlelight casting a warm glow over his features.

Rupa stretched back in her chair, a smirk forming. "Let's give him some peace. He'll crack it by tomorrow."

Annabel nodded, amused. "Yes, best to let him work his magic."

As they stood to leave, Cecelia met Kunal's gaze, warmth filling her chest. The events of the day—unraveling clues, unspoken bonds—felt like the start of something bigger, something she hadn't dared to dream of. Kunal's eyes met hers.

"Tomorrow?" he whispered, the words filled with promise.

"Tomorrow," Cecelia agreed, her heart fluttering.

They stepped out into the crisp evening air, the sun dipping low and casting long shadows over the cobbled path toward the castle. As they walked side by side, Cecelia allowed her fingers to brush lightly against Kunal's, her smile small but hopeful.

Tomorrow couldn't come soon enough.

Chapter Seventeen

TIGER

The morning sunlight filtered softly through Rupa's workshop windows, bringing a faint warmth to the crisp air. The familiar scents of wood shavings and oil mixed with the distant sounds of the bustling market, drifting faintly through the open panes. Rupa stood at her workbench, sleeves rolled to her elbows, focused on the intricate carvings before her. Cecelia, meanwhile, set about her tasks, sweeping the sawdust-covered floor with rhythmic strokes under Rupa's watchful eye.

The time passed with the steady hum of work. The silence, punctuated only by the scrape of sandpaper and the creak of shifting wood, felt comforting. Cecelia, pausing to wipe a layer of dust from her face and hands at the stone basin near the door, then settled into the corner. She pulled out her sketchbook and lost herself in the familiar dance of pencil across rough paper.

As the sun climbed higher, they took a break, sharing a simple meal of cheese, dark bread, and cider. Rupa, her focus unbroken, soon returned to her work. Cecelia joined her, the workshop gradually filling with the golden hues of late afternoon. A sudden knock at the door broke the tranquil routine. Rising to answer, Cecelia's heart skipped when she met Kunal's gaze.

"Ready to check in on Charlie?" he asked, an innocent playfulness in his tone, though his eyes lingered a moment longer than necessary.

Rupa dusted off her hands with a grin. "Let's go."

The three of them walked along the well-worn path toward Annabel and Charlie's cabin. At one point, Cecelia's hand brushed against Kunal's, sending a jolt through her. Their fingers grazed, and she caught his gaze—intense, searching, and just as startled as her own. They quickly looked away, but the fleeting contact left an unmistakable spark hanging between them.

Approaching the cabin, they were greeted by the warm glow of candlelight spilling through the windows. Inside, Annabel and Charlie sat at the table, the air filled with the inviting scents of mead and freshly baked bread. When they spotted their guests, both Annabel and Charlie broke into broad smiles, the weariness of their day's labor softened by shared joy.

"I've just finished the first draft of my play!" Annabel announced, her face glowing with excitement. "A whole week ahead of schedule."

"That's brilliant!" Cecelia exclaimed, her enthusiasm echoed by the clinking of earthenware cups as mead was poured.

Charlie leaned forward eagerly. "And I think I've cracked the code. It's not a simple cipher after all—it's the Vigenère cipher." He tapped his notebook with visible pride, his excitement infectious. "But now I need a keyword. Something that must have meant something to your ancestors, to your family."

Kunal's brow furrowed in thought. "A keyword? How many letters?"

"Less than ten," Charlie replied, drumming his fingers on the table, anticipation in his voice. "What do you think it could be?"

An uncertain silence settled over the room, broken only by the crackle of the fire. Then, with a sudden burst of inspiration, Rupa's eyes lit up. "Sutar!" she suggested, clapping her hands.

Charlie scribbled the name repeatedly beneath the coded letters, muttering calculations under his breath. Slowly, a triumphant grin spread across his face. "Rupa, you've done it. That's the key."

He quickly set about decoding the message. Kunal leaned closer, his voice low and tinged with wonder as he read aloud, "Find...the...root..."

"...to discover the branch," Rupa finished, her eyes wide with realization. "It's the rosewood writing desk!"

Annabel raised an intrigued eyebrow. "The what?"

"It's my family's desk," Kunal explained, a note of reverence in his voice. "It's been passed down for generations. The carvings depict a tree—roots below, branches above."

Cecelia felt a swell of admiration for the Sutar family's craftsmanship, a legacy carved into wood and passed down through time. Yet as the group prepared to leave, a sense of hesitation tugged at her. She fell into step beside Annabel. "They're so generous," she whispered. "The Sutars, I mean. Rupa didn't like me at first, but as soon as she realized you and I were friends, she took me in as her maid and lets me draw! Such help makes me... uneasy."

Annabel chuckled softly. "I know the feeling. When Sarala took me under her wing, I felt the same way. She still helps me with my writing, charging me half of what she charges others. You deserve kindness too, Cecelia. Let yourself accept it."

Taking a deep breath, Cecelia quickened her pace to rejoin Kunal and Rupa, who were animatedly discussing the desk's clues ahead of her. "Now that the mystery's solved, I suppose my help is no longer needed," she ventured with a light laugh, though uncertainty laced her tone.

Rupa spun around, her eyes gleaming with resolve. "Nonsense! You're part of this now, Cecelia. There's no turning back."

Cecelia's grin widened, the warmth of Rupa's words settling over her. The sun was beginning to dip low, casting golden hues across the path as they returned to the cabins. Inside Kunal's home, the rosewood desk awaited—majestic, its rich surface gleaming in the dim light. Cecelia's fingers traced the intricate inlays of mother-of-pearl, her touch reverent.

"It's the Tree of Life," Kunal murmured, his voice soft as he watched her admiration.

Meanwhile, Rupa was already exploring the drawers, sliding them open with swift precision. "We may need to turn it upside down," she suggested.

Kunal shot her a disapproving glare. "You are not flipping my desk, Rupa. It's endured centuries intact, and I'd like to keep it in that state. We'll find another way, surely."

Rupa smirked, unperturbed. "Don't let yourself become too boastful, my brother. You only just found the first clue after years of struggling."

With a scowl, Kunal resumed his search.

Gathering her courage, Cecelia crouched beside Kunal, the dim glow of the lantern reflecting a spark of determination in her eyes. "What if I slide underneath?" she suggested, her voice low but steady. "Even with the babe, I'm still small enough. There might be something hidden beneath."

Kunal's eyes lit up at her boldness. "Thank you," he said earnestly. He quickly laid his jacket over the dusty floor, creating a makeshift cushion for her. "Careful," he added, holding the lantern steady and adjusting its angle to illuminate the dark space beneath the desk.

Cecelia wriggled onto her back, the cold wood pressing against her spine as she squinted into the dim recesses. Strange shadows flickered along the carved wood, dancing eerily. She directed Kunal to shift the lantern closer, her voice hushed and urgent. Then, after a few moments of silent scrutiny, she gasped. "I see it!"

Kunal leaned forward, his excitement palpable. "What is it?" he asked, a tremble of anticipation in his voice.

"It's a tiger," she replied, her tone unexpectedly playful. "Quite a charming one, too."

At this, Rupa let out a soft laugh, her amusement echoing gently in the small room. "A tiger? Well then, that means we're off to see our parents again."

Cecelia's brow furrowed, confusion knitting her features. "Why a tiger?"

"Because," Kunal explained as he sat back on his heels, a grin on his face, "our family owns a chair carved with tiger heads on the armrests. I'll wager the next clue is there."

Realization dawned on Cecelia's face. "So, the clues are hidden within your family's heirlooms?" she asked, piecing it together slowly. "And since your family's kept everything, you should be able to find them all?"

"Exactly." Kunal's grin widened. "Mother has preserved every relic we've inherited, from the largest furniture piece to the smallest hatpin. It's sheer luck." His gaze softened as he looked at her. "Will you join us for dinner tomorrow? Meet the family?"

Cecelia hesitated, a faint blush coloring her cheeks. "I really shouldn't. It's a personal matter."

"Nonsense," Rupa interjected with a teasing wink. "You're already part of this adventure, Cecelia. Besides, I'll need your help preparing for dinner."

Despite herself, Cecelia's lips curved into a smile, her heart fluttering at the unexpected invitation. "In that case, I'd be honored."

"Good," Rupa said with a satisfied nod, surveying the dusty workshop with a critical eye. "Now, let's clean up a bit. Cecelia, could you arrange for two baths—one hot, one lukewarm? I need to freshen up before we head home."

"Of course," Cecelia replied promptly. Just as she turned to leave, an uneasy thought crept into her mind. "I only hope my mother isn't too suspicious. Kunal was right—she'll have questions about this sudden reassignment."

Rupa waved a dismissive hand, her voice light with amusement. "That's easy enough. Tell her something far worse first. Frighten her so thoroughly that when you reveal the truth, she'll be relieved. Mothers are like that."

Cecelia chuckled, her spirits lifted by the banter. As she made her way back toward the castle, there was a buoyancy in her step that hadn't been there before. The joy of newfound purpose brightened her mood, and a wide grin stretched across her face as she entered the bustling kitchen—only to be met by the stern figure of her mother.

Bridgette's narrowed eyes betrayed her suspicion. "What's this I hear?" she demanded, her tone sharp. "Frederick claims Rupa Sutar has asked for you as her personal maid. You're no longer under my instruction while the artists are here? What's going on, Cecelia?"

Cecelia managed an exaggerated expression of innocence. "Oh, Mumma," she began sweetly. "You'll never guess. I've found a husband, and rather than sailing to America, I'll be staying here with him. He's twice my age, wants a child right away, and the Sutars introduced us. I'll work for them until the wedding."

Bridgette's face drained of color, her eyes wide with horror. Cecelia couldn't help herself—she burst into laughter, unable to maintain the ruse.

"Who is this man?" Bridgette snapped, her voice sharp with urgency.

"There's no man, Mumma," Cecelia admitted through her giggles. "I was only teasing. The Sutars have offered me temporary work and extra coin, out of pity for a pregnant maid. I thought you'd be pleased to have the extra money."

"I see," Bridgette's expression shifted—was it anger, or something closer to reluctant amusement? "You had me fooled," she muttered, shaking her head with a grimace. Cecelia braced for a scolding, but Bridgette surprised her with a weary sigh. "Do what you must," she conceded, a begrudging fondness in her voice. "Enjoy the work while you can. But mark my words—two months from now, we leave for the colonies. No running off, no arguments."

Now was no time to argue, and relief surged through Cecelia, and she nodded eagerly. "Of course, mumma."

Bridgette's lips twitched with a smile, her tone still gruff but less harsh. "As if you'd ever give me a choice," she muttered. "Just try to behave yourself in the face of such esteemed merchants. The Baroness speaks highly of them, as does Lord Frederick. Even the silent Comtesse was impressed by their handiwork, and you know how the French are." With a laugh and a snort, she turned away.

A small smile spread across Cecelia's face. As she hurried toward the baths Rupa had requested, the castle hummed with the familiar rhythm of daily chores—whispers from servants, the soft thud of boots on stone, and the metallic clatter from the kitchens. But for once, Cecelia felt a sense of possibility, a sliver of freedom amid the routine.

The kitchen welcomed her with its warm, comforting chaos. The air was thick with the scent of fresh bread and roasted meats, the hearth blazing as the copper kettle over it belched steam. Cecelia wasted no time, filling smaller pots and placing them strategically around the fire to heat. The warmth wrapped around her, and she focused on the task, her fingers deftly inspecting the wooden tub for cracks. Rupa's discerning eye would demand perfection.

A familiar voice broke the moment. "What are you up to now, girl?" Maggie, the cook, emerged from the cellar, a sack of potatoes slung over her shoulder. Her eyes, though tired, twinkled with mischief.

Cecelia turned with a grin. "Just drawing a bath for the artists."

Maggie clicked her tongue. "No need for that. Benedict and Fenton will handle it." She gestured proudly as two stout, broad-shouldered men appeared, looking both eager and slightly lost. "New assistants," Maggie announced with satisfaction. "Lord Frederick finally granted me some help. 'Bout time."

Cecelia suppressed a sigh of relief, offering the men a grateful smile. "I'm sure they'll be a great help."

"Aye," Maggie agreed, wiping her hands on her apron. "Frederick wants me saving my strength for cooking, not fetching water."

Cecelia left them to their task, her thoughts turning toward more urgent matters. The air cooled as she approached the quieter wing of the castle, her steps echoing in the silence. Frederick's chambers loomed ahead, and she found him seated by the window, a book on his lap, his expression distant.

"My lord," she curtsied softly, her voice gentle. "You seem better today."

Frederick turned, a faint smile briefly lighting his weary face. "A good day, for now," he admitted, his voice raw but steadier. "But these physician's visits—they remind me of what's to come. It makes me sick all over again."

Cecelia hesitated, then ventured, "I came to ask about Comtesse Marguerite. My father told me you're aware of her situation."

His face darkened instantly, the burden settling back into his eyes. "I know everything," he murmured, his voice thick with regret. "But I don't know how to fix it." He paused, as if the weight of his words threatened to break him. "Henry conspired with her parents to have her committed," he added bitterly. "He took their money without a thought."

"That's monstrous," Cecelia breathed, her heart aching for Marguerite.

"She's only twenty-three," Frederick whispered, his tone filled with a quiet despair. "She told me she never wants to see them again. I can make Henry pay for his crimes, but how do I undo the damage he's done?"

Cecelia's mind raced, then steadied with sudden clarity. "You could offer to marry her," she suggested, her voice firm despite the audacity of the idea.

Frederick's eyes widened, a mix of surprise and desperate hope flickering across his face.

Chapter Eighteen

WARM BATH

Frederick blinked, his eyes wide with surprise. "Marry her?"

Cecelia nodded, her tone both soft and determined. "Yes. It would offer her protection, a chance to move forward. Her family sent her here to be 'cured,' but I doubt she wants to return to them. You could provide a fair contract—one that grants her control over her own finances and freedom. It would be a marriage in name only."

Frederick's brow furrowed as he processed her words. His gaze lingered on Cecelia, thoughtful and intent, as if testing the feasibility of her idea. Slowly, he nodded, his movements deliberate. "I hadn't considered that. You're right—it could be a way out for her." He sighed, the weight of such a decision settling across his face. "I'll think about it. Thank you, Cecelia."

She managed a small smile and excused herself, feeling an unexpected lightness. As she returned to the kitchen, the warmth of the hearth seemed almost welcoming, and a flicker of hope rose within her. Perhaps things could change—for her, for Comtesse Marguerite, and for others caught in the merciless grip of circumstance.

As steam began to rise, Cecelia directed Benedict, who strained under the weight of each heavy pot. The warm air was now heavy with the scent of firewood. They worked steadily, pouring the water until the copper tub was nearly full, its surface glistening in the glow of the fire. She tossed in a small pouch of dried lavender and rosemary, watching as the herbs released their calming fragrance into the steamy air. The scent added a sense of luxury to the otherwise simple chore, and she inhaled deeply.

With the tub filled, Fenton and Benedict grasped its sides, grunting as they lifted the sloshing container. They began their slow, cautious walk through the narrow corridors and out the servants' entrance, with Cecelia following closely behind. Her breath fogged the crisp morning air, the wisps vanishing as quickly as they appeared.

The recent rains had left the path to the studio a muddy quagmire, each step sinking their boots deeper into the muck. Fenton and Benedict struggled under the weight, moving at a labored pace, while Cecelia stayed close, steadying the tub whenever it threatened to tip. Despite her condition, she moved with surprising agility, navigating the uneven ground with practiced ease. Ahead, the small, thatched-roof studio came into view, golden light spilling from its windows, and Cecelia smiled in admiration as she caught sight of Rupa's intricate carvings inside. At the door, the men set down the tubs, their breath coming in heavy puffs of cold air.

Cecelia knocked lightly, and Rupa soon appeared, her hands dusted with sawdust and a warm smile on her face. "Thank you. This is exactly what I needed," she said as Fenton and Benedict maneuvered the tubs inside. Cecelia curtsied, her cheeks flushed from the chill and the effort.

"You're welcome, Miss Rupa. Is there anything else you require?" she asked politely.

Rupa's eyes twinkled mischievously. "Yes, actually. Come inside."

Cecelia hesitated, uncertainty flickering across her face, but then stepped in, grateful for the warmth that enveloped her as the door closed behind her. The air smelled of fresh wood shavings, oil, and lavender. Rupa led her to the back room, where a curtain separated the main studio from two smaller bathing areas.

Surprised, Cecelia turned to Rupa. "Do you… need me to wait on you? You and your brother?" Her voice was tentative, unsure of her role.

Rupa's chuckled softly. "Kunal's locked away in his studio, lost in whatever mad idea has taken hold of him. He won't be out for hours." She nodded toward the bath and shrugged, as if it were nothing. "No, this one's for you. You can't be meeting my family looking like that."

Cecelia's heart beat faster, a mix of gratitude and uncertainty swirling within. "A bath… for me?" she repeated, unable to hide her surprise. It seemed too extravagant, too generous for someone of her standing.

"Yes, Cecelia," Rupa replied with exaggerated patience, rolling her eyes playfully. "It's for you, and I won't hear another argument against it." With that, she disappeared behind her own curtain, the soft rustle signaling she was settling into her own bath.

Cecelia lingered for a moment, gazing at the steaming water. Her usual baths were nothing like this—more a chore than a luxury, done with a bucket of lukewarm water or a grimy shared tub that had seen better days. But this... this was something else, something rare. Hesitating only briefly, she dipped her fingers into the water. The warmth was inviting, the scent of lavender and rosemary both calming and comforting. Sighing, she began to undress, folding her clothes neatly on a nearby stool before slipping into the tub.

The water enveloped her like a soft embrace, soothing the aches in her back and legs. For a brief, precious moment, she let herself relax completely, the tension melting away. She closed her eyes, savoring the unfamiliar stillness. It was a luxury she never thought she would know.

"How is it?" came Rupa's voice from behind the curtain, pulling Cecelia from her reverie.

"It's wonderful," Cecelia admitted, her voice low and content. "I'll be out soon."

"Take your time," Rupa encouraged, the smile in her voice clear. "I still have plenty to do before we leave."

Cecelia let herself smile, sinking a little deeper into the water. It was like a dream—a small, unexpected gift in a life often filled with hardship. For the first time in what felt like forever, she felt cared for.

The warmth eventually began to fade, signaling the end of her brief escape. Reluctantly, Cecelia rose from the tub, shivering slightly as the cool air hit her skin. She reached for a towel, drying herself quickly and wrapping it tightly around her, feeling both refreshed and renewed. Somehow, the weight of her burdens seemed lighter now, buoyed by a newfound sense of hope.

As she prepared to dress, Rupa called out from the other side of the room. "I'm off to see the Comtesse about the wood for her commission. I'll be back soon, and then we can leave."

Cecelia's voice was soft. "Thank you, Miss Rupa. Truly, thank you."

"'Miss Rupa,'" came the amused reply. "We're past that formality, don't you think? Rupa is fine."

Feeling a deep sense of gratitude, Cecelia stepped out of the tub and dried herself off, dressing in the garments Rupa had laid out. The gown, made of soft linen, felt light and comfortable against her freshly cleaned skin. As she fastened the buttons, she marveled at the sensation of being properly bathed and dressed in clothes that hadn't yet been worn threadbare. The realization brought a bittersweet ache—she wished she could stay at the castle forever. But there was no time for tears; she quickly refocused, pulling her unruly curls into order with the towel.

Suddenly, the creak of the door made her heart jump. Expecting Rupa, she was startled to hear Kunal's voice. "Rupa?"

Panic seized her. She pressed a hand to her mouth, realizing the absurdity of her situation. He couldn't see her behind the curtain, but she felt vulnerable all the same. She fumbled to drape the towel over the edge of the tub, tugging on her gown hurriedly as its damp fabric clung awkwardly to her skin.

Just as she managed to tie the last string of her bonnet, the curtain was pulled aside. There stood Kunal, his face instantly reddening as he froze in surprise.

"Oh! I'm sorry..."

"No, I'm sorry," Cecelia whispered, her voice caught between surprise and awkwardness. "Rupa told me to bathe before visiting your parents."

Kunal's concern deepened, his expression softening. "Was it warm, not hot?" he asked cautiously.

"Yes," she answered, her brow furrowing. "But... how did you know?"

"Hot baths aren't safe for pregnant women," he explained gently. "My mother made sure I learned that."

Curiosity flickered in Cecelia's eyes. "How would your mother know that? I thought your family were woodcarvers."

Kunal's lips curved into a faint smile. "She had a different life before she married my father. She wore many hats. One was midwife, for a time—she helped bring many children into the world." He hesitated, then added quietly, "She isn't my mother by birth."

Cecelia's surprise was evident. "I... I didn't know."

"She chose us," he said, the words laced with gratitude. "My father was widowed, with two small children. She saw the burden he carried and decided to share it."

"She sounds extraordinary," Cecelia murmured, a sense of admiration softening her voice.

Kunal's gaze shifted, becoming more intimate as it swept over her. "You're extraordinary," he whispered, his eyes lingering on the simplicity of her gown, the freshness of her skin, and the vulnerability in her posture. "You're beautiful."

Heat rose in Cecelia's cheeks, and she stammered, "I'm just... clean, that's all. Rupa insisted."

He stepped closer, his tone dropping to a low murmur. "When will she be back?" There was a playful edge to his voice. "Because right now, I'd trade my life to be the fabric of that dress."

Cecelia's heart raced, a mixture of excitement and caution flaring within her. "We don't have time for... this," she said, though a mischievous smile betrayed her.

"Are you certain?" Kunal teased, inching closer, his gaze smoldering as it met hers.

"Rarely," she whispered, unable to resist as he closed the distance and captured her lips with his. The warmth of his kiss sent a shiver through her, a cascade of longing mixing with joy and uncertainty. Her hand instinctively rose to rest on his neck, fingers trembling against his skin. Emotion flooded her—desire mingling with a bittersweet ache, a vulnerability she hadn't anticipated. She cursed herself for being so moved, yet relished the tenderness of the moment.

A sudden gasp shattered the intimacy. They broke apart, startled, to find Rupa standing in the doorway, her expression caught between shock and irritation.

"How did you open the door so quietly?" Kunal stammered, his face draining of color.

"It wasn't quiet," Rupa replied sharply, her tone clipped. "Step away from my maid. What are you doing? Cecelia, are you alright?"

Embarrassment burned Cecelia's cheeks. "Yes," she squeaked, her voice barely audible. "I'm... sorry, Rupa. It isn't the first time, but I should have said something."

Kunal's tone turned defensive. "We haven't done anything wrong. I care for Cecelia, and I plan to court her, openly and honestly—when she's ready."

Rupa's eyes narrowed, her words biting. "You won't. You're not free, and neither is she. Both of you have obligations to attend to—it's reckless to entertain such notions now."

"I'll follow both my heart and my head, Rupa." Kunal's voice was firm, though there was a hint of desperation. "And I've chosen to pursue Cecelia. I'm not afraid of the consequences."

With arms crossed, Rupa countered, "Maa has a list of prospects waiting in Amber—a box filled with names for when our contract ends. You're expected to marry one of those women, not a French maid carrying another man's child." Her gaze softened slightly as she turned to Cecelia. "No offense, Cecelia. You deserve to know the reality of it."

Kunal's resolve wavered but did not break. "That may be the path set before me, but it's not the one I'm sure I'll take."

Rupa's skepticism was clear. "You've never defied our parents' wishes, not once. Why would you start now?"

He glanced at Cecelia, a mix of determination and regret in his eyes. "There's always a first," he said quietly. "If she'll have me."

Rupa raised an eyebrow, her tone dry. "So, you've asked, and she's refused?"

Kunal nodded, his shoulders slumping a bit. "She's afraid of the consequences. Of the difference in our stations."

Rupa's gaze shifted to Cecelia, a flicker of approval in her eyes. "You're wise, Cecelia. Very wise; perhaps wiser than the man who courts you." With a sigh, she motioned to the door. "Shall we go?"

Cecelia's voice trembled slightly. "Am I... still welcome?"

"Of course," Rupa answered with a casual wave. "But no talk of this kissing nonsense in front of my parents."

Chapter Nineteen

FAMILY DINNER

"Remember, Cecelia," Rupa's voice held a mixture of firm guidance and dry amusement as she reached over, adjusting a stray curl that had slipped from Cecelia's bonnet. "My parents will treat you kindly. They're not harsh, truly. But..." She paused, her fingers momentarily brushing Cecelia's shoulders. "If they sense any designs on my brother, you'll find their warmth vanishing swiftly. Keep that in mind—no hint of romance."

The casual tone did little to soften the impact; Rupa's words struck Cecelia like a sudden chill. She forced a smile, though it felt tight, strained at the edges. A cool draft carried the earthy scent of damp leaves and wood smoke through the window, a reminder that tonight would be unlike any other.

Behind them, Kunal shifted his stance. His gaze lingered on Cecelia's reflection in the mirror, unguarded yet unreadable. "Don't worry too much about the formalities," he offered, his voice steady but with a thread of tension beneath. "Just watch what we do, and you'll be fine."

His attempt at reassurance only seemed to amplify the flutter of nerves inside her. Noticing her slight tremor, Rupa began rummaging through a small chest. "Let's add a splash of color," she announced, her tone brisk. "I've something here that should suit you well."

Moments later, Rupa returned holding a shawl—an exquisite piece, vibrant with deep reds and golds, the intricate patterns unlike anything Cecelia had seen before. "This is from my grandmother in Amber," she said with a proud glint in her eyes. "It'll not only add color but warmth too. The night can be unforgiving." Rupa stepped away to prepare elsewhere, leaving Cecelia and Kunal alone.

The silence between them was thick, charged, the small room feeling suddenly too close, and Kunal leaned against the wall, folding his hands in front of him. His tone softened, becoming more intimate. "You look..." he began, pausing as if searching for the right words. "Ready." His dark eyes softened as he stepped closer, his voice dropping to a near whisper. "Not that you needed any help looking striking."

Heat crept up Cecelia's cheeks, but she tried to maintain her composure. Compliments were foreign to her, especially ones that carried such sincerity. "I'm just hoping not to trip over my own tongue," she replied, her tone tight, masking the fluster beneath.

A soft chuckle escaped Kunal, low and warm. His smile was faint but genuine. "If you do, I doubt anyone will notice. Besides..." He moved closer, the space between them shrinking, her pulse quickening. "It's not your words they'll be watching first."

His gaze lingered, and for a heartbeat, Cecelia felt the air thicken, her surroundings fading into insignificance. The room was too still, their connection too palpable, yet impossible to ignore. It was a dangerous feeling, but not unwelcome.

Rupa's sudden return shattered the moment. She moved briskly, draping the shawl over Cecelia's shoulders with practiced ease. The soft fabric and delicate embroidery were a stark contrast to the rough wool Cecelia was used to. It glimmered faintly in the firelight. "Now," Rupa declared, her critical gaze sweeping over Cecelia one last time, "you'll do just fine. Let's not keep my parents waiting."

Stepping outside, a biting wind greeted them, carrying the scent of wet earth and distant smoke. A carriage awaited in the darkness, its lanterns casting weak pools of light on the cobblestone as the coachman, wrapped in a thick cloak, opened the door with a nod.

Rupa entered first, her skirts rustling as she settled herself inside. Cecelia hesitated, adjusting the shawl once more before stepping in. The carriage's interior was upholstered in dark velvet, dimly lit by a swinging oil lamp. Kunal slid in beside her, his presence a steadying one, though the narrow space forced an awareness of their proximity.

The wheels rumbled over uneven ground, each jolt sending a shiver of uncertainty through Cecelia. But Rupa, unfazed by the bumpy ride, began to recount vivid tales of Amber—bright festivals, the heady scent of sandalwood, the glittering desert sky. Her lively words painted a rich tapestry, yet Cecelia's focus kept drifting back to Kunal, whose hand occasionally brushed hers as the carriage swayed.

At last, the carriage slowed, its wooden wheels crunching over gravel as it came to a halt before a large, sturdy house. It loomed like a ship in the mist, its weathered stone walls bearing marks of Yorkshire's relentless seasons. A single lantern hung by the door, casting long shadows across the drive.

Kunal stepped out first, turning to offer Cecelia his hand. His touch was warm, his grip firm as she climbed down. For a moment, he didn't let go; his fingers lingered, a subtle but unmistakable sign of reassurance. "You'll manage," he whispered, his breath warm in the chill night air. "I'm here."

Cecelia forced a smile, her heart hammering beneath her ribs. The grand home, adorned with rich draperies and fine furnishings, felt as foreign as it was beautiful. It stood in stark contrast to her usual surroundings, yet a warmth emanated from Rupa's parents that softened the daunting opulence. As they neared the door, light spilled across the gravel path, and the scent of spices—earthy, comforting—wrapped around her like a welcoming embrace.

Rupa, confident and poised, stepped forward, pride clear in her voice. "Mother, Father, this is Cecelia Rousseau. She's a friend of Annabel's and has been assisting me with my work at the castle."

Sarala, dressed in elegant silks, studied Cecelia with sharp yet kind eyes. "Welcome, Cecelia," she said, her embrace unexpectedly gentle.

Manik Sutar, his presence dignified yet warm, extended his hand. "Any friend of our children is a friend of ours," he declared, his handshake firm but respectful. Cecelia's palm was damp despite the heat radiating through the room.

As they stepped inside, the flickering lamplight cast long, dancing shadows against intricately carved wooden screens and vibrant tapestries. The house was a striking blend of Yorkshire's solid stonework and the Sutars' vibrant heritage. Bright silks draped alongside English brocades, while the smell of roasted meats mixed with the heady scent of cumin and coriander simmering in the kitchen.

"Please, sit," Sarala gestured gracefully toward a plush settee.

Settling onto the embroidered cushions, Cecelia tried to suppress her nerves, though the richness of her borrowed shawl seemed heavier now. She glanced at Kunal, noticing a mix of fondness and tension in his expression. The unspoken words between them hung in the air like a tangible presence.

Manik turned his attention to his children, a smile softening his face. "We've prepared a few of your favorites tonight," he said, glancing toward the kitchen. "Paneer tikka for Rupa, and rajma masala for you, Kunal."

Sarala's voice, light but nostalgic, added, "We've also heard from home. Your uncle writes that the monsoon has been kind this year."

The mention of their home sparked Cecelia's curiosity. "Paneer tikka... how is it made?" she asked before she could stop herself, but her curiosity seemed to please Rupa.

Rupa's eyes lit up. "Ah, Cecelia, it's a dish you must try. The paneer is marinated in a blend of spices—coriander, cumin, garam masala. It's then roasted until the edges are perfectly charred." Her eyes sparkled with enthusiasm. "It's all about balance."

"I'd love to learn," Cecelia admitted, the thought of spice-marinated cheese oddly fascinating.

Rupa's grin widened. "Then we'll get you into the kitchen soon. Cooking is an art of its own—you'd appreciate that."

As the conversation shifted to art and life at Castle Rowley, Cecelia felt a surprising ease settle over her. "Kunal and Rupa have taught me a lot," she said with genuine warmth. "Not just about art, but how to face uncertainty with grace."

Kunal's face softened, a shy smile curving his lips under the candlelight. Rupa, ever bold, beamed at the praise.

Yet, when talk turned to Cecelia's past, her expression dimmed. "I was involved in the arts back in France," she began hesitantly. "But adjusting to life here after losing everything has been... harder than I expected."

Sarala's gaze was steady, filled with understanding. "Every journey shapes us, even the most difficult ones," she said gently. "What matters is how we carry it forward."

Manik nodded approvingly, but Sarala's words stayed with Cecelia, a sense of reassurance settling in her chest. As the conversation shifted back to art and storytelling, Cecelia allowed herself to be drawn into the lively banter, charmed by the Sutars' blend of cultures and passions.

"Storytelling is like weaving a tapestry," Sarala mused. "Each thread tells a story, each color carries an emotion."

Cecelia, now fully engaged, found her voice. "Yes, exactly. Every artist weaves something unique, like Rupa's shawl—a blend of many elements, yet harmonious."

Rupa's eyes lit up with sudden excitement. "Speaking of weaving stories, we still need to inspect the tiger chair for the next clue, don't we?"

Sarala chuckled, a twinkle of amusement in her eyes. "Go on, then. Let me know what mysteries you uncover. Dinner will be ready soon."

With a sense of shared urgency, Cecelia, Rupa, and Kunal wound their way down a narrow, dimly lit corridor toward the study. The lantern in Kunal's hand flickered, casting long shadows that twisted across the carved wooden panels lining the walls in the cool, still air.

Cecelia felt a shiver of anticipation run through her.

When Kunal eased the heavy oak door open, it creaked like a whisper of the past, unveiling a room that felt suspended in time. Towering mahogany shelves reached up to the high ceilings, packed with scrolls, books, and relics—some ancient, others that seemed to be recently acquired. The rich scent of sandalwood mingled with the musty aroma of old parchment, filling the air with a sense of reverence.

At the heart of the room stood what had to be the armchair the siblings spoke of. It loomed behind a cluttered desk, its dark wooden frame adorned with carvings of tigers that seemed poised to spring to life. The worn velvet seat bore the marks of years gone by, adding to the sense of regality; indeed, the chair seemed more like a relic from a lost throne room than a piece of furniture. Cecelia's breath hitched.

"This is it," Kunal whispered, his voice tight with excitement. "The clue from the desk led us here."

Rupa circled the chair, her gaze sharp. "The tigers... the clue mentioned them," she mused. "There must be something hidden in these carvings."

Cecelia leaned closer, her fingertips brushing the intricately carved lion on one armrest. The craftsmanship was so fine that each curve felt almost alive beneath her touch. "Could there be a hidden mechanism?" she asked, lowering her voice as if not to disturb the sanctity of the space.

Kunal crouched beside the chair, inspecting it carefully. "We should try pressing the mouths of the tigers," he suggested, his voice steady but laced with hope.

The three exchanged a quick, determined glance. Cecelia and Kunal simultaneously pressed down on the lions' mouths. For a heartbeat, nothing happened. Disappointment swelled in Cecelia's chest, but then—a soft click broke the silence. The seat of the chair shifted, revealing a concealed compartment beneath.

Cecelia's gasp filled the air. "It worked."

Rupa's eyes widened with excitement as she reached inside, pulling out a small scroll wrapped in silk. The room seemed to hold its breath as she carefully unwrapped the delicate cloth, revealing hand-painted illustrations and flowing script.

"This has to be it," Rupa whispered, awe coloring her voice.

Kunal leaned closer, reading over her shoulder. "'Seek where the earth's embrace holds green, under the oldest one's serene,'" he read aloud, his tone both curious and wary.

A heavy silence followed, thick with contemplation. Then, Rupa's expression faltered. "It's the jade table."

Kunal's face darkened. "No. It can't be. We were so close."

"The jade table?" Cecelia asked, confused but eager to understand.

Rupa sighed, her shoulders slumping. "It was one of our family's most cherished pieces, passed down through generations. Inlaid with jade, carved from the oldest tree our ancestors knew. But when we moved here, it went missing."

"Stolen," Kunal added, his voice tight with anger. "Rupa swears it was in the front hall, but then it disappeared."

A deep sense of frustration washed over Cecelia. They had come so far only to reach yet another dead end. "Is there any chance of finding it?" she asked, trying to keep hope alive.

Rupa shook her head slowly, her anger barely contained. "I don't want to tell our parents yet. Not tonight."

Kunal frowned, puzzled. "Why not?"

"It's just that..." Rupa looked away. "I can't bear to disappoint them again."

Before anyone could respond, Sarala's voice called from the dining room. "Come, the food is ready!"

Cecelia forced a smile, trying to lift the mood. "Well, I don't know about you, but I'm starving. And your mother's cooking smells divine."

With that, they reluctantly closed the hidden compartment and left the study, the lost jade table hanging over them like a lingering shadow.

For now, however, they let the mystery fade into the background, allowing the warmth of the evening to take over.

The evening unfolded into something richer than Cecelia had anticipated. Kunal's unspoken turmoil simmered beneath the surface, yet the Sutar family's embrace of art, storytelling, and heritage drew her in. The warm glow of candlelight reflected off the patterned dishes, while the intoxicating aroma of spices filled the air, creating a sense of belonging Cecelia hadn't felt in a long time.

Seated beside Kunal, Cecelia marveled at the vibrant dishes spread before them—bowls of lentils spiced with cumin and turmeric, aromatic rice flecked with saffron, roasted vegetables glistening with oil, and freshly baked golden flatbread. Each dish seemed more exquisitely prepared than the last, mirroring the Sutars' meticulous approach to both food and life. Rupa, moving with her usual composed grace, poured water for everyone, the soft clink of her glass bangles adding a melodic backdrop to the meal. Manik and Kunal delved into conversation about a new woodcarving commission, their words filled with the fervor of artisans discussing their craft. Sarala watched them both, her eyes warm with pride yet tinged with a touch of amusement. Gentle laughter and the quiet scrape of silverware against porcelain filled the room, creating a sense of warmth and intimacy.

Amid the lively conversation, Cecelia noticed Kunal's increasing distraction. He pushed his food around on his plate, his eyes darting occasionally toward his mother, as if expecting an unspoken inevitability. The usual ease in his gestures was absent, replaced by an undercurrent of restlessness. Despite the fluid rhythm of family banter, something seemed to weigh heavily on him.

As the meal drew to a close, Sarala rose from her chair with a serene smile. Moments later, she returned carrying a polished wooden box, its carved surface gleaming under the flickering candlelight. The room fell into a curious hush as she gently placed the box on the table.

Kunal's brow furrowed. "What's this, Mother?" he asked, though his voice betrayed an edge of anticipation.

With measured elegance, Sarala opened the box to reveal a series of small, intricately painted wooden portraits. Each image depicted a young woman dressed in vibrant Indian attire, their expressions serene yet lively, with exquisite details capturing the delicate embroidery of their garments and the gleam of their jewelry.

"These," Sarala explained gently, "are eligible women from our community. Prospective matches for you, my dearest." Her tone was light, but the underlying expectation was clear. She lifted the first portrait and handed it to Kunal, her eyes never leaving his.

A palpable tension descended upon the room as Kunal examined the portrait, his face carefully blank. Sarala continued to introduce each woman in turn—Priya, a talented embroiderer from a family of merchants; Anjali, a poet known for her elegance; Meera, celebrated for her charitable work. As the portraits were passed around, Cecelia felt the weight of each introduction like a silent comparison.

When one of the portraits reached her, Cecelia's breath caught. The woman depicted was strikingly beautiful, with delicate features and an ornate bindi on her forehead. As Cecelia handed the image to Rupa, a wave of inadequacy washed over her. Here, surrounded by these poised and accomplished women, she felt like an outsider—a scullery maid trying to blend into a world of nobility and grace.

The final portrait was of Nisha, a renowned artist whose innovative work had earned her a reputation far beyond the local community. As the portrait was handed to Kunal, Cecelia felt her fingers tremble. She subtly reached beneath the table, finding Kunal's hand and giving it a quick squeeze. He returned the pressure, his touch both firm and reassuring—a silent promise in the midst of uncertainty.

Sarala's gaze rested on Kunal, a mix of hope and gentle pressure evident in her expression. "So, Kunal," she asked, her voice calm but expectant, "do any of these women appeal to you?"

Cecelia held her breath, her heart pounding in her chest. Kunal's face, normally open and warm, seemed to shutter, his composure faltering slightly. His gaze flickered to Cecelia before he answered, his voice steady but laced with tension.

"Mother," he began, choosing his words carefully, "I understand your intentions, and I'm grateful. But I'm not ready to consider marriage just yet. I need more time to focus on my craft and my responsibilities."

The room seemed to hold its breath, Sarala's poised demeanor softening with a hint of disappointment. Yet, she managed a gracious nod. "There's no rush, Kunal. When the time is right, you'll know."

The atmosphere relaxed slightly, the conversation resuming with tentative ease. Cecelia felt a surge of admiration for Kunal—his refusal was not an act of defiance, but one of quiet conviction. She squeezed his hand once more under the table, this time with a sense of solidarity and gratitude.

Though the evening's uncertainty lingered, the unspoken connection between Cecelia and Kunal seemed stronger than ever. For now, the future remained undefined, but as they sat side by side, Cecelia felt a quiet assurance—a shared understanding that whatever challenges lay ahead, at least for the immediate future, they could face them together.

CHAPTER TWENTY

INVENTORS

The next day, Cecelia worked in the artist's cabin, sweeping the cold stone floor in slow, rhythmic strokes. Her thoughts drifted, carried by the soft scrape of the broom's bristles against the ground. Finally, unable to contain her curiosity any longer, she glanced at Rupa, who was sanding a delicate wooden piece at her workbench. "Did you put me in this job just to help you with your family's clues?" Cecelia asked, her voice filled with a mix of suspicion and amusement.

Rupa looked up, her eyes gleaming with a playful glint. "Mostly," she replied with a sly smile. "But it's not doing us much good at the moment, is it? We've hit a dead end." Her gaze turned more pointed, her expression inquisitive. "Though I couldn't help noticing... something's still simmering between you and my brother."

Cecelia's cheeks burned as she focused intently on her sweeping, her movements suddenly more hurried. "There's nothing between us," she insisted, but the words felt thin and unconvincing.

"You really are a terrible liar," Rupa teased, leaning closer as if sharing a delicious secret. "Kunal talked about your lips like petals, you know. He even mentioned sweeping you off your feet." She paused, then added with a grin, "Oh, and something about being with you in this world and the next."

The broom froze mid-sweep, Cecelia's eyes widening. "He said that?"

Rupa burst out laughing. "No," she admitted, her laughter dancing in the air. "But you just confirmed everything for me."

Cecelia groaned, burying her face in her hands. "Oh, for heaven's sake," she muttered, her voice muffled. "It was only a few kisses and talk of courtship. Nothing serious. As I said before, our stations are not exactly compatible."

"Why the fiery denial?" Rupa asked, studying her with a curious tilt of her head. "A match with Kunal would be good for you, wouldn't it?"

A flicker of frustration crossed Cecelia's face. "Because I don't want to ruin him," she confessed, her voice dropping to a whisper. "He has a future—prospects I could never match. You may have granted me the pity of time to draw when my chores are done, but I am still just a maid. He deserves better than a tangle of obligations."

Rupa's expression softened. "There's no pity in my offer, Cecelia. You're sharp, clever—more so than many at court. Where did you learn words like 'notion'?"

Cecelia leaned against the wall, her broom now forgotten. A sigh escaped her, laden with memories. "I wasn't always a maid," she said quietly. "We were middle-class in France, but after the Edict of Nantes happened, everything fell apart." Her voice grew tighter. "We sold everything to clear the debts and fled to England to start over."

Rupa listened intently. "And then?"

"My mother tried to place me in lessons with the other children," Cecelia continued, her voice tinged with regret. "But I struggled to read. The letters never made sense, no matter how hard I tried. Eventually, they decided I was better suited for labor. I became a chambermaid, then a kitchen hand, and a laundry worker. I've scrubbed floors, polished boots, even joined the hunt to feed the household."

"That's unjust," Rupa said firmly, her brow furrowing. "You're bright, and your drawings are remarkable. Kunal showed me your sketches, and Annabel speaks most highly of you."

Cecelia blushed under the praise. "Annabel is helping me learn to read. It's slow, but she's patient."

Rupa's eyes brightened, an idea forming in her mind. "Have you heard about the gathering of inventors that Baron Rowley is hosting? Kunal and I plan to attend—just to observe, not participate. You should come with us."

Caught off guard by the invitation, Cecelia stuttered, "Me? But... I wouldn't even be able to take notes."

"Then draw," Rupa urged, waving a hand as if dismissing the problem. "Sketch anything that catches your eye. We're only there to observe, anyway."

Hesitation flickered in Cecelia's eyes, the thought of mingling with nobility and inventors both thrilling and terrifying. But the chance to be part of something beyond her usual duties was irresistible. "I'd love to," she whispered, a tentative but genuine smile breaking across her face.

Rupa's face lit up with a bright smile. "Good. It'll be a day worth remembering."

A faint breeze drifted through the artist's cabin, rustling the curtains as Cecelia swept the wooden floor. The scent of fresh-cut wood now laced together with the tang of varnish, grounding her senses. Rupa sat quietly at her worktable, her concentration evident as she carved intricate patterns into a block of wood.

"Could you fetch the other compass from the top drawer of my desk?" Rupa asked, holding up a small brass one as an example. "It's just like this."

Cecelia nodded and walked over to the desk. As she opened the drawer, her gaze fell upon a thick sheaf of papers tied with ribbon. A familiar scent rose from them—something floral, laced with a hint of aged parchment. It was unmistakable, stirring a memory that whisked her back to Paris, where she'd once stood, eight years old, in a luxurious hat shop with her mother. The memory enveloped her, almost tangible in its vividness.

Shaking off the reverie, she retrieved the compass and glanced briefly at the papers, noticing French script on the top page. Returning to Rupa, Cecelia placed the compass on the table, her voice light but laced with curiosity. "That scent—it reminded me of Paris. For a moment, I felt as though I'd traveled back there."

Rupa looked up, surprise flickering across her face. "Paris?"

"Yes," Cecelia continued, a touch of nervous laughter in her voice. "I caught a whiff of the paper's scent. It's... familiar. I hope I haven't intruded."

For a moment, Rupa's expression hardened, but then curiosity softened her features. "You recognized it by the scent alone?"

Cecelia's cheeks flushed. "I've seen enough French books and letters to recognize the look of the words, even if I can't read them well. And the scent... it was just like the fancy shops we visited before we left Paris."

Rupa's brow furrowed. "And you knew it was French?"

"I can read a *little*," Cecelia admitted, shifting awkwardly. "But mostly, I rely on what I remember from my time in France. I didn't mean to pry."

Rupa's posture eased, a hint of amusement touching her lips. "It's fine," she said, setting her work aside. "Those papers are letters from a friend in Paris. He's offered me a job there, but I haven't decided yet."

Cecelia's eyes widened. "A job? In Paris? What kind of work?"

A small smile curved Rupa's lips as she spoke. "His name is Étienne Moreau. His grandfather was a restorer of church frescoes, and Étienne studied art history and archaeology in Paris. Now, he owns Galerie Moreau in the Marais district—a gathering place for collectors of contemporary and ancient art."

"You can study art history?" Cecelia marveled, her voice full of wonder.

Rupa chuckled, nodding. "Étienne did. His gallery is well-known among French nobility, diplomats, and merchants. But it's more than just a business to him. He believes in connecting people to their heritage through art."

Cecelia's eyes sparkled. "There's no romance between you two?"

Rupa laughed at the suggestion. "No, not at all. Étienne is more like a mentor. We met when he came to England searching for unique pieces for his gallery. He was more intrigued by how we managed our inventory than by the carvings themselves." Her voice softened. "He found it fascinating—an artist who could also run a business."

"So, he's drawn to your mind," Cecelia said with a smile. "How wondrous."

Rupa's expression warmed. "He's helped me understand the art world in ways I never thought possible. I've even visited Paris a few times, though never alone. Kunal usually comes along to sketch while I work."

"Will you accept the job?" Cecelia asked gently, sensing a conflict beneath Rupa's composed exterior. "It sounds like a wonderful opportunity."

"It is," Rupa agreed, her tone more reflective. "Étienne wants me to manage his inventory and finances, and he's offered to sponsor my art. I'd have control over the profits." Her voice dipped, filled with uncertainty. "But once you start making art for money, it becomes... less yours."

Cecelia watched her closely. "Do you think it would make you happy? Would your family understand?"

"Understand?" Rupa let out a dry, humorless laugh. "Hardly. They'd see it as scandalous—their unmarried daughter moving to Paris to work for a Frenchman. My parents want me back in Amber, married to someone they've chosen, carving toys for my children." Her eyes clouded with a mix of defiance and resignation.

Before Cecelia could respond, a sharp knock on the cabin door startled them both. Rupa's gaze turned urgent as she whispered, "Not a word of this," before moving to answer the door.

The grand hall was a magnificent sight, bathed in the warm, golden light of countless candles flickering against dark, carved wood. The amber glow caught on the polished oak beams and highlighted the stern, ancestral portraits lining the walls, their gazes seeming to survey the evening's proceedings with detached interest. Shadows danced across the stone floors, adding a sense of both splendor and mystery to the space. Near the large marble hearth, Frederick stood with quiet authority, his posture relaxed yet alert. Beside him, a striking, well-coiffed woman with wide, curious eyes watched the proceedings attentively—Cecelia guessed this was Comtesse Marguerite.

Cecelia found herself between Kunal and Rupa, her pulse thrumming in the charged atmosphere. As she pulled out her sketchpad, her fingers trembled slightly, betraying her nerves. Sensing her unease, Kunal nudged her gently. His dark eyes flickered toward the pencil extender he had given her weeks ago, a knowing smile tugging at the corner of his lips.

"You kept it," he murmured, his voice low and warm, sending a jolt through Cecelia's veins.

"Of course," she replied, her voice taking on an unexpectedly sultry tone. Embarrassed, she cleared her throat. "It's quite useful."

His leg brushed against hers beneath the table, sending a delicious shiver up her spine. Cecelia kept her gaze focused on the front of the room, where the first inventor approached Frederick.

The line of inventors stretched through the hall, each face a mix of anticipation and anxiety. The scents of polished wood, burning tallow, and the earthy wool of worn tweed filled the air—an honest contrast to the extravagant silks and velvets of courtly affairs. These were practical clothes, belonging to craftsmen and creators, each determined to prove their worth.

The first inventor, a man of middle age with thin spectacles perched on his nose, stepped forward. He unveiled a brass-and-iron contraption adorned with intricate gears. "My lord," he began with a hint of hesitation, "this is an orrery, a mechanical model of the heavens. It represents the movements of the planets."

Frederick leaned forward, intrigued. "To capture the heavens in such a manner... a fascinating concept," he mused, clearly impressed. "This could enchant the guests of Rowley."

Cecelia's father, acting as Frederick's steward, scribbled notes rapidly on a piece of parchment.

A woman followed next, catching Cecelia's attention with her confident stride—an unusual sight among the male-dominated group. Dressed modestly, her lace cap held her hair neatly, yet her demeanor radiated determination. She presented two brass tubes.

"These are 'distance glasses,'" she announced, her voice clear. "They bring the far near, whether for studying the stars or aiding hunters."

Frederick raised the glasses to his eyes, his expression softening as he marveled at the distant view. "Extraordinary... to make the distant seem so close," he remarked. "We shall have them." His quick approval made the woman's shoulders relax in visible relief.

One by one, inventors presented their creations—grand mechanical devices or ingenious, practical improvements. Cecelia's hand moved swiftly over the paper, capturing each contraption's essence with fluid strokes. Lost in the rhythm of sketching, she felt a fleeting sense of freedom, drawn by the raw beauty of invention.

A wiry man stepped forward, holding up a mechanical joint. "This universal joint," he explained, "transfers motion at various angles. It could revolutionize machinery."

Frederick's brow furrowed thoughtfully. "How might it be applied on a larger scale?"

The man hesitated but found his courage. "In mills and textile machines, my lord. It allows for more flexible motion."

Next came a jovial Frenchman with a peculiar pot. "This is a pressure cooker, my lord," he declared. "It cooks food quickly, using steam to preserve nutrients."

Frederick exchanged a glance with Comtesse Marguerite, who smiled approvingly. "An intriguing concept," Frederick noted. "Faster cooking while retaining flavor and nourishment. Could it truly work in our kitchens?"

The Frenchman beamed. "Indeed, my lord. It could transform meal preparation."

As the inventors continued their presentations, Cecelia's sketches filled the pages, creating a visual diary of ingenuity. The room buzzed with a sense of possibility, each invention a glimpse of the future.

The moment everyone had anticipated arrived when Kunal left the hall briefly, returning with a towering longcase clock. Its oak casing was adorned with exquisite carvings representing the changing seasons—leaves, branches, and flowers forming a graceful arc.

"My lord," Kunal began with quiet confidence, "this is a longcase clock of my design. Its longer pendulum ensures greater timekeeping accuracy."

Frederick leaned closer, intrigued. "And how does it surpass our existing clocks?"

"The longer pendulum," Kunal explained passionately, "moves more slowly and steadily, minimizing the impact of external forces and improving precision."

Listening intently, Cecelia couldn't help but add in a soft voice, "It's more than a timekeeper... it's a guardian of time, standing still as the world rushes on."

Kunal's gaze locked with hers, a flicker of understanding and shared admiration passing between them. "Yes," he agreed quietly, "like the unchanging passage of seasons amidst the chaos of time."

Frederick, visibly impressed, nodded. "It shall have a place of honor in my study."

As the presentations concluded, the inventors departed, leaving behind the lingering scents of sawdust, ink, and the heady promise of progress. Kunal's clock was carefully wheeled away, its presence still palpable, a testament to craftsmanship and innovation.

Cecelia turned to Kunal, her heart racing with the thrill of the moment they had shared. Amidst the mechanical wonders and bold ideas, it was their silent, unspoken connection that left her breathless.

CHAPTER TWENTY-ONE

CELEBRATION OF LOVE

The morning air was crisp, nipping at Cecelia's cheeks as she approached Annabel and Charlie's cottage. She clutched a parcel of food under one arm, courtesy of Maggie. Her other hand rested instinctively on her growing belly—a small but unmistakable curve beneath her apron now. The reminder of what lay ahead was both reassuring and daunting. She paused briefly, imagining life as a single mother, but then steadied herself. She would find a way to provide for this child, whatever else the future might hold.

She rapped gently on the door, and Annabel's voice came from within, light and cheerful. "Come in!"

The cottage was warm and inviting, with a fire crackling gently in the hearth, its glow softening the rough stone walls. A stream murmured nearby, its presence a constant companion just beyond the cottage, infusing the air with a soothing rhythm. Annabel stood by a window, her silhouette framed by the morning light.

"Do you miss the bustle of the castle?" Cecelia asked, setting the parcel down on the well-worn wooden table. "Frederick says it feels quieter without you and Charlie."

Annabel turned, a broad smile lighting up her face. "We're enjoying the peace here," she admitted. "It's nice to have a bit of space. And it's not so far—close enough if the Rowleys needs us, but far enough to feel like our own little retreat."

Cecelia nodded, unwrapping the parcel to reveal a cake Maggie had sent along. As she sliced off a piece, the sweet aroma of sugar and spice filled the room.

Annabel, rummaging through a drawer, suddenly paused and turned, holding a small leather-bound book. Her expression was hesitant, with a spark of excitement in her eyes. "Cecelia, there's something I need to tell you."

A flash of worry crossed Cecelia's face. "It's not Charlie, is it? Is something wrong?"

Annabel quickly shook her head. "No, nothing like that. We're both fine. Come, sit down."

Relieved, Cecelia sank into a chair, nibbling at the cake. Annabel sat opposite her, the book resting in her lap, its pages slightly worn from use.

"I hope you don't mind," Annabel began cautiously, "but I've continued those storytelling sessions with Sarala, Rupa and Kunal's mother."

Cecelia's eyes brightened at the mention. "I remember. That's where you first began to write *Friends of the Vale*."

"Yes," Annabel confirmed, her voice filled with anticipation. "Sarala read it, and she loved it. She believes it has real promise."

Cecelia's brow furrowed in surprise. "Promise? But I thought it was just for us—something to share with our children one day. I've been drawing duplicates of each illustration, just in case."

Annabel leaned forward, her voice animated. "Well, Sarala has different plans. She's considering it for an anthology she's working on—a collection of stories by women, set to be published next year. She wants to include Friends of the Vale."

"In an actual book?" Cecelia's jaw dropped, her voice barely above a whisper.

"Yes, but it would be published anonymously," Annabel clarified. "Sarala knows how to sell discreetly, and if the anthology succeeds, there might be interest in individual stories."

"Does she really think our story is good enough?" Cecelia asked, still trying to grasp this unexpected turn.

Annabel's eyes sparkled. "She does. But I never intended for this to go beyond our original plan. It was meant to be personal. I'll understand if you don't want to be involved now that it's changing."

Cecelia's heart raced. "You still want me to illustrate it?"

"Absolutely," Annabel said with conviction. "Your drawings bring it to life. Besides, aren't you nearly finished?"

Cecelia nodded slowly. "Just three pages left."

"Good," Annabel reached across the table, taking Cecelia's hand. "There's one more thing."

"What is it?" Cecelia asked, bracing herself.

"Sarala suggested adding color to the illustrations," Annabel confessed, the words spilling out quickly. "She thinks children would respond well to it."

Cecelia's brow furrowed, her frustration evident. "Color? I've never done color before. And I don't have time to learn—especially with my departure looming in two months."

"I understand," Annabel said softly. "Perhaps we could compromise. Just the cover page in color, and the rest as sketches?"

Cecelia mulled over the idea, a tentative hope flickering amidst the uncertainty. "Perhaps... it could work," she admitted quietly, feeling an unexpected surge of possibility.

Hesitating briefly, she asked, "Just the cover page?"

Annabel nodded eagerly. "Yes! It'll draw the eye, make the whole book come alive."

Cecelia's lips curved into a slow smile. "All right. I'll do it."

Annabel's shoulders relaxed, her face lighting up with visible relief. "Thank you, Cecelia. I was worried you'd be upset, but I wanted to be honest with you."

"You've always been a good friend," Cecelia murmured, trying to swallow the bittersweet emotion tightening her throat. The impending farewell to this chapter of her life loomed heavily in her mind. "I've been fortunate to have you."

"And I, you." Annabel's eyes glistened as she squeezed Cecelia's hand.

For the next hour, the two women worked in companionable silence—Cecelia carefully sketching as Annabel's quill scratched softly on the page. Occasionally, Annabel would rise to polish a piece of furniture or adjust a misplaced trinket, her movements thoughtful, her gaze distant.

Suddenly, a firm knock broke the stillness, jolting them both. Annabel shot Cecelia a curious glance before moving toward the door.

"Charlie! And Rupa, Kunal—what a pleasant surprise! Please, come in," Annabel exclaimed, her voice brightening as she ushered the visitors inside. The firelight cast a soft, amber glow over the stone walls, wrapping the cozy cottage in a warm embrace.

"We come bearing gifts," Rupa announced with a grin, holding up a stout glass bottle. "And news."

As the cork was removed, a sharp, citrusy aroma wafted through the room, instantly recognizable. Cecelia inhaled deeply, savoring the refreshing scent.

"This is limonade," Rupa explained as she poured the fizzy drink into small wooden cups. "Made with real sugar and lemons straight from the market. There are several new vendors vying for Harold's old stall, each trying to bribe their way in with the best goods."

Kunal, handing Cecelia a cup, added, "It's become quite the favorite among the local merchants."

Cecelia took a hesitant sip, her eyes widening as the sweet-tart flavor burst on her tongue. It was invigorating and unexpected. "This is marvelous!"

"Isn't it?" Rupa said with a wistful sigh. "It's a shame Harold's family decided to let the stall go."

A sudden pang of sadness tugged at Cecelia's chest. "Harold? The vendor across from you... is he... gone?"

Rupa's voice softened. "Yes, he passed peacefully in his sleep. With no one else in the family inclined to art, they've decided to return to milling."

A lump formed in Cecelia's throat. Though her interactions with Harold had been brief, his gentle kindness lingered in her memory. She discreetly wiped a tear with her sleeve, needing a change of subject. Her gaze fell on the desk, cluttered with ink pots and scattered pages. "Annabel," she said, clearing her throat. "It looks like you've been busy. Do you finally have time to write all day now that you're settled here?"

Annabel laughed, as Charlie rested a hand on her shoulder. "I try, though I spend half the day rearranging this place to make it feel like home."

Charlie grinned. "She splits her time evenly—writing stories and fussing over every corner of the cottage."

"And you're no different," Annabel teased back. "Every creaky floorboard fixed, every chair mended. At this rate, it'll look new before long."

"It seems you've adjusted well," Kunal chimed in. "Speaking of adjustments, we've got some good news. Our father received word from a man named Kris Andreas, a colleague of Captain Harrington."

Annabel's eyes gleamed as she refilled the cups. "Is he a trader, too?"

"Not exactly," Kunal replied, his gaze brightening. "He manages a theater that specializes in the macabre."

Annabel's expression shifted, a hint of unease crossing her face. "Oh dear... I hope you being the occasional face of my pen name, Daegal Godwin, hasn't stirred up trouble for you."

"On the contrary," Kunal reassured her, his smile wide. "Kris is fascinated by your work. He's requesting three interlinked plays—Gothic and mysterious. I can deliver your manuscripts, or you might consider accompanying me on one of my trips to town. I brought my horse and cart, so I'll be around for a while."

Annabel's jaw dropped. "You're serious? My anonymous play has sparked more interest?"

"Absolutely," Kunal nodded. "You've managed to captivate the right people, even while hidden behind a pseudonym."

Annabel turned to Cecelia, her excitement palpable. "Can you believe it?"

Cecelia returned her smile warmly. "It seems you've left quite a mark, even under a false name. But what about Frederick's commissioned play? Will you use your real name for that?"

Annabel shook her head firmly. "No. I prefer to stay in the shadows. I'm not looking for fame—just the joy of writing. The money's reward enough."

Cecelia nodded thoughtfully. "I understand. I'll have the final illustrations ready by the end of the week, so everything will be set."

"I never doubted you," Annabel beamed.

Charlie cleared his throat, breaking the moment. "Speaking of news, has anyone told you that Frederick's engaged?"

Annabel gasped, eyes wide. "Engaged? To whom?"

Cecelia's hand flew to her mouth. "Comtesse Marguerite?"

Charlie nodded as he refilled his cup of lemonade. "Yes. He went to Rowley Manor to speak with his mother, then came back and proposed. She accepted, but you're all sworn to secrecy until it's official."

Kunal's brows knitted in concern. "Have you met her yet?"

"Briefly," Charlie admitted. "She keeps mostly to herself, only speaking to Frederick. She even asked him to pretend she's mute for now. It's clear she's more afraid of her family than of Henry."

The group fell silent, the weight of the news heavy in the air. The fire's flickering light danced on the walls, casting shifting shadows that mirrored the uncertainty of their thoughts.

"Well," Rupa said finally, breaking the tension, "we still have this delicious limonade. Let's make a toast."

"To new beginnings," Kunal said, lifting his glass. The others followed suit, their smiles returning, though a sense of unease lingered beneath the surface.

Cecelia sipped slowly, her mind whirling about Frederick's engagement and the path that lay before her. Did he remember his promise to find her a match? She hoped so; he had enough to worry about. Though the future seemed unclear, the warmth of their friendship had offered a moment of comfort amid the unknown, and she would always be grateful for it.

A sharp knock at the door pulled them from their thoughts. Annabel stood and moved to answer, her steps both cautious and light. A woman appeared in the doorway—her resemblance to Annabel striking, though the fine lines etched on her face hinted at years of quiet worry. Yet her eyes sparkled with warmth as she took in the scene.

"My darling girl," she said, voice catching slightly, "the arch is ready."

An hour later, after another round of limonade and slices of cake and gooseberry pie, Annabel linked arms with Rupa and Cecelia, leading them to her bedroom with her mother close behind. Once inside, Annabel's mother quickly took charge, her energy infectious as she clapped her hands together.

"Now, girls, guard the door while I help my daughter into her wedding dress," she instructed with a warm smile. "I'm Arva, Annabel's long-suffering mother who once introduced her to her first husband. But let's pretend he never existed." She winked playfully, her tone affectionate.

"Well, the marriage was thankfully annulled," Annabel called from behind the changing screen. "So, no, he doesn't."

The room, bathed in soft afternoon light, felt cozy and inviting. Cecelia admired its simplicity, while Rupa marveled at the intricately designed tapestries adorning the walls.

"What a lovely room, Annabel," Rupa said, her eyes lingering on the detailed patterns.

"These tapestries were Mara's, weren't they?" Cecelia asked, stepping closer for a better look.

Annabel, now partially dressed, nodded with a smile. "Yes, they were. I did my best to salvage them—some were beyond saving, but a few were too beautiful to leave hidden. Truth be told, some are strategically placed to cover blemishes on the walls." She laughed softly, contentment in her voice.

Her mother adjusted the gown over Annabel's shoulders, beaming with pride. "It's absolutely beautiful, my darling. I'm in awe of what you've accomplished with this little place. And to think, it's all yours! The deed, the home... everything."

Turning toward Cecelia and Rupa, Annabel's face lit up with joy. "And I have wonderful friends. I couldn't have done it without you both."

Moved by the warmth of the moment, Cecelia's eyes brimmed with emotion. She stepped forward and wrapped her arms around Annabel. "You look stunning. I'm so very happy for you and Charlie."

Pulling back slightly, Cecelia reached into her pocket, withdrawing a small wooden frame crafted by Kunal. Inside it was a carefully sketched portrait of Annabel and Charlie, their heads bent toward one another, sharing laughter over an open book. Handing it to Annabel, Cecelia spoke softly. "A small wedding gift for you. I thought it best to give it now, so you wouldn't have to carry it around later."

Annabel's breath caught as she took in the drawing, her fingers trembling slightly. "Cecelia... you made this for me? It's exquisite. I can't believe the detail—you must have spent hours on it."

"You've spent hours on me," Cecelia replied modestly, lowering her gaze. "You're the best friend I could ever ask for, and the two of you are the most wonderful couple I know. I'm so glad you found each other. I know you'll bring each other joy."

Standing nearby with a fond smile, Rupa nodded in agreement. "I've known Charlie since we were all ten years old, fresh from Amber. His family helped us find our footing here, learn the language, and understand the English ways. I always knew it would take someone truly special to capture his heart—and Annabel, you are that someone. Congratulations to you both."

Rupa then stepped forward, holding a small bundle in her hands. "I wanted to give you something as well, Annabel." She carefully unwrapped the package, revealing a small book with a gilded spine.

"This is a book about storytelling and writing. It's filled with exercises and ideas for crafting narratives." Her smile broadened as she revealed a second gift—a delicate wooden quill stand, carved with intricate floral designs. "And I made this for you. A little something for your writing desk."

Tears welled in Annabel's eyes as she accepted the gifts. "Rupa, thank you. This means so much. I've struggled to keep my writing organized—this will be a tremendous help."

Arva stepped forward, holding a box wrapped in soft cloth. "And one more thing." With careful hands, she unwrapped the cloth to reveal a delicate silver hairpin adorned with small pearls. "This was my mother's wedding gift to me, and now I'm giving it to you. It's not much, but it's been in our family for generations. It may not be fashionable now, but I hoped you might wear it today, for good fortune."

Annabel accepted the hairpin, her voice catching with emotion. "Oh, Mother, it's beautiful. I'll wear it proudly."

As Arva gently fastened the hairpin into Annabel's hair, a soft shimmer caught the light streaming through the window, casting a warm glow over the room. The pearls seemed to reflect the love that filled the space, radiating a quiet joy that enveloped them all.

With a deep, steadying breath, Annabel straightened her gown and glanced at her reflection in the mirror. A determined glint shone in her eye. "Shall we get me married, then, before I completely fall to pieces?"

Rupa and Cecelia shared a knowing smile as they linked arms with Annabel, ready to escort their friend into the next chapter of her life. Sunlight poured in through the window, casting a golden hue over the room, as if the day itself longed to witness the union that was about to take place.

Chapter Twenty-Two

FALLING FOR YOU

The next day dawned with a pale sun struggling to break through thick clouds, its light casting a muted glow over the courtyard. Cecelia awoke with a dull ache in her chest, a sense of disquiet that lingered from the intimate wedding of Annabel and Charlie. She had expected to feel joyful, yet the days since had been monotonous—filled with tedious chores in Rupa's outbuilding or napping, as her growing pregnancy drained her energy. Meanwhile, Kunal had disappeared into his work, spending long nights and early mornings in the studio, according to Rupa.

Despite herself, Cecelia's thoughts kept drifting back to him. He occupied her mind during quiet moments, filling them with a mix of hope and uncertainty as she imagined a life with him—if it were even possible. What am I doing? she chastised herself as she set a steaming bucket of water beside Rupa.

"Thanks," Rupa mumbled absentmindedly, her focus fixed on softening bark in a simmering pot. The project seemed to have captured her every thought. "This will take hours."

Cecelia sighed and sank onto the bench beside the table where they had recently played shatranj. Memories of Annabel and Charlie's love—evident in the smallest, yet most passionate gestures—tugged at her heart. "I want that too," she whispered, not realizing she had spoken aloud. Immediately, Kunal's face flashed in her mind, prompting an inward groan.

The heavy oak door creaked open just then, as if he had been conjured by her thoughts. Kunal's presence filled the room, and Cecelia found herself momentarily breathless.

"Cecelia," he said warmly, his voice carrying a familiar comfort. "I wanted to show you my progress on the castle carvings. Your insights would be valuable, given your years with the Rowley family."

Her heart raced as she smoothed her apron. "In your studio?"

"Yes," he replied with a pleasant smile. "Shall we?"

"Of course," Cecelia said, glancing at Rupa, who remained engrossed in her task.

The cool autumn air brushed against Cecelia's cheeks as they stepped outside, mingling with the distant sounds of castle life—laughter from servants, the rustle of leaves, and the soft clink of tools from other workshops. Kunal walked close enough for his arm to brush against hers, though he didn't touch her. She was acutely aware of his presence, the man who could shape wood into beauty and had unwittingly carved a place in her heart.

"I haven't seen you in days," Cecelia remarked, aiming for a casual tone.

"You asked me not to court you publicly," Kunal replied with a playful glint in his eyes. "I've been trying my best to respect that."

Her pulse quickened. "I've been working on Annabel's book. And... I've also started learning to read."

He raised an eyebrow, intrigued. "What book are you reading?"

She grimaced. "The Young Maiden's Tutor by Hannah Woolley. It's supposed to prepare women for higher society roles."

"Sounds dreadful." He made a face.

"Comtesse Marguerite threw it out a window," Cecelia admitted with a grin. "I rescued it from the mud. Figured it would be good practice."

Kunal laughed. "And what have you learned from it?"

"Etiquette, household management, and how to behave properly, for the most part," Cecelia sighed. "I thought perhaps I should be trying to improve myself, but it's frightfully dull."

He shook his head, his grin widening. "If I were learning to read, I'd start with poetry."

"Poetry?" Cecelia wrinkled her nose. "That sounds worse than etiquette."

"Not at all," Kunal insisted. "Poetry is short and satisfying. You can finish a poem in one sitting and feel accomplished."

As they reached his studio, Cecelia felt a sudden surge of courage. "Am I like a poem to you?" she asked, half-teasing. "Short and satisfying in small bursts?"

He paused, opening the door for her. "No," he said softly, his gaze steady. "You are far more than a poem. You are an anthology, a symphony—a dance that never ends."

Blushing deeply, Cecelia stepped inside the studio, her gaze sweeping over the room. It was already filled with carved masterpieces, each bathed in the soft, golden light of late afternoon. The air was thick with the scent of polished wood, beeswax, and sawdust—a warm, earthy aroma that seemed to envelop her in a familiar embrace. Scattered across the space were half-finished pieces, each more intricate than the last.

"You've been busy," Cecelia murmured, moving toward one of the larger pieces. It was an oak panel, beautifully detailed with the Rowley family crest intertwined with delicate floral motifs. The craftsmanship was breathtaking, the fine lines seeming almost alive beneath her fingertips. "These are remarkable, Kunal. The Rowleys will be honored."

Kunal stood beside her, his presence steady and attentive as she admired his work. "I've tried to capture their legacy and the essence of the castle in each carving," he said. His voice was low, thoughtful. Then, as if deciding something, he reached into his pocket. "But there's something else I wanted to show you."

Cecelia turned to find him holding a small velvet pouch, his expression suddenly serious. He opened it to reveal a finely crafted pendant. It was carved from rich rosewood, with inlaid silver vines spiraling around it. At the center were two small birds, their wings extended, facing one another with an air of tenderness and protection. The intricacy of the vines and birds was stunning—each curve and line shaped with evident care.

"I made this for you," Kunal said softly, offering the pendant. "I wanted you to have something personal, something that's a part of me." He paused, searching for the right words. "A reminder of... what I feel for you."

Emotion welled up in Cecelia's chest as she reached for the pendant, her fingers tracing the delicate inlays. "Kunal," she whispered, her voice catching. "It's beautiful. I... I don't know what to say."

"You don't have to," he reassured her. "Just wear it, keep it close. It's meant to be a part of your story now."

With a slight tremble, Cecelia fastened the pendant around her neck. Its warmth settled against her skin, a constant reminder of Kunal's affection. When she looked up, his gaze held hers, and for a moment, time seemed to stand still. Unspoken words filled the air, their connection deep and undeniable.

Trying to steady her emotions, Cecelia turned her attention to the rest of the studio. Her eyes fell on a magnificent rocking horse in the corner of the room. Its mahogany frame shone with a soft, polished glow, and its carved mane appeared to be swept by an imaginary wind. The lifelike texture, the gentle curve of its muscles, and the carefully stitched leather saddle all suggested readiness, as if it could gallop into life at any moment.

"This is exquisite," Cecelia breathed, her fingers grazing the smooth wood. "It feels alive somehow."

Kunal's smile softened as he watched her. "I wanted to create something that captured both the wildness of a real horse and the innocence of childhood—a balance of freedom and security."

Cecelia's gaze shifted to other pieces scattered around the room—a carved jewelry box adorned with tiny floral details, a half-finished bust of a stern-looking man, and several finely crafted furniture pieces. Each creation seemed to tell a story, brimming with Kunal's passion and artistry.

She turned back to him, her admiration evident. "You have a rare gift, Kunal. You bring life to everything you touch."

He stepped closer, his voice low, his expression earnest. "Cecelia, it's you who brings life to me. And even after our brief time together, our conversations, I think... no, I know I'm in love with you."

Kunal's confession landed softly between them, yet its weight was immense. Cecelia felt her heart stutter, the pendant around her neck suddenly heavy with meaning. Meeting his eyes, she saw a vulnerability there that matched her own.

Without thinking, she reached up to touch the pendant, her fingers lingering on the carved birds—so fragile, so full of promise. "Kunal..." she whispered, her voice barely audible. "You have to know that I didn't expect this. I... don't know what to say."

"You don't have to say anything," Kunal murmured, stepping closer. His presence radiated warmth and reassurance. "I just wanted you to know how I feel. Whatever happens, we can take it one step at a time."

In the quiet stillness of the studio, surrounded by Kunal's art, Cecelia felt her defenses start to melt. For the first time in years, she dared to imagine a future filled with more than just survival—a future with Kunal. She envisioned days of carving and sketching, of shared laughter and whispered confessions, of a life where their love could bloom in unexpected ways. Her fingers traced the contours of the rocking horse, lingering over the intricate craftsmanship. The horse's eyes, carved with a lifelike depth, seemed to hold a quiet wisdom. It was remarkable how much care he had infused into something meant to be a child's toy, each joint and curve masterfully shaped.

Kunal stepped beside her, his voice filled with pride. "The wood was chosen for its strength and grain. Each piece was selected to last for generations. I wanted it to feel alive, as if it's ready to gallop at any moment." He paused, watching her fingers run along the horse's smooth neck. "The design is a blend of my heritage and the new influences I've discovered here in England."

Cecelia smiled, charmed by his passion. "I can see that. It will be popular, I'm sure," she said, imagining children clamoring to ride it. "I wish I'd had something like this when I was a child."

Kunal's eyes lit up with mischief. "Why not try it now?"

She laughed, shaking her head. "Don't be absurd. I'd break it."

"You won't," he insisted, leaning casually against the workbench. "Trust me."

Her eyes narrowed skeptically, but curiosity won out. "Fine," she said with a playful sigh, carefully lifting her skirts. She swung one leg over the rocking horse and gingerly settled into the saddle. The wood creaked faintly beneath her weight, but it held firm. "Well, you were right," she admitted, her grin widening. "It's sturdier than I thought."

"Give it a proper ride," he encouraged, his eyes sparkling. "That's what it's made for."

Tentatively at first, she began to rock, a soft laugh escaping her as the motion grew more rhythmic. The childlike joy of the moment filled the studio, a carefree release of all the burdens that had weighed her down. But after a few seconds, she stopped, feeling self-conscious. "I really should get down before I break something."

With a mischievous glint in his eyes, Kunal teased, "Don't tempt me to join you."

"You wouldn't dare," she shot back, though her voice held a hint of challenge.

He grinned wider. "You clearly underestimate me. I'll be up there in an instant."

She giggled, glancing toward the door. "In that case, you'd better lock the door."

Kunal laughed, obliged, and secured the door. Returning, he swung his leg over the back of the rocking horse, towering behind her. His long legs reached the floor, making the moment more comical than romantic. They burst into laughter, the sound filling the studio.

"Keep us steady, Captain," Cecelia teased, her tone mock-serious as she mimed tipping an invisible hat. The playful banter eased the tension that had been simmering between them, allowing a brief reprieve.

"Are we riding a horse or sailing a ship?" Kunal chuckled, careful to keep a respectful distance. Yet his proximity sent a warm flush creeping up Cecelia's neck, especially when she felt the light brush of his breath near her ear.

Before the moment could deepen, Cecelia's stomach let out a loud rumble. Blushing, she slid off the horse with a sheepish grin. "Sorry about that."

Kunal laughed. "You offend my ears," he joked before retrieving a basket from the workbench. "Maa dropped off some samosas earlier. Care to share?"

Cecelia's gaze lingered on the food, her hunger warring with her pride. "I really shouldn't," she said, though her eyes betrayed her longing. "If I keep eating like this, none of my new dresses will fit." Yet, when he handed her one, she couldn't resist, taking a bite of the flaky pastry with a pleased sigh. "What's in this?"

"Pepper, cumin, and coriander," Kunal replied, settling beside her. "Peas, carrots, onions. And a generous amount of butter."

"It's delicious," Cecelia said, savoring the rich, spiced filling. She finished the first quickly, then accepted the second with a grateful smile. They ate in companionable silence.

Once the last crumbs were brushed from her hands, Kunal clapped his hands together with enthusiasm. "Ready to see the rest?"

Cecelia nodded, curiosity lighting up her eyes. Kunal handed her a pair of small leather gloves, a thoughtful gesture that made her smile. She slipped them on, finding they fit perfectly.

"These are some initial sketches," Kunal explained as he opened a large sketchbook. "I've been developing ideas for furniture designs."

"Let's start with beds," Cecelia teased.

Kunal raised an eyebrow, as if gauging her seriousness. But when she nodded encouragingly, he turned to a page filled with designs for four-poster beds. Each one was unique—some adorned with scenes from family histories, others featuring noble crests or intricate woodland carvings. He paused at a particularly ornate headboard. "This one draws inspiration from Indian mythology. The figures represent gods and goddesses from ancient tales."

Cecelia leaned in, tracing the detailed carvings with her eyes. "It's exquisite. And this one?" she asked, gesturing toward another sketch that featured a canopy adorned with delicate floral motifs.

Kunal's face lit up. "That design blends influences from both cultures. I wanted it to be both regal and inviting."

As she continued to browse, her admiration for Kunal's skill deepened. She paused before a line of miniature chairs—scaled-down versions of larger models. "You've done remarkable work, Kunal. The attention to detail is extraordinary."

"These are the most requested designs," he said modestly. "I'm working on a full children's line in the future as well."

Cecelia's gaze rested on the rocking horse, its polished surface gleaming under the soft light. Each curve was carved with such precision. The mane's curls seemed to shift in the light, and the body, sturdy yet graceful, was crafted with loving care.

"You've truly brought it to life," Cecelia murmured, her fingers gliding over the smooth wood. "It feels like it has a soul."

Kunal stood beside her, his voice low but filled with pride. "I've always believed that objects carry the spirit of their maker. Each piece I create holds more than its form—it holds a story."

Cecelia nodded, captivated not only by the beauty of his work but by the passion that drove it. "You've captured the spirit of the Rowleys," she said. "They'll be proud to display this." Her voice lowered. "Thank you for sharing this with me. You bring joy into my life, Kunal. I feel like... maybe I could belong in your world."

He stepped closer, his eyes never leaving hers. "You already do."

Before Cecelia could respond, he leaned in and kissed her gently. Her heart leapt, and she instinctively reached up, her fingers curling around the back of his neck. For a moment, the world outside the studio ceased to exist—no responsibilities, no uncertainties, just the warmth of Kunal's embrace.

When they finally pulled apart, Kunal's eyes were filled with a mix of tenderness and amusement. "I think I might need more practice at this," he said lightly, though his tone was sincere.

Cecelia laughed, her voice a bit breathless. "To echo your earlier sentiment, I I love you too," she whispered. "But if you ever find someone else to be your wife whom you prefer, who would fit in your world better—someone befitting your station—please, just tell me. We'll end it right then. I won't mind, I swear it."

"I would." Kunal's expression grew serious but remained playful. "I'm not looking for anyone else, Cecelia. What do you want for yourself?"

"I've been lonely for so long," she confessed quietly. "But you... you make me feel seen, like I matter. I've never felt truly wanted before. And I think... I need more of that."

"And I want you, Cecelia," Kunal whispered, his voice filled with conviction as he pulled her gently into his arms. "For exactly who you are."

In the warm glow of the studio, with the scent of polished wood lingering in the air, Cecelia felt a shift within her—a quiet certainty, a hope for the future she had never allowed herself to embrace.

Chapter Twenty-Three

KINDNESS

Cecelia arrived at Annabel's chambers with renewed determination, her steps purposeful despite the flutter of uncertainty in her chest. She wanted to conquer the elusive skill of reading, to make the printed words bend to her will. For hours, she stumbled through dense passages under Annabel's patient guidance, her voice faltering over unfamiliar syllables. Finally, Annabel closed the book with a soft thud and a warm smile.

"I think that's enough for today," Annabel said gently. "How are you feeling about it?"

"Better," Cecelia replied with a small nod, though the words felt inadequate. "I'm starting to understand the rules, but it's slow. Reading still feels like a mountain, and I keep tripping over every stone."

Annabel tapped her fingers thoughtfully on the book's cover. "Perhaps we should try something shorter next time? You don't need to master etiquette overnight. Maybe tomorrow we could focus on correspondence—practice writing letters instead. Tonight, perhaps practice writing in the journal I gave you. I put in lots of things to copy out and practice."

The suggestion struck a chord, echoing Kunal's earlier advice. Cecelia's lips curved into a genuine smile. "That would be wonderful. Thank you."

When Cecelia returned to her chambers, the sense of accomplishment began to fade. The dreaded blank writing journal Annabel had gifted awaited her on the desk, its pages stiff and unyielding, a reminder of the daunting expectations that lay ahead. She forced herself to open it, quill in hand, and began copying sentences with the meticulous precision of someone determined to succeed. The quill scratched across the parchment, each stroke slow and deliberate, but the repetitive words blurred together. By the time the sun dipped low, casting long, narrow shadows across the room, her mind felt as numb as her cramped fingers.

With a weary sigh, Cecelia set the quill down, rubbing her aching wrist. She longed for fresh air, for a respite from the oppressive stillness. Grabbing a box of Maggie's biscuits from the kitchen, she stepped outside, breathing deeply. The cool evening air filled her lungs, a momentary relief. Her feet seemed to have a will of their own, carrying her toward Kunal's studio.

When she reached the door, her pulse quickened, her nerves jangling. Why am I here? she wondered, but before she could retreat, her knuckles had already rapped softly against the wood. The door creaked open, and Cecelia's heart leapt as she almost dropped the box of biscuits.

Sarala stood before her, a figure of quiet authority. Her large brown eyes were both warm and perceptive, as if they could see through Cecelia's carefully composed expression. Her skin, deep and rich, seemed to glow in the fading light, and her silver-streaked hair was swept back neatly, adding to her regal air. Caught off guard, Cecelia hastily offered a small curtsey.

"Good evening, Cecelia," Sarala greeted, her voice gentle yet commanding. "May I help you?"

Cecelia cleared her throat, trying to regain her composure. "Good evening, Sarala. I brought these biscuits for Rupa... and Kunal, if he'd like some. I thought they would both be in here."

Sarala's eyes twinkled as she picked a biscuit from the box and took a delicate bite. "Thank you, my dear. These are delightful."

Cecelia's shoulders relaxed slightly, her nerves easing under Sarala's kind gaze. "Are you here for storytelling with Annabel, or to visit your children?"

"Storytelling, of course," Sarala replied with a knowing wink. "Though Frederick has also enlisted my help in organizing the library. I never miss a chance to visit."

Cecelia shifted awkwardly, the warmth of Sarala's presence making her feel both comforted and exposed. "Kunal isn't here, is he?"

Sarala shook her head gently. "He and Frederick went to meet a wood vendor. They should return later."

Cecelia's attempt to mask her disappointment was feeble. "I'll go check on Rupa, then. I'm sorry to have bothered you."

"You're no bother," Sarala assured her, her tone genuinely warm. "I believe you've come for the package Kunal left for you?" She gestured toward a low table inside. Cecelia hesitated, then stepped into the room, feeling the inviting warmth of the hearth and the faint scent of spices in the air. Sarala handed her a flat, carefully built board, neatly tied with a note bearing her name in Kunal's elegant script.

"Thank you," Cecelia said softly, taking the package with both hands. Her fingers trembled slightly, the unexpected weight of the gift making her feel both touched and uncertain.

Sarala studied her quietly for a moment, then smiled with gentle encouragement. "Would you like to join our storytelling group, Cecelia? Annabel said you might."

The invitation caught Cecelia off guard. "I... I'm still struggling to read and write," she admitted, her cheeks flushing. "I've been trying to learn from an etiquette book, but it's... maddening."

Sarala laughed, her voice warm and rich. "I'd feel the same if I had to study etiquette for hours. Let's find something more engaging." She walked toward a small, well-worn bookshelf, its contents a mix of English and Indian texts.

Cecelia's breath caught as Sarala pulled a richly bound, crimson book from the shelf. Its soft leather cover, worn at the edges and detailed with elegant gold embossing, seemed to whisper of secrets waiting to be uncovered. Cecelia accepted it with reverence, feeling the ancient tome's weight settle into her hands—a tangible reminder of history, of stories untold.

"The Faerie Queene," she read aloud, slowly tracing the gold-embossed title with a tentative finger.

Sarala's smile widened, her voice warm with encouragement. "It's a collection of poetry, a beautiful allegory written by Edmund Spenser. I read it when I was learning English, and it helped me immensely. But don't feel pressured to conquer it all at once. Take it poem by poem; each stands alone, yet they weave together a marvelous tale of knights, queens, and virtues."

Cecelia stared down at the book, feeling its weight like a challenge she wasn't certain she was ready for. "I've never read poetry before," she admitted, a mix of doubt and wonder threading her voice.

Sarala's expression softened, her eyes reflecting understanding. "Poetry is different," she assured. "It's not like the etiquette books that demand precision. Poetry asks you to linger over words, to let them paint vivid images in your mind. You'll find it more like a conversation than a lesson."

The book's faint scent of old parchment carried an air of mystery, and Cecelia ran her hand across the cover, feeling the delicate embossing under her fingertips. The idea of venturing into stories wrapped in verse both intrigued and intimidated her. "I'm not sure if I'll be able to follow it," she confessed, her voice barely above a whisper.

"You will," Sarala said, her tone gentle yet certain. "When you're ready, join us for storytelling. We gather at sunset every Thursday. There's no rush, no judgment—only shared stories, spoken and written. You would be most welcome."

A warmth blossomed in Cecelia's chest, and she suddenly felt a thrill at the idea of discovering a part of herself she hadn't known existed. "Thank you," she murmured, holding the book a little closer. "I'll try my best."

Sarala's gaze was kind, her words a reminder of freedom rather than obligation. "Reading should bring joy, not frustration. If it doesn't, then it's simply the wrong book."

Cecelia's smile grew, a mixture of relief and excitement. "I think I understand that now," she said, the weight of her earlier struggles lifting slightly.

After a moment's pause, Cecelia asked hesitantly, "Was learning English difficult for you?"

Sarala laughed softly, the sound rich and warm. "Only when I forced myself to read things like *The Young Maiden's Tutor*. That book could drive anyone to tears. No wonder the comptesse threw it out of the window."

"Indeed." Cecelia blushed, feeling foolish for her earlier efforts to persevere through dry lessons. "I thought it would be best for me to learn how to be better in other ways while I learnt to read.."

Sarala shook her head. "Learning should be a pleasure, especially when you're starting out. When it's enjoyable, it sticks. If not, it becomes just another chore."

With the parcel from Kunal and The Faerie Queene tucked securely under her arm, Cecelia prepared to leave. Sarala offered a final, warm smile. "You've earned a rest. Go enjoy the book—and if you like, come back for tea tomorrow."

Cecelia nodded, her heart lightening. "I'd love that."

Back in her chambers, excitement bubbled within her. She set the parcel on the end table, then sat down, carefully opening the box. Inside lay a set of finely carved shatranj pieces, a new one she hadn't seen, each figure delicate and intricate, telling its own story in wood. But it was something else that caught Cecelia's breath—a small journal and a note, neatly tied with a ribbon.

With a quiet gasp, she untied the ribbon and opened the journal. The first page was filled with Kunal's handwriting—clear, deliberate, and simple, designed for her to read.

Jouons à nouveau bientôt.

Let's play again soon.

The words stirred something deep within her—longing and anticipation, the memory of their games trailed by the promise of more to come. Her cheeks warmed as she flipped through the pages, her fingers brushing the paper in search of more secret notes. Suddenly, something small and slender slipped from the journal and fell into her lap—a pencil.

But this was no ordinary pencil.

Her breath hitched as she held it up to the light. Carved into the wood was a miniature figure—a fiery little woman with sharp features, windswept hair, and wings poised to take flight. Her tiny face was freckled, her expression determined, as if ready to face the world head-on.

It was her. Kunal had captured her likeness in wood—a whimsical, spirited version of herself, delicately carved into a pencil.

A wave of emotion washed over Cecelia, her heart swelling at the thought of him painstakingly creating this small, intimate token. She admired the fine details, her fingers tracing each curve and line with joy and disbelief. Just as she was turning the pencil over in her hands, a soft knock startled her. She quickly tucked the pencil back into the journal and hid it under her pillow, smoothing her skirts before calling out with a steady voice that masked her racing heart. "Come in."

The door creaked open, and Cecelia braced herself, still reeling from the quiet magic of Kunal's gift.

Bridgette entered with a familiar weariness in her eyes. Her brow was furrowed, as if carrying the weight of their family's future. "Hello, sweetheart," she greeted, her voice unusually soft as she sat on the edge of Cecelia's bed. Her gaze fell on the chessboard, and she reached out, but Cecelia pulled it away quickly.

"It's a gift," Cecelia said tersely, narrowing her eyes defensively. "Don't worry about it."

Bridgette's tone was knowing. "A gift from the artist?" she asked, her eyes sharp with a mixture of concern and curiosity. "Do you understand what you're getting yourself into, especially when you're meant to leave this place forever in just a few weeks?"

Cecelia's chest tightened. "Would you deny me a little joy before everything changes? Just this once, can you let me enjoy something without reminding me of your plans?" Her voice cracked with the strain, betraying her raw emotions. She expected Bridgette's usual dismissiveness, but this time her mother's expression softened.

"Are you really so unhappy about America?" Bridgette's voice was almost hesitant. "Can you imagine no joy in it at all?"

Cecelia sighed heavily, rubbing her temple. "I've liked every home we've had, Mumma. But for now, let me enjoy Kunal's company, even if it's fleeting."

Bridgette's frown deepened, her lips pressing into a thin line. "You're a young woman, Cecelia, and he's a man. Men often have intentions beyond what they show."

Cecelia half-laughed at the absurdity of her mother's warning. "He can't exactly get me pregnant, can he?" she said, her voice blunt. But instead of the expected outrage, Bridgette's face softened further.

"It's your heart I'm worried about," Bridgette whispered. "I don't want you to get it broken."

Cecelia's temper flared, sudden and sharp. "I'd love for my heart to be broken," she snapped. "At least then someone would have cared enough to try." Her arms folded across her chest defensively. "Now, what did you really come for? To remind me of my place again?"

Bridgette sighed deeply. "Your father has the tickets," she said quietly. "We leave in two weeks. Are you ready?"

Two weeks. The words rang in Cecelia's mind like a tolling bell, and her hand instinctively rested on her stomach. The faint curve there was a silent reminder of everything that was about to change.

"How long will the journey take?" she asked, her voice flat and resigned.

"Two months," Bridgette replied, waving a dismissive hand. "You're only four months along. You'll deliver two months after we arrive, easily."

"It doesn't sound easy." Cecelia grimaced, nausea rising in her throat at the thought of the long, uncertain sea journey.

Bridgette leaned closer, rubbing Cecelia's back with hesitant strokes. "It's going to be fine," she murmured, but her voice lacked the conviction Cecelia desperately needed to hear.

The queasiness surged, and Cecelia stood abruptly, her head spinning. "I need ginger," she whispered, bile rising. "I'm going to the kitchen for some. It should help."

"I can fetch it for you," Bridgette offered, reaching out, but Cecelia shook her head, her tone firmer than before.

"No," she insisted. "The walk will do me good."

Without another word, Cecelia left the room, her mind swirling with frustration, fear, and a stubborn resolve. Two weeks. Just two weeks to decide her future, to confront her feelings, and to face the reality of leaving everything behind, or giving into love while possibly ruining an artist's reputation.

The kitchen was dim and quiet when she entered, the hearth's embers humming softly. Maggie was nowhere to be seen. Cecelia began rummaging through the bins, her hands moving quickly. She found a small piece of dried ginger, placed it in her mouth, and let its sharp, earthy flavor spread, its warmth calming the storm in her stomach. She tucked another piece between parchment sheets and slipped it into the pocket beneath her skirts.

Suddenly, a stern voice sliced through the stillness.

"What on earth are you doing?"

Cecelia spun around, her heart jolting, to find the physician standing behind her. His graying hair seemed harsher in the low light, his sharp eyes glinting with disapproval.

"I—I was getting some ginger," she stammered, her voice thin. "For my stomach." She glanced at him, hoping for a hint of understanding, but his expression remained cold. "I'm pregnant," she added, as if that might soften him.

"I know you're pregnant," he snapped, stepping closer. "The castle knows."

"Fine." Cecelia's voice wavered, but she fought to control it. "Maggie doesn't mind if I take the ginger."

"Well, Maggie's not here, is she?" Doctor Fenton growled, contempt dripping from his tone. "It isn't the first time she's left things unattended. Perhaps I should report her to the Baroness for her lack of discipline."

"She isn't slacking," Cecelia countered quickly, her pulse hammering in her ears. "I've been helping her, and she's hard at work. What do you need?"

Doctor Fenton's scrutinizing gaze lingered on her, his silence heavy and uncomfortable. Finally, he shrugged, his tone clipped. "Frederick needs a strong, firm porridge."

"Fine," Cecelia repeated, turning to the stove, her skin prickling under his intense stare. She moved quickly, her hands steady despite the simmering anger beneath the surface. As she stirred the porridge, the physician's presence loomed, his cold, calculating eyes never leaving her. When she poured the porridge into a bowl, added a spoon, and placed it on a tray, he clapped his hands together mockingly.

"That took long enough," he sneered.

"A thousand pardons," Cecelia muttered, fatigue evident in her voice. "Shall I take it to him?"

"First, fetch a fresh stack of hand towels from the cellar," he ordered. "Then you may take it. The Baroness insists I watch him eat, as he's barely touched food in days."

Despite her distaste for the man, a pang of sympathy pierced Cecelia's heart. "Would you like to take the tray while I fetch the towels?"

He laughed, a high, stilted sound. "Good heavens, no."

Cecelia set down the tray carefully and hurried to the cellar, the memory of Frederick's wan face tugging at her. She half-hoped to find Lise there, but the storage room was emptier than usual, as if marked by her friend's departure. Dust hung in the still air, a cobweb glistening beneath Lise's abandoned bed. Cecelia gathered the towels quickly, her thoughts heavy with the loss of her friend.

Returning to the kitchen, she found the physician inspecting his nails with disdain. Before he could berate her, she raised a hand. "I know," she said wearily. "I took too long."

He huffed, then strode toward Frederick's room without another word. Cecelia picked up the tray, carefully balancing the porridge and towels. As she walked, a faint bitter scent reached her nose—subtle, almost imperceptible. She paused, sniffing cautiously. It was an almond-like aroma, earthy and nutty.

Her stomach churned, nausea rising swiftly. She shook her head, trying to dismiss the feeling. "What's wrong with me?" she muttered. "Bloody pregnancy. I'm smelling things that aren't there."

As she neared Frederick's room, her heart sank at the sight of him. He was paler, thinner, the dark circles under his eyes deepening his hollow look.

"Cecelia!" Frederick's voice was hoarse, but it held a spark of recognition. "What on earth is that?"

"Porridge," she answered softly, casting a wary glance at the physician. "It's good for you."

Frederick scowled, his lips curling in distaste. "I hate porridge," he grumbled. "This damned doctor won't let me do anything but eat and read when he's around. I'm losing my mind."

Cecelia set the tray on the bedside table, forcing a lighthearted smile. "Aren't you lucky?"

Frederick's weak laugh echoed faintly, but his eyes betrayed the weight of exhaustion and fear. "Sit with me," he urged. "Please. Doctor, you can go."

The physician's face hardened, his mouth a thin line of displeasure. "Your mother—"

"I'm still the Baron, am I not?" Frederick cut him off, his tone unexpectedly sharp. "Until my last breath, this house is mine to command. Go to the chapel and pray for me. That's an order."

Doctor Fenton's eyes flashed with barely concealed fury, but he bowed stiffly and left without another word. Frederick chuckled under his breath as Cecelia closed the door behind the man.

"You shouldn't provoke him like that," Cecelia whispered, leaning closer, her voice edged with concern. "He could make your end far worse than it needs to be."

A shudder ran through Frederick as he pulled the bowl of porridge into his lap. "I know," he admitted quietly, his voice raw with resignation. He took a bite, then grimaced, pushing the bowl away. "This tastes foul. Everything does."

Cecelia sighed, her heart heavy as she settled beside him. "What did you want me to stay for?"

Frederick's gaze fell to the bowl, his eyes dull and distant. "I can't believe I'm going to die within the year," he murmured, his words barely audible. "It doesn't feel real. I thought I was getting stronger for a few days there... but now, I can feel myself slipping again."

Cecelia reached out, gently clasping his hand. Her touch was steady, but her voice trembled with unspoken sorrow. "What do you want to do with the time you have left, Frederick?"

He sniffed, tears pooling in his eyes. "I'm afraid," he confessed, the words spilling out like a dam breaking. "Afraid of what comes after. Afraid that when I die, no one will remember me."

Cecelia's chest tightened with a profound ache, a deep empathy for the man who had struggled so valiantly to live. "People will remember you," she said softly, her voice filled with conviction. "You've done so much for those you love—more than most ever could. You've left a mark on this place... and on me. On Charlie and Annabel. You've done so much to make our lives better."

Frederick managed a watery smile, his grip on Cecelia's hand tightening slightly. "Thank you, Cecelia," he whispered, his voice thick with emotion. "That means more than you know."

They sat in silence, the weight of unspoken fears and fleeting moments hanging between them like fragile threads. Cecelia stayed until Frederick's breathing grew slow and even, his exhaustion finally overtaking him. She gently pulled her hand away, her heart aching with the knowledge that the man beside her was living on borrowed time.

But she couldn't shake the unsettling thought that the bitter scent in the room had lingered long after the physician had gone.

Chapter Twenty-Four

STOWAWAY

Days later, Cecelia knocked on Annabel's door with the urgency of a child bursting with secrets, shifting her weight from one foot to the other. The crisp evening air carried the sharp scent of woodsmoke, mingling with the dampness of fallen leaves underfoot. As the oaks whispered overhead, the door creaked open to reveal Annabel, her face brightening into a welcoming smile.

"I finished the pages!" Cecelia blurted, the usual reserve in her voice giving way to a rare burst of pride. She thrust the sketchpad forward as she stepped in, her voice softening. "I did the cover page... and even added a few of the other illustrations in color."

Annabel closed the door quickly, and her eyes widened as she flipped through the pages, her fingers tracing the fine lines. "Oh, Cecelia, these are breathtaking," she whispered. Her breath caught when she reached the colored illustrations. "This is stunning. It's perfect for *Friends of the Vale,* just perfect."

"The watercolors took longer than I thought," Cecelia admitted, a small laugh escaping her lips, though her eyes still held a touch of uncertainty. "Rupa showed me some tricks with the brushes."

Before Annabel could respond, an unexpected knock at the door jolted them both. Annabel raised an eyebrow and moved toward the entrance. "Good evening, Bridgette."

Cecelia's mother stepped in, looking weary but relieved. "Is my daughter here?"

"Yes, Mumma," Cecelia called out, her earlier joy dimming slightly at her mother's sudden arrival. "What's the matter?"

Bridgette's expression softened, but her eyes were tired. "There are some pieces missing in the castle and they're questioning everyone. There's whispered someone stole from the Baroness, or some other nonsense. I couldn't rest not knowing where you were, in case they'd thought to question you."

Cecelia sighed. "I'm here, Mumma. You know I wouldn't be involved in some thing like that."

Annabel, ever the peacemaker, stepped in with warm cheer. "Cecelia's been helping me with the book. In fact, I was hoping she could stay the night—we've still got work to finish, and I'd love her company."

"That's fine." Bridgette hesitated, her expression unreadable for a moment before she stepped forward and pulled Cecelia into a quick but firm hug. "I love you, sweetheart," she whispered, her voice unsteady.

Caught off guard, Cecelia returned the embrace, her voice soft. "I love you too, Mumma." She watched as her mother pulled away, clearly uneasy with such vulnerability.

As the door closed behind her, Cecelia let out a long breath, exchanging a relieved grin with Annabel. "That was easier than I thought."

"I'll get the kettle going," Annabel said, moving toward the hearth. "Let's get back to it."

Hours later, they were slumped in armchairs by the fire, surrounded by fabric swatches and scattered sketches. The fire crackled, casting a flickering glow, while the storm outside gathered force. Suddenly, a sharp knock jolted Cecelia awake. Charlie stood in the doorway, gently shaking Annabel.

"Sorry to wake you," Cecelia yawned, stretching her stiff limbs. "Annabel said I could stay. We were working on the book."

Charlie's smile was warm, his gaze resting on the strewn pages. "I can tell. Your illustrations are remarkable, Cecelia. They deserve to be published."

Cecelia beamed, her eyes brightening with pride. "Thank you."

Annabel, still half-asleep, tried to gather the scattered sketches. "I'll finish these later," she mumbled, her ears perking up as thunder rumbled through the house. "Is there a storm?"

Charlie nodded, glancing toward the rattling windows. "Just starting. I'm glad I got back before it worsened. I brought salt pork and apples in case anyone's hungry."

Annabel's gaze flicked anxiously to the rattling shutters. "Thank you, love. I think I'll have some hot water with lemon before bed."

"Goodnight, my love," Charlie murmured, pressing a gentle kiss to her forehead. He turned to Cecelia. "And goodnight to you, Cecelia. Annabel rarely lets anyone help her, but you seem to have managed it. Good for you both." He gave Cecelia an encouraging smile before heading off to bed.

As the storm's intensity grew, Annabel and Cecelia huddled closer on the chaise, steaming mugs in hand. The wind howled outside, rattling the shutters violently, and a sudden crack of lightning made Annabel jump.

When Charlie had gone to bed and both women had a warm mug in their hands, Annabel tucked a thick blanket over their laps as they settled on the chaise. A sharp crack of lightning split the air, making Annabel flinch. She wrapped the blanket tighter around her shoulders, her voice trembling slightly. "I won't pretend I'm not afraid. This house is sturdy, but it only takes one well-aimed branch through the roof to change that."

Cecelia glanced toward the rattling windows, her own nerves prickling. "Would you mind a story to distract us?" she asked tentatively. "I've been working on one about a squirrel, and I'd love your thoughts."

Annabel's face lit up, her unease momentarily forgotten. "Yes, please! Sarala told me you joined the storytelling group. I've been hoping to hear one of your tales."

Encouraged, Cecelia took a deep breath and began, "Once upon a time, there was a little old squirrel who lived alone in a small burrow deep in the woods. He kept to himself mostly, but every day he'd scurry around gathering acorns on the path that looped around the ancient oak tree."

Annabel relaxed, taking a sip of her tea. Her eyes finally drifted from the door to Cecelia.

"The squirrel was diligent," Cecelia continued, her voice steady. "He picked up more acorns than he ever ate, and when other squirrels came by, he pretended to be asleep. Soon, his burrow overflowed with a wealth of acorns, and no one knew."

Annabel's gaze softened, a touch of sympathy entering her eyes. "He sounds lonely."

Cecelia's tone turned teasing but laced with a hint of bitterness. "Only because you're used to company—siblings, lovers, one after another."

Annabel's smile turned wry. "Hardly something to envy. The vicar left me, Richard lied to me, and it's thanks to Agatha that I'm finally free of him. Not much of a legacy." She cleared her throat, glancing again toward the door. "Go on with Little Old Squirrel."

Cecelia pressed forward. "One day, Little Old Squirrel, feeling colder and wearier than usual, took a rest midway through his scurry. There, he met a younger squirrel and her family. They were kind, invited him for a holiday, and he accepted."

Annabel's eyes brightened. "How lovely."

Cecelia's expression remained serious. "While he was away, a tree fell on his burrow, destroying everything. Heartbroken, he returned to find his collection ruined. But the younger squirrel family welcomed him in permanently."

Annabel nodded thoughtfully. "Good of them."

"Later," Cecelia added, "when they visited the site of his old home, they found a few tiny saplings—acorn trees just starting to sprout. The old squirrel got a tear in his eye, then scoffed, saying it was foolish to be sentimental since the trees wouldn't bear fruit for years, but in a way it's nice, because he didn't have any family sprouts of his own. But the young squirrel simply said, 'Well, you do now.' The old squirrel replied, 'Indeed I do,' and placed a comforting arm over his new friend's shoulders."

There was a sob, and Cecelia looked at Annabel in surprise. "Have I truly moved you to years?"

"Your story was beautiful," whispered Annabel. "But that wasn't me."

There was a rustling under their feet, and Cecelia whipped her feet away from the floor and underneath her while she snatched a pillow to hold aloft. "Who's there?"

A dirty child crawled out in a tangle of limbs and blankets, and Annabel gasped. "Cassidy Rowley? Is that you?"

"I'm so sorry," Cassidy's shoulders shook.

"Oh, sweetheart," Annabel whispered, pulling the small girl up in to the couch. "What are you doing here?"

"I stowed away in the carriage," Cassidy whispered back. "Mother has been taking Geoffrey's carriage here every few days to spy on everyone in secret. This is the third time I've caught her doing it, and she didn't notice me climb into the luggage compartment. It was empty because she wasn't properly traveling."

"Spying," Cecelia hissed. "Why is Philippa doing such a thing?"

"Because Frederick kicked us all out of the house," Cassidy said incredulously. "Why on earth did he do that?"

"Keep your voice down. Charlie's asleep," Cecelia hissed. "Your mother pushed Charlie down the stairs, and Frederick said it would be better for your mother's recovery for you to go with her to Rowley Manor."

Annabel said softly. "But Cassidy, your mother must be worried sick, wondering where you are."

"She's not," Cassidy protested. "And I don't want to go. Castle Rowley is my home."

Cecelia shivered to hear the same words echoed back at her as she'd said to her mother. "Frederick and his fiancé Marguerite have grand plans for this place...I think you're really going to like what he's adding. A theater with plays and tumblers, a bigger library, a museum showing the treasures of your family, all cementing the Rowley legacy. You're going to love it when you see it." She smiled at Cassidy, letting the little girl lean back against her arm on the sofa.

"If he ever lets us come back," Cassidy sighed.

"You're supposed to come in the next month for Frederick's party," Annabel reminded her. "Your mother, Geoffrey and Talon will all come."

"What if I want to stay now?" Cassidy asked, her lip trembling. "What if I want to come back home and not stay in the drafty old manor? It's even more haunted than these soggy stones. The things you hear at night...it's not a screaming so much as a loud humming..."

"You can't stay here after you've run away," sighed Cecelia. "Your mother will be furious, and she will blame us. But if you own up to Frederick, and he brings you back, then perhaps ask Frederick's permission to visit—"

"Adding a healthy dose of appreciation, mind you," laughed Annabel.

"Naturally," snickered Cassidy.

"He might let you come back. He wants to please his mother, so you'll need to convince her that it's in your best interest," Cecelia said. "And perhaps you could endear her to the rest of us, while you are at it?"

"That's going to be quite difficult," moaned Cassidy.

"I've been learning to read, and that's been the most difficult thing I've ever done," remarked Cecelia. "If I can do that, even when I don't like it, knowing it's in my best interests, then you can do your part."

"Are you really learning to read?" Cassidy gasped. "That's wonderful! What are you reading?"

"A fussy old book on etiquette." Annabel waved her hand, and Cecelia blushed.

"Actually, Sarala lent me a book." She pressed her lips together, suddenly anxious. "The Faerie Queen. It's wonderful, all beautiful poems."

"Look at you," Annabel nodded approvingly. "I'm so proud." Turning back to Cassidy, she asked, "How long do we have before you're discovered missing?"

"Dawn," the girl replied.

"Then we'll tell Frederick now, and set out to arrive at dawn," sighed Annabel. "He may choose to send a messenger in the night. I'll be right back." She returned with Charlie, who looked at Cassidy with a question in his eyes.

The four of them made their way back to the castle with lanterns, and knocked on the kitchen door. A surprised Maggie let them in. "Young Cassidy what are you doing back here?"

Cassidy grinned. "I'm hoping for some apple cream."

Shaking her head, Annabel went to speak to the butler in hushed tones, who tossed a disapproving look their way before heading in the direction of Frederick's room.

"What's apple cream?" Charlie yawned.

Cassidy clasped her hands. "It's my favorite. Apples cooked with sugar and tossed in thick frothy cream. I could eat it all day."

"I haven't had that in ages," Annabel whispered. "And never with sugar."

"Please, Maggie?" Cassidy wheedled.

Cecelia gave the little girl a fond look. "I missed you, you know, kidlet."

Cassidy beamed. "I missed you too."

An hour later, they had all enjoyed apple creams sprinkled with precious cinnamon. Frederick had dressed, been briefed on the situation at hand, and was planning on escorting Cassidy back to Rowley Manor himself. Cecelia was helping Cassidy into her coat when Annabel came back up to her from speaking with Frederick with a funny expression on her face.

"Cecelia..." Annabel said softly. "Frederick said not to wake the usual morning carriage driver. He wants as few people around the castle to know about this as possible."

"And?" Cecelia shrugged.

"He wants you to go along to make sure Cassidy behaves." Annabel smiled, pressing her hand into the small of their back and pushing them out of the shadows towards the castle path. "And wants Kunal to take all of you there in his cart."

"What?" Cecelia gasped, as they stepped out into the light and came around the corner to see a horse and cart waiting, Kunal holding the reins and smiling sleepily at them.

CHAPTER TWENTY-FIVE

CARRIAGE RIDE

In the soft embrace of the twilight, Cecelia approached Kunal's cart, her gaze drinking in its charm. The cart was a small, open design, its frame made of polished wood that gleamed softly under the moon's gentle light. The woodwork was intricate, showcasing the skill of a master craftsman, with delicate carvings that depicted scenes of pastoral life. The wheels were sturdy, bound with iron for durability, yet they possessed an elegance that spoke of a time when even the most practical items were made with care.

The seating area was modest but inviting, with enough space to comfortably accommodate herself and Cassidy, whose eyes were already wide with wonder. The seats were simple wooden benches, their minimalistic design offset by the softness of their cushions. The cushions, covered in a fabric that bore a subtle floral pattern, added a touch of comfort and luxury to the otherwise unadorned cart.

As Cecelia helped Cassidy climb into the cart, the little girl's excitement was palpable. Bundled up in her warm cloak against the cool night air, Cassidy's cheeks were flushed with the thrill of this unexpected adventure. Frederick settled into the very back of the cart with a scowl on his tired face, his eyes obscured by a heavy cloak. Kunal winked at Cecelia behind his glasses and waited patiently as they settled in.

"Were you already awake?" Cecelia asked him, flustered to see him but also at the same time secretly delighted. "It's the middle of the night. I'm so sorry you were bothered."

"Baron Rowley has bothered me several times in the middle of the night, not wanting to merely write it down as he believes that removes authenticity from the idea," Kunal said dryly.

"I didn't know that," Cecelia whispered. "I think he can hear you."

"He's already asleep." Kunal looked back at the young Baron, as did Cecelia, and she saw that it was true. "I'm often up late working, so I don't mind. He said you needed to take a young child back to her home?" He threw a kindly look at Cassidy and did a double take as he took in her face. Slipping his gaze back to Cecelia, he asked nervously, "Isn't this one of the Rowley twins?"

"Oh, pay me no mind," Cassidy laughed from the middle seat behind them. "I'm just an old friend of Cecelia's." She regarded Kunal with interest. "Aren't you the handsome artist? I've heard of you."

"Hush," hissed Cecelia, ignoring Kunal's surprised face. "Don't speak to strangers."

"He's not a stranger," Cassidy said frankly. "Isn't he the man who you're sweet on? Annabel was just saying…"

"Start the cart, please," Cecelia murmured, red-faced, looking out the door. "Cassidy, please go to sleep. I'm sure you have lessons in the morning."

"This is far more interesting than lessons," Cassidy declared, but she settled back into her seat, and Cecelia felt a sense of peace. The openness of the cart allowed the night's beauty to envelop them, the stars twinkling above like a celestial tapestry. The horse, sensing its new passengers, shifted slightly, its muscles rippling gracefully under its sleek coat.

Once they were on their way, after a period of a few minutes of silence, Kunal asked from his seat directly in front of them, his deep voice carrying, "How did you and Cecelia become friends, Cassidy?"

"She's asleep," Cecelia hissed.

"I am not," Cassidy protested, a whine rising in her voice. "When we first met she told me that we were in the same boat because we both have curls and C names, so we had to look out for each other."

"I *see*," Kunal remarked, throwing her a grin, and Cassidy screamed with laughter.

"Don't encourage her," moaned Cecelia.

Frederick snorted in his sleep, and Cassidy jumped before she continued. "Oh, that's a good one! I think you could be an honorary member of the C party, since your name starts with the same sound," Cassidy continued. "She's also drawn Talon and I as the heroes from our books loads of times. She can't read them, but she can tell stories with her pictures."

"I'm learning to read," Cecelia sighed.

"That's right!" Cassidy exclaimed. "Good for you. Then you will be able to read to us, then, when we're back? I promise we'll convince Mother."

"We'll see." Cecelia continued to look out of the window, curling her coat more tightly around her.

"She's also helped us play loads of pranks here," Cassidy confided to Kunal. "Whenever someone came to visit the castle who we didn't like, we'd make it seem like it was haunted."

"Cassidy, Kunal doesn't want to hear about this," Cecelia hissed.

"I don't mind," he laughed. "I enjoy hearing about you."

"I've loads more," Cassidy cackled. "All my friends ask for Cecelia when they come to play. She does the best voices. She's tops at distracted Talon from being destructive. And she'll play any game you can teach her."

"That was a lifetime ago, now," Cecelia sighed, beginning to rifle through the parcel Annabel had sent with them.

"Do not pretend you don't like games. It wasn't so long ago, that we played shatranj," he reminded her.

"Is that a *new* game?" Cassidy asked in interest. "Will you teach me?"

"It is an *old* game," Cecelia muttered.

"Of course!" Kunal smiled. "Any time."

Reaching into her bag, Cecelia produced a small package of gingerbread. As she unwrapped it, the sweet, spicy aroma of gingerbread filled the air, mingling with the earthy scents of the countryside.

"Look, Cecelia, stars!" Cassidy exclaimed, her eyes reflecting the night sky as she took a bite of the gingerbread.

As the horse began to move, pulling the cart along the moonlit path, the gentle clatter of hooves against cobblestones created a rhythmic melody. Cecelia felt as if they were drifting through a dream, a world where time stood still, and the only reality was the beauty of the night and the warmth of the small, open cart that carried them under the stars.

"Ooh!" Cassidy took a piece and handed one up to Kunal. "This is the gingerbread that started it all, isn't it?"

"What do you mean?" Cecelia asked.

"That's right," Cassidy said thoughtfully. "You remember Richard, who was married to Annabel, well he stole Charlie's gingerbread, this very gingerbread here that's his mother Mara's recipe, and once Annabel found out that Richard was a thief..." Cassidy shook her head. "It was all over for him. Then as soon as Annabel found out that Richard's second wife Agatha was still alive and locked in the dungeon, she fell in love with Charlie and had Richard locked up for not paying his taxes and the marriage annulled." Cassidy shook her head, grinning. "Once Annabel moved here, everything got much more interesting."

"How on Earth do you know all this?" Kunal exclaimed. "You're a child."

"She listens at doors," Cecelia muttered.

"As though you don't?" Cassidy stuck her tongue out at Cecelia, then turned back to Kunal. "Do we have to go back to Rowley Manor? We could go anywhere in the world in this cart, almost."

"We're going back," Cecelia warned. "Your mother will have our heads, otherwise."

"She'll probably have it anyway," Cassidy sighed, yawning. "Where would you go, if you would go anywhere? Kunal, not Cecelia - I know you're going to awful America. You shouldn't. Your parents are going and that doesn't mean you have to. No offense."

"None taken," Cecelia scowled. "I don't understand it either, but my parents want me to come with them so they can help me look after the baby, they've got it all planned out, and who am I to look a gift horse in the mouth?"

"Do you know what the rest of that saying means?" Cassidy chortled. "The gift horse was filled with soldiers to kill the Greeks who received the gift horse. You should always look a gift horse in the mouth."

Cecelia sighed. "You may be too clever for your own good."

After a period of some silence, Cassidy piped up again. "Well? Where would you go?"

Kunal rubbed his chin thoughtfully. "If I could choose anywhere, it would be a place further than by cart. I'd go to France, the Netherlands, Spain or Portugal, the Ottoman Empire, even back to India. There's loads of adventures to be had that I've dreamed about. The sky's the limit."

"Wow," Cassidy said dreamily. "What would you even do in all those places? Could you find work in all of them? Or do you already have money?"

"It's not polite to talk about money, Cassidy," Cecelia admonished.

Cassidy waved her hand. "It's fine if you already have it."

"I'd go to Versailles in France to secure a commission from King Louis, and learn some advanced European techniques," Kunal mused. "I'd go to the Netherlands to create goods for maritime trade and decorations for ships—they're a center of innovation in woodworking tools, so I'd beef up my armory as well. I might stay there for a while."

The young girl nodded, spellbound. "What about Spain and Portugal?"

"They like their religious iconography. My grandmother back home would love me to embark on that adventure," he said ruefully. "Carvings I create there would export to the New World, increasing my reach and potential for more diverse commissions. I could go to the Ottoman Empire to learn carving techniques from Islamic culture, which would enable me to work on mosques and palaces throughout the empire."

"You've really thought about this," Cecelia managed, her head swimming in envy at the thought of the ability to travel and make money in all these amazing places. "What a lucky man you are with so many options. And you want to go back to Amber as well?"

"I daydream quite a lot." He grinned. "I haven't been back to Amber since we first came to England, and it would feel good to reconnect with my homeland. I have family and friends we left behind. And I'd love the chance to work in the courts of the Mughal Empire, where I could apply my skills learned in Europe to more traditional Amber designs."

"Don't you want a family?" Cassidy inquired. "Would you bring children to all those places with you, or have a nanny?"

"I want a family very much," he sighed. "But I won't have my own, I'm sure, for another couple of years. I'd bring them with me, though. It's good for children to travel and learn about the world."

"Your future children are lucky," Cassidy sighed wistfully. "Father never wanted to take us anywhere." Shrugging off the memory, she asked, "Do you know any stories?"

"I know some stories from folklore," he offered. "Those are probably the only ones I know by heart."

"Yes, please," she sighed, snuggling into Cecelia and closing her eyes.

"This is the story of Tenali Raman and the Three Dolls," Kunal murmured.

"Oh, good," she yawned. "Cecelia, I still have the doll you made me at home. I told Mother a French countess made it and she believed me."

She could hear a smile in his voice. "Once, a king from a neighboring kingdom sent three identical-looking dolls to King Krishnadevaraya of Vijayanagara. He challenged the king to find the differences between them. The king, puzzled by their identical appearance, turned to his wise courtier, Tenali Raman, for help.

Tenali Raman took the dolls and carefully examined them. After a while, he found a small hole in each of the dolls' ears. He then took a thin wire and inserted it into the ear of the first doll. The wire came out from the other ear. In the second doll, when he inserted the wire into the ear, it came out from the mouth. For the third doll, the wire did not come out at all.

Tenali Raman presented his findings to the king and explained, "Your Majesty, these dolls represent three types of people. The first doll, where the wire went in one ear and came out the other, represents those people who do not retain anything and let whatever they hear go in one ear and out the other.

The second doll, where the wire went in the ear and came out of the mouth, symbolizes people who listen and then talk about it. They are the ones who spread rumors and gossip.

The third doll, where the wire did not come out, represents those people who listen, understand, and then contemplate the knowledge in their heart. They are wise and thoughtful."

King Krishnadevaraya was impressed with Tenali Raman's cleverness and rewarded him for his wisdom, gifting him a splendid chariot adorned with mirrors reflecting the world in myriad ways. "As you journey in this Chariot of Reflection, may you continue to see the world from different perspectives and share your insightful reflections, enriching the minds of all who listen."

There was a silence, and Cecelia whispered, "I think she really is asleep now. Thank you."

They rode in silence the rest of the way, and when they arrived at last, Cecelia woke the small girl and brought her to her feet. Annabel roused Frederick. "What's the best way to sneak you in?"

"Side door," Cassidy said sleepily, rubbing her eyes. "Lucia sleeps in the kitchen."

After the grumpy guard that had been sitting in the back with Frederick, Rudolph, escorted them to the door, Frederick and Cecelia showed the archers they had the young child, and slipped her in through the side door to a familiar and surprised maid, Lucia. Smiling in relief, she knew Lucia would sneak Cassidy seamlessly back into bed. Thankfully, Philippa's servants seemed too afraid of waking her up to make noise about it, and Lucia recognized Frederick.

Cecelia raised her lantern once more as she watched Cassidy walk off with Lucia, and smiled when the young girls stopped and waved at Cecelia, then continued on. Suddenly as her eyes became used to the light, she peered at something just past Cecelia. A piece of furniture in the great hall. Was that... She squinted.

Was that a jade inlaid table?

CHAPTER TWENTY-SIX

HEARTBREAK

In the dim light of the moon, Cecelia climbed back into the cart, her thoughts swirling. She glanced at Kunal, uncertain whether to bring up the jade-inlaid table or let it rest for now. Had her eyes perhaps deceived her?

Instead, she smiled tightly, settling into the seat beside him, hearing Frederick and the guard settling into the back seat. "Thank you again for coming all the way out here to help me take her back."

"It's no trouble," Kunal replied, his voice low and smooth. "I like a good nighttime ride." His eyes sparkled mischievously as he added, "You can sit up here with me, if you'd like."

Her heart fluttered. Without thinking too much about it, she accepted his offer and clambered onto the cushioned bench beside him. She stumbled slightly as she found her balance, her hands brushing against his firm chest. He steadied her with a quiet laugh, and for a moment, their faces were close enough that she could see the warmth in his eyes.

After a few minutes of peaceful riding, the moonlit manor fading behind them, Kunal's voice broke the silence. "You know," he said, keeping his tone conversational, "Cassidy is right—you don't have to go to America. There are plenty of people here who would take care of you if you chose to stay."

Cecelia sighed, trying not to let his words tug too deeply at her. "My mother says this is the best chance I'll ever have for my future."

"It might seem like the best chance," Kunal replied, his voice gentle but firm. "But it's not your only chance. It's not your only choice."

"Then name another one," Cecelia said, a touch of frustration creeping into her voice. "I'm a penniless woman with no land, no assets. My only choices are the ones men offer me. I don't have the luxury of deciding my fate."

Kunal was quiet for a moment, and Cecelia's pulse quickened when she noticed him gather the reins into one hand and hold his other out, palm-up on his knee. Swallowing her pride, she slipped her hand into his. A surge of warmth shot through her when he gave it a light squeeze and glanced at her with a soft smile.

"I'm sorry," he murmured. "I know you've already decided. But Cecelia, if you wanted to stay, I would court you in public until you agreed to marry me. I'd build you a home, anywhere you wanted. Or we could live with my family—they'd welcome you with open arms."

Cecelia's heart skipped a beat, but she tried to keep her voice steady. "And what if I just enjoy kissing you on rocking horses but don't think seriously about a future?"

"I wouldn't believe you," Kunal said with a grin. "I think you've thought seriously about me, even if you try not to admit it."

"I have," Cecelia confessed quietly, squeezing his hand again. "I can't stop thinking about you, as much as I've tried. But I don't want to be a burden to you."

"You could never be a burden," he said softly. "I've never met anyone like you. If I don't do everything I can to keep you close, I'll regret it for the rest of my life."

"I'm practically illiterate," she reminded him, her voice heavy with self-doubt. "I'm a maid. I have calloused hands from scrubbing pots. I'm hardly a prize."

Kunal chuckled softly. "You illustrated an entire book, Cecelia. You're learning to read. You have more courage than anyone I know, and you always think of how to make things better and make the lives of those around you better, no matter what obstacles stand in your way. You may not realize it, but you're extraordinary."

She blinked, feeling a lump rise in her throat. "And what about this?" She placed her other hand on her belly, which had grown ever so slightly in recent weeks. "I'm carrying another man's child. Surely that's not part of the future you imagined for yourself."

Kunal looked at her with such tenderness it made her breath catch. "I've never spent much time imagining my future marriage. I always feared I'd end up with someone who would take me away from the things I love. But you..." He trailed off, his voice softening. "You make me feel like I wouldn't have to give up any part of myself. And as for the child—it's part of you. So I already love it, too."

Cecelia stared at him, speechless. "You love it?" she whispered.

"I do," Kunal said simply. "I'll wait as long as you need to before courting you publicly. But I won't hide how I feel. And I hope you're nearly ready, because I can't wait to start our life together."

Cecelia swallowed hard, her chest swelling with emotion. "I believe I'm nearly ready," she whispered, her voice trembling with the weight of the decision she hadn't yet fully made but now longed to embrace.

When they arrived at Castle Rowley, Cecelia did not sneak back to her family's farmhouse to sleep, but walked slowly with Kunal down the path, a decision she regretted when she saw Rupa and her parents standing in front of the castle, speaking to a nicely dressed man.

Kunal looked at her as she started to hang back. "Are you alright?"

"Who is that?" Cecelia whispered.

"Oh!" Kunal's face split joyfully into a smile. "It's Captain Harrington."

"Who?" Cecelia repeated.

"Our benefactor," Kunal explained. "Captain!"

Cecelia felt the stirrings of unease, but like a fool, she continued to walk forward with Kunal, albeit at a much slower pace.

"Kunal Sutar," The older gentleman had a mustache that was thicker than his beard, and a woolen hat and coat. "It's hard to believe you're already striking out on your own."

"Yes, my lord," Kunal beamed. "This commission has been a great gift. I understand it came on the wings of your recommendation, sir, which I thank you for."

"May it be the door to bigger and better things." Captain Harrington nodded at Cecelia. "And who is your young lady?"

"This is Cecelia Rousseau," Kunal said, slipping his hand to the small of her back, and she reflexively moved forward. "A wonderful fellow artist I hope to collaborate with."

Cecelia bent to curtsy, and heard a carriage stop behind her.

"I'm sorry..." The benefactor peered at her with amusement. "I'm sure I've seen you here before. If I'm not mistaken..."

"She works here," a voice came harshly, and Cecelia's blood turned to ice. It was unmistakably Philippa. "She is a maid at the castle. Cecelia, run along."

"She is my maid at the moment," piped up Rupa. "Cecelia has been assisting me for the past week. She's been as good as an apprentice. Kunal's right in that she's very talented."

"And yet, she is still a maid," Philippa said darkly. "One who should not be fraternizing nearly as often with these artists as she does. Your children are too kind to birds with broken wings," she told Manik and Sarala disapprovingly, and Cecelia's cheek's burned.

"Please do not disparage Cecelia, Baroness," Kunal said firmly, but Cecelia saw his hands shake. "She was once in a landowning family just like yourself, but fell upon hard times." He cleared his throat and added, a little more dangerously, "Hard time in which your late husband predicated. Or is he late?" His eyes flashed, and Cecelia felt as though her heart might stop at the tension. "No one's seen him lately."

"Are you in love with her?" Philippa hissed, her voice rising.

"Yes!" Kunal cried, and his parents looked shocked.

The benefactor surprised Cecelia by throwing back his head and laughing, long and hard, doubling over as great guffaws flew from his body until he finally straightened. "Well." He crossed his arms and look at Philippa. "If your maid and my artist are in love, we're not staying. Our business is done here."

"No." Philippa's voice was faint and her face paled. "You can't mean that. Our families have traded for years."

"That was before your staff corrupted mine," Captain Harrington laughed.

"Please, Captain," Manik began in bewilderment. "We had no idea of any of this. Let us speak to our son alone; I'm sure there's some sort of misunderstanding..."

"There's no misunderstanding," Kunal said, then looked at Cecelia. "Is there?" His voice grew softer as he whispered, "You may have to decide early."

Cecelia looked at the stricken faces of Manik and Sarala. She looked at the worried eyes of Rupa, with her hands clasped tightly in front of her chest. She looked into the furious faces of Philippa and Captain Harrington.

"I'm sorry," she squeaked, then cleared her throat. "There has been a misunderstanding. We are not in love. Kunal has many handsome prospects ahead of him, and I'm a maid of the castle who surely won't be here long." Her heart beat like a hummingbird's when Kunal look at her, and her stomach dropped when she saw the hurt on his face. Bowing her head, she repeated, "I'm sorry."

A bony hand gripped her arm and began to lead her away, and her heart raced when she saw it was the Baroness Rowley. "Your mother is at the market, and I'm taking you to her now to be dealt with." Philippa's voice was cold and clipped, her pace unrelenting as they moved swiftly through the darkened courtyard.

"What? But she should be in the dining hall by now," Cecelia protested, trying to slow down.

"Well, she's at the market," Philippa repeated sharply, her tone leaving no room for argument.

Before Cecelia could comprehend what was happening, they reached the carriage. Philippa practically shoved her inside with surprising force, the footman struggling to keep up as he opened the door. Once inside, the door was slammed behind her, the sound echoing ominously in the confined space.

Cecelia's hand trembled as she reached for the door, trying it in desperation, but a hand shot out from the shadows, gripping her wrist with chilling strength. She gasped, turning to find the physician seated across from her, a smug smile curling at the corners of his mouth.

"What are you doing here?" she demanded, her voice shaky, but filled with a mix of shock and anger.

The physician's smirk only deepened. "Securing your future, my dear," he said smoothly, his hand slipping into his bag resting on the seat. Cecelia barely had time to react before he lunged forward, something metal glinting in his hand.

With swift, practiced movements, he pulled a bridle-like device over her head—a scold's bridle, its iron frame wrapping tightly around her jaw, pressing against her cheeks and leaving her unable to speak. Cecelia tried to scream, but the bridle kept her mouth firmly shut. Her breaths came in sharp, panicked gasps through her nose as she fought against the restraint.

Before she could struggle further, the physician added a blindfold, tying it tightly over her eyes, plunging her into darkness, and pushed her down on what must have been the seat across from him in the carriage. Now she was trapped—unable to see, unable to speak. The carriage door opened and slammed again, and someone got in beside her. Cecelia's chest heaved with terror as the realization of her situation sank in, and her ears strained to listen.

"Let me make something perfectly clear," hissed Philippa's voice as the carriage began to move. "I know you carry my husband Henry Rowley's child. His only *true* child. The child he threw me in the dungeon for not producing."

Cecelia sat very still. *Perhaps this is it*, she thought. *This is the moment of my death.*

"I also know," Philippa continued, louder now. "You have stolen several artifacts from my personal collection, and spirited them away God knows where. I saw a ring fall from your pocket the other day."

Cecelia's face jolted in shock at the mention of stealing, but settled ruefully as she regretted ever pocketing that fool ring in the greenhouse. She was no thief, but her curiosity had cost her dearly. Hesitantly, she shook her head.

"And after the lies you spread about yourself and my son, now you conspire to burn bridges with my business contacts? I think not."

Philippa huffed angrily. "Pray keep still the rest of the ride, if you value your own life and those you hold dear." Cecelia felt the Baroness move away from her. "Switch places with me, Doctor."

The physician sat down too roughly against her, and his breath was soon hot in her ear. "You should've stayed in your place, little maid." He sounded almost hopeful, which she found a bit odd, even in her current state. "Now, you'll have to learn the hard way."

Cecelia's heart thundered louder than ever in her chest, each beat reverberating through her body as the carriage rattled down the road. Bound and silenced, her mind raced with fear, wondering what fate awaited her and how she could possibly escape this terrifying night-mare.

Chapter Twenty-Seven

Velvet Cage

Cecelia awoke with a start, her heart pounding as she took in her surroundings. She didn't remember falling asleep.

The room was beautiful—too beautiful. Her head throbbed as she rubbed her temples, trying to shake the fog from her mind. The sheets beneath her were softer than anything she had ever felt, far too luxurious for her to be anywhere familiar. She breathed deeply, steeling herself before daring to open her eyes again.

The room remained suspiciously elegant. She sat up slowly, her body aching as she moved, her breath catching in her throat as she scanned her surroundings. The bed was enormous, draped in silks, its posts ornately carved, and the linens felt foreign against her skin. Nervously, she glanced down, half expecting to find herself in a strange gown, but to her relief, she was still wearing her dress from the night before. Her thoughts immediately flashed back to the carriage—Philippa's accusing voice, the physician, the cold iron of the scold's bridle—and a shudder ran through her.

Peeling the covers back, Cecelia swung her legs over the side of the bed. Her feet touched the floor, and she immediately noticed the soft, rich fabric beneath her toes. She stood cautiously, the weight of the situation pressing down on her. A quick glance around the room revealed its beauty but also its eerie sense of entrapment. *No windows,* she realized with a sinking feeling.

Making her way to the door, Cecelia rapped on it, trying to inject her voice with confidence. "Hello! What am I doing in here?"

Silence.

She bit her lip, her chest tightening with frustration and fear. The room was too pristine, too carefully arranged. There was a small bookcase filled with dusty volumes, their spines worn but well-preserved. Two chaise lounges stood near a grand desk, and a tub sat invitingly in the corner, large enough for several people. But none of it offered an answer, and the door, of course, remained locked.

Defeated, she returned to the bed, the plush mattress almost mocking her as she collapsed into it. Exhaustion overtook her, pulling her back into an uneasy sleep.

When she woke again, hours had passed. A tray of food sat by the door, a chamber pot nearby. Cecelia's stomach growled, but unease gnawed at her more fiercely. The food was left for her while she slept. They were watching her—waiting until she was asleep to approach. The thought turned her stomach.

Cecelia knelt near the door, running her fingers along its surface, searching for something—anything—that might explain her imprisonment. Then, she spotted it. A Judas latch, just like the ones in the dungeons at Castle Rowley. Her mind raced with possibilities. She pressed her ear against the wood, listening for any signs of life, but there was nothing. Not even the faintest echo of footsteps.

The day dragged on in agonizing silence, the stillness gnawing at her. Cecelia paced the length of the room, her thoughts swirling. How long could she survive like this? What were they planning?

Then, just as the shadows began to lengthen, she heard it—the faintest sound of footsteps approaching. She froze, her heart racing as she backed away from the door. Moments later, the Judas latch slid open, and a hand appeared—missing a finger—setting down the tray. The latch snapped shut before she could utter a word.

Beneath the tray, nestled between the bowl of soup and a roll of bread, was a small folded note.

Her hands shaking, Cecelia grabbed the note, her eyes scanning the unfamiliar handwriting.

"Keep yourself healthy."

The words sent a chill down her spine. And who had left this message? The physician? Philippa? Someone else entirely?

Cecelia combed through each book in the room, her frustration growing with every failed attempt to understand the words. It felt like trying to catch smoke in her hands—nothing stuck. The more she tried, the more she missed Annabel, whose gentle patience had always made the task of learning bearable. "I need you here, Annabel," she whispered, feeling a pang of loneliness.

Her thoughts wandered to her friends. "I wonder if Annabel and Charlie have started a family by now," she murmured, her voice trembling as she fought back tears. Her thoughts shifted to Kunal, and she let out a bitter laugh. "He's probably married by now." She shook her head, feeling a wave of self-loathing rise up. "Of course, he is. You practically shoved him away, didn't you? Told him right to his face that you didn't love him. If he's smart, and you know he is, he's already back in India with a proper bride." The words tasted bitter on her tongue, and a flare of anger surged through her—at herself, at the world, at the locked door that kept her trapped.

Taking a deep breath, she tried to calm herself. "What would Annabel do?" she asked aloud, a rueful smile tugging at her lips. Annabel would find a way to make the most of it, she decided. "You'd have this whole library memorized by now, wouldn't you?" With a sigh, Cecelia pulled a book from the shelf, hoping for a distraction. The cover was intricate, showing a strange scene—an almost naked woman holding a star, a robed man lecturing another who appeared to be sleeping in front of a donkey. It was absurd enough to make Cecelia chuckle.

"Arte Gymnastica," she mumbled, sounding out the unfamiliar Latin. She flipped through the pages, quickly realizing the text was beyond her, though it gave her some comfort that even Annabel might struggle with this one. The illustrations caught her attention, though—people performing various exercises, their bodies stretching in poses that seemed oddly peaceful. With nothing else to occupy her, Cecelia began mimicking the movements, finding a small sense of relief in the rhythm of the stretches.

Days turned into weeks. She spoke only to her unborn child, the soft kicks in her belly the only connection she had to the outside world.

Her routine had become monotonous: waking up, finding the food tray, sometimes a filled bath, then flipping through the books and talking aloud to stave off the creeping madness of isolation. The lack of human contact gnawed at her, but each time the baby moved, she reminded herself she wasn't truly alone.

"Did my parents leave for America?" she wondered one day, her voice breaking the heavy silence of the room. "Mumma said they bought the tickets. Maybe they've found someone else to take my place. It'd be a relief, wouldn't it? I never wanted to go..." Her thoughts drifted to her family, to memories of her parents that felt both distant and intimate. For a moment, she allowed herself to re-member the happy times, before the reality of her situation came crashing back. "If I ever get out of here..." she whispered, her voice trailing off.

Then, suddenly, a sound broke the stillness—a soft creak, barely audible but unmistakable in the otherwise quiet room. Cecelia froze, her heart pounding in her chest. She scanned the room, eyes darting around, trying to locate the source. Finally, she spotted it—a wooden panel, slightly ajar, a sliver of space between it and the wall.

Holding her breath, Cecelia waited. No other sounds followed. After what felt like an eternity, she moved silently toward the panel and knelt down, cautiously pulling it open further.

Behind it, crouched in the narrow gap, was a small, older woman. Her wiry limbs seemed too frail for the dusty spectacles perched on her nose, and her eyes, wide with surprise, darted toward Cecelia with a mixture of fear and wariness. When their eyes met, the woman hesitated, retreating slightly into the shadows.

"Wait!" Cecelia whispered urgently. "Please, don't go."

The woman paused, her gaze sharp and suspicious. "Who are you?"

"I'm Cecelia Rousseau...of Castle Rowley," she replied quietly, still unsure of her own words. She squinted at the woman, a sudden recognition dawning. "Oh my goodness...you're not..."

"Little Cecelia Rousseau?" The woman gasped, her voice trembling. "You've grown so much!"

Cecelia's breath caught in her throat. "You can't be..."

The woman gave a sad, tired smile. "I'm afraid so." She extended her hand, and Cecelia, stunned, pulled her gently out of the hidden space. As the woman stepped into the light, Cecelia's heart pounded in disbelief.

Cecelia's voice trembled as she whispered, "Mara Wright," her shock palpable. "You're Charlie's mother...we all thought you were dead."

"Well, I'm not," Mara said matter-of-factly, smoothing her skirts as if this was just another ordinary day. "Henry told his brother Geoffrey that Lucas and I were criminals. Instead of killing us, as Henry ordered, Geoffrey's been holding us here, trying to get us to confess our supposed crimes for bloody years."

"Truly?" Cecelia asked, her curiosity piqued. "And what does he say your crimes are?"

"If only I knew," Mara sighed, her tone wry. "Every day I'm asked, and after months of pleading innocence, I started making up crimes. A new one each day." She gave a short, dry laugh. "I even keep a list, so I don't repeat myself. Still haven't guessed what they want to hear."

"You can write," Cecelia said wistfully, admiration mixing with her frustration. "You were a teacher."

Mara nodded, her expression softening. "That I was. You can't write yet?"

"I'm learning," Cecelia admitted, her voice faltering. "Or I was. Before I was...taken." Her hands drifted to her belly, and Mara's eyes followed, widening in horror.

"Oh dear," Mara breathed. "If they haven't told you why you're here, then it's clear—they plan to take your child once it's born."

Cecelia's heart clenched as Mara's words mirrored the darkest fears that had haunted her in the quiet of night. She bit her lip. "I've dreamt about that," she confessed in a trembling voice. "Nightmares, really."

"They'll kill you once the child is born," Mara said bluntly. "You know that, don't you?"

"Why would you say such a thing?" Cecelia snapped, her fear quickly turning to anger.

Mara shrugged nonchalantly, stepping back. "I could always crawl back into the wall if you prefer silence."

"No," Cecelia's voice softened, her desperation palpable. "Please don't leave."

In the months that followed, Mara became Cecelia's daily visitor and unexpected lifeline. Though Cecelia had tried to fit into the hidden passage once, her growing belly made it impossible. Mara, however, continued to slip in and out, each day bringing with her lessons in reading, writing, and even mathematics. The monotony of Cecelia's imprisonment was broken by Mara's patient instruction. Together, they delved into more subjects than she'd realized there were in the world.

For the first time in her life, Cecelia felt a sense of growing empowerment through knowledge, and the time to absorb it. The letters that once seemed like an impenetrable wall slowly became familiar friends. Her reading improved with each passing day, and the words that once slowed her down now flowed with ease. Mara's gentle corrections kept her from falling into frustration, and soon Cecelia was sounding out words and writing simple letters.

She began measuring her growing belly with a piece of string each day, comparing it to a ruler she had found in the desk. "Will you be a girl or a boy?" she wondered aloud to her unborn child, her voice carrying a mix of hope and trepidation. "Shall you have my unruly curls?"

To practice writing and to pour out her bottled emotions, Cecelia started penning letters. She wrote one to Annabel, recounting her days in the beautiful prison that had become her world. She wrote to her parents, though she knew they would likely never see it. And most of all, she wrote to Kunal, letter after letter, her heart spilling onto the pages with words she had never been brave enough to say aloud.

With each letter, Cecelia's thoughts became clearer, and she began to question her decisions. She had driven Kunal away, thinking it was for the best. But now, with Mara's guidance and her newfound sense of self-worth, Cecelia realized the weight of her mistake. She had loved him all along, but her fear had kept her from admitting it. The realization was bittersweet as she penned the letters, each one expressing the truth she had long buried.

Three months passed, and one morning, Cecelia woke earlier than usual. Her mind felt sharper, clearer, as if the fog that had settled over her for months had finally lifted. Rubbing her temples, she noticed the familiar sound of the slot in the door being opened—but this time, something was different.

It stayed open.

Her heart leapt as a familiar voice whispered, "Cecelia?"

She rushed to the door, peeking through the small opening. "Hattie!"

"I heard it was you," Hattie whispered, her eyes wide with disbelief. "I can't believe it."

Cecelia took the tray from her, setting it down carefully. "How much longer do you think I have before the baby comes?" she asked, trying to sound casual despite the tight knot of fear twisting in her chest.

Hattie's eyes flicked to Cecelia's swollen belly. "Not much longer. Weeks, maybe."

"Do you know when they'll let me out?" Cecelia pressed, her voice tinged with desperation.

Hattie shook her head, her face apologetic. "I don't. A few Rowley Manor servants are sick, so they brought me to assist."

"Are my parents still at the castle?" Cecelia asked, her voice barely above a whisper.

"No," Hattie said, her eyes darting nervously. "Philippa told everyone she sent the Rousseau family back to France."

Cecelia's heart dropped. "*France?*" she whispered, her voice catching. "What about Kunal? Has he returned home?"

"He's gone to France as well," Hattie replied, leaning closer.

"*He* has gone to France?" Cecelia repeated, stunned. "Why?"

"To find you," Hattie whispered, her voice hurried. "But he'll come back once he realizes you aren't there."

"France is a big place," Cecelia muttered, feeling a mixture of hope and dread. "Can you send word to him? Let him know I'm here?"

Hattie shook her head, her face pale with fear. "I daren't," she whispered. "I'm risking enough just talking to you."

Before Cecelia could protest, Hattie quickly closed the slot, leaving Cecelia alone once more with her thoughts, her heart heavy with uncertainty.

Chapter Twenty-Eight

REALIZATIONS

The following week was far more tempestuous than Cecelia had anticipated.

First, Mara's visits abruptly stopped. Cecelia had no idea why, and the uncertainty gnawed at her constantly. Had Mara been caught sneaking out to see her? Was she punished? Moved elsewhere? Cecelia found herself whispering to the empty room, "Maybe they've only moved her. Please, let that be all."

Second, Hattie didn't return to the slot the next day. Cecelia had been vigilant, catching the tray delivery and the removal of her chamber pot by the same hand missing a finger, which had become a familiar yet unsettling presence. Her nerves frayed, and she found herself chewing her lip, the taste of iron becoming all too familiar.

When the door finally creaked open one day while she was reading on the bed, Cecelia's heart soared with a flicker of hope—perhaps Mara, perhaps Hattie—but it quickly dissolved into dread as a figure stepped in, masked in the visage of a plague doctor, face obscured by the eerie beak-like mask. In one hand, the doctor held a leather strap; in the other, a scold's bridle. She shuddered. His voice, muffled beneath the mask, was as clinical as it was chilling. "I'm here to examine you."

Cecelia's pulse quickened. "What are those for?" she squeaked, her eyes darting to the bridle and strap.

"In case you're difficult," the doctor replied, his head tilting as if gauging her reaction.

"I won't be difficult," she said quickly. "You're here for the baby?"

The doctor nodded curtly. Cecelia hesitated, then lay down on the bed. The vulnerability of the moment made her skin prickle. "Here?" she asked, her voice barely a whisper.

"That will suffice," the doctor said, dragging a stool closer. The examination was clinical and brief, yet the invasive nature of it left Cecelia feeling exposed and cold. When he was done, the doctor stood and scribbled something into a small notebook.

"Is the baby alright?" Cecelia ventured, her voice soft with apprehension.

"Healthy," the doctor confirmed. "It's positioned well—should be no complications, barring any unforeseen events. You should deliver in about a month."

Cecelia blinked, confused. "A month? Aren't you taking me out of here?" She sat up, her chest tight with hope. "You're not leaving me here?"

The doctor paused, visibly startled even through the mask. "You're to stay," he said shortly, his fingers twitching toward the bottle and handkerchief again, as if reminding her of their purpose. "I'm only here to report to the Baroness."

"So she does plan to take my baby," Cecelia whispered, her stomach knotting. "How can you allow that? How can you stand by and let it happen?"

The doctor scowled beneath his mask, gave three sharp raps on the door, and swiftly exited without answering her. When the door locked behind him, Cecelia's heart sank.

The days blurred together in the following week. No one visited. No Mara, no Hattie. She heard the occasional footsteps beyond her door but was met only with silence. The isolation gnawed at her, each day stretching into an eternity. She strained her ears for any sound, any hint of human connection. When a meal tray clattered through the slot one day, she swore she heard Hattie's voice somewhere distant in the hall, but the echo quickly faded, leaving her with a pang of loneliness that settled deep in her bones.

Books became her only solace. She devoured every one in the room, reading with a voracity she hadn't known she possessed. Mara's patient teaching had made all the difference; now, even though the act of reading still brought moments of frustration, Cecelia found that once the words clicked, they offered an escape—albeit a brief one—from the velvet-lined prison that surrounded her.

But as the weeks dragged on, the collection of books dwindled. One day, her eyes drifted upward, toward the high shelf built into the wall where the ceiling met the stone. There were seven dusty, forgotten volumes perched up there, just out of reach. Determination sparked in her, a flash of rebellious energy.

She rummaged through the room, grabbing what she could—a mop, a broom, a swath of fabric—fashioning them into a makeshift sling. Her pulse quickened, not with fear but with purpose, as she wielded the mop and broom to prod the book that stuck out furthest. Slowly, it edged toward the brink.

With a triumphant grin, Cecelia maneuvered the book into the fabric sling, catching it just before it tumbled to the floor. As she lowered the book onto a nearby pillow, her heart raced—not just from the effort, but from the sheer joy of having accomplished something.

A noise behind her made her spin around, her heart leaping into her throat. But it was only Mara, emerging from the hidden panel. Cecelia smiled, her spirits lifting as she proudly showed off her prize.

"Did you see that?" she exclaimed, still catching her breath.

Mara shook her head, smiling despite herself. "You've gone mad. What are you doing? Have you finally lost it in here?"

Cecelia, grinning, shrugged playfully. "Maybe. But I got the book, didn't I?"

Mara's laughter softened as she pulled Cecelia into a careful embrace, mindful of the growing child between them. "You've always been clever, child," she said warmly. "Madness or not, you always find a way."

"I've read every book in the lower shelf," Cecelia sighed, gesturing to the now-familiar rows of spines. "I wanted more to read, and those on the upper shelf are the only ones I haven't gotten to yet."

Mara blinked in surprise as she glanced at the bookcase. "You've read all of these?" She crouched to inspect the titles. "There must be nearly thirty here."

Cecelia nodded with a shy smile. "There's nothing else to do but exercise." She picked up a book from the desk and waved it playfully. "And look! This one's in Latin, but it has pictures about gymnastics!"

"Look at you," Mara smiled fondly. "I'm so proud of how far your reading has come."

"That's all thanks to you," Cecelia said softly, handing her a blanket. "Stay for a while, won't you? I was beginning to think something had happened to you."

Mara's face clouded for a moment. "I had a bit of trouble. Got caught unwashed after coming through the tunnel, and the physician came in for a health inspection."

"Was he wearing a plague hood?" Cecelia asked with a grimace.

Mara nodded, her expression darkening. "Same one, I'd guess."

"Yes," Cecelia muttered. The memory made her stomach turn.

"The good news is," Mara continued, her voice brightening, "after that little incident, they put Lucas in the same room with me. He's alive, Cecelia—he's thin as a reed, but alive."

"Oh, Mara!" Cecelia threw her arms around her, tears springing to her eyes. "Thank goodness for that. They put you in together?"

Mara nodded, her eyes shining. "He's been a model prisoner, you know. Geoffrey keeps him locked up in his wing, using him as a quiet companion. Lucas reads him poetry whenever Geoffrey gets lonely." She snorted with derision. "He offered me the same arrangement when I arrived, but I changed the poetry into... well, let's say it wasn't to his taste. So he's left me alone." Mara's face grew serious. "Lucas thinks we should kill him with kindness, make him see us as harmless. But I fear my defiance is a death sentence."

Cecelia shivered. "And you think you'll be able to... escape?"

"Perhaps," Mara sighed, her voice filled with uncertainty. "But tell me, what did the physician say about your baby?"

Cecelia's hands instinctively moved to her belly. "He says the baby's healthy. Due in a month. It's positioned well, thank God. But I'm terrified of doing anything too strenuous—what if I make it turn the wrong way?"

Mara placed a reassuring hand on Cecelia's arm. "You'll do just fine, sweetheart. You're stronger than you know."

Tears pricked Cecelia's eyes again, but this time, she let them fall. "You don't know that," she whispered. "They'll take my child and then... then they'll kill me. That's what you said."

Mara took a deep breath, her face drawn with sorrow. "Let's not think of that now. What's this book you've pulled down?"

Cecelia sniffed, brushing away her tears, and held up the book she had retrieved from the high shelf. A laugh bubbled up in her chest. "The Compleat History of Druggs."

"For heaven's sake!" Mara chuckled. "What do you plan to do with that?"

Cecelia shrugged, flipping it open. "It's fascinating—everything is, really. Maybe I'll find something to dull the pain of childbirth."

"With what? The air?" Mara raised an eyebrow, glancing around the sparse room.

"I suppose I'll find out," Cecelia muttered, her lips quirking into a faint smile.

Mara shook her head, laughing softly. "Read all you like, dear. My Charlie was just like you. He loved learning about plants and herbs, anything that could heal—or harm. Smart boy, my Charlie."

Cecelia looked up, her expression softening. "You always said you didn't want to talk about Charlie. But of course, he's a very smart man."

Mara's eyes flickered with desperation. "Do you think I'll ever see him again? Sometimes I wonder if I'm mad for thinking they'll let us see him before... before they kill us." Her voice faltered, her hands trembling as she spoke.

Cecelia reached out, her voice steady. "You're not mad. We have to plan for every possibility. We'll need every idea, every opportunity. So when something changes, we'll be ready."

Mara nodded, though a trace of doubt lingered in her eyes. Cecelia's words, though softly spoken, seemed to offer a fragile sliver of hope in the uncertain darkness of their confinement.

"Right then." Mara placed her hands on Cecelia's back. "You're all knots, love. That's no good for a pregnant woman. Let me help loosen you up."

"That would be lovely." Cecelia's thoughts drifted to Kunal, the last person who had done this for her. The memory of his touch brought a sudden surge of emotion, and she swallowed down a sob as she lay on her side, the weight of the book in her hands. Mara sat beside her, working her hands gently along her back. "I wonder if I'll ever see him again."

Mara's voice held a knowing smile. "Your young man, the artist with the woodcarving family and their riddles? The one you said you didn't deserve?"

"That's the one," Cecelia murmured. "Being trapped here makes everything seem clearer. I was a fool to let him think I didn't believe in us. I was too afraid, too caught up in what people might say, or how different we are. I folded the moment he finally stood up for me—against his own family."

Mara's hands paused for a moment. "And if you had the choice again?" she asked gently.

"I'd tell him I love him," Cecelia whispered, her voice thick with regret. "I'd try. Even if it didn't work out, at least I wouldn't be left with this hollow feeling, like a part of me's been ripped apart. It's like being torn to shreds by a wild animal."

Mara rose to her feet, her expression thoughtful. "Don't lose hope. My dear Lucas, bless him, believes Geoffrey will protect us, that he'll stand up to Philippa. Geoffrey may have a softer heart, but he's not exactly one to take a stand."

Cecelia's thoughts shifted. "Hattie's still around," she remembered, relaying their conversation. "Perhaps we could find a way to involve her in a plan—something that won't put her at risk."

Mara nodded slowly. "Let's think on it."

They sat in silence for a while, the weight of their thoughts hanging between them like the quiet before a storm. Cecelia absently turned the pages of the book in her lap.

Mara looked over with curiosity. "Are you actually reading that?"

"I like to skim it first," Cecelia admitted. "Get a sense of what's coming, what to expect. I like that about books—you know it's all there, waiting to be discovered." She smiled, glancing back at Mara. "Then I go back and read it properly. Am I mad, or are books supposed to feel like old friends?"

Mara's smile softened, a touch of warmth in her eyes. "No, love. You've got it just right."

Cecelia continued reading through the book in bits and pieces, her eyes suddenly catching on a phrase: the smell of bitter almonds. Her pulse quickened as memories of the Castle Rowley kitchen flooded back. The porridge. It had never smelled like that before. A pang of homesick longing hit her, but alongside it came suspicion. Frederick had always hated almonds, and yet, that smell had clung to the dish. She had made the porridge herself, using the usual ingredients. But she'd left the kitchen to fetch towels, leaving the physician alone.

Her hands trembled as she flipped back through the pages, her eyes widening as she read more closely. A chill crept up her spine. "Mara..." Cecelia's voice was barely a whisper, fear lacing every word.

"Hmmm?" Mara, still massaging her back, didn't look up. "What is it?"

"It says here…" Cecelia swallowed, her mouth dry. She reached for a prune from her breakfast tray and nibbled it nervously. "It says that surgeons often mix arsenic with cyanide, and the smell is of bitter almonds."

Mara paused, her brow furrowing. "I see… and what of it?"

Cecelia sat up straight, the realization dawning on her in a rush of horror. "Small amounts of the mixture kill slowly, over time. And it causes the exact symptoms that Frederick's been suffering." Her voice grew urgent. "Mara, I think the Rowley physician has been poisoning Frederick!"

Mara's hands froze mid-motion. "What?"

Cecelia explained about the bitter almond scent in the porridge, how it had stood out to her only now. And the days Frederick had been healthy and the days he had been sick fell into place in her head. "Frederick's condition improves when he leaves Castle Rowley," she added, rubbing her hands together as she pieced it all together. "But every time he returns, after a few days of the physician's care, he falls ill again."

Mara shuddered. "If you're right, this is beyond sinister. But what can we do about it?"

Cecelia hesitated, then lowered her voice, glancing at Mara cautiously. "You do know that Frederick is... Lucas's son, not Henry's, don't you?"

Mara's expression didn't change. She scowled. "Of course I know. Lucas told me when Philippa came to him, asking for a child. We were too frightened to refuse. And not long after we made plans to leave Castle Rowley, they locked us away here."

Cecelia let out a relieved breath. "Frederick knows too. He found letters between Philippa and Lucas and shared them with Charlie. Philippa knows Charlie has the letters."

Mara's face turned pale. "Why didn't you tell me this sooner?"

"You said you didn't want to talk about Charlie," Cecelia reminded her gently.

"But..." Mara sank into the chair, her face crumpling with worry. "If Philippa knows Charlie has that knowledge, she'll kill him if she gets the chance."

Cecelia winced, recalling the fall down the stairs. "She already tried. I'm sorry, I should have told you earlier."

Mara's expression darkened with rage, her hands clenched tightly in her lap. "Tell me everything now."

Cecelia nodded, sitting up straighter. "I have an idea," she said, grabbing the heel of bread off her tray and placing it aside. She flipped the tray over, her fingers tracing its surface. "If Hattie is in the kitchens, there's a chance she'll notice something if we send a message."

Mara leaned in, curious. "What kind of message?"

Cecelia frowned, her mind working quickly. "We need symbols. Something to represent the physician, the poison, and Frederick."

"A staff of Asclepius," Mara suggested. "For the physician."

Cecelia raised an eyebrow. "That's the staff with the snake, isn't it?"

Mara smiled. "Yes. Where did you learn that?"

"A translation of Pharmacopoeia Londinensis," Cecelia replied. "Published by the Royal College of Physicians in 1618." She paused, thinking. "We could use a skull and crossbones for the poison."

"Well done," Mara said approvingly. "And for Frederick... perhaps the Rowley crest."

"The falcon," Cecelia mused. "Maybe with the letter F, to make sure it's clear we mean Frederick."

Mara's eyes widened. "Henry's still alive?"

Groaning, Cecelia nodded. "Unfortunately."

She moved to the desk, rummaging for the bent quill pens she'd found earlier. Grimacing, she began carefully etching the symbols into the back of the tray, her concentration sharp as she worked. Mara watched in silence as Cecelia carved each symbol with determination.

As Cecelia worked, she glanced up at Mara. "Let me tell you every-thing."

Chapter Twenty-Nine

HOPE

After they took the tray Cecelia had painstakingly etched, she waited anxiously. The next day, a different tray was delivered—no sign of the message. Undeterred, she etched the new one and sent it back. This continued for five trays, each sent off with the same cautious hope, until at last, she heard Hattie's familiar whisper through the slot.

"Cecelia!"

Cecelia scrambled to the door as quickly as her growing belly allowed, relief flooding her. "Hattie! Thank God you're all right!" she whispered back, pressing her ear to the door. "Did you see the trays?"

"Yes, I saw the bloody trays," Hattie hissed, her tone sharp with urgency. "I had to trip your food runner Leon just to get in here—he twisted his ankle. You can't mean what you're saying, Cecelia... that the physician's been poisoning Frederick? Is that what that bloody scrawl means?"

"That's exactly what it means," Cecelia replied, her heart racing. "You have to tell Frederick."

Hattie let out a short laugh. "Tell Frederick? No one can get near him now. He's either in the infirmary or the chapel. I thought you'd want me to tell Kunal."

"Kunal?" Cecelia gasped, her heart skipping. "I thought he was in France."

"Well, he's back," Hattie said casually. "He came with Captain Harrington. They've been raising quite a fuss, searching for you."

Cecelia's heart swelled with warmth. "Can you tell him I'm here?"

Hattie's voice was quick to shut that down. "I can't. He'd storm in, and I'd lose my position faster than you could blink. But... I'll tell him about the poisoning. And Philippa."

"Yes, tell her! Please, Hattie," Cecelia whispered, fighting back tears of gratitude.

With a soft click, Hattie closed the slot. Cecelia let out a shuddering breath, sinking to the floor. The cold stone beneath her was grounding, but it couldn't ease the swirling anxiety within. She hugged her belly, feeling the gentle movements of the baby. "I hope this works," she whispered, her voice shaky. Slowly, she forced herself to eat what was on the tray, before stretching her aching limbs and climbing back into bed.

When Cecelia woke the next morning, something felt different. She had no windows, but there was an unsettling stillness in the room, as if the very air had changed. Disoriented, she lit the candles that were delivered with her weekly meal tray and sat up slowly, her senses on high alert.

The door to her room creaked open, and a shadowed figure slipped inside, closing it quietly behind them. Cecelia's hand instinctively went to her stomach, her grip tightening in fear. Was she about to be killed? Or rescued?

Then she heard the voice.

"Cecelia?"

"Kunal?" she whispered, her voice trembling with disbelief. "It cannot be you... Please, speak again."

"I'm here, Cecelia," he replied, his voice closer now. In the darkness, she felt the fabric of his sleeve brush against her. His hand found hers, and she let out a shuddering breath, her heart thundering.

Their lips met in the dark, and for a moment, the world fell away. The tension, the fear—it all dissolved as Cecelia melted into the warmth of his embrace. He smelled of fresh linen and sawdust, the familiar scent overwhelming her with memories of safety and home. His beard had grown thicker, the roughness of it grazing her skin as he kissed her neck and shoulders, cradling her head with tenderness.

Her smile grew impossibly wide as the baby kicked, making her squeak with surprise. They pulled back, both breathless, the moment filled with a quiet joy. "Have you come to take me from this place?" Cecelia asked, her voice cracking. "I swear I stole nothing. I found a dirty old ring in the greenhouse, but I stole no artifacts from the Baroness..."

"We know," Kunal whispered. "The Baroness found the physician who poisoned Frederick, Doctor Fenton, trying to send the artifacts to a family member. She also found plenty of proof of the poisoning. Thank God you realized."

"Thank God and thank *you*, my love," she cried. "I feared I'd have to give birth here, and then they'd... kill me."

"Perish the thought, my love, my heart, Cecelia..." Kunal murmured, pulling her into a tighter embrace. Cecelia buried her face in his shoulder, her body shaking with quiet sobs. "You've been in this room all this time?" His voice was filled with disbelief. "You were never in France? The Baroness told me she sent your entire family away there."

"I've been here the whole time," she confessed, pulling away slightly to look at him in the dim light. "Kunal, I'm so sorry... for not standing up for us, for not fighting. I was a fool."

Kunal kissed her hand tenderly, his fingers warm against her skin. "You're forgiven, Cecelia. We've both had to learn how to fight our battles. But we must leave now," he whispered urgently. "Hattie told

Philippa about the physician's treachery. He's been locked in the dungeon, and Philippa is questioning him as we speak."

Cecelia nodded, her heart racing. "Then we must hurry. How did you come to find me?" Cecelia hurriedly lac up her shoes. The cold of the stone floor sent a shiver up her spine, a stark reminder of how long she had been trapped in that room. "Did Hattie tell you?"

"Not at first," Kunal admitted, his voice low as they moved in the shadows. "But she came to the castle. She was hesitant, but Annabel and Lise pressed her, and eventually, Hattie told us about the Baroness and Geoffrey keeping you here. She showed us the room after dark."

"Lise is back?" Cecelia frowned in surprise, fastening her cloak. "I thought she left for good."

"She returned as soon as she heard you'd gone missing," Kunal explained. "So did Agatha. Annabel and Charlie have been frantic—everyone's been searching for you, Cecelia."

Tears welled in her eyes, her heart tightening with a mixture of disbelief and gratitude. She gripped Kunal's hands, feeling the warmth of his skin ground her. "I... I'm so glad you're here."

"Frederick is with me too," Kunal continued, his voice steady. "Geoffrey's agreed to let you leave with us, but he wants it done quietly. No fuss, no talk amongst the staff." He shook his head. "I would have agreed to almost anything to get you back."

Cecelia, pulling her cloak tightly around her shoulders, was stuffing a few belongings into a satchel when she froze, a realization settling over her. "We can't leave without Mara and Lucas."

"Mara and Lucas Wright? Charlie's parents?" Kunal's voice was filled with disbelief. "Cecelia, my love... They've been dead for years."

"They're here," Cecelia insisted, her voice urgent. "Mara found a hidden panel in my room. She's been visiting me through it for months, teaching me to read. She said Lucas had been moved in with her not long ago. I would have lost my mind without her." Her voice cracked slightly. "We can't leave them behind."

A long silence followed, the weight of her words lingering between them. Kunal hesitated, then his voice softened. "And you're certain? You weren't imagining it, after being kept alone for so long?"

"I know what I saw, Kunal," Cecelia said, her tone firm. "Mara is alive."

Kunal cleared his throat, nodding. "We'll talk to Geoffrey." He took her arm, guiding her through the door. "But first, let's get you out of this room."

As they stepped out into the corridor, the dim light of torches flickered off the cold stone walls, casting long shadows that danced eerily along the passage. Cecelia blinked, her eyes adjusting to the faint glow after so long in the darkness. Kunal's hand tightened around hers, his steady presence anchoring her as they walked, the distant hum of the manor muted in the quiet night.

They made their way to the great hall, where Geoffrey sat hunched over a long wooden table. The room was bathed in a muted glow, the fire from the hearth casting an amber light across the room. Geoffrey's shoulders were slumped, his face pale and haggard, as though the weight of his actions had finally begun to crush him.

Cecelia's heart pounded quicker in her chest as they approached.

"Lord Geoffrey." Cecelia's voice rang out, surprising even herself. The hall fell silent as Geoffrey looked up, startled, his weary eyes meeting hers. Kunal turned to Cecelia in surprise but didn't interrupt, sensing the weight of her words. She stepped forward, her hands resting protectively over her swollen belly, her gaze fierce, her curls bouncing with every step. Geoffrey seemed to shrink under the intensity of her stare. "I am Cecelia Rousseau, formerly of Lyon and Castle Rowley. Your family has destroyed mine." Her voice was steady, carrying the anger of years, and Geoffrey, visibly shaken, sank deeper into his chair.

"If you do not release Mara and Lucas Rowley," she continued, fire in her eyes, "then when I die, I will return as a ghost and *haunt you for the rest of your miserable days.*"

"Miss Rousseau," Geoffrey's voice trembled, his fingers nervously twisting the handkerchief in his lap. "I have already destroyed my own family. I have no power here. Surely, you can see that?"

Cecelia remained silent, her arms crossed over her belly, staring him down as the tension in the room thickened.

"After my brother Henry returned from his... encounter with your mother," Geoffrey began, his voice shaking. Kunal gasped audibly at the revelation, his wide eyes darting to Cecelia, and Geoffrey seemed to realize Kunal had been left in the dark. "He doesn't know, does he?"

"If I had to tell him every sordid thing your family has done, we'd be here for centuries," Cecelia retorted coldly. "Now tell me—how did you ruin your family?"

Geoffrey's hands shook as he pulled out his handkerchief, dabbing his brow. "After Henry came back, we played polo one morning. I... I hit him with my mallet." His voice faltered, and he gestured awkwardly to the area below his belt. "I, uh, injured him—badly. He could never father children after that. And so the Baroness—Philippa—sought children elsewhere. Henry's... inability to father children made him cruel. He took it out on everyone."

"Elsewhere?" Cecelia raised an eyebrow, her voice tinged with irony. "Odd choice of words."

Geoffrey's face paled. "What are you implying?"

"I'm saying I know Lucas is Frederick's father," Cecelia said, and both Frederick and Lucas flinched while Mara sighed. "But you sired the twins. The resemblance is plain, and the gossips has whispered about it for years."

Geoffrey's face drained of all color. "That can't be."

"Oh, it can," Cecelia shot back. "The castle inhabitants all know. Did the Baroness never tell you when she came to 'rest' at the manor? Frederick thought she came here to tell you everything."

"No," Geoffrey muttered, rubbing his temples. "She spent her time speaking to Lucas through the door. I was kept away, not allowed to listen." His face crumpled in realization. "I thought she brought them here for punishment. But I may have been just a pawn in her schemes."

"Well," Cecelia let out a low whistle, sharing an incredulous look with Kunal. "Perhaps you can start making amends by releasing Lucas and Mara." She straightened, her voice steady but filled with determination. "Then you could ride with us to Castle Rowley, stand up to Philippa, and tell her they don't deserve to be punished for your family's misdeeds."

Geoffrey seemed to wither under the weight of her words, and a sigh escaped him. "I've already agreed to release Mara and Lucas," he muttered. "Frederick is with them now, but I doubt he'll ever forgive me for keeping them imprisoned."

"They were locked up in your house," Kunal said pointedly. "That makes it hard not to blame you."

"Henry forced me," Geoffrey protested, his voice rising. "He said they had committed unspeakable crimes, and if I released them, he'd see me hanged for crimes I hadn't committed. He's always done that—our parents believed everything he said, every lie he told."

"We're turning Henry in," Frederick's voice cut through the room like ice. He stepped into the hall, Lucas and Mara beside him, his expression hard as he regarded his uncle. "This ends now, Geoffrey. We're going to the castle, and we're leaving tonight."

CHAPTER THIRTY

FAMILY

Frederick and Geoffrey were to ride in the carriage, while Lucas and Mara took their place in the back of the cart with Kunal. Frederick's word was final, and to Cecelia's surprise, there were no objections.

"When we return to the castle," Frederick announced, standing tall before the group outside in the brisk air, "Geoffrey and I will speak to Mother. She'll have no choice but to hand Henry over to the constable, and as for the physician, we'll turn him in for poisoning me. Then, I'll resume my role as Baron, and all of this nonsense will finally be put to rest."

Though no one spoke against the plan, Cecelia exchanged a wary glance with Kunal, her brow furrowed. Without saying a word, she climbed into the front of the cart, motioning for Lucas and Mara to join her in the back.

Kunal mounted the cart beside Cecelia and took the reins. "Ready?" he asked quietly, his eyes scanning the group as though waiting for someone to raise a concern.

Cecelia nodded, her mind still spinning, and as the cart began to roll forward, the sound of Mara humming a soft, lilting tune filled the air. It was an oddly cheerful melody, one that seemed out of place in the current moment. Cecelia's ears pricked up, and she turned, curiosity dancing across her face.

"Mara," Cecelia called over her shoulder, "what is that tune?"

Mara paused, slightly surprised. "What tune?"

"The one you're humming," Cecelia insisted, her voice sharp with impatience. "Where's it from?"

"Oh, that?" Mara hummed a few notes, thinking. "I've heard it in the castle for months now. It's rather lovely, don't you think? I used to think it was you, Cecelia."

A wave of realization struck Cecelia like a sudden gust of wind. "Stop the cart!" she shouted, her voice urgent.

Kunal, startled but quick to act, pulled the reins tight, halting the horse. Cecelia jumped from the cart and began shouting after the carriage that was now steadily moving ahead, her voice barely reaching its occupants. But before she could panic, a sharp whistle pierced the air. She turned, eyes wide, to see Kunal blowing into a wooden whistle hanging around his neck. The carriage came to an abrupt stop.

Kunal shrugged at Cecelia's look of surprise. "Always good to have a whistle."

Frederick emerged from the halted carriage, visibly confused. "What is it?" he asked, his voice laced with impatience.

Cecelia pointed back toward the distant house. "My parents—they're still in there. That's a tune my mum always sang me, ever since I was a child."

"Geoffrey!" Frederick's voice boomed, and his uncle hurried out of the carriage, his face drained of color. "Are Bridgette and James Rousseau in your house?"

Geoffrey grimaced, glancing briefly at Cecelia before muttering, "I suppose they are."

"For God's sake," Frederick growled, his temper rising. "Fetch them immediately. And while you're at it," he added, his voice brimming with cold fury, "remember this: our family needs to learn to settle disputes without locking people away."

As Geoffrey hurried off, Cecelia called after him, "And bring the jade table from your foyer!"

Geoffrey's head whipped around, his eyes wide in surprise, but he nodded.

Kunal turned to Cecelia, his voice low with alarm. "What?"

"I saw it in there," Cecelia explained, her voice tight with urgency. "I think Henry stole your family's table and gave it to Geoffrey to hide."

Kunal's brow furrowed, confusion clouding his face. "To what end? Why go to such lengths for a table?"

Cecelia's voice dropped to a murmur as she pieced the puzzle together. "Henry likely did it to punish your family—for helping Charlie in court. Henry is always seeking retribution."

Before Kunal could respond, Geoffrey returned with Cecelia's parents and a servant pulling the jade-inlaid table on a hand cart. As soon as Bridgette saw her, she rushed forward and wrapped Cecelia in an embrace that was far gentler than Cecelia had ever known from her. It took Cecelia by surprise—her mother was not one for tender displays—and for a moment, she let herself melt into it.

"Thank you, sweetheart," her mother whispered, her voice thick with emotion. "Thank you so much."

Meanwhile, Kunal was carefully inspecting the jade table, his expression sharp and focused. "This is ours, all right," he said grimly. "Bloody thief, that Henry." Without hesitation, he heaved the table onto the cart.

Frederick gave a tight-lipped smile, though his eyes remained watchful. "Excellent. Now, let's move forward. The Rousseaus will go with Kunal, and Lucas and Mara can ride with us."

Mara stiffened, her eyes narrowing. "You want us to ride in the same carriage with the man who imprisoned us?" she demanded, her voice incredulous. "Have you lost your mind?"

Frederick took a deep breath, steadying himself. "I beg you, my lady, please join us in the carriage. It's the swiftest way to the castle, and I promise, no harm will come to you. You'll be reunited with your son and his fiancée soon enough."

"Fiancée?" Lucas gasped from the back of the cart. "Charlie is wed?"

"I'll explain everything on the way," Frederick replied, and with a reluctant sigh, Mara climbed into the carriage beside Lucas. Cecelia, her parents, and Kunal took their places in the cart, with Cecelia in the front beside Kunal and her parents settled in the back. As Kunal took the reins and set the horse into motion, the group resumed their journey toward the castle.

"You must be nearing the end of your time, aren't you?" Bridgette, remarked, her gaze fixed on her daughter's swollen belly. "Did they send a doctor to see you while you were imprisoned?"

"Yes," Cecelia nodded, recalling the cold examination in her prison room. "He said I have a few weeks left. Thanks to Kunal..." She glanced at him shyly, her voice softening. "I won't have to give birth in that horrible, windowless room. I even learned to read while I was locked up. Mara found a way into my room and taught me. I've read thirty books."

"Thirty?" James gasped, exchanging a look with Bridgette. "I thought you said she'd never manage it."

"I thought she wouldn't," Bridgette admitted, her cheeks reddening. "That's what the tutor said. The other children made fun of her, and I thought it best for her to stick to things she could do."

Cecelia took a deep breath, her expression softening as she turned toward her mother. "You were wrong, but I forgive you."

With a small smile, she took Kunal's hand, then looked back at her parents. "I'm not going to America."

Kunal coughed awkwardly. "About that," he said, casting a sidelong glance at Cecelia. "I went to France with Captain Harrington."

Cecelia raised an eyebrow, intrigued. "I heard something about that."

"I wasn't on a wild goose chase," Kunal explained. "Philippa told everyone you and your family had been sent to France, and we believed her. But I wasn't just looking for you... Captain Harrington went with me because I told him everything—about you, about us. I laid it all on the line."

"What happened?" Cecelia asked, sensing there was more to the story.

Kunal smiled. "Captain Harrington had been in love with a woman for years but never told her. After hearing me out, he decided to act on his feelings. He confessed his love to her, and they married. When he returned, he was a changed man, ready to repay the 'debt of love,' as he put it."

Cecelia smiled warmly but sighed. "I'm sorry you didn't find me in France, that you made the trip for nothing."

"On the contrary," Kunal said, shaking his head. "The trip was far from a waste. While I was there, I discovered something. Your father's land, the one you lost in that bad investment? The agreement was found to be fraudulent, and the property was seized. The others involved were given a chance to buy back their land for a fraction of the original cost."

James looked stricken. "I had no idea... I was never told."

Kunal nodded. "It seems Baron Henry Rowley intercepted the letters that should have reached you."

James balled his hands into fists. "That swindler."

Kunal cleared his throat. "I realize this might be imposing, but... I bought the land back for you."

There was a stunned silence in the cart. Kunal rushed to explain, "I did it with you in mind—your family. The deed is in your name, not mine. You can move back whenever you like. Your home is still standing, your farm untouched."

Cecelia's father was speechless for a moment before he turned to his daughter with a broad grin. "Cecelia, I could kiss your fiancé, right at this moment!"

Kunal laughed, the tension breaking with the moment. Cecelia blinked in surprise, her cheeks flushing. "Fiancé?" she echoed. "We're not engaged."

James's face fell in embarrassment. "I'm sorry—I didn't realize you hadn't..."

Kunal smiled gently and looked at Cecelia, his eyes soft. "I've already asked your father for your hand. And your mother, too."

Cecelia's heart swelled, a warmth spreading through her chest as she held Kunal's gaze. "Did you really ask them?" she whispered, her voice almost childlike in its vulnerability. "Even after I was so awful?"

"You weren't awful," Kunal said gently, his eyes searching hers. "You were protecting yourself. It wasn't the life you imagined, and you were right to be realistic." He paused, as if gathering his courage. "I was ready to run back home... but then something changed." He looked over at Bridgette, whose eyes were shiny with unshed tears. "Just before your parents disappeared, your mother showed me your sketch pad."

Cecelia's jaw dropped. "You... what?" She turned to her mother, disbelief mingled with a curious tenderness. "Why would you do that?"

Bridgette's expression softened, her voice shaky yet firm. "You'd drawn so many pictures of him, Cecelia. I thought he must know where you were... or at least why you left so suddenly." She hesitated, then added with a tender smile, "It was clear from those drawings that you love him deeply, darling. I wanted him to see it, to understand how much he meant to you."

Cecelia's cheeks flushed, caught between embarrassment and the sweetness of the moment. She reached for Kunal's hand, holding it tightly. "Well... I suppose that's true enough," she admitted softly. She felt a deep sense of release in admitting it aloud—not just to Kunal, but to her parents as well. For the first time, she felt free of the burden of trying to seem indifferent.

James cleared his throat, his voice unusually gentle. "We never really wanted to go to America, you know." He looked at Bridgette, who nodded in agreement, her face a mix of regret and relief. "We thought we had to, that it was our only chance at a fresh start, at survival. But leaving you behind... it never felt right."

"It felt like a betrayal," Bridgette confessed, her voice breaking. "But we were scared. The world seemed to be collapsing around us, and America felt like a desperate way out. We just thought... maybe it would be a new beginning."

Cecelia's eyes filled with tears, the weight of all that had been left unsaid finally lifting. "I understand now," she said, her voice choked with emotion. "And I don't blame you."

Her father's face softened, his eyes brimming with unspoken love. "We were wrong," he said, reaching out to touch her hand. "We should have fought harder to stay, to keep our family together."

Kunal's voice, low and sincere, filled the quiet space. "You have a home here," he promised. "A place where you're wanted, where you belong. And that's all that matters."

Bridgette's hand joined her husband's, forming a circle of warmth around Cecelia's. "We're a family, Cecelia," she said, her voice thick with emotion. "We may have lost our way, but we've found it again. And we'll face whatever comes next together."

Tears flowed freely down Cecelia's cheeks as she looked at each of them in turn—her parents, Kunal. For the first time in a long while, she felt truly anchored. "I love you all," she whispered, the words filled with a fierce, untamed joy.

"We love you too," James replied, his voice strong and clear.

Kunal's hand squeezed hers gently, his gaze steady and filled with unspoken promises. "And I love you, Cecelia Rousseau," he said softly, his voice steady. "More than I could ever put into words."

Cecelia's smile widened, radiant even through the tears. "Then let's go home," she said simply, feeling the fullness of the moment, the shared promise of a new beginning—for all of them.

CHAPTER THIRTY-ONE

RECKONING

When they arrived at Castle Rowley, the imposing structure loomed under a brooding sky, its stone walls etched with centuries of damp Yorkshire weather. A wind swept across the courtyard, rustling leaves and setting an ominous tone, as if the very land sensed the tension to come.

At the center of this foreboding scene was Philippa Rowley, astride an enormous, battle-scarred stallion. The beast—Hercules—was famous for his stubbornness and strength, a fitting mount for the resolute Baroness. Her posture was rigid, and the cold, calculating gaze she leveled at the arrivals was as piercing as the chilly air.

"She's brought out her favorite horse," Cecelia murmured to Kunal, her breath visible in the morning chill. "She's trying to appear unshakeable." Her voice held an edge of fear. "What could she be planning?"

"Perhaps she simply felt like riding," James offered, though his eyes betrayed his unease. He tightened his grip on Bridgette's hand as the cart slowed to a halt.

Frederick and Geoffrey's carriage came to a creaking stop beside them. Frederick descended first, his face set with a mixture of determination and weariness. When Geoffrey followed, he appeared a ghost of his former self, his head bowed, a broken man.

The true spectacle was Mara and Lucas's emergence. Mara stepped down slowly, her eyes locking defiantly with Philippa's. The Baroness's expression wavered, her surprise so palpable that for a fleeting moment, she looked almost vulnerable. But that softness was quickly replaced by the hard mask of control she wore like armor.

Kunal leapt from the cart, securing their horse before returning to help Cecelia down. Her legs felt shaky beneath her as she took in the scene. "Baroness Rowley," Kunal announced clearly, "may I present the Rousseau family of Lyon, landowners once more—free from your service and obligations."

Philippa's eyes flicked to James. "Leaving us, are you?" she asked archly, her voice tinged with bitter sarcasm. "No hope of retaining your loyalty?"

"We have our own land again," Bridgette answered, her tone steely. "We're no longer bound to your service, and we'll be returning to France as soon as possible."

"Is that so?" Philippa's expression shifted, shadows of uncertainty playing across her face. Her gaze lingered on Cecelia, a silent reckoning passing between them. "And I understand now that Cecelia is innocent of the accusations I made," she said flatly, almost reluctant in her admission. "The physician confessed—after I... persuaded him—to both poisoning my son and fabricating evidence of theft."

"Mother," Frederick interjected sharply. "I told you not to imprison anyone else."

Philippa turned to her son, her voice suddenly raw. "But you never forbade torture. And after months of poisoning you, am I not owed a measure of justice?" Her tone teetered between defiance and desperation.

Frederick's expression hardened. "We will discuss that later," he said, his voice tight. "Right now, we're turning Henry over to the constable."

At this, Philippa's face blanched. "Oh, Frederick." Her voice cracked as tears welled up. She clutched the reins, her knuckles white. "Don't you see? Once we do this, the façade of normalcy is shattered. The entire region will know of our shame, that Henry Rowley—supposedly the father of three children—has committed such horrors. Our name will be ruined." Her lower lip trembled, her voice dropping to a whisper. "We will be the laughingstock of Yorkshire."

Frederick stepped forward, his voice surprisingly gentle. "Mother, I am relieved to hear you speak the truth at last."

The Baroness's mouth fell open in shock, caught off-guard by his words.

"What I mean," Frederick continued carefully, "is that our reputation has already been tarnished by ghosts and dark tales. The stories are out there. We cannot fall further than we already have." He paused, his eyes steady. "The only way left is up."

Philippa's face twisted with conflicting emotions, but something in her son's words seemed to reach her, like a crack appearing in a fortress wall. As she struggled to regain her composure, a fragile, almost desperate hope flickered in her eyes.

Cecelia watched the exchange, her heart caught between pity and anger. This was a moment of reckoning for Philippa Rowley, a woman whose iron will had driven so many of the tragedies that had unfolded. She felt Kunal's reassuring touch on her arm, grounding her as the final confrontation loomed ahead.

The tension in the courtyard was thick enough to slice, the air cold and damp with a lingering morning mist that clung to everything, casting a ghostly pall over the castle grounds. Horses snorted restlessly, their breath clouding in the chilly air. The distant caw of a crow seemed a fitting backdrop as Philippa stared at Frederick, her eyes dark and unreadable.

The seconds stretched. Cecelia could see Philippa's lips tighten, the weight of her decision like a stone in the air. Finally, the Baroness inhaled deeply. "John?"

From the shadows of the dense trees, a giant of a man stepped forward. His sheer size was intimidating, his posture both vigilant and unyielding. Frederick's brow furrowed, his hand instinctively moving closer to his sword hilt. "Who the devil are you?"

"Call me John," the man replied, his voice deep and rough. "Good morning, Baron Rowley."

"He's my personal guard," Philippa interjected, a hint of pride in her voice. "After the physician's betrayal, I needed someone I could trust, someone... I chose myself." She smirked, as if she'd bested them all by securing this formidable ally.

A shiver ran down Cecelia's spine, her hand tightening around Kunal's.

Philippa's eyes never left her son's. "John was ready to cut all of you down on my command," she admitted with eerie calm. "But I'm starting to believe Frederick might be right. Revenge has its limits, even for me." Her mouth curved into a bitter smile. "Onward and upward, as they say."

The looming man, John, nodded at her command. "Shall I fetch him, Baroness?"

"Yes," Philippa said slowly, her voice dripping with anticipation. "Go and fetch Henry."

As John moved toward the castle with long, deliberate strides, the heavy clink of keys resonated from his side pouch. The front doors creaked open, and he disappeared into the dark interior.

Meanwhile, a sudden cry echoed from the path beyond the gate, drawing Cecelia's attention. Her heart lifted at the sight of Annabel and Charlie, their faces a mix of confusion and hope. Cecelia's voice rang out, her joy irrepressible. "Come here! It's Mara and Lucas!"

Kunal watched her, warmth in his gaze. "All's well that ends well?"

"Don't jinx it," Cecelia warned, her tone half-serious. "Besides, we haven't even solved your family's riddles yet."

"Thanks for the reminder," he teased. "I'll fetch that jade table."

As Kunal moved to the cart, Annabel and Charlie reached the group, their reunion a whirlwind of embraces and tears. Mara clung to her son, while Annabel wept openly, her relief palpable.

But the moment of joy was abruptly shattered as the castle doors swung open with a resounding bang. All eyes turned toward the imposing figure now stepping into view. Henry, shackled and disheveled, had been dragged from the castle dungeon. His once-imposing frame had withered, his face sunken and pale. He hobbled down the steps, his feet dragging on the cobblestones as John propelled him forward.

Cecelia's eyes met Henry's, and a flash of hatred burned within his. He looked smaller, diminished, yet still dangerous. "You!" he spat, his voice hoarse but dripping with venom.

Cecelia tensed, a knot of fear coiling in her stomach. She glanced at John, hoping the man had a strong hold on the disgraced baron. But as if reading her thoughts, Henry's body suddenly surged with adrenaline. In a frenzied burst of strength, he wrenched free from John's grasp, shoving the hulking man aside with surprising force.

"Cecelia!" Kunal shouted, already abandoning the table and breaking into a run.

Cecelia's instincts kicked in, and she turned to flee, though her waddle was no match for the madman's wild charge. Panic surged—she was unarmed. How could she outrun him in her condition?

The ground was rough beneath her shoes as she pushed herself forward, her breath ragged and desperate. But before she could even comprehend what was happening, there was a loud, sickening crunch.

She spun around, her heart pounding, fearing the worst.

But there, sprawled on the ground, was Henry—his leg twisted at a grotesque angle. Above him loomed Philippa, still mounted on her massive stallion, Hercules. The horse's iron-clad hooves had come down hard, and Philippa's face was a mask of cold triumph. Henry lay on the cobblestones, groaning in pain, completely at her mercy.

Cecelia stood frozen, her body shaking from the sudden rush of adrenaline. Kunal reached her, pulling her into a fierce embrace. "Cecelia," he breathed, his voice thick with relief. "Every moment I feared I'd lose you."

She managed a shaky smile, the terror ebbing away. "And what are you planning to do about it?"

Without hesitation, Kunal dropped to one knee on the cobblestones, his gaze unwavering. "Cecelia Rousseau of Lyon and Castle Rowley," he began, his voice steady and earnest. "Will you marry me?"

Cecelia's breath caught, her heart swelling with a rush of joy and disbelief. Tears blurred her vision, and she bit her lip to keep from bursting into sobs of happiness. "Yes," she whispered, her voice breaking. "Yes, I will."

The courtyard erupted into applause—an unexpected, heartfelt release of emotion from all who had gathered. Even Philippa, still perched on Hercules, looked momentarily softened by the scene before her.

In that instant, with the castle behind them and the future ahead, Cecelia felt a profound sense of redemption, not just for herself, but for the fractured family that stood together at last.

Chapter Thirty-Two

FOUND FAMILY

Henry's leg was a mangled mess, twisted in multiple places. Hercules, had collided with him with a force that had knocked him cold, and heavy hooves had kicked the cruel former Baron mercilessly as he fell. Despite the grim injuries, Philippa showed no hesitation. She ordered Henry's limp body dragged into the carriage, sending him and the physician straight to the constable. Her face betrayed no regret, just a grim satisfaction that justice was finally in motion.

Cecelia felt Annabel's arms wrap around her, the embrace warm and familiar, a balm against the chaos of the day. Annabel's voice was hushed but filled with a fierce love. "You've had enough adventures for a lifetime, Cecelia," she whispered. "Your little one will need a whole book just to understand their mother's stories."

Cecelia hugged her friend back, inhaling the familiar scent of lavender that clung to Annabel's dress. "You have no idea how much I missed you," Cecelia murmured, her voice breaking.

"And I, you," Annabel said, as if it were the most natural thing in the world. "We never doubted you were alive, not for a moment. We couldn't go forward without you, Cecelia. And now..." Her eyes shone with unshed tears. "Now Charlie's parents can bear witness as we start our family, too. It feels like a fairy tale."

"It really does." Cecelia's eyes darted around, searching. "But where is Kunal?"

Charlie stepped forward then, his embrace feeling like the protective warmth of a brother. "He went to fetch something for you," he said, his voice heavy with emotion. "My mother told me you were the one who kept her sane in that room. And when Kunal found you and you insisted on rescuing my parents before yourself... I don't know how I'll ever repay you."

Cecelia smiled through her tears, resting her hands on her belly. "Perhaps you and Annabel could babysit now and then? I could use the help."

Charlie's grin widened. "You have my word."

Cecelia felt a hand on her shoulder and turned to see Kunal standing there, looking exhausted but radiant. His eyes were filled with tenderness. "We were just talking about you," she said with a wry smile.

"Cecelia," Kunal began, taking a deep breath. "One of the reasons I didn't propose immediately after rescuing you is that I wanted to give you this first."

He held out a small wooden chest, its surface aged but polished, the lock undone. Cecelia's brow furrowed. "That's your family chest."

Kunal nodded, lifting the lid to reveal a collection of slips of parchment and small pieces of bark, each bearing neat handwriting or small illustrations. "These are choices, Cecelia," he said quietly, his voice raw with emotion. "While I was searching for you, I realized I needed to think beyond my own happiness and consider what would make you happy."

Tears pricked Cecelia's eyes. "Oh, Kunal," she whispered, her heart swelling.

"I decided that the greatest gift I could give you was the freedom to choose." Kunal's voice trembled. "You've always told me I had all the options, while you had none. So, I've written down choices, things you might want to do or become. And I promise, whatever you choose, I'll support you in making it happen." His eyes were bright, a hint of a smile playing at his lips. "I was going to read them to you, but now... I suppose you can do that yourself."

Cecelia nodded, her throat too tight for words. She took the chest in her hands, its weight surprisingly comforting, and sat down on a nearby tree stump. She began reading through the slips, each one like a new horizon unfolding before her:

- Become a Business Partner
- Start an Inn or Tavern
- Become an Artist Publicly
- Join a Convent
- Apprenticeship in a Trade
- Work as a Governess
- Become a Herbalist or Midwife
- Become a Craftswoman
- Go to India for an Indian Wedding
- Go to France to Stay with your Parents
- Write More Books With Annabel
- Go to Amsterdam...

The options seemed endless, each one imbued with the promise of a different life. Her vision blurred with tears, and she looked up at him, her voice barely audible. "How long did this take you?"

"I needed to do something to keep sane while I searched for you," Kunal admitted, his voice hoarse. "I was consumed with worry, but writing these gave me hope, knowing that your life could be about more than survival."

"You are a wonderful man," Cecelia said softly, overwhelmed by the depth of his love.

Kunal knelt before her, the gravel crunching under his boots. "And you are a wonderful woman, Cecelia," he said earnestly. "But I want you to be more than wonderful—I want you to be free to choose."

Cecelia leaned forward, her lips brushing his gently. "I don't need a hundred choices," she whispered, her voice filled with certainty. "I just need one." She smiled at him, feeling lighter than she had in years. "And that choice is you."

Kunal's face broke into a wide grin, his eyes shining with joy. "Then let's make our own story, Cecelia—one of love, family, and everything else we choose together."

From the back of the cart, James and Bridgette exchanged glances, their expressions a mix of pride and realization. Bridgette's voice was low but clear as she spoke to her husband. "You know, James... I never really wanted to go to America. I just thought it was the only way."

James squeezed her hand, his own eyes moist. "Nor did I, Bridgette. I just wanted to keep us all together, whatever it took."

Cecelia overheard them, and her heart swelled with a new understanding. She turned back to Kunal, her voice thick with emotion. "Maybe we're not just building a life for us, Kunal. Maybe it's for all of us—for the family I was afraid I'd lost."

He pulled her close, their foreheads touching. "And for the family we're going to create, Cecelia. A new one, built on love, trust, and choice."

"I will truly help you accomplish anything on that list," Kunal vowed. "I'll use my connections, Captain Harrington's, or even my parents'. Though," he added, puffing his chest with pride, "I no longer work for my father."

Cecelia's brows shot up. "What? How?"

"Captain Harrington listened to my pitches during the journey, heard out all my ideas," Kunal explained, his eyes alight with excitement. "He wants to hire me directly to design and decorate his new house in London." His smile widened, the words tumbling out in a rush. "And the best part? I can do the work from here. When we're ready, we can take on commissions anywhere—together."

Cecelia's heart swelled at his infectious joy. "That's incredible, Kunal. Truly."

He coughed, his demeanor shifting to a mix of eagerness and hesitation. "Of course, it depends on what you choose..." His voice trailed off as he pointed to a slip of parchment. "That one, for instance."

Cecelia peered at the slip, a laugh bubbling up. It read: Find a Husband who looks like the true Father.

"Oh, really?" she teased. "You'd just help me find a replacement, a Tom, Dick, or Harry, like that?"

Kunal's face took on a mock-serious expression. "If that's your choice, I'll make it happen. As much as it would pain me." His eyes darted playfully, then his voice dropped to a low rumble. "But who are these Tom or Harry fellows you speak of? Show me where they are, so I can run them through."

Cecelia laughed, a sound that felt both familiar and liberating. "Do you even have a sword on you?"

Kunal's expression softened, his eyes warm with love. "You're teasing me."

"Of course," Cecelia admitted, unable to hold back her grin. She rummaged through the slips in the chest, pulling out a small bundle. "I choose these five."

"Five?" Kunal's eyes widened, a grin breaking across his face. "Ambitious, are we? But..." His voice trembled with hope. "You truly do want to marry me? To raise this child together? To build our lives side by side?"

Cecelia's voice was steady and full of conviction. "Kunal, there's nothing I want more. I want all of it—our marriage, our family, and a future we choose for ourselves."

His eyes shone with joy, and he took her hand, threading his fingers through hers. "Then let's go to the chapel," he said, his voice low and urgent. "Before you have this baby."

Cecelia blinked, a mix of shock and elation making her head spin. "Are you serious? You want to marry me right now?"

"Absolutely," he replied, tightening his grip on her hand. "Your parents are waiting at the chapel, and mine are at the studio. We can still have a proper Amber wedding later if we visit home, but if we marry now, I'll be the legal father of your child—and your husband."

He paused, searching her eyes. "We have many hurdles ahead, Cecelia, but this will make things easier for the three of us."

"The three of us," Cecelia repeated, the words like a warm, comforting embrace. She squeezed his hand, feeling a sense of belonging she hadn't dared hope for. "It feels so wonderful to say. After everything, I never thought we'd make it to this point." She beamed up at him, her eyes bright with happiness.

As they approached the studio, she caught sight of Sarala opening the door, her face beaming with pride. Behind her, Kunal's father, Manik, stood with an awkward smile, holding a small garland of marigolds in his hands. Her parents were not far behind, their eyes alight with a blend of relief and anticipation.

Sarala stepped forward, placing the garland gently around Cecelia's neck. "Welcome, my daughter."

The gesture brought tears to Cecelia's eyes. She looked around at the small gathering, this unexpected family that had formed out of love, trust, and the most unexpected of alliances. It was not grand or formal, but it was theirs—a beginning they had forged together.

Kunal leaned closer, his voice low and reverent. "Are you ready?"

Cecelia nodded, feeling more ready than she had ever been. "Yes," she whispered. "Yes, I am."

And as the doors to the chapel creaked open, the soft strains of a violin filled the air. Cecelia's heart swelled with joy, anticipation, and the promise of a life lived on her own terms. They stepped forward together, hand in hand, toward a future they would shape as one—filled with love, trust, and endless choices yet to come.

He pulled her close again, their foreheads meeting gently, as the warmth of family surrounded them. "Cecelia," Sarala whispered, her voice filled with emotion as she embraced Cecelia tightly, "Welcome to the family, my darling girl. We are so, so happy to have you."

Kunal's eyes shone with love as he leaned in. "Maa, Cecelia also wants to have an Amber wedding in a year or two when we return there. It was one of her choices from the chest."

Sarala's face lit up with joy, the kind that makes her eyes crinkle at the corners, and Manik broke into a broad grin. "Oh, it will be such a wonderful occasion! I'll start planning it now. The colors, the music, the rituals! You will love them."

Cecelia's heart swelled at the enthusiasm, but the joyous moment was unexpectedly interrupted by Rupa's firm voice cutting through the gathering. "I'm going to Paris with my benefactor." The abruptness of her words drew everyone's eyes to her.

Cecelia reached for Rupa's hand, squeezing it gently. "Rupa, that's wonderful."

But Rupa's gaze was conflicted, her cheeks burning with emotion. "I'm so sorry. I don't mean to take the spotlight, but I've been so afraid of disappointing all of you, especially you, Maa." Her voice cracked.

"To see you happy for Kunal today made me realize I need to say it before I lose my nerve."

Sarala, however, was unfazed. "Oh, thank goodness," she exclaimed, clapping her hands together in genuine relief.

Rupa's mouth fell open. "You're not... upset?"

Sarala's eyes softened with maternal understanding. "My darling girl, I've known for a while. I... may have snooped through your desk." She winced with guilt. "When I found your plans for Paris, I realized how ambitious you've been, how brave."

"Maa!" Rupa's face was a picture of astonishment mixed with amusement.

Sarala laughed, her eyes twinkling with mischief. "I was so relieved, you know. I feared something worse."

Cecelia couldn't resist a grin. "Like an illegitimate pregnancy?"

The family burst into laughter, and the tension that had gathered around Rupa's confession melted away. Rupa wiped her eyes, a small smile tugging at her lips. "Cecelia, you've been such an inspiration. Without our conversations, I might not have found the courage to speak my mind."

Cecelia's voice was tender, her admiration evident. "And you, Rupa, inspired me to embrace my own dreams—no matter how impossible they seemed."

Manik turned to Cecelia with gratitude. "And speaking of dreams, thank you for recovering our jade-inlaid table. Rupa has just examined it."

Rupa beamed. "I found a clue underneath, just like you did with the desk, Cecelia. It spoke of reflection and looking inward." She gestured toward Sarala, who carefully drew a small mirror from her pocket.

"The mirror had a secret compartment," Sarala explained, her hands shaking slightly as she opened it to reveal an exquisite jade ring, intricately carved with tiny motifs of feathers and lotus blossoms. Cecelia gasped as she noticed a small peacock etched delicately on the side.

"It's stunning," Cecelia breathed, tracing the delicate details with reverence.

Rupa's voice was filled with wonder. "The inscription says, Dhany-ate Bhāgyena—'Blessed by Fortune' in Sanskrit."

"It's a treasure worth every step of the journey," Cecelia agreed, her eyes shining.

But Rupa hesitated before holding out the ring to Kunal. "This culmination of the riddles passed down through generations is yours to share with Cecelia and your children. You should be the one to pass it along."

Kunal met Rupa's gaze, his voice choked with emotion. "This ring is not mine to give. It's yours, Rupa."

Rupa's eyes widened, her hand still outstretched. "What?"

Kunal's voice was full of brotherly love. "For years, I kept that chest hidden away, barely thinking of it. But you, Rupa, always nudged me to open it, to solve its mysteries. You've been with me every step of this journey. It's yours, by right and effort."

Rupa looked from the ring to her brother, her smile quivering with disbelief. "Are you certain?"

Kunal nodded, his eyes warm and steady. "If our ancestors had valued passing riddles to women, they would have done so long ago. But they didn't, so I'm correcting that now."

Rupa slowly slipped the ring onto her finger, her voice breaking. "It fits."

"Of course it does," Kunal said with a smile. "It was always meant for you."

Sarala's eyes filled with tears as she wrapped her arms around her children. "What a blessed mother I am, to have children who give so freely to each other."

Manik patted Kunal on the back, then rested his hand on Cecelia's shoulder. "And what a blessing to have another artist join our family."

Cecelia felt a rush of warmth. "Cecelia Sutar," she whispered to herself, testing the sound. "It sounds like music."

Kunal leaned closer, his voice low and filled with wonder. "And so would Sophie Sutar, or any of the other ideas you wrote down."

Cecelia's eyes widened in surprise. "You knew?"

Kunal's cheeks reddened. "Your mother showed me your sketchbook, and I saw the names there."

Cecelia's hands instinctively rested on her stomach. "I can't explain it, but... it feels like a girl."

Kunal's eyes sparkled with joy. "Then let's welcome her with a wedding that will honor all the choices that brought us here."

And with that, they stepped forward together, toward a new chapter filled with love, resilience, and choices that were truly theirs to make.

As Kunal and Cecelia stepped out of the studio, the warm sunlight bathed them in a golden glow, making the moment feel almost enchanted. The soft hum of castle life surrounded them—servants bustling about, birds chirping overhead, and the faint rustle of autumn leaves.

Before Cecelia could take it all in, Annabel and Lise burst from the castle's front doors, their skirts billowing with urgency and their cheeks flushed from excitement.

"Cecelia!" Annabel cried breathlessly, her voice carrying a melody of joy. She threw her arms around Cecelia, squeezing tightly. When she finally pulled back, she pressed a beautiful bouquet into Cecelia's hands. It was a wild assortment of blooms—lavender, daisies, and some late roses, tied together with a bit of ribbon. "I couldn't let you get married without flowers. You deserve a bouquet as wild and lovely as your spirit."

Cecelia's eyes glistened as she admired the colorful arrangement. "It's perfect, Annabel. Just like you."

Lise stepped forward next, holding a bonnet with delicate blue embroidery that matched Cecelia's eyes. "May I?" she asked softly, her voice filled with the tenderness of a dear friend.

Cecelia nodded, smiling, and stood still as Lise gently finger-combed her curls. Her touch was soft, like the feeling of childhood memories being brought to life—their secret meetings in the courtyard, whispering of dreams and mischief. As Lise pinned Cecelia's hair back, she murmured, "You've always been the bravest of us, Cecelia. I know you'll make a fine wife, mother, and artist." She placed the bonnet over Cecelia's wild curls, securing it with care. "There," Lise whispered with a grin. "As radiant as ever."

Cecelia reached up to touch the bonnet's embroidered petals, feeling a surge of love for her friends. "Thank you, Lise. I will cherish this."

With a knowing smile, Lise held out a small pouch next. "This is also from me," she said, her tone a mixture of shyness and sincerity. "It's lavender oil. To soothe the baby, and your nerves, when needed."

Cecelia laughed lightly, taking the pouch and tucking it into her basket. "You know me well, Lise. Thank you."

Rupa pulled out a tiny silver locket. "This was mine when I was a girl... I want your child to have it one day." She pressed it into Cecelia's hand, her eyes misty with emotion. "For good luck, and a reminder of friendship that stands the test of time."

Tears welled in Cecelia's eyes as she clutched the locket, its cool metal warming in her palm. "You both mean the world to me. I never imagined having friends who'd give so freely of their hearts."

Annabel's face was glowing. "We wouldn't let you do this alone, Cecelia. You deserve every bit of happiness that's coming your way."

Kunal, standing quietly nearby, watched the exchange with a soft smile. He stepped forward, placing his hand gently on Cecelia's back. "Shall we?" he asked, his voice low and full of promise. "There's a wedding waiting for us."

Cecelia took a deep breath, her heart full to bursting. She reached out to squeeze Annabel and Lise's hands one last time, then lifted her chin, feeling both strong and deeply loved.

"Yes," she said, turning toward the castle with a smile that held the hope of every new beginning. "Let's go get married."

They walked together toward the towering stone steps of Castle Rowley. For Cecelia, each step felt like a closing chapter and an open door—a door that led not just to a future with Kunal, but also to the enduring love and loyalty of friends who had helped her find her way home.

Chapter Thirty-Three

IT'S TIME

"Oh no," Cecelia gasped, clutching her belly as a sudden wetness spread beneath her skirts. "It's happening."

"What is?" Kunal turned sharply, worry etched on his face as he tried to read her expression. His hands were still sticky with oil from the crates he had been arranging beside him. "Did you hurt yourself? Twist your ankle?"

"No," she managed, her voice tight with disbelief. "My water... my water has broken."

Kunal's eyes went wide, and the color seemed to drain from his face. "No!" he cried out instinctively, yanking the reins to bring the cart to an abrupt stop. "We're not ready. We only said our vows six hours ago! We're still miles from my parents' house, and the cart is loaded with half my studio."

Cecelia gripped the edge of the wooden cart, pain already starting to spread like wildfire across her abdomen. "It seems the little one doesn't care about plans," she groaned. "This child is coming now."

"Now?" Kunal's voice wavered, his bravado crumbling. "Are you sure?"

"As sure as I am of anything," she gasped. Her voice faltered, raw with fear. "Kunal, I... I don't know if I can do this."

He reached for her hand, holding it tightly, his gaze steady despite the panic flickering in his eyes. "You're the bravest person I know," he said quietly, his voice thick with emotion. "We've faced worse than this, together. And we're going to get through this too. I promise."

The sound of approaching hoofbeats suddenly broke through the tension. Kunal's head snapped up, and his grip on the reins tightened as he steered the horse off the path slightly. "Stay calm," he murmured, his voice low and protective. "Let's hope they mean no trouble."

Just then, Cecelia felt the first real contraction—a sharp, wrenching pain that made her gasp and double over. Her body seemed to seize from within, her breath hitching as she clutched at her belly, fingers digging into the rough fabric of her gown. "For all that is holy..."

The forest seemed to hold its breath, the usual cacophony of birds and rustling leaves replaced by an eerie silence. Even the breeze seemed to still, as if nature itself understood the gravity of the moment. Cecelia's vision blurred, and for a brief moment, she saw a small butterfly flit past her face, its iridescent wings catching the dappled sunlight. It landed delicately on a wildflower nearby, a fragile symbol of resilience amidst the chaos. She drew a deep breath, finding an unexpected calm in the tiny creature's presence.

As the contraction ebbed, leaving her breathless and trembling, Cecelia straightened slightly, her resolve firming. She could do this. She had to.

Kunal was still watching the approaching carriage with a wary eye, but when he saw the familiar figures inside, his shoulders sagged with relief. "It's Annabel and Charlie," he said, his voice breaking into a relieved laugh. "They've brought the rest of your things. It seems fate is on our side, after all."

"Annabel!" Cecelia called out, her voice breaking with a mix of pain and hope.

The carriage came to a quick halt, and Annabel practically leapt out, her skirts swishing around her as she ran toward Cecelia. "Oh my goodness, Cecelia!" she exclaimed, her face flushed with concern. "Are you all right?"

"Not quite," Cecelia panted, feeling another wave of pressure build within her. "The baby... it's coming."

Annabel's eyes widened, but her training as a midwife took over. "All right," she said, her voice brisk and determined. "We're going to make do here. Charlie, get the blankets and towels from the back, and bring that bottle of brandy. This could take some time."

Charlie, momentarily stunned, snapped back to action. He rummaged through the cart, his hands moving with a mix of urgency and care. Annabel turned back to Cecelia, her touch both soothing and strong as she helped her friend shift to a more comfortable position. "Just keep breathing, Cecelia. We'll get through this together."

As the next contraction hit, Cecelia's whole body tensed, her muscles screaming with effort. The rough wool of the cart's blanket pressed into her palms, grounding her amidst the pain. She felt Kunal's hand squeeze hers tighter, and she locked eyes with Annabel. Her friend's steady gaze felt like a lifeline.

"You're not alone," Annabel whispered, brushing Cecelia's damp hair away from her flushed face. "Focus on your breathing. You're doing incredibly well."

With a slight grimace, Kunal helped Charlie lay the thick woolen blankets on the grass beside the cart, creating a makeshift birthing area that was soft and warm. "You're strong, Cecelia," Kunal murmured, his voice steady despite the clear terror in his eyes. "You've got this, my love."

Charlie returned, carrying a clay jug of water, a bundle of herbs, and clean linens wrapped carefully in a cloth, and Annabel arranged the herbs and linens beside Cecelia. "We'll make a herbal infusion," she explained, setting aside chamomile and yarrow. "It'll help with the pain and keep you strong."

Cecelia's cries grew louder, punctuated by ragged breaths. Her body trembled, soaked in sweat, but she gritted her teeth, finding strength in Kunal's steady hand and Annabel's confident commands. "Just one contraction at a time," Annabel coached, her voice calm but firm. "Each one brings you closer to holding your baby."

The hours seemed to stretch, marked by the rhythm of contractions, each more brutal than the last. The sun was now low, casting a warm golden hue over the forest, and Cecelia's body was nearly at its breaking point. Suddenly, Annabel's expression shifted, a crease forming between her brows.

"Cecelia," Annabel said urgently, her voice still soothing but now tinged with concern. "The baby's shoulder is stuck, and we need to act fast."

Kunal's heart lurched, but he forced himself to stay focused. He tightened his grip on Cecelia's hand, whispering fiercely, "You're strong, my love. Just keep breathing and focus on me."

Annabel remained calm and decisive. "Charlie," she instructed, "bring me the slippery elm bark from the bag. We'll use it to help ease the baby's passage."

Charlie nodded, moving swiftly. Annabel's fingers worked quickly, applying the slippery elm around Cecelia's birthing area. "This will help, Cecelia," Annabel reassured her. "I need you to turn onto your hands and knees—it's the best way to give the baby more room."

With a deep breath and a nod from Kunal, Cecelia mustered the last of her energy, shifting to the new position. Her muscles screamed in protest, but she gritted her teeth and focused on Annabel's voice.

"When the next contraction comes," Annabel urged, "give it everything you've got. Push as hard as you can."

Cecelia's face contorted with effort as the contraction surged again. She pushed with a ferocity that felt both primal and determined. Annabel's hands guided the baby's shoulder free, and Cecelia could feel a shift—a release.

"That's it, Cecelia," Annabel said, her voice filled with relief. "You've got it. Now keep pushing!"

With a final, desperate effort, Cecelia bore down, every fiber of her being focused on this moment. A raw, guttural cry escaped her as the baby finally emerged, the sound reverberating through the trees.

Annabel cradled the newborn in her arms, her face breaking into a wide, triumphant smile. "It's a girl, Cecelia," she announced, her voice filled with joy and relief. "You've done it. She's here."

Cecelia's breath hitched as she reached for her daughter. Her exhaustion melted away, replaced by a flood of emotions she couldn't contain. Tears streamed down her cheeks, and she laughed, her voice soft and awestruck. "She's here," she whispered, pulling the baby close.

Annabel handed the infant over gently, her smile radiant. "She's strong," she said with a hint of pride. "And perfect."

Kunal stood close, his eyes shining with a mixture of disbelief and overwhelming joy. He leaned forward, tenderly kissing Cecelia's forehead and then brushing his lips against the baby's tiny head. "Our little miracle," he murmured.

Annabel reached into her bag and pulled out a small cloth pouch. "Here," she said, handing it to Kunal. "Rub this on her gums—it's a mix of honey and chamomile. It'll calm her."

Kunal's hands trembled slightly as he opened the bag and gently rubbed a bit of the mixture on the baby's gums. His face was wet with tears, his voice barely a whisper. "She's perfect, Cecelia. Truly perfect."

Cecelia watched as her husband's hands, usually so skilled at shaping wood, delicately cradled their child. "Mira," Cecelia whispered, the name flowing like a soft melody. "Her name is Mira. It means... wonder in French, and sea in Sanskrit."

Kunal's face lit up, a broad smile spreading across his lips. "Welcome to the world, Mira," he said gently. "You have no idea how much we've been waiting for you."

Charlie and Annabel stepped back, giving the new family a moment of privacy. Annabel, ever the attentive friend, prepared an infusion of raspberry leaf tea for Cecelia, knowing it would help her regain strength. As the tea steeped, she exchanged a tearful, joyful look with Charlie. They both understood that this was more than just a birth—it was a beginning.

Cecelia, feeling a surge of maternal protectiveness, cradled Mira against her chest, marveling at the tiny fingers that grasped weakly at her shift. Her heart swelled, her body still aching from the ordeal but her spirit soaring.

"You are loved beyond measure, Mira," Cecelia whispered, her voice filled with tenderness. She kissed the baby's soft cheek, her lips lingering there as if to anchor this moment in time.

Kunal wrapped an arm around Cecelia's shoulders, and they leaned into each other, foreheads touching. The world around them seemed to pause—the rustling leaves of the forest, the warm rays of the sun filtering through the trees, and the soft chirps of birds created a sanctuary of serenity.

"Can you believe we made it here?" Cecelia murmured, looking up at Kunal. "After everything..."

He nodded slowly, his voice thick with emotion. "I can. Because you are the strongest person I've ever known."

As Annabel approached with the steaming cup of raspberry leaf tea, Cecelia looked up, smiling gratefully. "Thank you," she said, her voice hoarse but steady.

Annabel placed the cup in Cecelia's free hand. "Drink up," she said with a wink. "You've got a lot of stories to tell Mira."

Cecelia took a careful sip, the warmth spreading through her weary body. "I don't know where to start," she admitted, glancing down at Mira's tiny face.

Charlie, his voice warm and teasing, chimed in, "Start with the one where you saved everyone, even when you were carrying this little one."

Cecelia laughed softly, a sound filled with joy and relief. "I suppose that's one way to begin."

With Kunal's arm still wrapped around her, she leaned back, feeling the strength of his support. "Yes, Mira," she said, looking down at the baby. "We've come a long way to find you, my little wonder."

And as the sun set, casting a soft golden glow over the forest clearing, the new family remained cocooned in their moment, filled with hope, love, and the promise of the future that lay ahead.

CHAPTER THIRTY-FOUR

AT LAST

The weeks following Mira's birth were a blur of exhaustion and love, more intense than anything Cecelia had ever known. The Sutar family insisted that Cecelia, Kunal, and the baby move into their home, setting up a charming guest room filled with soft, hand-woven blankets, embroidered cushions, and rich wooden furniture. The windows overlooked the sprawling gardens, and a faint scent of jasmine drifted in through the open panes. Cecelia was grateful for the support, especially Sarala's presence, which was comforting in its familiarity.

Sarala, practical yet compassionate, had suggested hiring a wet nurse, but Cecelia, after months of isolation in Rowley Manor, couldn't bear to part with Mira, even for a moment. The idea of handing her baby to another woman felt like giving up a piece of herself. She wanted to experience every moment—the softness of Mira's skin, the gentle sounds she made, and the way her tiny, delicate mouth searched for sustenance.

Cecelia cherished the quiet moments when Mira, with her feathery red curls and round cheeks, latched on with surprising strength. Mira's ruddy hand would wrap around Cecelia's finger, her grip so tight it made Cecelia smile with pride. *She's going to be fierce*, Cecelia thought, marveling at the determination in such a small creature. And when Kunal entered the room, Mira would stretch her tiny hand toward him, as if recognizing the warmth of her father's presence.

One evening, as Cecelia watched Kunal lean over the crib, speaking to Mira in a soothing voice, Cecelia felt her love for him deepen, this time infused with a new layer of tenderness. She admired how he instinctively knew when she needed a break, rubbing her feet without a word or pacing the room with Mira until she dozed off. Kunal's dedication to their daughter was palpable, and it made Cecelia's heart swell each time she saw him coax their little one to sleep, his voice a gentle murmur that seemed to calm both mother and child.

In the meantime, Kunal had completed the Rowley commission—an ambitious project that had required the finishing touches of gilded moldings, elaborate frescoes, and intricately carved panels that spoke to the castle's twisted history. Frederick Rowley, true to his promise, had embraced the castle's dark past rather than shy away from it. On his birthday, he unveiled an exhibit in the newly renovated library, showcasing the relics his mother had hidden, accompanied by detailed reproductions of the riddles that had led them to the secret chamber of treasures.

The library itself had been meticulously organized by a team of professionals, with a section dedicated to the public. It was named the Cassidy Rowley Room, a tribute that brought Frederick's sister to tears. Cecelia had intended to attend the celebration, but exhaustion won out, and she'd reluctantly stayed behind. Frederick didn't seem to mind, though. He visited the Sutar home shortly after Mira's birth, bringing gifts wrapped in fine linen and a warm smile.

"The best gift you've given me is my own life, Cecelia," he said sincerely. "The rest is mere embellishment."

Cecelia grinned. "And now? Will you travel? Oh!" Her eyes widened as she remembered. "Your fiancée. Did you marry yet?"

Frederick's smile faded, replaced by a resigned look. "I have to tell her I'm not going to die soon after all, and if she likes, we can end the engagement." He shrugged, trying to mask his lingering sadness. "But I've decided to travel once I regain my strength. I've already convinced your father to stay on as estate manager."

Cecelia's jaw dropped. "You're serious? I thought he'd return to France."

"I made him an offer he couldn't refuse," Frederick explained proudly. "A substantial promotion, a raise, and the chance to visit France often. It gives me the freedom to explore."

It seemed that everything had fallen into place, like the final pieces of a well-crafted puzzle. Yet Cecelia couldn't shake an underlying unease—a whispering sense that something was still unsettled.

As if sensing her anxiety, a soft yawn came from the crib, and Cecelia's thoughts scattered. She rose from the bed with surprising ease—her body, once aching and strained, now felt strong again. She crossed the room and reached into the oak crib that Manik had carved so lovingly. Mira, half-awake, reached instinctively for Cecelia's hand, snuggling against her mother's touch.

Cecelia watched her daughter, her heart swelling with a fierce love. "You are my wonder," she whispered, a promise made in the hushed intimacy of the nursery.

There was a light knock at the door. Cecelia looked up to see Sarala standing there, her face warm with a smile. "Little one stirring?"

Cecelia nodded, instinctively checking her chest, then flushing as she realized she'd done it in front of her elegant mother-in-law. "I'm so sorry. I was just—"

"No need for apologies," Sarala reassured, her voice gentle. There was a hint of something deeper in her eyes, a flicker of vulnerability Cecelia hadn't seen before.

A beat passed, and then Sarala's voice grew softer, more confessional. "Cecelia, did you know I cannot have children?"

Cecelia's eyes widened. "No, I didn't. Kunal told me about your happily blended family, but not about this."

Sarala smiled, but it was tinged with a bittersweetness that lingered like old memories. "I tried very hard during my first marriage," she confessed. "Five years of trying... and failing." Her words were steady, but Cecelia saw the years of pain etched in her expression. "When my husband passed, I thought my chances at a family had ended too. And then I met Manik." She glanced lovingly toward the window, as if he might materialize there. "He brought a new kind of joy into my life. We found a different way to have a family—one that was built from love, rather than blood."

Sarala's hand settled gently on Cecelia's shoulder, her grip warm and reassuring. "Kunal loves this child with all his heart," she said, her voice full of certainty.

Cecelia's gaze softened, turning to Mira, who had opened her large, curious eyes. "I know," Cecelia whispered. "I couldn't have asked for a better husband, or a better family. I love you all so much."

Sarala pulled Cecelia into a half-embrace. "And we love you, my dear," she whispered, her words filled with maternal warmth.

A playful voice broke the tenderness of the moment. "We certainly do," Rupa chimed in from the doorway, leaning against the frame with a grin. "Thank goodness Kunal chose wisely."

"Oh, you," Sarala teased, swatting playfully at Rupa. "Don't think I'm not planning a dowry box for you as soon as you return from Paris."

"I never worry about you, Maa." Rupa winked, stepping over to the crib and placing a soft kiss on Mira's forehead. The baby let out a squeaky sound, somewhere between a giggle and a coo, prompting all three women to laugh along with her. "Cecelia, your husband awaits."

"Where?" Cecelia asked, a curious smile playing on her lips.

"I'll show you," Rupa offered, pressing a quick kiss to her mother's cheek before leading Cecelia toward the door.

Cecelia turned back to Sarala, hesitation clouding her eyes. "I can't thank you enough for watching her tonight. It's harder to leave than I thought."

Sarala nodded knowingly. "It always is, the first time." Cecelia's hand lingered over Mira's blanket, and in a sudden burst of longing, she scooped her daughter into her arms, inhaling the sweet scent of her head. Mira's tiny fingers tangled in Cecelia's hair, prompting a squeal of laughter.

"Easy there, little one," Sarala chuckled, expertly freeing Cecelia's curls from Mira's grip.

Cecelia kissed Mira's forehead, then wrapped her carefully in the patchwork quilt Lise had made. With one last lingering embrace, she reluctantly handed Mira over to Sarala, who produced a small wooden rattle from her apron pocket. "Go on, Cecelia," Sarala whispered, gently shaking the rattle to distract the baby. "I'll bring her to you in a few hours, or give her a bit of barley water if she wakes."

Cecelia paused, torn. "Bring her to me," she said quietly. "Even if I'm asleep, I'll wake for her."

Sarala nodded. "I will."

As Cecelia stepped out with Rupa, she felt a pang of separation, as though she were leaving a part of herself behind. The hallway stretched before them, lined with paintings of ancestors in rich oil tones. Rupa kept a lively pace, her gown rustling against the polished floorboards, but Cecelia's mind was still back in the nursery.

The anticipation in her stomach was like a flutter of wings as they approached the east wing of the house. The candles flickered, casting warm pools of light on the intricate tapestries. Cecelia's hand instinctively rested on her stomach—no longer full with child, but now filled with a different kind of expectation.

They had arrived. Rupa stopped, turning back to Cecelia with an earnest smile. "Enjoy your evening. I mean it." She enveloped Cecelia in a fierce hug, clinging like a sister saying farewell for longer than she wanted. "I'm truly going to miss you when I leave for Paris next month."

"Then expect a visit from us as soon as you're settled," Cecelia promised. "I've already proven that I can leave my child in another room. Any day now, I'll be ready to conquer Europe."

Rupa laughed, a carefree sound that made the hall feel a little less empty. "You come whenever you're ready, and I swear you'll have a place to stay with me, my sister."

Cecelia watched Rupa disappear down the corridor, her heart full. It was an odd sensation, feeling the weight of both new beginnings and farewells all at once. Taking a deep breath, she turned back to the door in front of her, squared her shoulders, and pushed it open.

The warm glow of a dozen candles greeted her, filling the room with a soft amber light. The scent of lavender lingered faintly in the air, and the room, adorned with a simple elegance, exuded a quiet intimacy. Kunal stood by the table, his warm brown eyes soft and inviting, the flickering candlelight catching the warmth in his gaze. "Welcome, my love," he murmured.

"Thank you," Cecelia whispered, a sudden wave of shyness washing over her. Her voice felt small, tentative. "Have you... planned something for tonight?"

He nodded, a gentle smile curving his lips. He gestured toward a small spread on the table: figs, cheese, and a handful of nuts arranged thoughtfully. "I thought we could eat a little, and talk."

Cecelia bit her lip, feeling a surge of vulnerability she hadn't expected. "I—I'm nervous about being with you." The words spilled out unbidden, and she winced. "I know it's silly, but... I just had a child, and—"

Kunal's expression was tender as he reached for her hand, guiding her gently to the chair. "What makes you feel nervous, my love?" he asked, his voice low and soothing as he began to massage her shoulders. "You can tell me anything."

She hesitated, then blurted, "You've only known me pregnant. What if that's what drew you to me?" Her cheeks burned, and she immediately regretted saying it. "It's foolish, I know. But I can't help it."

Kunal's hands stilled, his voice filled with gentle curiosity. "Do you really believe that?"

She sighed, her shoulders sagging beneath the weight of her confession. "Women often imagine the worst, Kunal. It's how we protect ourselves. Please, don't hold my fears against me."

He shook his head slowly. "Never. I understand more than you think." He leaned down, his breath warm against her ear. "But let me assure you—my love for you is not about the child you carried. It's about the woman who carried her."

Her lips quirked into a hesitant smile. "And how did I carry her, exactly?"

"With confidence," he replied, brushing a kiss along her neck. "And strength," he added, his lips lingering just beneath her ear. She shivered, a flush of warmth spreading through her as the intensity of the moment built between them. "And grace... so much grace."

"Kunal..." she whispered, her voice husky, his name an invitation as well as a promise.

Her whisper seemed to ignite something in him, a raw need that matched her own. "Do we really have to wait to eat?" she asked, her tone half-teasing, half-serious.

"Not at all," he murmured, his voice thick with desire. In one swift, fluid motion, he slid an arm beneath her legs and lifted her effortlessly. Cecelia giggled, clinging to his neck as he carried her to the bed.

He laid her down gently, brushing stray strands of hair from her face as he leaned over, the intimacy between them deepening. "I want to make you feel loved, Cecelia," he whispered, his voice warm and tender, every word weighted with the sincerity of a vow.

"You already do," she whispered back, her heart swelling as she reached up, pulling him closer.

His expression shifted, a flash of uncertainty crossing his features. "Can I tell you what I'm afraid of?"

"What is it?" she asked softly.

"That it will be over too quickly," he admitted, his cheeks flushing with embarrassment. "Or worse, that I might hurt you... so soon after you've had Mira."

Her heart ached at his vulnerability. "I promise you," she whispered, her voice firm yet reassuring. "I'm ready. And if it's over quickly..." She flashed a playful wink. "Then we'll eat the food and try again until it lasts longer."

Kunal's grin was slow but genuine, and he leaned down to kiss her again. His lips brushed over hers with renewed hunger, a spark twinkling in his eyes. "It seems you no longer dress like a maid, now that you're the wife of an artist."

Cecelia stuck her tongue out playfully, her eyes glinting with mischief. "What's your point, good sir?"

"There is... considerably more clothing to remove," he murmured, his voice a low rumble that sent a thrill through her.

"My attire is indeed elaborate and structured," she whispered, "befitting a lady. Shall I guide you, so you'll know how to undress me in the future?"

"Please," he breathed, the raw anticipation in his voice making her shiver.

"Start with the pins," she directed softly, arching her neck to expose the back of her head. "They're expertly stuck in my hair."

His fingers traced the line of her neck, seeking out the pins. "There must be dozens..."

"You'll never find them all," she teased, her voice breathy. "But you can start by unbuckling my shoes."

He swiftly complied, pulling off her shoes with a flourish and tossing them aside. As his hands returned to her hair, he meticulously worked through each pin, dropping them one by one onto the bedside table. Once her curls fell free, his fingers sank into them, gently tugging, and Cecelia sighed with pleasure. "What's next?" he asked, his voice rough with desire.

"Stockings," she moaned, her breath hitching. "They're tied to my garters with ribbons."

With a hungry gaze, Kunal slid his hands down to her legs, lifting one gently. He pressed a kiss to her ankle through the silk stocking, and Cecelia felt a jolt of desire ripple through her. He trailed kisses up the inside of her calf, to the soft skin behind her knee, his mouth warm and insistent. Then he untied the ribbons with deft fingers, peeling the stocking off slowly, the fabric whispering against her skin as he cast it aside. He shifted so that his chest was over hers, his weight solid and warm.

"Kunal," she murmured, her voice low and inviting. "You are truly magnificent."

"You took the words right out of my mouth," he replied, his lips brushing the tops of her breasts exposed by her chemise. "Cecelia, I ache to have you."

She chuckled, a deep, throaty sound. "I still have sleeves and a stomacher to untie, a gown to unhook, a petticoat, bodice, and chemise to remove."

He groaned, burying his face against her chest. "That is most unwelcome news."

"Is this unwelcome?" she teased, guiding his hand beneath her, pressing it against the bare skin of her back.

Kunal's breath hitched, his eyes darkening. "Cecelia, please..." He pulled back slightly, as though wrestling with himself, his jaw tight with restraint. "I... I cannot watch you undress further, or it will be over before it even begins."

Her lips curved into a sly smile. "There is a simpler way."

His curiosity piqued, he whispered, "What is it?"

Without breaking eye contact, she leaned over him, pressing soft kisses down the expanse of his chest beneath his open shirt. She shifted her weight, lifting the heavy layers of her skirts until she straddled him.

In the dim candlelight, she could see the hunger etched across his face. "Like this?" she whispered, her voice tinged with playfulness.

He inhaled sharply, his hands finding her hips, pulling her down against him. "Exactly like this," he murmured, his voice hoarse with need.

"This is it," she whispered, shifting her skirts just enough so he could feel her bare skin against his. The warmth of her body pressed intimately against him, sending a shiver of anticipation up his spine.

"Ooh," he groaned, his voice a deep, guttural sound. "Yes, that feels..."

Before he could finish, she bent down and claimed his lips again, their kiss raw and hungry. His teeth grazed her bottom lip, and she responded with equal fervor, savoring the mixture of urgency and tenderness. The taste of him, a mix of musk and faint sweat, was intoxicating. She let out a low moan, feeling the heat building inside her, primal and unrelenting.

Her hands found his breeches, tugging them open, and as their mouths remained fused, their hips aligned, and her legs wrapped around his waist. Her body sank down onto his, enveloping him fully. The sensation was intense, and she rocked her hips slowly, their rhythm building with each thrust.

"Ohhhhh," Kunal groaned, his voice raw. "Cecelia... I don't know how long I can last..."

"You'd better," she teased, her voice a whisper against his ear. She quickened her pace, her movements fluid yet driven, until they found a rhythm that sent sparks flying between them. Her hips moved faster, and she felt a surge of pleasure rising like a wave within her.

Kunal's grip on her hands tightened, and he let out a deep, almost desperate moan as he reached his climax. Her own body pulsed with pleasure, bringing her close to her own edge. She finally stilled, letting out a soft gasp as she felt him release beneath her.

"Cecelia," he whispered, his voice thick with awe. "My God... that was incredible. I'm so sorry it didn't last longer..."

She laughed softly, giving him a playful squeeze before slipping off him. "You did wonderfully," she assured him, shifting to lie beside him. She guided his hand beneath her skirts, her voice low and teasing. "But you're not quite finished."

He grinned, his fingers eager to explore her once more. "I can manage that," he murmured, his touch deliberate and tender as he sought out the spots that made her breath hitch. As his hand moved skillfully, he whispered words of love and encouragement, his voice hushed but full of warmth.

When she whispered her secret fantasy, he hesitated only briefly before lowering himself between her thighs, eager to fulfill her desires. His beard tickled at first, but she guided him with gentle words and playful instruction, her laughter mingling with sighs of pleasure.

"Can you remember the poem you read to me?" she asked, her voice soft but commanding.

"Yes," he replied, his breath hot against her.

"Then spell it out," she instructed, her voice both amused and breathy, "with your tongue... until one of us is finished."

He obeyed, his tongue tracing letters and words against her most sensitive skin, each stroke igniting a fresh wave of pleasure. As she finally reached her climax, her cries were full of blissful abandon, her body trembling beneath his determined ministrations.

When they finally lay spent, tangled in the sheets, Cecelia nestled into the curve of his body, his arm draped protectively around her. She closed her eyes, feeling the warmth of his chest against her back, the steady rhythm of his breathing lulling her into a contented haze.

"You are everything to me," he whispered into her hair, his voice rough with emotion.

"And you to me," she murmured, pressing a soft kiss to his arm. "Always."

CHAPTER THIRTY-FIVE

HAPPY

Cecelia jolted awake as the first pale light of dawn filtered through the heavy drapes. She glanced toward the bassinet beside their bed, her heartbeat slowing at the sight of Mira's wide, curious eyes. "Good morning, little one," she murmured, lifting the baby gently into her arms. With practiced ease, she opened the discreet panels in her nightgown that Sarala had designed, allowing Mira to latch.

The relief was immediate as Mira began to nurse, and Cecelia relaxed into the mattress, the tension in her back easing. She fixed her gaze on the pale, diffused light trickling into the room, determined to keep herself from nodding off. But Mira had other plans—a sudden sharp pinch made Cecelia flinch. "Little minx," she muttered, adjusting the baby to the other breast.

"Good morning," came Kunal's drowsy voice beside her. "You're amazing, you know that?"

Cecelia glanced over her shoulder, her lips curving into a soft smile. "I love you."

"I love you, too," he replied, shifting closer. He watched her, an almost reverent expression on his face. "Do you need anything? Water, perhaps?"

"Could you hand me a fig from last night?" she whispered.

Kunal eased himself out of bed, careful not to disturb the mattress, and Mira let out a tiny, disgruntled squeak at the movement. He returned with a fig, realizing her hands were occupied, so he held it to her lips. She nibbled at it delicately, her mouth brushing his fingers. After the first bite, she took another, the simple act feeling unexpectedly intimate.

Once Mira finished nursing, she drifted back to sleep. Cecelia tucked herself back into her gown, her movements slow and careful. As if on cue, a light knock came at the door.

"Come in," Cecelia called softly.

Sarala entered, her face lighting up at the sight of Mira. "Has our little Mirabai finished her breakfast? May I steal her away for a bit of morning storytelling with her grandfather?"

"Yes, please." Cecelia kissed Mira's forehead, her heart swelling with a mix of love and longing as she handed her over. Kunal did the same, brushing his lips tenderly against their daughter's soft cheek.

"Take some time to yourself," Sarala suggested, bouncing Mira gently. "Rest, read, whatever you like before breakfast. You'll need to be fresh for tomorrow."

Cecelia's breath caught. "Oh, right... tomorrow."

Sarala's expression softened as she headed toward the door. "You'll do splendidly. Just be yourself."

As soon as the door clicked shut, Kunal leaned closer to Cecelia. "You're worried about tomorrow, aren't you?"

"It's just..." Cecelia hesitated. "It's strange to think that people might actually want me to illustrate their family stories, cookbooks, or even lost artifacts."

"You've proven you're more than capable," Kunal assured her. "I've seen your drawings—they're not just accurate; they're full of life. You bring history back to people."

"I feel like a fraud," she admitted, her voice barely above a whisper. "What if it's all a fluke? Or what if something happens—an accident, and I can't draw anymore?"

Kunal took her hands gently, lifting them to his lips and pressing a kiss to each fingertip. "Then you'll learn to draw with your other hand. Or even your feet, if necessary."

Despite herself, Cecelia laughed. "I'm being serious."

"So am I," Kunal insisted, his voice low and tender as he kissed along the inside of her arm, the roughness of his stubble sending a shiver down her spine. "Anything could happen... but that's what makes it worthwhile."

She let out a deep sigh, leaning her head against his shoulder. "Can't we just stay here with Mira?"

Kunal's gaze softened. "I know returning to Castle Rowley makes you nervous, but our friends want to see you, and you've been looking forward to the new museum."

Cecelia's jaw tightened. "I know... but the Rowleys have a long memory. What if something happens again? Philippa and Geoffrey never seemed the forgiving sort."

Kunal's eyes were steady, his voice firm. "I won't let anything happen to you, Cecelia. Not this time. I promise."

"She already took me once," Cecelia said, her voice barely steady. "Right under your nose. One minute I was there, and the next, I was gone."

He tightened his grip on her hand. "I know, and I still ache over it. But Philippa won't catch us off guard again. We're going back on our own terms, and you'll have your work to focus on."

Cecelia nodded slowly, uncertainty lingering in her eyes. "All right... but you'll stay close?"

Kunal leaned in, his forehead touching hers. "Always, my love."

There was another quiet knock on the door, and Kunal opened it to see Sarala, an apologetic look on her face. "I promise, I only meant to listen for a moment."

"Maa..." Kunal laughed. "We are married now...we could have been doing anything. Why are you listening at doors?"

"If you're not ready to go back to the castle yet, why don't we have the event at the literary house that I sponsor?" Sarala asked frankly. "We can shut it down for a day for a private event, and likely get higher bids for new commissions than at that drafty old castle."

"That's so kind of you to think of," Cecelia smiled, looking at Kunal.

He nodded. "They are indeed. My point was only to say that we cannot live in fear of Philippa kidnapping you, not if we plan to travel."

Cecelia nodded, her thoughts swirling as she watched Mira in Sarala's arms.

"Cecelia?" Manik appeared by Sarala's side. "There is a messenger downstairs with something for you."

"What is it?" Cecelia asked suspiciously. "Who is the messenger?"

"It's Barnaby, from Castle Rowley," Manik said, handing her a large leather pouch. "He says it's important. Nervous lad, that one."

"He is," Cecelia muttered as she opened the letter and groaned, closing it again. "It's from Baroness Philippa Rowley."

"Well, you won't go see her, and we won't have her here after what happened," Sarala shrugged. "You know she's asked for an audience with you. I suppose this is how she thinks gets ahold of you."

Cecelia scowled, opening the letter again and sitting down on the bed to read it. With a weary gaze, she read:

Dear Cecelia,

I'm sorry.

She paused, incredulous. "She actually says she's sorry."

Kunal blinked, a hint of disbelief in his voice. "That's a twist. Could it be genuine?"

Cecelia continued reading, her voice edged with curiosity:

What must you think of me after all this time? My husband paid your mother to conceive you, then I resented you and your family for it. Add to that the fact that Henry, who I thought unable to father more children after an accident he never forgave me for, saw you as his one proof of potency, and punished you accordingly. I was complicit in every cruelty, and I tried to grind you down when he wasn't around.

Thank God, we failed.

Cecelia's voice caught, and she paused, a rush of unexpected emotion in her chest. Kunal reached for her hand, and she squeezed it before reading on:

You saved my son's life, Cecelia. Without your intervention, Frederick would have been lost to me. For that, I owe you a debt I can never repay. Frederick has fully recovered and is now set to marry the Comtesse Marguerite de Villeneuve, daughter of a nobleman with vast estates near Versailles. The Comte is close to the French crown, managing royal finances, and Frederick has impressed him with his intelligence and command of French—skills, I understand, that she helped him practice. Thank you for suggesting to him that they wed, and it seems he listened to you more than to myself. It seems others have hidden your kindness from me, fearing it would upset me.

Marguerite will soon move to Castle Rowley, where she intends to help restore it. I have married Geoffrey, and we will raise our children at Rowley Manor. Enclosed is a deed to some land for your daughter. I wish I could offer more, but Castle Rowley's debts are severe, the result of Henry's reckless management.

I will do everything in my power to rebuild our family's standing and support yours in turn.

Cecelia reached into the pouch and withdrew the folded parchment—a deed to land near Castle Rowley. She looked back at the letter, her eyes widening:

Please accept this land. It's not much, but it's a beginning. I hope you'll see it as my first attempt to set things right.

Warmest regards,

Baroness Philippa Rowley

Cecelia sat back, the letter slipping from her fingers as she let out a shaky laugh. "All these years, I've waited for acknowledgment from Philippa. And now that it's here, it feels... strangely hollow."

Kunal, sitting beside her on the sun-drenched window seat, watched her carefully. "Because you've created something more real than a title or land," he said softly. "You've made your own choices—built your own life."

"Yes," Cecelia murmured, her voice thick with emotion. "For the first time, the past doesn't feel like a weight around my neck." She glanced toward the open window, where a soft breeze rustled the curtains and filled the room with the scent of summer wildflowers.

Kunal reached for her hand, his touch warm and reassuring. "And the land Philippa offered?"

Cecelia's eyes brightened with a hint of mischief. "It can be Mira's one day. A place for her to explore, to sketch, to find her own refuge... like I found in that old greenhouse."

Kunal smiled, a slow, heartfelt smile that made Cecelia's heart swell. "A garden for Mira," he echoed. "And maybe a little cottage, for when we visit England between travels. Somewhere to plant roots, but never be confined."

Cecelia nodded, tears pricking at her eyes—not of sadness, but of a deep joy. "And in the meantime, we'll keep to our travel plans?"

"Wherever we go, it will always be home," Kunal said, his voice tender, "as long as we're together."

They fell into a comfortable silence, both gazing out the window at the Yorkshire countryside that had once seemed so suffocating. Now, it was a symbol of what they had overcome—what they had reclaimed for themselves. The world outside felt wide open, a canvas waiting for their next brushstrokes.

Mira's soft cooing from the nearby bassinet pulled them from their reverie. Cecelia rose, cradling the baby gently in her arms, brushing her lips over Mira's downy red curls. "Look at her, Kunal," she whispered. "She's a part of this place, yet free from its shadows."

Kunal wrapped his arms around them both, resting his chin atop Cecelia's head. "Just like her mother," he said, his voice filled with love and pride.

Cecelia leaned into him, closing her eyes for a moment. "I never thought I'd find this," she admitted. "A family, a future... peace."

"And yet, here we are," Kunal whispered, tightening his embrace.

They stood there for a long time, savoring the warmth of the sun's rays and the simple joy of holding their daughter. The future stretched before them, as uncertain as ever but no longer daunting.

She closed her eyes for a moment, taking in the scent of the wild-flowers drifting in from the open window, the soft rustle of leaves—a promise of freedom. The world felt wide open, not as a threat, but as a thrilling opportunity.

Mira's quiet cooing from the nearby bassinet drew their attention. Cecelia rose, cradling the baby close to her chest, brushing her lips across Mira's downy curls. "Look at her, Kunal," she murmured, her voice filled with wonder. "She's the beginning of everything we hoped for."

Kunal wrapped his arms around both mother and child, resting his forehead against Cecelia's. "Just like you were the beginning of everything I never dared to hope for," he said, his voice full of love.

Cecelia nestled against him, feeling the strength and warmth of his embrace. "I never imagined it would turn out this way," she admitted, her voice a mix of gratitude and disbelief. "I've spent so much of my life hiding—hiding from the past, from shame, from uncertainty. But now... now I just want to live."

"And live we shall," Kunal whispered, pressing a tender kiss to her temple. "Together."

For a long moment, they stood in a comfortable silence, the morning light enveloping them in a warm, golden glow. The castle walls that had once loomed so heavily in Cecelia's life now seemed far away, a reminder of how far she had come.

With a sudden, mischievous smile, she turned to Kunal. "Well then," she teased, her eyes alight with mischief, "what say you to the idea of going forth as two brave, defiant artists who are ready to conquer the world?"

Kunal's laughter rang through the room, full and joyous. "I can think of no greater honor."

And as he leaned down to kiss her—slowly, sweetly, as if sealing a promise they both understood—the world outside seemed to pause, granting them this small moment of happiness.

Whatever awaited them, they knew they were ready—side by side, as equals, as partners, as a family.

MANY THANKS

There are so many people who helped make the book possible.

My husband Chris, who can build a fire within seconds, never fails to make me laugh, and whose smile and love keeps my heart full.

My parents Michael and Katherine who taught me the value of museums, doodling, and art just for yourself.

My sister Rachel, who is a constant reminder never to give up.

My art mentor Nicola who encourages me to be weird and inventive in my creations.

My beta readers Tehniat Shuja and Hina Patel for their much appreciated feedback which shaped the final version of this book.

My Panic! at the Art Zoom friends, because even when we have no time at all, we connect once a month to talk about art.

My local book club, who helps me get outside to talk about books in person, which I can't recommend enough.

My Moms Who Write offshoot critique group, fierce wonderful women storytellers who tell me like it is and have improved my writing tremendously. If you like this book better than the first one, it's because of them.

Thank you so much for all you do to inspire me constantly.

About the Author

Matilda Lockwood is a historical romance author and illustrator living in a small town an hour from Seattle by ferryboat. She enjoys penning characters who draw strength from creativity. When not writing or sketching, she can be found frying up eggs from her backyard chickens for her family, reading in the woods, or swimming in nearby Puget Sound.